THE STANSTEAD INCIDENT

A Novel of International Politics and National Security

Neil Currie

-BERWICK BOOKS-

To my Canadian-American wife Karin with love.
A gracious symbol of the unity of two great lands.

PREFACE

Experience teaches that terrorists tend to establish bases in out-of-the-way failed states from which they can emerge to inflict some atrocity. Why not in a better located state that with a determined push could fail?

In 1980 a referendum was held in Québec on whether to separate from the rest of Canada. It lost by 19%. Fifteen years later a second referendum was held on the same question. That time it only lost by 1%. Our story takes place amidst a third try.

While most questions of border security have focused on America's southern border, the northern border with Québec—just 300 miles from Manhattan—is largely ignored by the press, although those charged with the nation's security have long been concerned by its vulnerability.

On September 27, 2007 undercover agents of the General Accountability Office, the investigative arm of Congress, told a U.S. Senate committee that they had been able "...to cross the Canadian border unchallenged, successfully simulating the movement of radioactive materials into the U.S. from Canada."

Preventing that requires government agencies to "connect the dots." But, before they can, they first need to find the dots. That requires initiative and imagination, commodities not always associated with bureaucracies or with the politicians who direct them.

Prologue

Hôtel de Ville, Montréal
Thursday, June 25th
7:32pm EDT

Storm clouds were approaching from the west. He clucked to the big bay, urging it to a faster pace. He would have said something reassuring to his passengers but they didn't speak French or English... Chinese apparently. He shrugged. It was making his last run of the day easy. No questions. Not like his fellow Québécoise, although their questions were predictable. They always wanted to know why there was a statue to the Englishman Nelson opposite City Hall in the heart of French Montréal...and not just a simple statue but a life-sized figure atop a sixty foot column. Over the years he had devised an answer that offered something for most everyone: "Nelson defeated the French at Trafalgar but he was killed there by a French sniper."

He again glanced toward the west as the calèche rounded the corner of Rue Notre-Dame beside Nelson's column. The lights that outlined the cross on Mount Royal had come on as the sky darkened. For four hundred years a cross had stood there, watching over the city below. Now, as he watched, the cross was suddenly enveloped in a blinding white light. Lightning? Inexplicably, the words of the rosary came to him: "nunc et in hóra mórtis nóstræ...now and in the hour of our death."

Outremont
Thursday, June 25th
7:32pm EDT

He was angry with himself. He hadn't summoned the nerve to ask her to dance, afraid she might say "no", afraid the other guys would razz him if he ventured across the floor to ask. So, instead, he had just watched from a distance, envious of everyone who spoke to her, emboldened when she threw a glance his way, but never quite enough to approach. And now it was almost too late. The music had ended and the push to the door had begun. He hung back as much as he could in the milling crowd of teens until she came alongside.

She must know he liked her. After all, through the intermediary of a friend of her younger brother he had sent a note asking whether she was planning to attend the dance tonight. Her return note was terse but encouraging: "Yes. Maybe I'll see you there."

So it was now or never. Summoning all his courage he turned to her and said "hi." She pretended surprise at seeing him but then, amazingly, placed her hand on his arm and leaned close to speak through the din.

"We're going to Martin's," she said. "Are you?" The pâtisserie was a favored after-dance destination. Before he could answer, a gust of wind sent a sudden shower of raindrops into the foyer. "Oh," she cried, assuming his answer, "We're going to have to run for it!"

Acting on a sudden impulse, he grabbed her hand and pulled her through the throng hesitating at the door. She didn't try to hold back or withdraw her hand...nor would she ever.

Bourse de Montréal
Thursday, June 25th
7:32pm EDT

He flicked his cigarette into the middle of the trash-strewn alley, leaned away from the wall and stretched. The freshening breeze carried the imminent threat of rain. *Might as well go inside and get on with it.* Other than the restrooms it wasn't a bad job. Mostly picking up trash and carting it out here to the dumpster which meant several times a night he could linger and have a smoke.

Apart from a couple of cleaning ladies, who mostly kept to themselves, there usually was no one around after six; certainly no one to beef about his cigarette breaks. He had counted himself lucky to get the job. But then, as the heavy steel utility door clanged shut behind him, blocking the stiffening breeze, he reflected that he'd always been lucky. He once got four numbers in the lottery and won $150.00.

As the freight elevator began its slow climb what must have been a clap of thunder shook the building. Lucky again. By the time he finished work the storm should be over.

Chapter One

24 Sussex Drive, Ottawa
Thursday, June 25th
7:32pm EDT

Thunderheads had been building all afternoon but it wasn't until an hour before they had to leave for the reception that the first large drops of rain fell, followed by a traffic-snarling torrent. He listened to a few minutes of news on the car radio but it didn't tell him anything he didn't already know: traffic was a mess and the first polls on the newly announced Québec referendum were inconclusive. The separatists—or sovereignists as they called themselves—were ahead, but one week into what would be a four month campaign their lead was only a little more than the margin of error. If it stayed that close, turnout would tell the story. As for tonight's turnout ... she obviously didn't want to.

With the radio off they had made the rest of the ride in thick silence. Now, as they neared its end, occasional shafts of sunlight shot between the departing clouds to glance off the windows of stately homes set far back from Sussex Drive behind ornamental iron fences that weren't entirely ornamental. First came the residence of the British High Commissioner. Commonwealth countries, which shared a common monarch, had high commissioners. Everybody else had ambassadors.

A half-mile on was the French embassy. Despite being the other parent of the Canadian confederation France was given no special standing, that discrimination having been determined long ago on the Plains of Abraham. But in a city where proximity to power conveyed status, the French ambassador had the consolation of being next door neighbor to whomever the voters in their wisdom decided should live at number 24 Sussex.

He slowed as they approached its gates. A policeman in an orange rain coat and plastic-covered hat saw the turn signal and stopped the in-bound traffic to allow the prime minister's guest to cross over. A pair of constables from the RCMP's Protective Operations unit stood just far enough back from the road to allow two cars at a time to await entry without blocking traffic. One held his hand out, waist high, palm down, indicating the driver should stop. As he did, he lowered his window. The outside air was surprisingly cool. *Although,* he thought without looking at his companion, *it's pretty chilly inside, too.*

"Good evening, sir." Even as the constable spoke his eyes scanned the car and its occupants. The driver was well dressed, perhaps in his mid forties, full hair neatly trimmed, slightly grayed at the temples, no glasses, white shirt, striped tie with a Windsor knot, dark suit with a small lapel pin in the shape of a maple leaf. The woman in the passenger seat was younger than the man by a good bit; dark hair in a perky cut framing a narrow, high-boned face, black cocktail dress offset by a simple gold necklace...a latter day Audrey Hepburn... elegant, chic, expensive.

The officer leaned toward the open window holding a clipboard. His companion stood on the opposite side of the car in the driver's blind spot, thumbs loosely hooked over the broad, black belt that held his holster. Had he been visible to the occupants of the car they might have noticed the holster's leather cover was unsnapped in subtle recognition that times had changed. "May I have your names please?" He asked even though he knew who the man was, having seen him any number of times on TV. You didn't get into trouble by following regulations.

"Andrew Fraser" the man replied "and"—with a nod toward his companion—"my wife."

The constable checked his clipboard. About a dozen names from the top he saw "Hon. Andrew Fraser/Marie-Paule Fraser". He made a mark beside it with a pencil tethered on a short length of string. "And may I see some identification, sir?"

The driver tugged a passport case from his inside jacket pocket and, extracting a parliamentary ID card, handed it to the constable who scrutinized it carefully, glancing back as if to assure himself that the picture and the person were one and the same. Satisfied, he returned it. "And you ma'am?"

"I'm with him," she replied. Her tone suggested she wasn't necessarily pleased by the admission.

"Yes, ma'am, but I'm afraid I'll have to see some identification."

"Well I don't have any," she answered not looking at the officer but staring straight ahead at the large gray stone house at the end of the drive. Guests were already making their way up its steps as an umbrella-toting attendant stood guard against further rain.

Damn her! He could feel himself tense. The invitation had clearly stated "ID required". Another car pulled up behind them. She was having her moment; one of many. Head held stiffly, chin tilted up, non-compliance clearly stamped on her face. He spoke quietly but firmly, as one might to a recalcitrant child, "Marie-Paule, show him your ID."

"I don't think I brought any," she replied in a dull tone. He reached over and took the small, black clutch bag from her lap. It contained only a few items: a comb, a gold vanity case, a lipstick, a key case, a few dollars…maybe more…but no ID. He felt around inside the purse. It was soft to the touch and gave off a slight springtime fragrance.

Damn it! The reception began at 7:00. They were already late, the traffic having made what should have been a ten minute ride a half hour trek. There was no way he could go back to the hotel, get her ID—or drop her off—and return. The reception would be half over by then making it look as though he were ill mannered or, even worst, that he was making some political statement by a late arrival. He could feel himself beginning to perspire despite the chill air when his hand struck something hard in the change pocket of the purse—her driver's license. He thrust it out the window at the constable who took it with unhurried formality and studied it. Then he bent down and looked at her profile for a long moment before handing it back. "Thank you, sir." He seemed to put a little extra emphasis on the "sir" as if to differentiate between the levels of cooperation from the occupants of the car. "Have a pleasant evening."

Nodding thanks he dropped the purse and license in her lap and, leaving the window down, began to move forward through the open gate. He was tempted to say something cutting but all that came to mind was *are you satisfied* which was pointless since he knew the answer.

There was a slight bump as they drove across an iron bollard recessed in the driveway, the civilian equivalent of a tank trap to prevent an unwanted visitor from going any further. An RCMP patrol car was parked on the lawn angled toward them, motor running, two men in the front seat quietly observing each vehicle that passed. He drove slowly, tires crunching on the gravel.

An attendant opened the passenger door while another waited on the driver's side to whisk the car to a parking area some distance from the house. Three or four flagstone steps led up to the front door where a liveried attendant bade them good evening in English and French while a maid in black dress, white cap and apron stood just inside, ready to receive a raincoat or umbrella.

He had been to 24 Sussex before and, like most ministers of the crown, wondered what it would be like to live here; portraits of those who had looked down from soft pools of light on the walls. A youthful RCMP constable stood stiffly at the foot of a broad staircase that curved upward from the back of the entrance hall, his dress uniform adding a splash of color. Oriental runners marked a path across the well-buffed floor to an open set of double doors where a jumble of conversation, punctuated by occasional laughter, spilled out.

Just inside the doors the prime minister and his wife chatted with Finance Minister David Osgood and his wife as they waited for their other guests. The PM had a remarkable ability to feign interest. The finance minister was easily the most boring man in politics. The working theory in the press gallery was that his constituents didn't vote him into office but out of town. Snippets of his monologue occasionally penetrated the ambient noise. Something about European interest rates.

Beyond the prime minister small knots of men and women stood holding drinks and chatting about the weather, their children, plans for the coming holiday weekend; everything except the subject that most concerned them. He couldn't help but note how tired the PM seemed and wondered if the whispers about his health might be true. Although the government still had two years to go and a comfortable majority in the Commons to insure they'd make it, there was speculation whether it would be with the same leader.

At 71 McKinley Marston was rounding out a forty-year political career that had seen him advance from city councilman to provincial legislator to the backbenches of the Commons. His progress had been slow but steady, much like the man himself. In years when the party was in the majority he was given some sinecure. In opposition his advancement came more quickly since, by definition, his side had lost seats and with them potential competitors. In time he became finance minister although he had no special training or aptitude for it. It turned out he had something far more valuable: luck. He took office in heady days when a booming economy carried the country along and he was smart enough not to get in its way. His speeches, written for him by the party central office when it was a political occasion or by a senior civil servant when it was a ministerial one, were carefully vetted to avoid any controversy. That suited him perfectly. And in a television age it didn't hurt that McKinley Marston looked like a prime minister—neat and trim with sleekly combed white hair and an impeccable British Army mustache.

"Andrew, how good of you to come," the PM intoned, offering his hand for the briefest of moments. It felt cold and frail. "And Mrs. Fraser, I am so pleased you could join us this evening." He inclined his head toward Marie-Paule who returned the gesture in a near parody.

"Merci à vous, premier ministre, Andrew a voulu que je l'accompagne." The PM looked very directly at her for just a moment before replying. "I hope it was your wish as well." She did not answer.

"Ah, Andrew." Osgood could not be avoided as he stood so close by the PM as to suggest, erroneously, that he was part of the official welcoming party.

"David, my good fortune that we meet twice in the same day." He managed a thin smile as he slipped his hand onto the small of Marie-Paule's back and gently pressured her to keep walking.

"Bonjour Madam Fraser," David bowed in Marie-Paule's direction. *"Vous regardez très chic ce soir."* One had to wonder how many language classes it had taken him to learn that. A few more and he might get it right.

"Hello," she replied. Her tone was disinterested, bordering on rude. In theoretically bilingual Canada manners dictated that you reply in the same language in which you were addressed. When she did not it was intentional. Andrew had called her on it before. Her answer was "If I want to talk to them, I'll talk to them in any language *they* want. If I don't, I won't talk to them in any language *I* want."

Osgood was not about to let him get away easily. He held the perfunctory handshake while adding his other hand to Andrew's forearm in an immobilizing suggestion of sincerity. "I do hope you understand my concerns this morning were strictly fiscal. I quite agree with you that we need to take a look at our defense spending and, if it were just up to me, I'd make it a priority to do so." As a political statement it failed in both the present and future tenses. David Osgood had never seen a military spending bill he hadn't wanted to cut and he never lost an opportunity in cabinet to make the effort, which he would then later restate for the press as a choice between guns, which made people worse, or health care which, theoretically, made them better. Whatever his political ambitions, absent some miracle it seemed unlikely he would ever realize them. The party central office routinely commissioned polls to test public reaction to various potential stars. Some tested positive, a few negative. Osgood generally drew a blank.

That, of course, left open the question of who would become prime minister when McKinley Marston or his government expired. Most of the likely candidates were in this room or soon would be along with a few promising backbenchers who were probably headed to the front. There were also some party functionaries plus a press baron whose newspapers reached nearly half the voters in the country. They were complemented by several businessmen whose advice found the ear of the prime minister and whose contributions found their way to the party coffers.

Originally this gathering was to have marked the end of the parliamentary session but it had morphed into a referendum rally. If all went well this fall in Québec they could return to business as usual. If not, it was anybody's guess what would happen next. The referendum didn't actually provide for Québec's immediate secession but asked the voters whether negotiations should be held with Ottawa to reset the terms for continued participation in the Canadian confederation. A second referendum, presumably in the spring, would decide whether to accept those terms. This two step process had prompted more than one cynic to suggest it had less to do with separation and more to do with revenue sharing and "cultural status". That last item was widely seen in English Canada as code for a political quota system.

Québec argued that sovereignty ought to be shared equally between the two founding cultures, French and English. English Canadians countered that went against the tradition of "one man, one vote" in a country that was three-quarters non-French. Québec rejoined that the issue wasn't individuals but cultures, of which there were just two, conveniently ignoring the Inuits, who actually came first, and the Pakistanis, Indians, Jamaicans and East Europeans who had arrived more recently.

With effort he disengaged himself from David's grasp only half hearing his protestations of immense goodwill but budgetary impotence. "I quite understand David, but I'm not sure our friends in NATO will. They don't think we're carrying our weight. But that's a discussion for another time."

Marie-Paule, who had moved on as he had urged, was flirting with two waiters who manned a long white table crowded with trays of glasses and a dozen or more bottles at the ready to extend the prime minister's hospitality to his guests. She held a glass of white wine they had poured for her. "Ah," she said, looking up at Andrew as he came alongside, "did your friend buy you a tank or a boat?" He ignored her and ordered a very light whiskey soda.

Marcel Gigiere, the elegant-looking natural resources minister and fellow Montréaler, detached himself from the group where he had been holding court. "Good evening my friend," he beamed. Marie-Paule suddenly lost interest in the waiters and joined them. "And good evening to you Marie-Paule. You look charming as always." He did not wait for her reply. "So why are we here Andy? Auditioning?"

"Perhaps."

"And what role will you play in this little drama?"

"None. I'm quite content where I am," he replied looking at Marie-Paule who had taken his arm and was hugging it in an uncommon display of affection.

"Ah, a politician without ambition; how very unusual. Do you not agree, Marie-Paule?"

"I don't know," she replied. "Andrew does the politics. I do other things."

"What sort of other things?" Marcel asked. She in turn raised her eyebrows and gave a throaty laugh while looking up at her husband in seeming adoration.

"Do you think I should tell?" she asked him. Then deciding to answer her own question, she quickly added, "No, I think I should not." The laugh that punctuated her decision was pitched an octave lower than usual. Andrew recognized the symptoms.

"My friend, I should like to drop by when you have a bit of time available." Despite his smile Marcel's tone suggested it wouldn't be a social call. It was no secret that he wanted regular naval patrols of the Northwest Passage. Pack ice, long Canada's arctic ally, was disappearing taking with it the constraint that had denied the waterway being considered a usable international strait. The solution was a more robust Canadian presence, but coming up with the money when other priorities were already straining the defense budget was difficult. If negotiations with Québec ended up taking more out of the treasury that would only compound the difficulty.

"I think I can guess what you want to talk about Marcel but I'm afraid I've got to head home in the morning."

"Perhaps we could ride down together if Marie-Paule wouldn't mind and have a little chat on the way." He turned to her as if to seek permission.

He got a pout in reply. "That means you two will talk politics all the way to Montréal."

Not all the way," Marcel assured her. "I promise we'll stop at the bridge." It was not much of a concession. The Île aux Tourtes Bridge connecting the island of Montréal with the mainland was 90% of the way home. Although Marie-Paule made a face, she voiced no objection.

"Then that's agreed," Marcel said turning back to Andrew. "If we meet at nine we'll be home before noon, enough time to look around our ridings."

Andrew's riding, the historic term for a constituency, was centered on Westmount, a once exclusively English-speaking enclave within Montréal. Marcel's was on the opposite slope of Mount Royal and included the boroughs of Outremont, portions of

Notre-Dame-de-Grâce and the Town of Mount Royal. The latter two, generally known by their initials, were also originally English but, beginning with the separatist bombings of the 1970s and increasingly with the language laws of the '80s, many of their residents had pulled up stakes and moved away, mostly to Ontario. Their carefully maintained homes sold for a fraction of their original cost to an emerging French middle class and the once English areas gradually became French. It was a similar story in Andrew's riding except that the new residents there included many immigrants from Eastern Europe who had come this far to be Canadians, not Québécoise.

A few more people had entered the room. It looked as though the entire cabinet was present. He decided to get a refill while it was still politic to do so. "Would you like me to freshen your drink?" he asked Marie-Paule, who had relinquished his arm now that Marcel had moved on. She looked studiously at her glass, head tilted to one side, almond-shaped eyes narrowed, giving the question her most careful consideration.

"No," she said, turning on her heel as she did, "I'll get it." In a moment she was gone, her insouciant walk leaving heads turned in her wake, still as compelling as the day he first met her.

* * *

It was a Friday and he had hurried into the bank just moments before the close to deposit the meager paycheck of an assistant professor of political science. "Five minutes more and you would have been broke all weekend" the teller said as he slipped his check under the grill. "Maybe you would have had to go hungry and stand outside the gate with a sign around your neck like that little bear in the story book. 'Feed this professor' it would say." He had fumbled for a clever reply. Later, trying to replay the moment from memory, he had no idea what he actually had said. He couldn't take his eyes off her. Even in a city justifiably renowned for its beautiful women she was extraordinary.

His deposit slip called for a little cash back. Marie-Paule Gagnon, as the nameplate by the teller's window identified her, made a show of counting out the bills first in French and then in English. "I just want to see if it comes out the same," she laughed. "There, now you have enough money to take me out to dinner this evening!" She offered it as a joke. Heart in mouth he seized it as an opportunity.

"Would you like to?" he asked.

"Will your wife come, too?" she replied, eyes sparkling with laughter.

"I'm not married," he answered shaking his head for emphasis. Marie-Paule tilted hers to one side and pretended to consider the situation she had created.

"I don't know that the bank would like me to go out with a customer."

"I'm not a very good customer," he replied.

"No," she laughed, looking at the little pile of bills stacked between them, "you're not."

"When do you get off?" he asked.

"Not for another two hours. "I still have to settle my accounts." And pretending annoyance, she added "But I can't start until all the customers are gone so I may be here very late tonight!"

"What if I meet you at six at Le Vieux Logis?"

"That is not such a cheap restaurant," she replied, looking at his stack of bills. "Perhaps you would like to cash a little more of your check, non?" And again she laughed. He was totally enthralled. She was lovely and funny and free-spirited. In the space of five minutes he had fallen in love.

* * *

Someone tapping on a glass wrenched him back to the present. The prime minister stood waiting by a fireplace nearly as tall as he. A round of laughter from a group of businessmen who had not heard the summons sounded suddenly out of place in the quickly quieting room. He looked around for Marie-Paule. She was standing by the bar. His instinct was to move in her direction but the moment was lost.

"Good evening my friends." The PM's thin, reedy voice sounded as though it had been carried in on a chill gust of wind. "Mrs. Marston and I are so pleased you were able to join us this evening, the efforts of the weatherman notwithstanding. We are gathered as our national holiday nears in anticipation of what I most earnestly trust will be good tidings in coming months that we shall continue as one nation. It goes without saying—although I shall say it—that a vote for common sense this fall will require the unstinting efforts of each and every one of us to make the case for Canada. In that regard I must make special mention of our ministers from Montréal, Andrew Fraser and Marcel Gigiere. They will be carrying the case for Canada to every corner of Québec in the weeks ahead and I know I speak for all of you in saying we could not have more able emissaries."

Without looking in her direction he could feel Marie-Paule's eyes. His anticipated efforts, which were being politely applauded, would leave her alone too many nights and weekends. "Of course," the PM continued, "they have a stirring story to tell. There is much in our confederation that is praiseworthy." He then proceeded to itemize it and praise it. Those who had drinks sipped, those near enough the snacks, snacked. Those caught without either were forced to listen.

He had once been asked why McKinley Marston was prime minister and had replied without thinking "because he was there." It didn't sound like much of an answer but it was the truth. After a particularly close election, the party found itself in opposition with its leadership undecided between two evenly matched stars. Someone supposedly devoid of ambition was needed to act as interim leader until the next party conference could sort things out. McKinley Marston was deemed an acceptable compromise.

No one could have foreseen the sudden collapse of the governing coalition over what at the time seemed a minor scandal. Rather than call another election the governor general invited McKinley Marston, as interim leader of the opposition, to try to form a government.

To everyone's surprise the presumed placeholder showed an aptitude for assembling a viable cabinet from un-ambitious party elders, a few little-known backbenchers and even an opposition renegade who crossed the House for the opportunity to be a minister, albeit of Indian Affairs. By the time elections were   required McKinley

Marston was a familiar presence that aroused no particular passions for or against and as Canadians are want to do when there's no compelling reason for a change, they left well enough alone. The Marston government subsequently was returned with a modest majority.

Over the next few years he brought in some younger talent including Andrew and Marcel. And so he had become one of Canada's longer-serving prime ministers without ever advancing a controversial policy, taking a principled stand or turning a robust phrase. Indeed, as one commentator observed, McKinley Marston was living proof that the meek do inherit the earth.

Inherit it, but not occupy it forever, Andrew thought. The PM was getting old and, what's more, he was showing it tonight. Even by Marston's admittedly modest rhetorical standards this fell well short of being the pep rally he had intended on the eve of yet another question mark over Canada's continuation as a unified country.

The first sign that anything unusual might be going on beyond the gates of 24 Sussex was the chirping of a cell phone. Mac James, the public safety minister, fumbled in his pocket to silence it as he slipped toward the doors at the rear of the room. The PM carried on without seeming to notice although he was known to consider cell phones especially rude devices. A moment later another phone sounded. This time the slightest shadow of a frown crossed the prime minister's face.

A quiver in his own pocket made him start. At least he'd had the foresight to set his phone to silent ring. He glanced at the calling number. He would have to take this one. With apologetic nods to those around him he moved quietly toward an adjacent drawing room keying in the return number as he did so. It was immediately answered by the duty officer. "Sir, four bombs have exploded in Montréal. There are casualties."

Andrew felt his stomach tighten. "When?" he asked.

"About twenty minutes ago, sir. About 7:30."

"Where?"

"City hall, a community center in Outremont, the stock exchange, and the cross on top of Mount Royal. Most of the casualties appear to be at the community center and at city hall."

"Any numbers?"

"Not at this point, sir. It's pretty chaotic down there and making it worse there's a heavy storm passing through."

"Do they have any idea who did it?"

"No sir."

"Tell me about city hall and the stock exchange." They were in his riding. "Weren't they closed?"

"Yes, sir. The casualties at city hall were out-of-doors, apparently some tourists. There were no casualties that we know of at the stock exchange. But it's pretty chaotic, as I said."

"Keep me informed," Andrew directed, then rang off and stood in silence for a long moment not quite certain what his next move should be when the murmur of voices caught his attention: Mac James and René St. Pierre, the other two phones that had rung. As public safety minister, Mac was in charge of the RCMP—the Royal Canadian Mounted Police—who long ago had dismounted for all but ceremonial occasions and subsequently grew into one of the world's premiere security forces. As deputy prime minister, René wasn't actually in charge of anything, a minister without portfolio, but he had the prime minister's confidence and hence his ear.

"Montréal?" Mac asked quietly.

Andrew nodded. "Any idea of casualties?"

"At least a half dozen dead but some of those they're taking to hospital probably won't make it." Mac's look was a mix of anger and discouragement. "I really thought that sort of shit was behind us."

There had been a time in the '60s and '70s when militant Québec separatists planted bombs in mailboxes and other symbols of the federal government. The bombs didn't differentiate between federalists and separatists, Anglophiles and Francophones, visitors and residents. The only thing their victims shared in common was a desire to mail a letter, check up on their pension at a government office or walk quietly down a city street.

"You really think they're back in business?" Andrew asked.

"I don't know but it's a hell of a kick-off to the referendum."

"Has anyone told the PM?"

"René is just about to." Through the open doorway they could hear the prime minister wrapping up his remarks. He was speaking of common sense and decency as true Canadian values and his confidence that on reflection their confreres in Québec would prove reluctant to throw away nearly a century and a half of progress. "And then again," Mac muttered under his breath, "maybe they won't." Stiffening his shoulders he added "I guess we'd better go in. The old man will have some questions. I hope he'll understand I don't have many answers."

A polite smattering of applause and a sudden migration to the bar greeted the end of the prime minister's remarks. David Osgood was already at the PM's elbow, telling him how inspirational his remarks had been. René interrupted the flow. "Prime Minister," he said leaning closely to speak directly into McKinley Marston's ear, "if we may have a word with you."

The prime minister didn't seem to understand. "Yes, yes, of course. I shall be in all morning."

"No sir, I'm afraid we must speak right now." Mac and Andrew waited to one side. They beckoned for Marcel to join them. The community center was in his riding.

"Well, I really shouldn't leave my guests but if you do need a moment I suppose we could step across the hall." He led the way toward a small waiting room dominated by a marble fireplace, a gilt-framed mirror extending from its mantel to the ceiling. It was not a cozy room nor was it intended to be. This was where you waited to see the prime minister when you had disturbed him at home. Its chilly formality suggested that whatever brought you there had better be of sufficient import to warrant the intrusion.

The four men followed him into the room. Andrew, the last to enter, quietly closed the door behind him. "Well now gentlemen," the prime minister said turning toward them, "you look rather serious. I trust this is not a coup?" Mac ignored the PM's attempt at humor and proceeded directly to the point, detailing what had happened in Montréal.

"Oh dear, oh dear." The prime minister looked paler than usual. Incongruously a loud burst of laughter could be heard at that moment from the reception across the hall. He glanced toward the door, concern etched into his face. "I shall have to let them know." It would not do for the inevitable news story to say the cabinet was partying in Ottawa while bombs were bursting in Montréal. "I don't think we…" He suspended whatever it was he was going to say as Mac's phone chirped.

He answered with a simple "yes" then listened intently. "I see. You can tell them I am with the prime minister now, as is the deputy prime minister…" He paused and raised an eyebrow in Andrew's direction who shook his head slightly. Mac didn't finish the list. No need to raise undue concern by acknowledging the presence of the defense minister. "Keep me advised. Thank you." He returned the phone to his pocket before reporting to the others. "The death toll is up to eleven; five at city hall; six at the community center. At least a dozen have been taken to hospital. Some of them may not make it. The bomb went off just as kids were leaving some event at the community center. They walked right into it. At city hall the bomb was actually across the street. Even so it shattered most of the windows in the front of the building and killed the driver and four tourists in one of those horse-drawn carriages. There was damage but apparently no casualties at the stock exchange. The cross on the mountain was also toppled. So far no one's claimed responsibility for any of it."

The prime minister looked shaken. "Well, then, gentlemen, if you'll permit me a moment to inform my guests and unfortunately send them home on a very different note than…" He shook his head and didn't finish the sentence. Andrew followed him out in search of Marie-Paule.

She was on the far side of the room talking with the bartender. He interrupted. "I'm afraid I'm going to have to attend a meeting with the prime minister. I don't know how long it will be but I'll make arrangements to get you back to the hotel."

"No need," she replied, flashing a grin that lay somewhere between coquettish and tipsy. Addressing the bartender she said "You'll give me a ride, won't you?" Before he could answer, she wheeled back to her husband to explain, "We're both named Paul only he's a boy and I'm a girl. Isn't that funny?"

Andrew looked firmly at the masculine Paul. "Thank you but I'll make arrangements for my wife. I'm sure you have other things to attend to."

Suddenly she was in his face. The grin was gone and the voice was rising. "I told you I have already made arrangements. I do not need you to tell me what to do. You dragged me here because of your politics and you are leaving me here because of your politics. So now I'll take care of myself without any politics!" Conversation among those closest to Marie-Paule ceased, crowded out by the drama unfolding in front of them; a cabinet minister being chewed out in public by his slightly tipsy wife.

It was the very sort of scene he had tried to head off all evening. But to confront her would only make matters worse and there wasn't time to take her aside and try to calm her. They were already calling for quiet so the prime minister could speak. He therefore said nothing further but turned and walked out of the room. The Mountie was still stationed at the foot of the stairs to the prime minister's private quarters. "Excuse me constable. I'm Andrew Fraser." The officer came to attention. "I need to ask you a favor. I have to attend a meeting with the prime minister leaving my wife with no way of getting back to our hotel. Could you please ask your commander to see that she gets there safely?"

"Certainly, sir. Which is she?"

"She's standing by the bar. Short dark hair. Black cocktail dress." He wanted to add "the most beautiful woman in the room" but the constable could see that for himself. He did add, "I would have her take our car but I'm afraid she's had a bit of wine and it might not be wise."

"Yes sir. I'll get word to the duty officer and we'll take care of it sir." Andrew gave him the name of the hotel.

As he left to rejoin the meeting in the ante room, he turned and added, "I trust she won't give you any problem."

"No sir," the young corporal replied.

He's got a surprise coming, he thought. *But then, so has she.*

An hour later as he waited on the steps for his car to be brought around he looked toward the city which occupied one of the most dramatic settings of any world capital. Atop the cliffs that determined the Ottawa River's course the floodlit Houses of Parliament clustered beneath a brooding northern sky looking for all the world like some medieval fortress. The thin spire of the Peace Tower, rising from their midst, spoke of national aspirations while the river below symbolized present realities with mostly English Ontario on one side, mostly French Québec on the other.

4861 Chemin de la Côte-des-Neiges, Montréal
Friday, June 26th
12:30am EDT

Not surprisingly there had been no sign of Marie-Paule at the hotel although there was ample evidence the RCMP had delivered their charge. The room was a shambles. He'd gathered his things into his suitcase, left a generous tip for the maid, who didn't deserve the mess she would inherit, and headed down to the lobby to meet Marcel. After the evening's events they knew their place was at home. He had answered Marcel's unspoken question by saying Marie-Paule would take the train down in the morning, that she was tired and didn't want to travel tonight. Marcel seemed to have accepted "tired" as a reasonable synonym.

Now, apart from a brief pause at the lobby, the elevator climbed without interruption from the parking garage to an 8th floor hallway that was neither hostile nor welcoming. The floral carpet was serviceable but bland. The walls, covered in a beige and silver striped paper, were unrelieved by anything more than a bi-lingual exit sign. He'd once suggested to the condo committee that some pictures would break up the monotony, perhaps prints of old Montréal. They listened respectfully—he was a Member of Parliament after all—but, not unlike his frequent experience in Ottawa, nothing happened.

In any event, they hadn't bought the apartment for the hallway. It was the view that had decided them; that and the heady expectation of evenings spent in the softness of the big chesterfield overlooking the sparkle of the city as it stretched toward the dark band of the river and the U.S. border an hour beyond. And, for a time, that was how it was. Over more than one breakfast they had laughed they could rent out the bedrooms since they so infrequently used them.

In those early days, as he began his political career, he would often return late from a constituency meeting and Marie-Paule would be there waiting for him, sometimes wide awake, eager to share a story from her day, other times curled up asleep amongst the pillows, unable to maintain her watch any longer. But in recent years he more often would find her asleep in the master bedroom which in time became "her" room, a separation that began with sleepy protests when he tiptoed in late. At first he took to changing in the dark and washing up in the guest bath, before slipping into bed beside her. But, when that was followed by complaints at how she had been unable to get back to sleep, one night he just stayed in the guest room rather than disturb her. In time, it became "his" room.

A red light on the answering machine blinked insistently advising there had been three calls in his absence. His first thought was that they could wait until morning but as the machine was on their unpublished private line, he punched the playback button with a sigh of resignation. An electronic voice said the first call had been received at "ten-oh-four a.m." That was yesterday now. Phyllis, who handled his constituency scheduling, had a change to report. He noted it on his calendar. The next call was for Marie-Paule. Her car was ready. He hadn't known there was anything wrong with it. He jotted a note for her.

The third call had been received at 11:23, a little over an hour ago. "Hey mate; just thought I'd touch base." There was a note of concern beneath the casual friendliness of the man's voice. "I understand you've had some trouble up there. If you get a chance, give me a holler. I'm in the office. I'll be here for a while."

It had been that way for nearly twenty years. Somehow, whenever one of them hit a rough spot, there would be a call from the other... like the evening he'd rung up intending nothing more than to needle Mark about the trouncing his team had just taken at the hands of the Canadiens only to learn his mother had died that day. They had ended up talking for the better part of an hour, trying to make sense out of why a loving God would make a world in which, inevitably, we lose those we love most.

And it wasn't just the rough spots, either. The evening he first won a seat in parliament he'd returned to the apartment, sharing sips of the second or third bottle of champagne with Marie-Paule, to find the phone ringing. It was Mark calling with congratulations. While Marie-Paule fell asleep on the chesterfield the former college roommates had talked into the night about what it meant to be in government. It was a serious discussion worthy of a graduate level seminar. Now, Mark had again sensed the need to call and had taken the time to do so.

Despite the lateness of the hour he punched in his friend's number. In the distant darkness a phone rang in the night. It was answered on the second ring: "The White House."

Chapter Two

Ferme St. Germaine Freres
Friday, June 26th
6:00am EDT

Only the measured tick of the wall clock greeted him as he descended the back stairs to the kitchen he'd left just a few hours earlier, too tired to watch any more of the news coverage. Once he'd thought it would be exciting to live in Montréal but now he was glad he didn't.

No more lettered than any other farm boy who had fidgeted through Ecole Ste. Anne until sixteen and freedom, Fernand St. Germaine began each day accepting of the work that would fill it. The nuns had urged he stay another year and graduate and, who knows, perhaps go to   seminary and make a future for himself. There was nothing wrong with their suggestion except that it came much too late. By sixteen he had already been working alongside his father and his uncle for half his life. At first it was to scamper up the stairs to the loft in the pre-dawn darkness and push bales of hay over the side to fill the feed racks. Later, when he was taller and stronger, it was to carry pails of warm frothy milk to the collection tank at the front of the barn. And, eventually, it was to do some of the milking himself. All that happened each morning long before the nuns ever laid eyes on him.

Even now, twenty years later, with the farm and its problems his alone, he didn't spend much time rethinking the past. Not his schooling; not his decision to sell off the herd. Dairy farming was a marginal business at best. When one winter an unusually severe ice storm prevented the co-op's tanker from making its rounds for more than a week, his course became unarguable. In his memory he could still see the steam rising off the manure pile behind the barn as he dumped bucket after bucket of warm milk, throwing away his income while the cows still had to be fed and the bills paid.

Some of his neighbors went to the Caisse Populaire and in a few weeks took out savings it had taken years to put in. Others borrowed against their farms. He couldn't do either. His savings, plus a substantial mortgage, had gone to buy out his brother Raymond's share of the farm. Raymond had married the eldest daughter of a farmer who had only daughters. As he couldn't work two farms twenty miles apart, the answer was to sell his share in the smaller, weaker one to Fernand.

In retrospect the decision to get rid of the cows had been a good one. While those who hung onto their herds struggled with high feed costs and low milk prices, once freed of much of the daily farm routine, he still found himself with as much work as he wanted or needed. It began with a call from a neighboring farmer's wife. *Her husband had hurt himself and would be laid up for a couple of weeks. Could Fernand help out? She would pay him.* That had led to other paying jobs when farmers or their hands needed time off. It suited him just fine. Sometimes he worked a lot; sometimes he had several days free to go hunting or fishing.

It was on one of those hunting days spent with Raymond that he first learned of the "back door" to the States. A few hundred yards past a farm house on Route 141 a narrow track led away from the highway. It was really no more than a memory of a road, two ruts of dirt and stones paralleling a weathered split-rail fence that eventually disappeared into the forest. They had walked about a mile when Raymond pointed to a small stone pillar. Years of rain and snow had nearly erased the message it once carried. "Maybe we should hunt in Vermont," he'd laughed. "It won't count against our Québec limit!"

"That's the border?" Fernand was impressed. Somehow it seemed there should be something more to indicate they were about to cross into another country. He circled it slowly, trailing his hand across its rough surface before looking up. "Where does this road go?" he asked.

"Another half mile or so," Raymond told him, "and it runs into a paved one a couple of miles west of Canaan."

"In the States?"

Raymond nodded. "Vermont."

"Who built it?"

"I don't know," Raymond said, "Probably loggers. Now it's kept open as a fire road. They come through in the spring and clear any trees that fell during the winter and dump some gravel in the washouts. It's good for hunting and it crosses a stream that's good for fishing. But I don't usually go over. There's enough to hunt on this side."

And there still was when the day ended. As a hunting expedition it had not been a great success but discovering the little track across the fields seemed reward enough. Before returning to his truck Fernand stood beside the stone marker for a long moment looking back at the cool, pine-covered hills on the American side of the border. Then he turned to face the rich, rolling farmlands of Québec, still warm from the late afternoon sun, and nodded his approval of whoever had long ago decided where to draw the line.

Just as he had unexpectedly come onto the old border track so he had unexpectedly come onto a new business. A farmer who hired him to help with the first cutting of his hay had a disappointing yield. *Would Fernand be willing to sell his hay now that he didn't have any cows?* He would. It provided enough cash to take care of his mortgage for a couple of months. That fall he sowed all his fields in alfalfa. The result was a bumper crop with three rich cuttings through the next summer. Every square foot of the barn was filled with big, fragrant bales. Unfortunately, all his neighbors had bumper crops, too.

Then one evening the TV weatherman noted that while the storm systems that had moved up the St. Lawrence Valley from the

Great Lakes had brought Québec ample rainfall that summer, to the south in New York and New England it was a very different story. Fields were parched and hay lofts nearly empty. Farmers were going great distances to find hay and paying top dollar when they did.

A few phone calls got him the name of a broker near Schenectady, New York. He was offering $200 a ton. That worked out to almost $8.00 a bale, nearly double what it had fetched last year from his neighbors although he had to go farther to deliver it. The broker had explained what was needed to cross the border. Since he was only selling his own hay and was carrying it in a farm truck there wasn't much required.

An afternoon of backbreaking labor lugging 80 pound bales to the door of the loft where he dropped them onto an old stake truck with the faded letters *Ferme St. Germaine Frères* still visible on its doors and he was loaded for the trip south. A tarpaulin secured by strong ropes assured the load would stay dry and wouldn't shift.

That first trip had been long. He had directions, but uncertain of the way, he drove slowly. Nonetheless it was a profitable journey. They liked the quality of his hay, had men to help unload it and, when he deposited the $1760 check they gave him, he discovered it translated to almost $2000 Canadian. In time he learned to leave with a near empty tank and fill up with cheaper U.S. gas once he was across the border and to top up again on his way home. Even with the fuel factored in, he still cleared a tidy profit on each trip beginning in September and continuing until the barn was empty.

Although the drought of that first year didn't return, a lot of farms in the States, especially those close to big cities, were being squeezed by encroaching development and no longer could lease enough land to grow all their own hay. They had to buy some and the sweet Canadian alfalfa with its high protein content was a favorite. While the price per ton and the exchange rate fluctuated it remained a profitable business, unlike dairying.

In time he became a known commodity at the border. A few perfunctory questions, a glance by the customs officer at the bales of tightly stacked hay, perhaps a tug on one of the ropes to make sure the tarp was as secure as it looked and he was waved through.

Soon he developed a routine that worked well for him. Weather permitting, he would spend Saturday loading the truck and on Sunday go to bed shortly after supper to get up early enough Monday morning to be on the road at dawn. That way he could make his deliveries by early afternoon and still head back in daylight arriving home by nine or ten. The truck was old so he took slower, less-traveled state roads, avoiding the interstate and a costly tow if he broke down.

The day after he got back from a hay run he'd sleep in and then head to town to deposit his money in the Caisse Populaire and have lunch at the café across the street. The rest of the week he tended to the things that needed doing around the farm, took an odd job or, depending on the season, went hunting. In summer, when his clients were pasturing their herds and his hay was growing he worked as a groundskeeper at the Fairhaven boat club, a private preserve for mostly English families from Montréal who had cottages on the lake.

All together he was able to keep the mortgage paid and gradually grow his bank account. Even so, Raymond routinely urged him to sell the farm and come work with him. "You're only working for the bank," he'd say. In a sense that was true and Fernand knew it, but there was more to it than that. It was important to own land and in the process keep the family farm intact. And, who knows, perhaps someday when milk prices were stronger he would build a new herd and maybe find someone who wanted to live on the farm with him and raise sons who would help him as he had helped his father. It could be lonely in a farmhouse that had once been filled with family.

Perhaps that loneliness had something to do with his reaction when he first saw Marie-Paule at the boat club. She was impossible not to notice. Not only was she very French in a very English place, but she was in constant motion, entertaining an admiring male audience on the veranda of the old club house, teasing one about his swimming, another about his pretensions of being a ladies' man. The smooth tan of her long legs contrasted smartly with her white shorts and sandals as she sat on the railing, now and again pretending to slip backwards to everyone's amusement. The dark green bathing suit that disappeared into the shorts displayed her figure to advantage, especially when a breeze off the lake pushed a cloud in front of the sun causing a momentary chill that made her nipples strain against the fabric. Her dark hair was gathered into a little pony tail that poked through the back of a baseball cap. She obviously liked to flirt and, just as obviously, was very good at it.

Once she looked in his direction, almond-shaped eyes flashing green above high cheekbones, an aquiline nose adding elegance to a mouth shaped for laughter or love, and he found his breath caught between his head and his heart.

It had taken some time for him to find both the courage and the opportunity to speak to her. That, in itself, was not surprising. A groundskeeper would not normally have reason to speak to a member. Then one languid summer afternoon when the opportunity did present itself, he nearly blew it. In fact, it was she who saved the moment.

He had taken advantage of the club's policy that allowed staff to use the beach after four p.m. on Mondays when few members would be around following the weekend. He swam toward the white raft that rocked gently atop a half dozen empty metal drums a short distance offshore. From a swimmer's vantage it was not possible to see the top of the raft so it was to his surprise when he clambered up the ladder to discover her lying in the sun tanning. He caught himself before he stepped on her but he couldn't help showering her with droplets of cold water which made her sit upright with a little exclamation. The opportunity to speak to her was at hand but his courage wasn't. He started to turn to dive back into the protective cover of the water but her questioning "Hello?" stopped him, a single word whose inflection suggested both surprise and curiosity. He tried not to stare but *Mon Dieu* she was beautiful.

"Who are *you*?" she asked, the directness of the question eased to some extent by her smile. Still, it was clear that since he had intruded on her territory he should identify himself. He answered although afterward he couldn't remember what, no matter how often he replayed the encounter in his mind. Although her initial question had been put in English, his accented reply caused her to switch to French, her tone softening at the same time. "Are you a member?" she asked.

He shook his head no. "I work here," he said.

"Oh good," she replied. "Then you can do some work for me." And she held out a small tube of sun screen at the same time turning her back to him.

He stood dumbfounded. She wanted him to touch her? "C'mon," she told him indicating her back, "I won't bite." He reached out as if in a daze and took the tube from her. For her part she reached back and gathered her pony tail on top of her head leaving her neck and shoulders bare. "Go ahead," she urged him. "I don't want to peel." He fumbled the cap back and squeezed some of the white cream into his hands suddenly realizing how big and rough they were; farmer's hands that had never known skin cream. He was uncertain what to do but at her instruction patted a bit on her neck. A tremor ran through his entire body as he made contact with her. She was so soft and warm. "Rub it in a little," she commanded. He obeyed, gingerly at first, then, when it brought a sigh of pleasure from her, more firmly.

"You have big hands," she said. He couldn't tell whether it was a compliment or a complaint so he said nothing. "A little lower," she directed. "He moved his attention to the zone between her long, slender neck with its soft down and the elastic edge of her bathing suit. He was beginning to get the hang of it now and applied the cream with more vigor. But, when she suddenly turned, his hand accidentally brushed her breasts. He pulled back as if stung. She seemed not to notice and held out her hand for the tube. "I can take it from here," she said. "Thank you."

He nodded, incapable of thinking of anything to say. But the words he couldn't muster were clearly written on his face for her to read.

"Do you live around here?" she asked. He nodded again.

"If we are going to have a conversation, you have to speak," she said in a tone suggesting aunt with nephew.

"Ste. Herménégilde," he replied.

"That's one I haven't heard of," she laughed. "What do you do in Ste. Herménégilde?" She wrinkled up her nose as she struggled with the cumbersome name.

"I have a farm."

"What kind of farm?"

"It used to be a dairy farm but now I just raise hay."

"Who eats the hay?"

"Cows."

"I thought you didn't have cows anymore. Or are you saving the hay for when you do?"

"I sell the hay to farms down in the States."

"Ah," she said, perhaps appraising him rather differently for her tone took on a crisper, more interested tone.

"Do people pay a lot of money for hay?"

"Not so much," he replied, "that's why I work here during the summer."

"What do you do in the winter?"

"Odd jobs but mostly just get ready for spring."

And so it went for the next several minutes. She asking question after question about him and him answering each in turn but not asking anything of her. At last she said she had to be going. And, slipping the tube of sun cream into the top of her bathing suit between her breasts, she rose and stepped to the edge of the raft ready to dive in for the swim to shore. But first, she paused and then smiled back at him, "I'm glad I met you Fernand St. Germaine." And then she was gone.

He shivered. Perhaps it was the freshening breeze that blew across the lake, perhaps it was because the raft suddenly seemed very empty and a long way from shore. Fernand watched as she splashed out of the water onto the beach and paused to wring out her pony tail. Then, with a quick look back at the raft, she gave a little wave and lightly ran up the steps of the clubhouse to disappear inside. He didn't want her to think he was following so he sat on the edge of the raft and waited for what seemed a sufficient time before slipping over the side and swimming back. Of course he didn't go into the clubhouse but walked around the side to the tool shed not understanding why he felt like both laughing and crying.

The next day it rained and she didn't come to the beach. Wednesday noon she arrived with a half dozen other people in a convertible driven by a young man who laughed a lot and kept putting his arm around her. Fernand tried to stay out of sight, mulching the flower beds on the street side of the club house. But when they left after only an hour she saw him on his knees by the corner of the building and gave him a little wave and a smile. She was wearing a big, floppy sun hat that framed her face like the halos around the heads of the saints in the window at Ste. Anne's.

After that he didn't see her again until the following Thursday afternoon when she walked up behind him as he stood on a stepladder painting the white trim around the windows. "Hello up there, Fernand St. Germaine," she said with a grin. "Do you have to paint the whole place?" He nodded.

"Oh my," she said in mock dismay," I thought we got you talking." She pouted in his direction before dissolving into laughter. "I'm going for a swim. Why don't you join me when you're done painting? I'll be on the raft looking for somebody with big hands."

"I can't today," he said.

"Why not?"

"We are only allowed to swim on Mondays."

She looked up at him with her head tilted to one side as if to catch a distant sound. "You can only swim on Mondays? Why?"

He shrugged. "It's the rules."

"And what will they do if they catch you in the water?" she asked.

Again he shrugged, "I don't know."

She turned and looked out across the lake as if searching for something. "They don't own the whole lake," she pointed out.

"They own this beach."

"But they don't own the whole lake and they don't own the whole shore. What if you swam out from there?" She pointed toward a rocky outcropping with a few pine trees farther along the shoreline where the road to the cottages came almost to the water's edge.

"Swim to where?"

"To the raft."

"They own the raft."

"But they can't tell at this distance who's on it." She pursed her lips and raised her eyebrows as if to ask a question but instead turned and walked down to the water.

It would be almost another hour before he was done; a very long hour. Every time he looked he could see her on the raft. At first there were some other people there, too, but after a while they swam back to shore and she stretched out the way he had first found her that Monday.

At last he put his tools and the ladder away. From the door of the shed he could see two boys playing tennis on the courts beside the club house. An elderly couple sat in white, wicker rockers on the veranda. The sound of a ping pong ball and occasional bursts of youthful laughter came from inside the clubhouse.

He debated for only a moment and then quickly stripped off his paint-splattered dungarees and his shorts. His swim trunks hung on a wooden peg near the door of the shed. He tugged them on and scuffed his feet into an old pair of sneakers. He next exchanged his work shirt for a clean tee shirt from his locker. It had the club insignia on the breast pocket. Then, he pulled a pair of khakis over the bathing suit, gathered up his keys and wallet and, tugging the door closed behind him, headed toward his pickup truck parked behind the shed.

The swim from the rocks to the raft was no farther than from the beach to the raft. As he climbed the ladder Marie Paule looked up and smiled. "Hello Fernand St. Germaine. I was thinking, perhaps you should bring a paint brush with you next time you come and if they ask 'what are you doing here?' "—she deepened her voice to a growl in imitation of a club grandee—"you could wave the brush at them and say you were painting."

Fernand replied in kind, "But then they'd ask 'where is your paint?'"

"Here!" she replied, pulling the tube of sun cream from its travel position and handing it to him And with that she turned her back and waited. As he took the tube from her and began applying the cream he felt himself becoming aroused.

As one summer afternoon followed another he increasingly focused on the white raft bobbing on the deep blue of the lake. Some days she didn't come to the club. Some days it rained. And some perfect, warm sunny days there would be a parcel of teenagers noisily crowding the raft. There were, in fact, only a few times when it was vacant and she would swim out and he would follow, on Mondays from the beach, other times from the rocky point. And, despite his initial worries, no one seemed to pay any attention and nothing was ever said to him, even the day he essentially got caught.

It was midweek, a no-swimming day for staff, and as soon as five o'clock came he had hurried to change into his bathing trunks. He glanced out at the raft to reassure himself that she was still there and alone. He didn't give the parking lot a second look as he drove the short distance to the rocky outcrop. There, having shed his shirt, pants and canvas shoes, he slipped into the water and struck out for the raft. A smile welcomed his arrival along with a funny story about her adventures buying corn at a local farm that morning. She talked as he, now rather more expertly than on the first occasion, applied the sun cream to her smoothly tanned shoulders and back without being asked. That done, she turned and stretched on her stomach in the sun, her arms providing a pillow for her head as she looked out toward the hills beyond the far end of the lake. Fernand sat nearby, legs dangling over the side, and answered her questions about his farm and his trips to the States. He wondered if he should invite her to come see the farm. *But if she did come, would she be put off by it? She lived a very glamorous life and he did not.* As his thoughts silently wove themselves through the ebb and flow of their conversation there was a sudden splash and for a moment the raft tilted as someone grabbed hold of its ladder.

"Andrew," she exclaimed, "what are you doing here?" Even in bathing trunks and with his hair plastered down by the water her husband exuded a presence. Somehow you sensed he was important. He leaned over and gave her a light kiss on the cheek, ignoring Fernand.

"Things wrapped up early so I thought I'd drive down, have a swim and take you someplace nice for dinner this evening…that is, if you're free." He laughed as he added the caveat, at the same time turning toward the other occupant of the raft, hand extended "Hi, I'm Andrew Fraser."

Fernand reached awkwardly to shake his hand, in the process forgetting to answer. Andrew, still gripping his hand, cocked an eyebrow, waiting for a response. Marie-Paule came to the rescue.

"This is Fernand St. Germaine. He's my manservant," she laughed. "Don't you think it was nice of the club to provide him?"

"Indeed," Andrew replied. "I take it then you are not a member?" Fernand shook his head no. Andrew continued to look intently at him as if memorizing his features or, perhaps, bringing the rules about staff swim times to mind. After a long moment he let his hand go and in a brisk tone of voice that suggested a change of subject, turned his full attention to Marie-Paule, settling down beside her facing toward the club. "Anyone interesting up this week?" Clearly that did not include Fernand and in a few moments he quietly slipped over the side and swam back to the rocks, unnoticed.

Chapter Three

He could hear the phone ringing somewhere in the distance but couldn't rouse himself enough to answer it. Twice more it rang before stopping in mid-peal allowing him to slip back into half sleep only to be re-awakened a moment later by Marie-Paule's hand shaking his shoulder. "Andrew, it's for you." He mumbled his thanks and took the handset from her but didn't immediately answer, needing time to collect his thoughts.

The Prime Minister's reception seemed days ago, not mere hours. And then, when he did get home, sometime after midnight, he'd returned the phone call from Mark. They had talked for a while… more an exchange of concerns rather than information, which was in short supply. As he told him, the bombing sites didn't really make sense but maybe as more information—or more bombs—were found they would. When they eventually rang off he had wandered into the living room where for a time he sat staring unseeing at the once romantic but now vaguely threatening lights of the sleeping city before kicking off his shoes and sagging onto the chesterfield where Marie-Paule found him.

A thin "Hello" from the phone he was holding brought him back to the moment.

"Yes?"

"Andrew." It was Mac James, the public safety minister.

"Good morning, Mac. Sorry to have kept you." He fought to stifle a yawn.

"Sorry to disturb *you* but I thought I ought to bring you up-to-date before your day begins." As members of the cabinet it was important they speak with one voice. He glanced at his watch: 7:30. He'd been asleep for a little over six hours. He ought to feel better than this.

"Right."

"Two more kids from the community center died during the night. Three are still in intensive care. The others should make it."

"Any claim of responsibility?"

"No. But we're setting up an intergovernmental coordinating committee with the city and province. It's going to meet later today. The PM wants you and Marcel to be on it. I'm also sending the RCMP district superintendent. That should at least blunt any of the usual 'us-against-them' bullshit."

"I agree. Who's going to run it?

"Emile Ganeau."

That made sense. The Montréal mayor was probably the only person who could chair such a meeting as he had long ago distanced himself from Québec City, whose separatists he openly derided as buffoons and from Ottawa, whose bureaucrats he decried as unimaginative and inflexible. Having actually run a business before trying to run a city his attitude toward government—and especially meetings—was "just get on with it."

"A couple of other things Andy. The PM's also going to form a cabinet committee to track developments and again wants both of you on it. René's people will contact your office with details." He paused as if carefully selecting his next words. "We're also providing you and Marcel with a protective detail. I know you've rarely used security but we don't yet know who or what we're dealing with and until we do we're not taking any chances. They're on their way over to your place now. Please don't go out without them."

"Understood Mac, but do you really think that's necessary?"

"Necessary? Hopefully not. Prudent? Definitely."

When the call from Ottawa ended, he sat awash in the bright sunlight that poured in the windows, lost in thought. A noise behind him made him aware that Marie-Paule had returned and was watching him. "Do you want some coffee?" she asked.

"Yes, please," he replied. Actually he wanted more than coffee. He wanted to know where she'd spent the night and how and when she got home but this was no time for a confrontation. He stood up, gathered his discarded shoes, retrieved his suitcase from the hall and headed for the guest room.

With the coffee, a shower, shave, and fresh clothes, his grogginess was replaced by a growing anxiety to get going, to do something. He could hear Marie-Paule moving about in the master bedroom... her room. She had left the radio on the kitchen counter tuned to a French news/talk station. Thanks to her his French was fluent. Even his accent was good.

It was just coming up on 8 o'clock as he put a couple of pieces of bread in the toaster and poured himself a second cup of coffee. A talk show host was promising that the telephone lines would be open after the news so listeners could call in "to discuss the terrorist attacks and who you think is *really* responsible."

"The government, who else?" he muttered to himself.

The news sounder reclaimed his attention. "The toll from last night's terrorist attacks has climbed to thirteen with the death of two more children at the Jewish community center in Outremont. Powerful bombs, apparently timed to explode simultaneously, also toppled the historic cross on Mount Royal and damaged the stock exchange and city hall where a surveillance camera recorded the blast as occurring at 7:32 p.m. While that was well after most employees had gone for the day four Japanese tourists and the driver of the calèche in which they were riding were killed by the force of the bomb placed in *Place Jacques Cartier*. In addition to the dead, nineteen people were injured and remain in hospital, three in critical condition. Mayor Emile Ganeau says the city will post a $50,000 reward for information leading to the arrest and conviction of the bombers." The voice of the mayor could be heard over some traffic noise and a jumble of other voices. He expressed outrage over the bombings, sympathy for the victims and their families and, as promised, offered the reward. The newscaster then called on reporters at each of the bomb sites for descriptions of the scene on this morning-after.

Marie-Paule appeared in the kitchen doorway. She looked remarkably well considering her condition when he'd handed her off to the RCMP last night. "I have to go out," she said in a matter of fact voice that didn't invite further conversation.

"I may not be here when you get back," he replied, glancing toward the radio.

"I know," she said. "But if you're late, don't sleep on the couch." There was a hint of softness in her voice that seemed to border on sympathy. He nodded. It had been some time since she had expressed concern for him or had it just been some time since he'd been aware of it? He wondered if she was suggesting he should move back into the master bedroom. "It's not a bed and I don't want it to start smelling like one." Having answered his unspoken question she turned toward the door, the rhythmic tap of her heels across the marble foyer punctuating her departure.

He wanted to snap back, to point out that at least she knew where he had slept last night but at the same time he realized there were only two responses she could make: get angry and fight, which might push what remained of their relationship over the edge; or say nothing, thereby allowing his fears to fester. *Or...* the thought fleetingly crossing his mind *...or perhaps she took the train down and got home first.* She had better than an hour's head start and he hadn't actually checked to see. The hall door shuddered slightly in its frame as she left, its latch snapping with a metallic finality. In any event, he told himself, this wasn't the time or place for a showdown. Should that moment come, it would require a setting where arguments couldn't be ended by stalking out.

"Damn it!" The toast popped up as if on cue to punctuate his frustration. She was right though about not sleeping on the couch. His back ached.

As he slathered some peanut butter on the toast, a taste that had outlasted his youth, he reflected that there was never any time to *just be*. That was probably ninety percent of what was wrong between them. Any relationship, especially a marriage, required an investment of time and his account was seriously overdrawn. No wonder she was distant. He was hardly ever here and when he was he had a dispatch box full of work that kept him isolated in his study.

It hadn't always been that way. In the first years they were married, even though she'd kept her job at the bank and he'd continued to teach, they still found time for each other even as he got more politically involved. And when the chance came to stand for a seat in parliament she had campaigned alongside him. Although the French vote in the riding was small back then, he had no doubt she was responsible for what he got of it, certainly among the men as she proved as funny and flirtatious on the stump as in person.

It wasn't until a couple of election cycles had passed and he began to move toward the front benches that he finally took a leave of absence from the university. And when he became a member of the cabinet in the reshuffle that inaugurated the current government, the social requirements of his position demanded that Marie-Paule finally resign her bank job and join him in Ottawa to, as she put it, "become a party girl." At first she threw herself into the role but as most of the entertaining was in the evenings, she became bored with empty days in Ottawa which, for all its charm, was not Montréal.

Little by little she began to disengage. First it was a polite note of regret to a luncheon or tea. Then it was the occasional evening affair, which sometimes proved awkward as the newly-minted defense minister was forced to make a solo appearance. But now her boycott had very nearly included a prime ministerial event and her behavior there could not have gone unnoticed. It was time for a serious talk, a talk that no doubt would include her new-found passion, *La nouvelle Galerie*.

He suspected it was the artists that had caught her interest as it surely couldn't have been their art. To his eye most of the canvases weren't actually pictures of anything, a quality he had thought as necessary to painting as rhyme was to a poem. In any event he bought a small canvas for $150 which he chalked up as an equal contribution to the arts and to his marriage. Marie-Paule got it framed and hung it in his study. Perhaps that was the start of her involvement in fund-raising for the gallery which occupied a smallish storefront on one of the warren of narrow streets that lay between the autoroute and the Lachine Canal. While the neighborhood looked questionable, it was in fact quite safe. So far as he could tell the same was true of the gallery's habitués. The men favored pony tails and facial hair in their grooming, dungarees and sandals in their wardrobe and superlatives in their speech. He doubted that any of them had ever voted for him but they seemed as harmless as they were penniless.

More than once Marie-Paule had asked him to intervene with the Arts Council to get a grant for the gallery. He tried to explain why he couldn't—that political pressure would be resisted by the Council which jealously guarded its independence. She not only had rejected his explanation but surreptitiously used his official stationary to write a plea to the Council. That prompted a harrumphing reply from the Council chairman that fortunately had not ended up in the newspapers. In any event, the result was that he protectively distanced himself from the gallery even as Marie-Paule distanced herself from politics, thus further distancing themselves from each other.

Hôtel de Ville
Friday, June 26th
2:30pm EDT

As a member of parliament he knew it was important to visit the bomb sites in his riding. Accordingly his first stop of the day had been at the stock exchange where a police lieutenant showed him the alley behind the building. Frankly the physical damage didn't seem to amount to much. The political damage was far greater. Confirmation of that came from a CTV video crew which spotted him. They noted that the defense minister may have felt more comfortable travelling about the city than its other residents because unlike them he had a security detail.

Although Mount Royal technically wasn't in his riding he had also stopped there. The road leading to the summit was closed to the public but his security team was waved through. They parked a respectful distance away from the bomb site among several police vehicles and walked the rest of the way to a clearing fenced off by yellow crime scene tape.

The tangle of twisted metal in the center of the clearing seemed incompatible with the symbol of peace that in various incarnations had watched over the city since 1643. Over those years countless proposals of marriage had been offered before it, ashes of loved ones had been scattered about it and troubled hearts freighted with unanswerable questions had sought solace beneath its outstretched arms. But now it lay in ruins, the victim of political passions run amuck. That much he understood. What he didn't understand was the timing of the attack. The referendum was still nearly four months away, time enough for memories to fade and passions to cool...unless this was just a first installment.

Presumably there might be some answers forthcoming at this inaugural meeting of the intergovernmental coordinating committee. Having city, provincial and federal officials gather at one of the bombing sites was supposed to send a message of defiant unity. In point of fact it sent a mixed message at best as it was from the city hall balcony that Charles de Gaulle had delivered his defiant cry of "Vive le Québec Libre" in 1967, a challenge to Canadian unity separatists had not forgotten and federalists had not forgiven.

Here too yellow police tape cordoned off the street as workmen carted away broken glass and other debris. The bomb had actually been placed a hundred yards away at the base of the Nelson Column. At that distance it was no match for the sheer mass of the building whose 19th century architects believed in symbolizing political strength with structural strength. The horse-drawn sight-seeing carriage, unwittingly having picked precisely the wrong moment to pass between building and bomb, had offered no such resistance. Its occupants became what, in other conflicts, would be termed "collateral damage".

As he entered the conference room, he saw Marcel talking with the mayor. The RCMP division superintendant was there, as Mac had promised, as was a district commander of the Québec Provincial Police—the Sûreté—and the city police chief, Louis Ribaud. The overlapping police jurisdictions were a potential problem. The purpose of this meeting was to make sure they weren't.

Familiar with the mayor's penchant for brevity, Chief Ribaud gave an admirably short summary of where the investigation had taken them so far; in essence, not far. They knew what type of explosive had been used; Semtex, originally a Czech product but now available from any number of sources, all unsavory. "It doesn't take much to do a lot of damage," he explained. "Pan Am 103 was brought down by a few ounces. A few pounds would have been enough for everything that happened last night." He drew in a deep, audible breath before adding, "And there could be a lot more wherever that came from."

"Do we have any claim of responsibility?" the provincial premier's representative asked, perhaps a little anxiously lest the name of one of his party's stalwarts should surface.

"Including the Internet," Mayor Ganeau replied, "eleven."

"Serious ones?"

"Not if spelling counts." The mayor looked around the table for the next question. "Mr. Fraser?"

"Do we have any suspects?" Andrew directed his question to the chief.

"Do we have any specific individual, someone we can attach a name to? No. Not yet. But we are combing employment records at all four sites to see if the same name turns up in more than one place—perhaps someone with a grievance—and we've got undercover personnel listening for leads."

"Were there any security cameras anywhere?" someone wanted to know.

"Here and at the stock exchange. They had one in the alley where the blast occurred. We're reviewing the tapes but frankly spotting someone planting something in full view of the camera would be a long shot. We could get lucky but ..." His voice trailed off ending in a shrug.

"What about here?" The mayor asked.

"The cameras here were focused on the building, not the park."

Andrew had another question. "Chief, if the news reports are correct, all four explosions occurred at more or less the same time—apparently within a few minutes of each other—certainly not enough time for a person to get from one place to another. Does that mean the bombs were on timers or was there more than one bomber?"

"We suspect timers but we don't know yet. We're going through the debris now trying to determine that."

"Do you think whoever did it will strike again?"

The chief squinted in thought. "I dunno. That's up to them. If they think they got the job done, maybe not. If they don't, then maybe yes. Or..."

"Or?"

"Or maybe there wasn't any 'them'. Maybe it was just a lone weirdo...like an arsonist who wants to make things burn so he can watch the fire trucks come...I dunno."

Andrew slowly shook his head. "Somehow I don't think so, chief."

The chief stared back very hard before answering. "Me neither."

4861 Chemin de la Côte-des-Neiges, Montréal
Friday, June 26th
6:30pm EDT

His return to the apartment had been greeted by a one line note on the hall table from Marie-Paule announcing that she had gone down to the cottage for the weekend. Depending on how he chose to read it, it could be an invitation to join her...or not.

They had bought the cottage in the Eastern Townships long before he ran for parliament. It wasn't very big—two bedrooms, a bath, a tiny kitchen and a living room they had made larger by knocking out a partition letting it absorb the smaller of the bedrooms. That meant no overnight guests. It also meant that at the end of the day there was no place to take a disagreement except to bed. More than one issue that might have festered in Montréal dissolved overnight at the cottage. Perhaps that would happen again if he drove down tomorrow and didn't bring any work along. They could have dinner at the boat club or maybe go to some little restaurant where they could be alone and talk and get to know each other again.

But for now a ham sandwich and a bottle of beer were supper and his companions were a gaggle of pundits in an Ottawa TV studio who were filling time until separatist leader Lucien Renard was due to speak to a labor meeting in Montréal. Their consensus was that the renewal of separatist violence would push the referendum over the top even as it sank Québec's economy. Some saw a repeat of the 1960s and '70s when the *Front de libération du Québec's* bombing campaign drove out many English speaking people who took their companies with them and the jobs they provided. Consequently, as the separatists gained political power, Québec lost economic power. Toronto soon surpassed Montréal not only in population but as the financial center of the country. When the next Québec elections were held the issue was not sovereignty but jobs. The separatists lost.

Other of the panelists argued that in the intervening years Québec had changed in fundamental ways. Business was increasingly the purview of an emerging French middle class scornful of the provincialism and socialism of the separatists. But, if the doors to commerce in Montréal now read "Entrée", once inside the *nouveaux entrepreneurs* often discovered the exits were locked. Whereas the English could flee to Toronto, there was no place in North America where Montréal's new French business class could go if things turned sour without leaving their language and culture behind. Therefore, the panelists reasoned, they would oppose separatism.

With that introduction the picture shifted to a school gymnasium in the east end of Montréal where the president of the *Fédération des travailleurs du Québec* was wrapping up his remarks. Renard sat on a metal chair behind him waiting his turn.

Renard was aptly named. He looked like a fox with a narrow face, slightly protruding eyes and long reddish-brown hair. His voice emerged as a bark—rough and insistent, demanding you listen even if you didn't want to. Nonetheless he was effective and, in some quarters, even admired. He'd come up through the dockworkers union where his father had been a steward. But, unlike his father, he had never actually labored on the docks moving heavy loads between ship and shore. He'd worked in the union office, beginning summers as a clerk when he came home from college, first Laval and then Insead, the elite French business school. Later, he became the union teller, the man who matched jobs with bodies. It was there that he distinguished himself. With never enough jobs to go around, he proved to be scrupulously fair, seeing that every dues-paying member got some of the available work and he didn't take bribes to skew the assignments. Everyone shared and the older men weren't sent down into the holds of the bulk carriers where speed and agility meant the difference between loading the cargo and becoming part of the cargo. He wasn't one of them but he was respected by them and that was what he needed for a start.

It was often remarked that not all French were separatists but all separatists were French. Less often remarked was that a lot of them were also socialists. They talked in public about dignity and being master in their own house but, like much of the current crop of environmentalists, when you scratched away the slogans you often found hard left philosophies underneath. Renard was no exception. His Laval economics major had given him grounding in academic Marxism. Combined with a minor in history that focused on Québec's grievances, his future course was all but predestined. Nothing he learned at Insead dissuaded him from it.

It was not long before he was arguing to anyone who would listen that the tyranny of English Canada was all that stood between them and a fair share of Québec's natural riches. In his telling, English-speaking Toronto was the enemy. "We should not send our timber and our ore and our power to Bay Street," he would argue. "They can't get it if we Québécois don't cut the trees and dig the mines and dam the rivers. We do the work. They get rich. *Québec pour les Québécois! Québec pour les Québécois! Québec pour les Québécois!* he would shout at the end of each speech until his audience picked up the chant.

In time the chant grew louder as his audiences grew larger. And his voice carried farther when he won a seat in the National Assembly, the ambitiously named provincial legislature. There, as a member of a still young separatist party, his power grew until now, as premier, he was again challenging Québec to separate from Canada.

"Citoyens du Québec..." Renard had taken the podium and begun to speak. Cries to be quiet could be heard off camera along with a chorus of shhhhs. He started again. "Citoyens du Québec..."

His voice faded into the background and a disembodied woman's voice devoid of any emotion began a simultaneous English translation which, as was often observed, presumably shouldn't be needed in an officially bilingual country.

Andrew listened intently. "A great tragedy occurred 24 hours ago in Montréal. The lives of a dozen people—some of them mere children—were taken from them in a series of brutal bombings. For them and for their families and friends we grieve and our tears join with theirs. For those wounded in these vicious attacks our thoughts and prayers go out to you." His head was bowed as he spoke. He never looked directly into the camera after his opening words. In this mode he talked for another minute or so and then stopped. After a tense silence he slowly raised his head until he was staring directly into the camera. His eyes were cold and hard, his words clipped and angry, bizarrely at variance with the quiet monotone of the translator. Those following Renard in French thus heard a measurably different message than those listening to the English translation. Andrew was tempted to change the channel to hear him free of translation but didn't.

"In a little more than a hundred days we are to have a referendum on our future. Can we believe these events occurred without any awareness of that? Can we believe this was not an attempt to influence that decision? At the very hour this outrage occurred the leaders of Canada were gathered in their prime minister's house plotting the defeat of our campaign to restore their heritage to an oppressed people." He said "Canada" as though it were a foreign country and if not an actual enemy then at least an indifferent sovereign.

"And who do you think they will blame for this tragedy?" He paused as if waiting for an answer. Then, with a twitch of his eyebrows, answered his question with another: "Why would those who are about to win their long fight for freedom and justice attack those for whom they wage the fight? That..." he concluded in a suddenly softer voice "...that is not reasonable."

"And we must also ask how could anyone strike in secret not once but four times in the heart of a great city? Are there not guards at the borders to keep evil-doers out and watchers among us to warn of what bad people are plotting? Are there not taxes collected to pay those who are charged with guarding our borders and watching over us?" He sighed and looked down at the floor in seeming despair. "Perhaps there is too much to guard. Perhaps there are too many to watch. Canada is a very large place. It houses many people from many countries speaking many languages. Perhaps the job is too big for its government. Perhaps it is too far away. Perhaps a government closer to its people can more effectively protect them."

His right fist now began rhythmically pounding the palm of his left hand, his voice rasping beneath the translator, his jaw clamping on each word, his look filled with fury. "Why did Canada not prevent this slaughter of French innocents? Why could they not find a few pennies to protect the people who earn the dollars they tax? With their army and police and spies why could they not prevent this assault on our people?"

He radiated an anger that was both threatening and compelling. Even in translation the man was spellbinding. He knew when to speak and when to use silence to build intensity. His listeners would find themselves growing anxious during his silences so that when he finally spoke it became an emotional catharsis.

The quiet, detached English translation was now nearly buried beneath a furious torrent of French in the background. The visage of an angry man filled the screen. "I'll tell you why they could not safeguard our people because they are not *of* our people! They do not *know* our people but they do know what time it is and they are afraid. They know their time is up! Their time is up! And they know it! Soon an oppressed people will declare with one voice that it is time for three centuries of tyranny to end!" At that the audience erupted in cheers. Renard ignored them, again looking down toward the floor, deliberately breaking off contact with his audience, leaving his viewers alone, confused, perhaps even afraid of what was to come next. But when he resumed speaking his voice was calm and quiet under the translator, all emotion seemingly drained from it.

"They think we will flee in terror. They are wrong. We will not flee. This is our home. We have nowhere else to go and we wish to go nowhere else. We only wish to be safe in our homes and free of fear in our streets. And if their government cannot protect us, then we must have a government of our own that can!" The last word emerged as a barely audible growl. He stood silently for a long moment and then, surrounded by a phalanx of guards, turned and walked out of the room as cheers again erupted behind him.

Andrew muted the sound and sat in silence for a long moment. Renaud's disavowal of responsibility for the bombings was powerful, even convincing, but strikingly he had only blamed the government for not preventing the attacks, not for committing them. So the question remained: if not the separatists and not the federalists, then who?

Chapter Four

Chateau Cher
Saturday, June 27th
2:30 p.m. CEDT

The luncheon had gone exceedingly well. From the Soup au Pistou with its accents of basil to the Poulet Provencal and the crisp un-oaked Sauvignon Blanc from a neighboring Sancerre vineyard, the menu was perfectly suited to the day. A soft breeze made certain the bright sunshine did not become too warm for his dozen or so guests. Better yet, the luncheon conversation had confirmed that there were powerful men who shared his vision…or at least as much of it as he had shared with them. He must remember to find some token of gratitude for Philippe who had invested much time and effort in assembling the guest list. He had, as always, done a superb job.

And, let it be noted, he had done rather well himself; diplomatic allusions but nothing more. Certainly nothing that could come back to trouble him should one of his guests be so indiscrete as to repeat his words in unfriendly ears. One did not get to be President of the Republic by being indelicate, unlike one guest who had thoughtlessly noted that Sauvignon Blanc was not actually native to the region having been grafted onto American stock in the late 1800s after phylloxera had devastated the local vineyards. As host he had gently turned aside the rude observation by suggesting it was in keeping with Lafayette's precedent that the French should improve what came from America.

The appreciative ripple of laughter that greeted his sally had provided opportunity to move seamlessly to other, somewhat allied, topics.

The conversation subsequently ranged from the importance that the European Union speak with a French accent to the need to contain American influence as once the Americans had sought to contain Soviet influence, albeit not always with French help. Someone quoted Henry Kissinger that diplomacy is the art of restraining power, a maxim the Americans in their missionary zeal never seemed to remember. That brought his trenchant observation that Kissinger was, after all, European not American, and a Jew at that. The chuckles that came in response provided the perfect note on which to end the luncheon and repair to the veranda for cigars.

The chap now descending the steps to the garden with him obviously understood the value of discretion. His approach had been impeccable. One moment there was a small gathering at which nothing of consequence was being said, and then there was a brief moment when it was just the two of them. His guest had taken that opportunity to suggest that a little stroll in the garden might be agreeable after so excellent a luncheon. Thus they set out on what might be regarded as a voyage of exploration.

Of the several assets Marie-Therese had brought to their marriage this estate on the River Cher two hours south of Paris was the crown jewel. In her family for all but a few years during the revolution it bespoke a heritage that he envied and, while it would never be his, thanks to the Code Napoléon, it would in time, be his son's. Among her further assets was sufficient income to maintain the property and promote the political talents of her husband. What she may have lacked in other areas was easily satisfied from among the camp followers that any successful politician was sure to attract. Again, of course, he was very discrete.

"…as you did so effectively as mayor." His thoughts had wandered. The other man had been speaking in that lilting, lightly accented French found among the better-educated classes of the

Littoral. While he couldn't put a name to the round, olive-toned face with its sleepy eyelids he did remember that he was in banking in Lebanon or Syria or some such place.

Until now his guest had been complimenting him on the elegance of the garden to which he had responded with murmurs of appreciation without really listening. For exploring the garden, of course, was not the purpose of their stroll. It was, at best, only the aperitif. The main course no doubt would follow in good time; otherwise a nap would be most pleasant about now. A good meal, an excellent wine, a fine cigar and a warm day could do that to you.

But rest would have to wait. His political antenna was signaling him to be alert. "While I did not have the pleasure of making your acquaintance when you were a mayor, I have heard much of your great success in that office," the banker continued, "especially of your remarkable ability to understand differing needs and to fashion a comfortable 'living space' for everyone, if I may use such a term...a talent that I see you are now putting to the service of the nation. If in any way I may be of some assistance in that effort, I would be honored if you would call on me."

In his early political career André Legrande had indeed exhibited a remarkable talent for creating "living space" for competing interests: labor and management, church and state, left and right, law and order. That last one had been key for on it depended all the other balancing acts a big city mayor must be able to perform. It had been his genius to realize early on that law and order were not necessarily coupled as most people assumed. Law was one thing. Order was quite another. And, of the two, the average citizen by far preferred order. Law only came into the formula once order was disturbed, often too late for any but remedial effect.

That was why, even before he ever ran for mayor, he reached certain understandings with various interests ranging from the Church to those who were unlikely to have ever seen the insides of one. Each interest group had certain objectives. And he had patiently and convincingly explained to each how his election as mayor would make their attainment of those objectives more likely. Some, like law and order, had proven relatively easy. Others, like labor and management, had been more difficult. Left and right were nearly impossible.

Law and order had simply been a matter of the aforementioned "living space." In discrete meetings with a number of influential men he had made it clear that the law would not show undue interest in certain of their activities in return for an end to other activities that offended the community's sense of order. It proved to be a very profitable bargain for everyone concerned. Two years into his administration a popular national magazine had noted that his city defied the national trend as every category of crime declined in its precincts except so called "crimes of passion". Some things, after all, were not negotiable.

A seat in the National Assembly soon followed where he learned to play on a larger stage. Not only was the Elysée Palace in the hands of the conservatives, of whom he was nominally one, and the Assembly in the hands of the socialists, whom he cordially detested, but both the right and the left were riven by internal disagreements. In such an environment he thrived.

Whereas at home he had spoken of living space, in Paris he called it "co-habitation". The idea was the same. What made it so much more difficult in Paris was that everything was viewed through a political prism. A new play was praised or denounced not for the quality of its drama but for whatever political shadings some critic found in its lines. Cleaning up an eyesore became a doctrinal conflict between leftist greens and laissez faire rightists. Nonetheless the concept delighted the chattering classes who dominated the TV talk shows and op-ed pages. Consequently André Legrande's name was frequently on their lips.

Naturally the zealots of the right and the left railed against co-habitation as a sell-out of principle. But that only served to convince the others that "if *they* don't like it, it must be good." By extension, they also felt inclined to think well of the man who promoted the concept. From there a series of increasingly important cabinet posts and a tough but ultimately successful run for the presidency were only a matter of time and a generous application of Marie-Therese's inheritance.

"Monsieur le president," the banker's voice brought him back to the present. "I was greatly impressed by your comments over that excellent luncheon. I very much share your vision. As you so correctly noted, France and the world need 'a third way' whereas it would appear that presently there are only two. That was how it was during the Cold War. You could be with the Soviets or with the Americans. Not much to choose from there until de Gaulle blazed a third way." The banker paused to look at the opening to the neatly trimmed boxwood maze, seemingly uncertain whether to enter. "Tito and Nehru realized he had created an exit from bi-polar politics and the non-aligned movement was born. It gave them freedom from vassalage to either camp and in the process, provided a little bargaining room—a little 'living space' as you so aptly describe it." Turning to face the President of the Republic the banker added, "And I do believe you would like to further that concept both at home and on the international stage. Or am I mistaken?"

The president did not offer a simple *oui* or *non*. His answer, as always, was more nuanced. "I believe you are quite correct in your memory of the history of that time," he said, "and indeed there have been other occasions when it might have been useful to have had some alternative to, shall we say, joining the posse or those who flee its embrace." They both smiled at his little jest. His supposedly off-mic comment at a recent G-7 summit about "American cowboys" had received wide circulation in the press and was, in some measure, thought to have helped his re-election. Whatever the authenticity of his indiscretion, the sentiments behind it were real and passionately held in the Gaullist tradition. In the popular imagining the Americans remained cowboys, riding into town in a cloud of dust, shooting

up everything in sight and leaving a mess behind. He had repeatedly pressed the European Union for greater independence from the
Americans but with only limited success. There was too much history and too much commerce to nudge them away from Washington
although privately several leaders told him they agreed with his concern that the Americans would drag them into another cold war, if
not with the now oil-rich Russians, then with Islam. But just when
he thought he had a convert to "the third way" they'd wriggle off
the hook and mumble something about their hopes that the next
American election would serve up someone more...well...European.
If they would only review the history of the post war years with a clear
eye, as he had done, they would realize de Gaulle had been right to
disengage France from NATO and seek a European-centered defense,
even as Schumann before him had been right to seek a European-
centered economy. France's rejoining NATO was, in his eyes, an error
only awaiting an opportunity to be corrected.

"Quite so monsieur le president," the banker was purring. "Quite
so. And it is on that point of agreement that I would venture to note
there are others who feel as you do and have quietly asked me to so
advise you." André's political antenna began to vibrate. Who might
engage a banker of undoubtedly substantial means—Philippe would
not have invited him if that were not the case—to carry such a message for them?

"I appreciate your letting me know," he told the banker. That was
the truth. He wondered when he would find out what his guest might
expect in return for the unspecified support of his unnamed friends.
He did not have long to wait.

"They are men with certain interests," the banker continued,
"who, like most of us, find it much easier to conduct one's affairs in
an orderly climate than in one filled with turmoil. To that end they
would be most supportive of a 'third way' in those areas where their
interests lie."

The banker's circumspect language required a bit of definition. "Are we speaking of the Levant?" he inquired.

"There indeed," the banker replied, pausing, whether for effect or deliberation, before adding "but also in other areas where some of the same circumstances might pertain."

"Such as?"

"Ah," the cigar added a bit of color and fragrance to his exhalation, "that is perhaps more for you to say than for me to suggest, monsieur le president. If I understand the success of your third way correctly, it consists in some part in identifying areas where interests do not directly compete and hence where assignments may be made to offset concessions in areas where they *do* compete. Excuse me if I overly simplify what is, of course, a far more subtle and complex process, but alas, I am just a businessman and you are, may we say it, a statesman, one who resolves the interests over which others compete and thus improves the quality of life for all."

The man's flattery was being applied with a palette knife rather than a brush but the result was none the less appealing. Of course, there were many details to be identified; what "interests" was he referring to; what areas did they wish to occupy; and, not insignificantly, what compensation might result from some yet unspecified effort on his part? As they strolled through the garden the pieces and the pattern they formed gradually became clearer. Simply put, the interests the banker claimed to represent were finding the situation in the Middle East increasingly ill suited to the conduct of business as a heavy-handed American policy driven more by political considerations at home than any appreciation for the subtleties of life in the region confronted a virulent strain of Islam. The Americans vetted their policies with Washington's influential "Jewish lobby" which, once largely confined to liberal Democrats, had in recent years acquired strong support among Republican evangelical Christians.

A few prescient voices in the Middle East deplored where the resulting polarization was leading the region but had nothing beyond pious aspirations to offer as an alternative. He could see the need for a third way. What he could not yet see was what was in it for him... or for France, if it came to that. It was there that the banker was able to shed some light, albeit, illuminating a few rather disturbing images in the process.

"If I recall correctly, monsieur le president, you were able to establish order as mayor by indicating new locales for certain activities you did not wish to see flourishing in certain precincts." That was true. The red light district, which had been a blight on the center city, found a new home in a neighborhood where any sort of industry was tolerated if not actually welcomed. Once relocated, the former red light district underwent gentrification and in time, generated taxes instead of bribes with a salubrious effect on the city's architecture, exchequer and official standards of conduct. It was a win for much of the city, if not necessarily for all.

"There has been a certain amount of concern expressed of recent," the banker continued, "at the potential for what is termed 'radicalization' of certain ethnic groups who make their home in France." That observation so engaged the president that he stopped and turned to look down from his nearly two meter height on the considerably shorter banker, peering intently at him as if to determine whether he had just signaled a threat or an opening. His companion seemed not to notice. "Your government's Commission of Inquiry following the recent unpleasantness in Clichy-sous-Bois found that high unemployment among the youth and inflammatory rhetoric in the mosques had combined to create some—as they put it— 'alienation'."

It most assuredly had. Hundreds of automobiles were torched and although no one was killed in the rioting and remarkably few were injured, the flames blazed for days on TV sets around the world leading to cancelled hotel rooms and café tables. Tourism, which brought money earned elsewhere to fill French pockets, was off by nearly half in the three months following that long weekend of violence. Only several sharply worded addresses on television insisting on law and order had kept his poll numbers from being incinerated along with the automobiles. And while the wrecks had been quickly towed away and the insurance companies importuned, the view of his administration had been significantly altered in ways he did not appreciate. The strident interior minister had become a hero in certain quarters while the detested socialists enjoyed an uptick in popularity with their mushy talk of a "social compact" for the forgotten and disadvantaged which, when dissected, simply amounted to higher taxes on the most productive segments of society to buy off the least productive, many of whom had not even bothered to learn the language since washing up on French shores. How in heaven's name could they expect to hold a job if they couldn't communicate with their employer or his customers? There were schools. Why didn't they go there and learn something other than how to stuff a rag in the gas pipe of an automobile that cost more than they could earn in a year? But while the commission was far too soft on personal responsibility for what had happened, it was right when it blamed the imams for inciting them to riot.

"I believe we might be able to have some effect on both those challenges your commission identified: the lack of gainful employment and the intoxicating speech of the clerics." The banker had his full attention. "We are aware of certain industries that might be willing to consider locating in what I believe they termed 'disadvantaged districts' if certain circumstances were otherwise favorable."

His government had already tried to get some low end French manufacturers to relocate in return for various government incentives including seeing that overseers stayed away, but with little success. However, he had not looked outside the country which this chap apparently was prepared to do. It was an interesting idea but much too soon in the conversation for anything more than an oblique "I see" in response. After all, the fellow had not yet said how he might be able to tone down those imams and the rabble they aroused, or more importantly, what he would want in return for doing so.

"The sometimes unfortunate rhetorical excesses of the clerics can misdirect impressionable young people, as they did in my own country," the banker continued, prompting André to again wonder just which country that was. He must remember to ask Philippe who was busy keeping the other guests on the veranda to allow this little voyage of discovery to continue uninterrupted long enough to reach some shore.

"Of course, some of these teachers and their students are beyond reason and are best encouraged to seek elsewhere to fulfill their ambitions but generally it has been our experience that mosques, like any other business, have bills to pay and are not inattentive to those who make it possible for them to do so." So that was his answer: buy off the imams which was more efficient and doubtless more effective than trying to deport them or shut them up with laws sure to be challenged in court as the stupid British were doing. He was impressed with the quiet tidiness of the package that was being offered—jobs and bribes—or "contributions" as his companion called them. A tidy package indeed but surely not without some offsetting cost elsewhere. After all, for a banker the books must balance.

"That," André observed, "might suggest some interesting options for what you correctly discern is a domestic concern. But I believe you also mentioned a wider sphere of action."

"Indeed, I did," the banker agreed with a heartiness that suggested he felt the first stage of an agreement had been concluded although his host had not actually said so, nor would he ever. Some agreements were best made with a slight incline of the head rather than words that could someday turn and echo in places one would prefer they not be heard. "While my associates wish to establish a presence within the European Community and consider France its natural center, their interests are not limited to Europe. Nor, if I may be so bold as to suggest, are yours." That observation did not require any particular insight. He had made no secret of his hope that the francophone world would one day rival the British Commonwealth if not MacDonald's and Wal-Mart for international ascendancy.

The banker retained his attention as over the next few minutes he described a process by which the same business interests that would transform troublesome suburbs would also reach out to the wider world under the French flag much as ships ranged the seas under flags of convenience…a process he colorfully described as "the opportunity for merchant caravans to follow the French flag and to prosper in its shade." To the banker's surprise, it was at that point that his host extended his hands in a gesture of sorrowful resignation. "Alas, monsieur," he said, "I regret that I must break off our discussion, but as you can see, I have other guests and I must not neglect them however much I may find myself intrigued by your ideas. Perhaps we can continue our conversation at another time." He savored the look that flashed across the banker's face. Whatever the man thought the president would do in response to his overture, he did not think he would terminate the conversation. It was thus "advantage André" with further sets to be played.

Philippe saw them turn back and immediately suggested to the two men whose conversation he had monitored if not actually engaged, that they might like to join the president in the garden. Thus, on André's return to the veranda a few minutes later it was as one of a group that did not include the banker and raised few eyebrows. During the next hour he took time to speak with each guest. He also found a moment to suggest quietly to Philippe that the banker might be invited to linger behind to continue their conversation and that the Cardinal be asked to join them.

It was a columnist in *Le Figaro* who had dubbed Professor Jean-Pierre Dumont "The Cardinal"—not because of his piety but for his physical and political resemblance to Cardinal Richelieu, the powerful advisor to Louis XIII, who cemented the foundations of the Bourbon dynasty at home and the French empire abroad. The sobriquet stuck, as well it ought to. For had the chattering classes looked beyond the day's headlines, they might have found some interesting parallels between the thin-faced, hawk-nosed man in de Champaigne's portrait of the original cardinal and the one who would take his place beside the seat of power four centuries on.

With the other guests departed, that seat of power proved to be a large wing chair to one side of the fireplace in the library next to the president with the banker seated opposite. It was too warm for a fire but cool enough with a late afternoon breeze to make the library preferable to the veranda. The empire clock on the mantel chimed softly as if to mark a moment of special significance as the three took their seats. Drinks had been offered but declined. Cigars had long since burnt themselves to ash. There thus were no diversions at hand, no pretense that they had met for any purpose other than the one the president would reference once the formalities were observed. "M. Khashan" he said—Philippe having equipped him with the name and a few other details he had not remembered during the walk in the garden—"may I introduce Professor Dumont. He is a most valued advisor. With your permission, I should like him to join us."

"I would be delighted," the banker replied. "M. Dumont's reputation precedes him." Turning to the Cardinal he thrust out his hand, adding, "I am most honored, monsieur. Your presence assures me that I shall not leave here without having learned something of great value."

Not for the first time that afternoon André raised an eyebrow at the heavy application of flattery although he noticed the Cardinal didn't seem put off by it. But then, he was an academic so that should come as no surprise. "M. Khashan and I began an exploration of some ideas earlier this afternoon but had to break off so that I could attend to my other guests. I asked him to stay on a bit as I must admit I am curious to discover where his ideas might lead. Now," he added addressing the banker, "perhaps you could bring M. Dumont up to date."

"Indeed, M. le President, with great pleasure," Khashan said, turning toward the Cardinal. "I had noted with great approbation that the president has demonstrated a rare ability to find a third way between seemingly irreconcilable polarities in domestic affairs and I observed that such a gift might be most welcome in the larger arena of world affairs. I further suggested that should he agree to undertake such an initiative beyond the borders of the republic, I was quite confident that significant commerce could result with benefits accruing to France and to those who invest in her leadership." The Cardinal thought that last bit intriguing and wondered in what sense this balding, olive-toned man meant it. He further noted that despite the man's tendency to decorate his sentences with rhetorical embellishments and to gesture as he spoke, his eyes did not waver beneath their heavy lids. It was as if he were reading from a script only he could see. Whatever hyperbole might excite his speech, his eyes remained calm, windows on a very purposeful mind perhaps playing out a charade. That further intrigued the Cardinal, an inveterate worker of puzzles.

"While such a commercial potential already exists within the European Union," the banker continued, "alas, what is true of France is also true for every other E.U. member. So one might say there is no French advantage, especially since Brussels believes its duty is to deny any member an advantage thus devaluing French ingenuity and, might I suggest, compromising French sovereignty. In the final reckoning, France within Europe can only be as great as the Brussels bureaucrats and the most timid member states allow." He paused and looked expectantly at André who, however, said nothing. Therefore, the banker continued.

"As for the special trade relations France maintains outside the common market, most are with relatively impoverished nations, principally in Africa. One day they may prove to be profitable markets, but for now, they offer only modest opportunities although your commerce, of course, speaks to noble purposes. As for Asia," he continued in his cataloguing of French commerce, "Japan, China, India and some other smaller economies offer more valuable prospects but they bring with them a competition injurious to French industry. I speak of product piracy, low wages and artificial currency valuations which make for very uneven playing fields."

"If what you say about Europe, Africa and Asia is true," the Cardinal interjected, "where then, do you see an opportunity for France, M. Khashan?"

"North America."

The president stirred in his chair. The cardinal raised an eyebrow. "With all due respect, sir," he said, "we already have significant trade with the United States even in such matters as aircraft where several American airlines fly our Airbus."

"True enough," the banker replied, "you do trade with the United States but unfortunately you do it on an essentially level playing field."

André was confused. "But I thought you said that was the goal; that the problem was uneven playing fields."

"No, sir," the banker replied. "I must apologize if I gave that impression." He paused a moment before adding, "I am suggesting a level playing field is the problem. You should tilt the field...in favor of France."

"And how would you propose we do that?" André asked, pursing his lips.

"Regain Quebec."

Chapter Five

The White House
Monday, June 29th
8:30am EDT

As he climbed the granite steps from the glorified parking lot that had once been West Executive Avenue carrying a plastic-wrapped plate of scrambled eggs, toast and bacon in one hand and a Styrofoam cup of coffee in the other, he kept a careful pace behind two young women who were heading in the same direction. When they tugged open the heavy oak door of what was formally known as the Eisenhower Executive Office Building he slipped between them with a cheery "thank you." Now all that stood between him and breakfast was a guard, a flight of stairs and the door to his office. None proved an obstacle. The guard glanced at his ID tag not for the name on it—Mark Rayberg—nor even for its unflattering photo but for its background color which told him the level of its bearer's security clearance. This one was free to go where he wanted.

Repeated efforts to tear down the EEOB and replace it with something more functional had been rebuffed by preservationists. They had a point. It had seen a lot of history once having simultaneously housed both the departments of State and War. He sometimes wondered whether they had gotten along any better when they were under one roof than they did now sitting on opposite sides of the Potomac. Apart from the five months when James Monroe simultaneously headed both departments, probably not. And that, of course, was the reason his office had been created. The National Security Council was supposed to be above Washington's turf wars. Sometimes it was. Other times it was just the most prized turf.

Having successfully, if awkwardly, navigated his office door, he put the plate down on a desk that was clear of any papers. Security wouldn't allow otherwise, not even for as long as it took to pop over to the Navy mess in the White House basement. Next he uncovered the coffee and took a trial sip. Good. Still hot. Then he retrieved *The New York Times* and the *Washington Post* from the table by the couch, separating the Post sports section from the rest of the paper. As he dug into breakfast he scanned the baseball standings to see how the Nationals were faring. If they could play 500 ball their fans would continue to support them. Below that and, like Cinderella, they might wake up one morning back where they started wearing their old clothes, which in their case meant in Montréal wearing Expo uniforms.

The thought of Montréal shifted his attention to the "A" sections of the papers. The Times had a few paragraphs on the bottom of the front page about Sunday's memorial service for the bombing victims. On the jump page they had an AP photo of the bombed out Jewish community center and a small map of Montréal with an arrow pointing to Outremont. The rest of the story was mostly filler: the general background of the separatist movement and the F.L.Q.'s 1960s bombing campaign. With a quick check of the editorial page he turned to the Post.

They'd put the story inside with lots of quotes from a Laval University professor who explained the referendum and suggested why an independent Québec might be in the U.S. interest. He didn't say why it might not be in Québec's interest. That was covered in an op-ed by a Post columnist who still had distant cousins in Québec although most of his family had left for the New England textile mills long before he was born. He noted that the separatist agitation largely came from a small, leftist elite that presumed it would be in charge once ties to Canada were severed. They argued that the French were doomed to second class status in the Canadian confederation. The Post columnist asked what status they thought they'd have on their own in an American-dominated, English-speaking continent. Given their relative numbers, he wrote, at best they'd have to settle for a distant third place behind the Latinos. "Going it alone in an ever more integrated world is a bad idea in any language," he concluded.

An independent Québec might be a romantic notion based on a mixture of real and inflated historical and cultural grievances, Mark mused, but it was also an opportunity for mischief. Like Cuba in the heyday of communism, it could provide a base for outsiders with malign intent. That would be where his office might come in, although not yet as there was nothing solid to go on, just the same niggling concern Andy had expressed Thursday night that things didn't add up.

His reading was interrupted by the telephone. Could he spare the National Security Advisor a few minutes? Courtly manners were a hallmark of this administration after years when such courtesies were largely absent from public life. As the president-elect had told his senior staff at a pre-inaugural meeting "civility is the lubricant that enables the machinery of government to function smoothly."

While he and the rest of the NSC staff worked in the EEOB, the National Security Advisor had an office in the West Wing, just a few doors away from the Oval Office. To get there you could take a small elevator up one level or climb a narrow flight of stairs. He always opted for the stairs in the belief they would compensate for his no longer taking long morning runs across the Mall, his running time having been consumed by his working time.

He was often struck by how different the real West Wing was from the typical movie version. Though busy, there was no frenzy of activity. It had the look and feel of the executive suite of a private bank.

A neat, gray-haired woman in a conservatively cut suit sat at a small mahogany desk angled in the hallway opposite the stairs. Some of the junior staff surreptitiously referred to her as the "hall monitor." A few paces away a uniformed Secret Service officer stood watching the comings and goings. The lady at the desk flashed a welcoming smile. "I believe Mr. Hamilton is expecting you Mr. Rayberg." Her words might have been construed to mean "go on up" but her tone said "wait" as she dialed a three digit internal number. "Mr. Rayberg is here," she reported. Her eyes did not leave him. He sometimes wondered who would prove the tougher foe in a showdown, the hall monitor or the secret service officer. She again smiled. "You may go ahead Mr. Rayberg."

Although already announced, protocol dictated that he tap gently before entering the National Security Advisor's suite. A pleasant, middle aged woman who exuded quiet competence greeted him with a warmth that suggested he was one of her favorites. While inquiring how he was doing she, in turn, tapped on an inner door, opening it partway as she did. "Mr. Rayberg to see you, sir."

DeWitt Hamilton, whose bloodlines endowed him with both names, had been a partner in a Wall Street law firm his grandfather had co-founded. That was before his former Harvard classmate had summoned him to become an advisor to his campaign and now his presidency. Witt Hamilton had traveled extensively for the law firm whose moneyed clients could have formed their own United Nations had they been more inclined to talk than action. In any event, they occasionally provided him with bits of information he might find useful and sometimes forwarded a quiet word from him. He could have had the State Department in the new administration but he had suggested another name, a respected former ambassador and college president who knew all the diplomatic niceties and yet was expert at academic infighting, an essential skill at State. He opted instead for National Security Advisor which not only covered a broader spectrum but was less encumbered with ceremony. And so it was that Witt Hamilton and his Rolodex had moved into the West Wing two years ago.

Among the names in his Rolodex was that of the president of a Washington think tank who suggested that one of his staffers, a bright, young, former aide to the Senate Foreign Relations Committee, might be useful. Further inquiry confirmed that judgment and two days before his 38th birthday Mark Rayberg stepped through Washington's famous revolving door moving from quasi-academic status to again being a player. While one of the younger members of the Council, he quickly discovered that the team Dewitt Hamilton had assembled was more interested in the quality of a person's ideas than how many years he or she had taken to develop them. One of his ideas had made its way into print in a book the *New York Times* praised for its understanding that, for all the statistics and computer modeling that inform modern government, history and the emotions it evokes still play an outsized role in decision making.

As he entered the National Security Advisor's office, Witt Hamilton was standing by one of its tall windows that looked onto a stretch of what had once been busy Pennsylvania Avenue but since 9-11 had been transformed into a pedestrian mall. There was some debate as to how much safer it made the White House but no one disputed that it made it quieter. He turned as his guest was announced. "Good morning Mark. Thank you so much for coming over." He motioned his aide to a waiting chair while taking his own seat behind an elegant Winthrop desk. "I will not keep you long but the situation in Québec came up this morning and I thought it would be useful to hear your views on it." He did not say where the situation in Québec had come up or with whom but it didn't require much imagination to guess. "It presumably was the work of the separatists?"

"Presumably sir…" He hesitated before continuing, "But possibly not."

The National Security Advisor steepled his hands in front of him, fingertips touching his nose, elbows on the desk, all attention focused on Mark. "And what raises your doubts?"

"Two things: the choice of targets and the history of separatism in Québec. Three of the targets could be seen as an effort to suppress the federalist vote; the fourth—the cross on Mount Royal—doesn't fit that scenario. It's a symbol of *French* Canada, not *English* Canada. And then, there's the matter of who this generation of separatists is. These are not "farmers with pitchforks" to borrow a phrase. For the most part they're a college-educated elite."

"The separatist leader I saw on TV this weekend didn't seem to fit that description," Hamilton dryly observed.

"Yes and no, sir. Lucien Renard comes from a working class background but he is unusually well-educated—Laval and Insead. "

"He hides his erudition well."

"Yes, sir. He is very good at role-playing for the cameras and the crowd."

"Are you suggesting that because of his education he is incapable of brutality? I'm afraid history would challenge such an assumption."

"No, sir. I am suggesting that because of his education and his knowledge of history he is unlikely to use violence, a course that had already failed."

"Perhaps unlikely but, I suspect you would agree, not impossible."

"It is, of course, possible sir," Mark conceded, wondered as he did whether Hamilton might be right.

"So you find the situation...?" Hamilton's voice trailed off leaving it for Mark to answer.

"Inconclusive, but worrisome." He proceeded to run through not only what he knew of the bombings but his concern at the prospect of unrest on America's undefended northern border.

When he finished, Dewitt Hamilton swiveled his high-backed chair a quarter turn so he could again look out the window toward Blair House on the far side of Pennsylvania Avenue. After a long moment, he turned back to his desk and, picking up a bone-handled letter opener, thoughtfully tapped it against the top of the desk, as if deliberating how to proceed. Then, apparently having reached a decision, continued.

"I received a call this morning from Jean-Pierre Dumont, the advisor to André the Grand." Hamilton's jab at the notoriously vain French president was tempered by a mischievous smile. "Jean-Pierre and I have known each other for years, long before either of us acquired our present jobs," Hamilton continued. "After his usual circumlocution, he began to question me about our view of what's happening in Québec. He seemed particularly interested in what our response would be if the referendum were to win approval."

"May I ask what you told him, sir?"

"I was purposely vague in reply. So far as I know State hasn't determined a response and while I no doubt will have some opportunity to weigh in on whatever in their wisdom they may decide, so far the question hasn't come up. In point of fact, that's something I may need to change. In any event, when I asked *his* views he didn't answer but changed the subject, asking what we thought of Russia's claims to the Arctic; did it worry us as an Arctic power? I said we took a dim view of their claims but thought they would probably be resolved diplomatically although, of course, I could not speak for Canada, Denmark, Iceland or Norway who also claim parts of the Arctic."

"If you don't mind my asking, sir, why would France care? They're not an 'Arctic power' as he put it."

"Well that perplexed me, too, so I asked. His response was that they were signatories to the Law of the Sea Treaty which he noted gave authority over exploitation of resources beyond a 200 mile exclusion zone to the International Seabed Authority, which is true enough. The French have done a lot with submersibles and they already have a license from the ISA to explore in the North Pacific for polymetallic nodules, chunks of raw metal that lie on the ocean floor, coughed up by undersea volcanoes ages ago. Perhaps they're thinking of trying something similar in the Arctic. Indeed, I asked him whether they were."

"To which he replied?"

"If you knew the Cardinal, you'd know he rarely replies directly to anything. He said something about how one never knew and it was always useful to keep an open mind about the future but of course the opinions of friends must be weighed in the balance and so on. It's a shame you haven't met him. It's very rare that one encounters a true 17th century mind these days."

"Do you think France has an eye on the Arctic?"

"It's possible. He did make a little joke about Arctic warming and how one day perhaps Alaska might have its own Riviera. It was said with humor and I took it as such. Perhaps I should not have." He paused, seeming to replay that part of the conversation in his mind before he continued. "In any event, what I wanted to ask you was, can you quietly find out what a line 200 miles from the bordering states would leave unclaimed, especially 200 miles from Alaska? "

"Before or after the new Russian claim?" Mark asked.

"Ah…an interesting question. Let's rephrase that: If the Russian claim were to be upheld how much open seabed would be left? And, as long as you're taking measurements, let's also measure Canada's claims both with and without Québec. I must confess my knowledge of geography in that part of the world is very modest."

Mark's expression clearly telegraphed his amazement. "Are you suggesting sir that the French or the Russians might be trying to influence what's happening in Québec?"

"No. What I am saying is Dumont raised a tangential issue which exceeds my grasp of geography. So I'm assigning one of my brightest staff members to quietly search out that information. We have an obvious interest in what happens in Québec—indeed, in all of Canada—but we also have an interest—perhaps even a greater interest—in what happens off our northern shore, distant and chilly though it may presently be. Prudhoe Bay on that shore accounts for fully 15% of all the oil we use. Anything that might impact that production or potential future production constitutes a national security issue which, after all, is what this office is supposed to be concerned with."

"Yes sir," Mark replied. "I'll get on it right away." As he prepared to get up, Dewitt Hamilton held out a restraining hand.

"There's one other thing. I don't know whether it has anything to do with what we've been discussing, but he also mentioned parenthetically that their aircraft carrier, the *de Gaulle*, will be making a port call at St. Pierre and Miquelon in August. As I say, I don't know what, if anything, such a visit to their islands might have to do with any of this but I've learned over the years to listen to the parentheses in Jean-Pierre's sentences. What he puts inside them is often as important as what he leaves outside. So, with what may be an excess of caution, I shall pass the information along to the navy and others who, like yourself, may find it of interest. Do keep me informed."

Chapter Six

55 Rue du Faubourg Saint-Honore, Paris
Tuesday, June 30th
9:30am CEDT

The Cardinal's presence at the 9:30 meeting was strictly for show. Since he had already seen the agenda he knew nothing vital was going to come up. Indeed, a meeting of thirty politicians and senior bureaucrats was not the place to raise important questions but a place to rally support for decisions already taken. In any event, only a handful of those attending would actually state their views. The majority would wait to determine the president's preferences which, while useful, was hardly informative; hence, no vital issues. Certainly not the one he had been mulling over since it had been raised by the little Lebanese banker the previous Saturday at Chateau Cher.

"Would you not agree M. Dumont?" That horrid woman who had been given the education ministry to keep some troublesome constituency on board was addressing him and he had not the slightest idea to what she was referring. He therefore answered obliquely.

"Ah Madam, it is not for me to agree or disagree. I am only an advisor, not a decision maker, unlike you." He smiled his most charming smile as he brushed her off. But, as she looked inclined to press whatever point she had raised, he turned to the finance minister, who detested her, and suggested he might wish to answer her. It worked. As expected, he promptly said "No, never, it's vastly too expensive," and she slumped back in her chair glaring not at the Cardinal but at the finance minister.

For his part, the president appeared deeply engaged in what was going on around the table and perhaps he was. One could never tell for sure. Time and again the Cardinal had seen people with diametrically opposed views leave a meeting each firmly convinced the president favored their position. It was a talent that had been on full display Saturday with the Lebanese banker Khashan who no doubt left Cher thinking his extraordinary proposal to reunite France and Québec after 250 years apart had won presidential approval. In point of fact it had not, although neither had it been rejected.

There were serious questions to be considered before taking such a step, even though the banker had anticipated many of them, including some that the Québec separatists seemed to have ignored. Calling them "socialist romantics" he had argued that they had not thought through the ramifications of separation from Canada. "They assume that life will go on as before but with them in charge rather than Ottawa bureaucrats or Toronto bankers," he observed. "Precedent suggests they are wrong." Perhaps significantly he didn't identify an alternative. "They will also demand that only French is spoken in Québec but they forget Québec is a relatively small island in a very large English sea. The Americans are notoriously monolingual and, of course, with Québec's departure from Canada, the imperative for the rest of Canada to learn French would cease. In short, gentlemen, though the separatists may not presently realize it, they need France for both their economic and cultural survival."

And, when asked, he had seemed convinced the separatist referendum would succeed.

"History favors it. In 1980, when first put to the test, separation failed by 19 percent. In 1995 it failed by just one percent. That trend suggests the third try is unlikely to fail...plus much groundwork has been laid."

The Cardinal had been about to ask what groundwork but thought better of it. There could be some things he did not want to know. Instead, playing the role of skeptic, as he so often did in defense of the presidency against various schemes that might compromise it; he had merely noted that Québec was already a member of the Francophone Union with an official presence in Paris. "With all due respect sir," the banker had responded, "that makes them no different than Niger or the Comoros islands, hardly models to which anyone would willingly aspire. I am suggesting that Québec become an actual part of France, an overseas *département* such as is now the case with Guadeloupe, Martinique and Réunion. They each elect members of the National Assembly and the Senate as well as the European Parliament and use the Euro as their currency. But, more importantly," he had gone on to argue, "even as Québec would be in France, France would be in Québec. A company established at either end of this Atlantic bridge would, perforce, be a domestic French company subject to French law and a contributor to the French economy. The precedent, gentlemen, is there." he had concluded, "and it is internationally recognized." That was the moment when André's silence may have suggested to the banker that his extraordinary idea had not been rejected.

Thus, moving quickly to secure what he took as tentative approval, Khashan had added. "In providing Québec with a 'third way' you secure for France an economic strength that will assure Europe speaks with a French accent, not a German or English one, even as you go a long way toward restoring the grandeur that won de Gaulle the respect of his countrymen." That had finally brought an audible response from André.

"Not all of them," he had dryly observed. "Some thought it was hauteur, not grandeur."

"Well then," the banker had conceded with a shrug, "I amend my statement to say it won de Gaulle a sufficient number of votes from his countrymen to retain office for a decade."

Thinking back over the conversation at Cher, the Cardinal was struck how at that point Khashan's speech had suddenly became free of its rococo embellishments and his words, though as carefully chosen as before, lacked their previous languor. He had advanced a lot of numbers, as might be expected from a banker, contending that Québec's economy would immediately add 10% to the gross national product of France with future growth on the order of 20 or 25% which would put France on a par with Germany if not somewhat ahead.

André had expressed doubt. "Even assuming Québec should wish to rejoin France after so long an absence, would it not have to surrender its place in NAFTA as it would no longer be part of Canada and thus lose much of its economic advantage?"

The banker had conceded that Québec might not be able to retain membership in the North American free trade bloc but argued that some advantageous arrangement short of actual membership was assured as both Canadian and U.S. interests had large investments in Québec which they would want to protect. André had absorbed Khashan's argument without comment but then asked "What makes you think the United States would stand meekly by were we to engage in such an undertaking in their back yard?"

The Cardinal had seconded André's concern. "The Americans do have their Monroe Doctrine which supposedly closed the western hemisphere to Europe two hundred years ago."

"Indeed," the banker had replied, "*supposedly*". "You will of course recall that on Christmas Eve of 1941 de Gaulle's Free French invaded Vichy-controlled St. Pierre and Miquelon off the Newfoundland coast and the United States did nothing."

"That was during the Second World War which left them otherwise occupied," the Cardinal had replied.

"True enough," the banker rejoined, "They were otherwise occupied then. So might they be again."

"You intend to start another world war?" André had asked, a smile playing around the corners of his mouth.

"Nothing so extreme as that, sir," the banker had answered, "Let us just say a little diversion."

"What diversion would be sufficient for the Americans not to notice a French fleet landing at Montréal?" The president's smile had turned into laughter that contained a clearly dismissive tone. And, indeed, a moment later he left the library but the Cardinal had remained, not convinced but curious. He repeated André's question.

"What indeed would be so diverting as to make the Americans fail to notice a French fleet landing at Montréal, as the president put it?"

"Oh, I doubt an entire fleet would be needed—at most perhaps a ship or two at an opportune moment to show the flag—and while they would certainly notice it," the banker had replied, "the Americans would not necessarily object if it were seen to be advancing their interests."

"Their interests? Was that not what their Monroe Doctrine was all about; a statement of their interests?"

The banker had shrugged at that. "Times change."

"What has changed?"

"Two things: the climate and the neighborhood. While the cause may be debatable, the Arctic is getting warmer making its waters open to navigation more months of the year which makes U.S. dreams of transporting Alaskan oil to East Coast refineries more plausible should their environmentalists ever let them drill. And the Russians, also aware of the changing climate, now contend they own much of the Arctic and accordingly are increasingly active in the neighborhood. The Canadians, of course, always assumed the Arctic was theirs and are building bases and constructing a fleet of coast guard cutters to enforce their claim. That puts Canada into contention with both Russia and the United States while France, which has long backed freedom of navigation and, more recently, open resource recovery under the Law of the Sea Convention, lines up with the United States rather than Canada on both issues. And that I believe would prove sufficient to win U.S. acceptance of the transfer of Québec sovereignty from one NATO ally to another as being in their interests."

Despite his doubts the Cardinal had discovered he was finding the conversation increasingly interesting as he examined the banker's proposal. "Accepting for the moment your premise that there are economic benefits to be had by Québec becoming an overseas *département* of France and that the United States would not necessarily protest more than form requires, what makes you think Canada would let Québec go?"

"Constitutionally they have no grounds to stop it. Canada is a confederation, not a union. Emotionally some might bemoan redrawing the map after all these years, but more—probably a lot more— would not be unhappy to see Québec go. It has long been an irritant to many in English-speaking Canada."

The Cardinal had continued to probe. "Your points may be well taken, although quite frankly, I am not presently prepared to say they are. But, just for the moment, if we may continue thinking aloud, how would you see such a process unfolding? There is no way France could be seen to initiate it. Any overt move on our part would surely prove counterproductive."

"That sir," the banker had replied," is where certain interests with which I am familiar would be prepared to act as... precipitators." He had said the word as though he had given its choice much consideration. "It would be their task to create circumstances which would encourage the separatists to broach what they would believe to be their own idea."

"Which would be?"

"Which would be, as I noted earlier to the president, the opportunity for merchant caravans to follow the French flag and to prosper in its shade." At that moment a breeze had stirred the curtains at the still open doors to the veranda as if prodded into life by the thought of an oasis ahead.

"And nothing more?" The Cardinal was by nature a cautious man.

"Perhaps to savor some secret pleasure in playing the game. Some of the principals I represent are not particularly fond of the Americans or the British or their surrogates. They might take certain pleasure at seeing the balance redressed. As I suggested to the president, there are many in the world who would welcome a 'third way.' "

The shuffling of papers and scraping of chairs brought the Cardinal back to the present. With ruffled feathers smoothed and armed with talking points for the press, the members of the Tuesday Club, as the papers called it, were officially excused although few chose to leave while the president lingered to exchange pleasantries. At last Philippe finally said "Time M. le President, time please." Thus with apparently great reluctance André again thanked them for sparing him this hour from their busy schedule and with the slightest of nods to the Cardinal stepped into his adjoining office. In a moment his most trusted advisor followed him and was seen to do so, for therein lay the Cardinal's power.

"Ah, Jean-Pierre, a not uninteresting meeting do you not agree?" The Cardinal knew better than to try to parse the sentence. The president's use of multiple negatives was generally an indication the sentence had no meaning at all and therefore its subject need not be pursued. His assumption was subsequently verified as the president veered where he really wanted to go. "I see the public opinion polls suggest our friends in Québec remain inclined to step away from Canada. What do you make of that?"

"Not much."

"Not much? Indeed!" The president appeared bemused. "And why not?"

"Because, as you noted, if they do—and that's by no means certain as there are still nearly four months until the referendum—but, if they do, it would constitute a step *away* from something but not necessarily a step *toward* anything. All their referendum says is that they will now consider what to do next and—if and when they reach a conclusion—they may put that conclusion to another vote. If precedent is any guide, they will use the process to try to extract concessions from Ottawa and, having done so, forget the second referendum."

"How can they do that? If what I read is correct, there is a six month deadline before round two."

"Deadlines are bargaining chips in which postponement—a cost free commodity—can be traded for something of value."

The president looked thoughtfully at the Cardinal thinking, not for the first time, that he was a very useful teacher, although publicly he would never have phrased it quite that way. "So you think our Lebanese visitor misunderstood what is at stake and thus overstated its potential?"

"Not at all. If anything, he probably, purposefully, understated it." The presidential eyebrows bespoke the next question which the Cardinal proceeded to answer. "I strongly suspect he...no let me rephrase that...*I am quite certain* he has more than the aggrandizement of France on his mind. I would not be at all surprised to learn that he has hedged his conversations with us to his ultimate benefit."

"A shyster?"

"Oh, much more than that; I think he schemes on a far grander scale. If one could browse among his thoughts I suspect you would find several volumes of history in addition to some economic texts and a very long shelf of adventure novels. That well-rounded figure we met may conceal a Napoleon or two, perhaps even a James Bond and almost certainly a cowboy."

The president smiled broadly at the Cardinal's description of the little banker. "And if we know this about him, what might we *not* know?"

"From what inquiries I have been able to make so far, I suspect quite a lot."

"Ah, so what have you found?" the president asked.

"Essentially nothing."

"Nothing?"

"Nothing beyond the expected: took his baccalaureate at St. Joseph's in Beirut and an MBA at Insead—which, of course, doesn't mean he's a Christian or a capitalist—heads a very private investment bank in the 16th arrondissement; credit rating—excellent; a few mentions on the business pages—generally favorable; a piece he wrote some years ago for *Politique internationale* lamenting the destruction of Beirut. Nothing really."

"What had you hoped to find?"

"An outstanding warrant or two from some vengeful Middle Eastern ruler...an allusion to some unsavory associate...or at least a membership in some questionable fraternity."

"And that you did not, is that such a bad thing?"

"Possibly. It certainly means he is proceeding with the utmost caution. And, prudently, one must wonder why."

"He's a banker. They tend to be a cautious lot," the president replied.

"Perhaps."

"But you do not think so."

"Not entirely."

"So," the president said, moving behind his desk, "you think we should drop the idea." He said it as a statement but the Cardinal chose to take it as a question.

"No, I don't. I think we ought to take some prudent steps of our own and, indeed, as you suggested Saturday, I have begun doing just that."

"Do tell."

"I rang up an old acquaintance yesterday—Dewitt Hamilton—who is presently the national security advisor to the American president as well as a personal friend of his." The Cardinal had the full attention of M. Legrande. "After the customary courtesies I asked his views on the Québec situation."

"And he said...?"

"Next to nothing. I had the distinct impression the Americans really haven't given it any thought. But when I raised the question of the Russians in the Arctic that brought an immediate response—negative I hardly need add. However, as we suspected, the Americans' northern concerns have little to do with Canada and much to do with their own economic and security needs. I suspect they take Canada for granted. It has been a stable, non-threatening neighbor for a very long time and they can't conceive of that changing."

"But it might."

"Indeed…at least part of it."

"And if it did, wouldn't they be inclined to over-react as they often do…I think of what followed 9-11."

"Most assuredly….which is good."

"How so?"

"Not having thought about Canada in a great while, they are likely to embrace the first plausible suggestion for restoring something approximating the status quo. I suggest that would be the moment when we step forward with a solution: Canada remains Canadian and Québec remains French, albeit, a different sort of French."

The president cocked his head and not for the first time looked admiringly at the Cardinal. "Would I be correct in surmising we will not take that step for some time?"

"Most assuredly. Québec City and Ottawa will first have to play out their well-rehearsed roles seeking some negotiated settlement which will again nudge Québec a little further away from Canada. Only when that fails—as it must since there is little of value left to be traded in return for nominal allegiance—only then will they begin to look for alternatives and only then will the Americans begin to pay attention."

"And we in the meantime…?" The president left the question hanging in midair where the Cardinal retrieved it.

"In the meantime, I suggest we align ourselves with the larger American interests in the Arctic and with the separatists when opportunities arise—or can be created—so that when it comes time for them to set aside their romanticism and face the real world everybody will realize we are their default position."

"That alignment with American interests...I gather you are speaking of the maritime right of passage which Khashan mentioned?"

"That surely but also the Russian claims which, as I said, provoked an immediate response from Hamilton suggesting they are not viewed favorably by the Americans. Indeed, he said as much and of course, as I expected, he asked why I raised the question."

The president chuckled. "I should have liked to have heard that answer."

"It was easy. I simply told him the truth."

"Ahhh, the ultimate default position!"

They both laughed. "I noted our license from the Seabed Authority for mining rights in the North Pacific which he naturally took to mean we have an interest in similar undertakings in the Arctic. From that he will undoubtedly proceed to assume we share his apprehension of the Russians' exaggerated territorial claims as they would impinge on our economic aspirations. It is, after all, quite understandable that one regards his enemy's enemy as his friend, although real life is rarely that simple."

"Not your life anyway, my friend," Andre laughed. "So, what's next?"

"Since the *de Gaulle* is sailing in that direction anyway, I suggest a slight diversion."

"To?"

"Perhaps a bit beyond St. Pierre and Miquelon."

"To what end?"

"With your permission, I intend to place a call to Lucien Renard, a little show of Francophone solidarity. In the course of the call I will make some allusion to the *de Gaulle's* plans to be in the neighborhood and would hope that he might have opportunity to visit her if his busy schedule permits."

"Won't he ask why she 'plans to be in the neighborhood' as you put it?"

"Probably. In which case I shall note that St. Pierre and Miquelon are overseas *départements* of France. I probably need not go beyond that notation. Just plant a few seeds, not seek a harvest before it's ripe." The Cardinal was not certain his patron had heard that last comment. He seemed to have moved on to something else.

"This referendum, if Québec did vote to separate, what then?"

The Cardinal thought a long moment before responding. "I don't think M. Khashan would say 'if'. He suggests sufficient groundwork has been laid to assure a vote for separation. I, of course, did not seek specifics. But, to answer your question, I presume Québec would awaken one morning to discover they are lonely."

"So why wouldn't they join the United States?"

"If it were just a matter of economics, they might, although the socialists who infest the separatist movement wouldn't like the idea. But emotionally separatism is all about language. The United States basically doesn't speak anything but English and, some would say, that none too well." That elicited a soft chuckle from the president. "Isn't it remarkable," the Cardinal continued in a philosophical tone, "when the Bible wanted to illustrate the divisions that afflict mankind the writer chose the tower of Babel and the confusion of languages. Why not sex or age or color, all of which are equally apparent? Could it be because language is ultimately more divisive as it underlies culture and understanding? It is, after all, ultimately philosophy."

The president did not follow the Cardinal down that path. "You are suggesting that having severed its family ties, Québec will come to bemoan its orphan status?" Although not a philosopher, André Legrande appreciated and often used a nicely turned metaphor.

"That might be an apt description."

"So the question for us would be: do we take in orphans?"

"Perhaps not right away. But we might wish to leave the door ajar. Besides, we have other interests to consider."

"The Muslims?"

"Indeed."

"Do you think Khashan's jobs and bribes scheme will work?"

"Jobs, bribes *and relocation*. He didn't emphasize relocation but he did mention it as an alternative for those who won't work and can't be bought."

"Relocate where? Québec?"

The Cardinal shrugged. "Maybe...but probably not. Too cold. Perhaps someplace a little warmer."

André thought about that for a moment. "And what do you think our banker will be doing while we consider our response to his rather extraordinary proposal?"

"Making money...that's what bankers do. I suspect certain investments have already been made and he's looking to insure them."

AUGUST/AOÛT

Chapter Seven

The White House
Thursday, August 6th
5:00pm EDT

Joshua Ireland would not have been central casting's idea of a four star admiral. Short and thin with grey hair combed straight back, wire-rimmed glasses perched above a hawk-like nose; he more nearly resembled the senior teller at a bank than the commander of the most powerful fleet in the world. His reedy voice belied the mind that carefully chose each word it uttered. He did not get to become Chief of Naval Operations by making incautious remarks. Third in his class at the Academy, PhD from Princeton, author of numerous carefully reasoned articles in the *Proceedings of the U.S. Naval Institute* and a two volume set detailing the history of naval tactics since the ascendancy of steam over sail…when Joshua Ireland spoke, others listened, as Dewitt Hamilton and Mark Rayberg were now doing.

"It was my understanding from what you told me last month, Mr. Hamilton, the French were sending the *de Gaulle* to pay a visit to their islands of St. Pierre and Miquelon."

Hamilton nodded his agreement. "That is what a senior advisor to their president told me then but we have not spoken since. Has there been a change?"

The admiral only grunted in reply. Unfolding a paper he pulled from his jacket pocket, he read aloud. "At 23-hundred hours on 5

August the French aircraft carrier *Charles de Gaulle* transited the Cabot Strait and entered the Gulf of St. Lawrence." He peered over the rim of his glasses at the NSC chairman. "Either they have a very poor navigator or they're going somewhere else."

"And where do you think that might be?"

"I don't know but given the draft of the ship it couldn't be much further upstream than Quebec City."

The National Security Advisor sat silent behind his desk. The CNO refolded the paper and returned it to his pocket, then cleared his throat, not in preparation for speaking but perhaps to prompt someone else to speak. At length, Hamilton did. "That does make one wonder what other little surprises the French may have up their sleeve. I must admit that I wondered at the time at the *de Gaulle* sailing—if that's the right term for a nuclear-powered ship—all the way across the Atlantic just to look in on the good people of St. Pierre and Miquelon. There can't be very many of them."

"Fewer than ten thousand," Mark offered.

"And in any event, the Cabot Strait is a good 250 miles beyond St. Pierre and Miquelon," the admiral added, "nearly halfway to the mouth of the St. Lawrence."

"I believe I have been outfoxed," Hamilton said, "and it's not a very agreeable feeling. That senior advisor I mentioned said the *de Gaulle* was going to make a stop at St. Pierre and Miquelon and I didn't think to ask where else it might be going, not that he likely would have told me, but at least for forms sake the question should have been asked."

Mark had a query. "Admiral, do we know whether the *de Gaulle* actually did stop at St. Pierre and Miquelon?"

"No we do not. Given the information we had been provided we had no cause to track the flagship of a friendly power operating in its own waters."

"Its own waters?" Mark looked quizzically at the CNO.

"Yes, it goes back to a dispute some years ago between Canada and France. Basically France said since St. Pierre and Miquelon is an overseas department it's entitled to the same coastal zone as any other part of France, at that time, twelve miles. However, as the islands lie only ten miles off Newfoundland, Canada argued that's impossible and the islands should be treated like rocks in the ocean with no coastal zone. In the end it was taken to a court of arbitration which gave France a small economic zone around the islands with a corridor to the south that would allow it access to the islands without having to enter Canadian waters."

"And how did it work out?"

"We don't know. It never really got a chance to be tested. A year or two later, when the Law of the Sea Convention came into effect, it provided a 200 mile economic zone that theoretically put the corridor back inside Canadian waters."

"Since the issue has not crossed my desk, I assume nobody's challenged it?" Hamilton asked.

"Up to now, that is correct," the admiral replied.

"It is truly amazing how many problems can be resolved if you ignore them," Hamilton mused. "But," he added, "I suspect this may not be one of them. There apparently is no question the ship is now in Canadian waters?"

"Actually there is," the CNO shifted in his chair, seeking a more comfortable position for the discussion he sensed was coming. "The Law of the Sea Convention provides for a right of innocent passage through straits and waters more than 12 miles from shore. The Cabot Strait is approximately 60 miles wide. I would presume the French took a middle course. In any event, there are some further rights for military ships; basically, they have to be non-threatening and keep moving but, once the *de Gaulle* enters the St. Lawrence River—if that is her destination—the rules change and we could get involved even though we have not ratified the Convention. As you know, the St. Lawrence Seaway, of which the river is part, is jointly administered by Canada and us. It's open to commercial traffic but there is no automatic right of access for a warship. That requires an invitation, something not commonly given."

"So," Hamilton asked, "what happens next?"

"That would seem to be up to the Canadians. Do we know whether they invited the *de Gaulle*?"

"No, in point of fact we don't, although I can't imagine why they would."

"Well, it seems to me," the admiral said, "the next step would be to find out."

"And if their answer is no?"

"Well, then it would seem they ought to convey that message to the skipper of the *de Gaulle* and his government."

"And if he does not take appropriate action, such as turn around and go home, what then?"

"I suggest we not cross that bridge until we come to it. You don't get to be captain of a flag ship by being stupid."

"Well, admiral, that is indeed interesting. I thank you for bringing it to my attention and for now I suggest that's where we leave it. I assume you'll be keeping an eye on the *de Gaulle's* progress and will keep me informed. In the meantime, we'll try to get some answers to the questions you raised." Correctly interpreting that as the end of their meeting, the admiral gave a stiff-necked nod in acknowledgement and left.

"When the door had closed, Hamilton turned to Mark. "You have to wonder what our French friends are up to. What's the point of antagonizing Ottawa?"

"This may sound loopy sir, but the French are romantics. More than once they've denied the obvious and opted for the unlikely. The Marginot Line may be the best known example but there are others...their nuclear '*Force de frappe*'...their whole '*third way*' foreign policy, especially under Legrande. The list is long."

"And you think Québec could be part of it?"

Mark took a deep breath before answering. "I think it's very possible, sir. They may be encouraging Renard out of some romantic notion of revenging Montcalm's defeat. After all, if the *de Gaulle* goes as far as the admiral says it can, then it would be dropping anchor right under the very cliffs where the battle took place. As you yourself said of Dumont, "It's rare these days that one encounters a true 17th century mind.""

"*Touché!* But do you really think a port call by a French ship—even a nuclear-powered aircraft carrier—would have much of an impact on the referendum?"

"Much? No. Some? Possibly."

The frown that had been growing on Dewitt Hamilton's face had become a pursued-lip scowl. He stood and paced toward the window where he gazed out at Pennsylvania Avenue—what White House regulars called the DMZ as it stood between the executive mansion and the perennial collection of protestors camped in Lafayette Park. At length he turned and asked Mark, "If Canada hasn't invited the French—and for the moment let's assume they haven't—what could the French possibly hope to gain?"

Mark shrugged. "Ingratiate themselves with a future independent Québec? I don't know. Perhaps I should give a call to my friend in Ottawa and find out what he knows—unofficially as well as officially."

"Yes, do that," Hamilton slowly replied. "We have practical interests that I would prefer not to have upset by some Gallic flight of fancy."

"Yes sir, but I suggest we also need to give some thought as to where the *de Gaulle* might be headed after Québec."

"Presumably home?"

"Presumably, but not necessarily."

"They still have some islands in the Caribbean."

"Yes sir. But given the Cardinal's comments about Arctic mining, I can't help but wonder..."

"I wouldn't think you'd use an aircraft carrier for a mining expedition, especially since with their Cousteau legacy they have some very advanced undersea explorers." Hamilton slowly shook his head before adding, "by the way, that was an impressive bit of research you did on the Arctic boundaries. It suggests that if the Russians get their way there won't be much room left for the French or anyone else to poke about." Then, suddenly re-energized, he said in a brisk, dismissive tone, "Why don't you make that call to your friend and see what you can find out. But be circumspect...Ottawa's interests are not necessarily ours."

Thursday, August 6th
7:00pm EDT

Like most of his days this one had been a blur of meetings, phone calls, e-mails, memos to be read, responses to be written and visitors with questions about everything from government policy to lunch plans (sandwich at desk). It was all part of the warp and woof of government that was supposed to be glamorous but often didn't rise above tedious. Knowing that Andrew's day was probably being consumed in much the same manner Mark purposely held off calling until an hour when their conversation wouldn't have to be sandwiched between other demands. That way there might be opportunity to get some of the "unofficial" information to go along with the "official."

As he punched in Andy's private number in Montréal he half hoped Marie-Paule would answer. Last time he'd called she'd purred into the telephone, "Ah Mark, you are perhaps busy making a little war, *non*? And you want to borrow one of Andrew's tanks, *oui*? Maybe we can come take it for a little (she pronounced it lee-tle) test drive, *non*? Wouldn't that be fun?" And then she laughed that deep, sexy laugh of hers.

The voice that answered his call was deep but not sexy. In the single word "hello" it managed to convey the unmistakable impression you were interrupting something far more important than whatever had prompted your call. Had he been a telemarketer this would have been a definite "no sale".

"Hey sport, how goes it?"

"Ah...at last, a friendly voice. You are friendly, aren't you?"

"Within the limits of my brief, yes, but I'm heartbroken that Marie-Paule didn't answer. She's lots more fun on the phone than you. Probably in person, too...*non*?"

"I wouldn't know. She's down at the lake. I've got to be back in Ottawa in the morning." He didn't sound particularly happy about it.

"This referendum's really got you on the run, has it?"

"You could say that. There's hardly a day I don't have a speech somewhere. In fact that's why I'm here tonight. By the end of this thing I doubt there will be many places in the province I haven't visited at least once."

"Well with that kind of exposure, maybe you can run for king of the new country." They shared a laugh before Mark added with concern evident in his voice "How's it going?"

"I wish I could say 'good' but the polls are more or less remain stuck where they've been all along..."

"And that is...?"

"A single digit lead for Renard but in reality probably too close to call; virtually a three way tie among pro, anti and undecided. It's the undecideds who have me worried. Our polling says they're mostly young, educated, urban, upscale or headed that way but still only a generation removed from the farms and provincial towns they grew up in. I don't know if they're really undecided or just embarrassed to admit how they're going to vote."

"You must be pointing out the economic facts of life to them."

"I am but then they look at Renard and his MBA and listen to his argument that if Québec were an independent country it would have something like the 30th largest GDP in the world and he says they would be in charge of it, not Ottawa and certainly not Toronto."

"But if Québec left Canada it probably wouldn't remain 30th. A lot of the companies that are there now would probably move to Ontario to keep access to NAFTA".

"You know," Andrew replied, "that's a logical argument and I make it repeatedly but I'm finding logic doesn't have much to do with where people come down on this. There's a lot of emotion and an incredible amount of misinformation being peddled on the Internet. But if I started trying to shoot down every bit of bullshit that appears on the web, I'd be spending all my time playing on their end of the field. So, I continue to try to make the case that it's Canada that allows Québec to be Québec...prosperous, French, covered by a health care system you guys may not like but which Québec does and could never afford on its own. And, as defense minister, I'm able to point out what it costs to maintain even as much of a military as we have and ask how they would pay for that. They're all honest arguments backed up by verifiable figures but all Renard has to say is 'Bay Street bankers' and half of those who were listening to me stop listening. And his campaign is well-financed. They're raising a lot of money."

"Where from?"

"I don't know. Some undoubtedly is from small contributions at rallies but people who expect to take Bay Street's place in the new order may be kicking in the real change." There was a pause before he added in a weary voice, "It's a little discouraging. It makes you wonder whether one-man, one-vote is just a polite name for grand larceny."

Mark didn't respond immediately. When he did, he felt like he was piling on at a time when his friend needed a boost. "You mentioned the cost of Québec fielding a military. I'm not quite sure how to broach this but Renard may be about to trump you on that one."

"How so?"

Mark took a deep breath and plunged ahead. "Are you aware of the French aircraft carrier *de Gaulle*?

"I am. Ugliest damn ship I've ever seen. Must have been designed by the same people who did the Citroen."

"Do you know where it is?"

"Not a clue. Should I?"

"It's in the Gulf of St. Lawrence."

"The *where*?" Andrew's bellow was so loud Mark had to hold the phone away from his ear. "Are you bloody well kidding me?"

"I'm afraid not."

"What the hell is it doing there?"

"I don't know. Our Chief of Naval Operations told us this morning that it passed through the Cabot Strait last night. We had thought it was heading to St. Pierre and Miquelon."

"You knew it was in the neighborhood?"

"More or less." Mark was beginning to feel the conversation was heading in an unpleasant direction. "We assumed you knew."

"You assumed wrongly." Andrew's voice suddenly sounded more like the man who answered the phone than the old friend who had been chatting on it. "When, may I ask, did you first learn the French were coming?" For a giddy moment Mark thought of the Peter Sellers movie *The Russians Are Coming* and had to suppress a nervous but inappropriate desire to laugh.

"It was mentioned in passing to my boss about a month ago in a phone call from one of Legrande's advisors. The call was on a totally different subject. He just tossed off the *de Gaulle*'s summer plans to visit St. Pierre and Miquelon as an 'oh, by the way'... We didn't give it any thought, just routinely passed it along to the Navy on an FYI basis. It wasn't until the CNO showed up this morning that we learned where it was."

Andrew took a deep breath and struggled to think rationally. "Did your guy indicate where they're going?"

"No. We asked him that and he said given the draft of the ship it couldn't go much further up river than Québec City but legally it could only do that with an invitation from you and concurrence from us. That's when Hamilton raised the question whether you guys knew. I said I'd call you."

"And eventually you did." There was near ice in Andrew's voice.

"It's been a hectic day and, as I said, I assumed you knew about it. You've presumably got ships in the area."

"For the record, we've got seven frigates in the entire Atlantic fleet. They're first class ships with excellent crews but three of them are on NATO duty ranging from pirate patrols off the coast of Somalia to training exercises off the coast of Scandinavia. One is in Haiti on a UN mission. Two are actually on Atlantic patrol and one is tied up in Halifax for refitting alongside a couple of 40 year old destroyers, some second-hand British submarines and a half dozen CDVs— Coastal Defense Vessels—about the size of a minesweeper, lightly armed and crewed by reservists who spend most of their time making sure fishermen don't fish; all-in-all 5000 men, fifteen ships and a trio of leaky subs to patrol two million square miles of ocean." He fairly spat out the statistics. "Maybe Renard is right. It wouldn't cost much to duplicate that effort." He paused and took a deep breath. "Look, I'm sorry I'm snapping at you. Let me ring off and pass the word. Maybe someone knows something and hasn't told me. I've been on the go all day. You going to be in for a while?"

"Yeah."

"I'll ring you back. Thanks for the heads up."

Mark found himself a little shaken as he replaced the handset. They had been close friends for twenty years. He didn't want to ruin that. He hadn't called earlier because he wanted time to talk at length about the Québec situation and there weren't enough minutes free in either of their days to put their feet up on the desk and chat. And he really had assumed—wrongly—that Andy probably knew about the *de Gaulle*. Ye Gods, what a position to be in: fifteen ships and three subs. While there were more on the west coast it was a far cry from the 400 ship Canadian navy that escorted convoys across the North Atlantic during the Second World War. Granted, the U.S. Navy was down to half its Cold War size but even at that it was still ten times as large as Canada's and, with nearly a dozen aircraft carriers and their battle groups, it had thousands of times more firepower. The Canadian forces were good—their ground units had punched far above their weight in Afghanistan—but ultimately you couldn't be in two places at once and, as the second largest country on earth, Canada had a lot of places it needed to be. Several minutes went by before the phone rang. He took a breath and tried to put some warmth in his voice. "Rayberg."

"Hey, I'm sorry I snapped at the messenger. I was upset at the message and wished the messenger had brought it sooner."

"No problem. I understand. What did you find out?"

"One of our coast guard cutters spotted the *de Gaulle* this afternoon. It had three support ships with her….a patrol frigate forward and a couple of destroyers flanking, one a Cassard class and the other an F67. That's half her usual complement so we're looking for the others. When we find them we may have a better idea where she's headed." The plaintiff note of weariness that had colored his earlier comments on the referendum crept back into his voice. "And the reason I didn't know? The Coast Guard is part of the Department of Fisheries; not Defense. They reported up their chain of command which then took its sweet time calling across town to let us know. I'd like to threaten there'll be hell to pay but, in reality, Fisheries has more political clout than Defense so the most I'd get would be some clucking about the need to connect the dots because after all, we're all on the same team, aren't we?" He did a reasonably good impression of the prime minister.

"Well," Mark replied, "if it's any comfort to you—and I know it isn't—we have the same problem. I could cite chapter and verse in which agencies don't talk to each other. You may recall Professor Bailey of our schoolboy days used to quote Sir Francis Bacon that 'knowledge is power'. Bailey no doubt thought that might encourage us to acquire some but what any bureaucrat could have told the good professor was that knowledge is power only so long as you keep it to yourself. Share it and you level the playing field."

"So true."

"So what are you going to do about it?"

"I don't know. I've kicked it upstairs with a recommendation that we make clear to the French that we have our eye on the *de Gaulle* and remind them that the St. Lawrence Seaway, which includes the river, is a demilitarized zone and off limits to all warships. The next move will be up to the PM."

"Do you think Renard is behind this?"

"Undoubtedly. It could, as you say, undercut my military cost argument except I don't know how the average Québecker would feel about the French military. They didn't do so well the last time they were here."

"We all have our off days," Mark rejoined. "I'll recommend to Hamilton that we send the same message to the French as joint administrators of the Seaway."

"Thank you. That might be helpful." Andrew sounded calmer.

"I'll try. You know that line about fishing in troubled waters? Maybe between us we can give the French a little trouble digesting their catch."

Chapter Eight

80 Wellington Street, Ottawa
Friday, August 7th
11:15am EDT

Whatever hopes he had entertained of getting an early start on the weekend and joining Marie-Paule at the lake had been dashed by the prime minister's summons to a meeting of the Cabinet Coordinating Committee even though in the several meetings held in the weeks since the bombings there had been precious little to coordinate. The security cameras hadn't shown anything out of the ordinary and apart from the initial finding that the explosive agent was Semtex, the bomb fragments had yielded few clues beyond bits and pieces of batteries available in any hardware store along with cheap alarm clocks, all presumably set to go off at the same time. Since that could be as much as twelve hours ahead of the blasts, it left open the possibility the bombings might have been the act of a single person moving leisurely about the city and not a coordinated conspiracy which would explain why the police had failed to pick up any leads. One person acting alone need not say anything to anyone. Two or more people acting in concert must at least confide in each other thus doubling the chances of a leak.

Not only had there been no leak, there had been no public claim of responsibility. That baffled him. Why would someone stage such an attack and not attempt to score propaganda points from it? When the Palestinians exploded a bomb in Tel Aviv or the Chechens in Moscow, they were eager to claim responsibility and attach a long list of grievances to their claim. It seemed to defy human nature not to boast of what you'd done. But, so far, there was only silence on the part of whoever had planted the Montréal bombs.

But if the bombers had remained silent, Renard had not. He opened every speech by noting how many days had elapsed with no arrests, darkly declaring that if "others" couldn't effectively defend Québec perhaps it was time for Québec to defend itself. That had produced a flurry of speculation whether he was advocating some sort of beefed up Sûreté or even a U.S.-style National Guard. Separatist supporters argued such steps were necessary; opponents worried they could open the door to the sort of quasi dictatorship Québec had known in the post war years in what became known as *La Grande Noirceur*—"The Great Darkness".

And now matters had been further complicated by the presence of the French carrier in the gulf. Public messages from Ottawa and Washington reminding the skipper and the Quai d'Orsay that the St. Lawrence Seaway was a demilitarized zone, off limits to warships of any nation, had been met with a politely worded reply from Paris assuring the two governments that France was fully cognizant of the status of the Seaway and had no intention of violating it. That, of course, left open the question why the ship was there and what, if anything, could or should be done about it.

Perhaps that was why he and his colleagues had been summoned to this conference room in the Langevin Block opposite the houses of Parliament where they sipped coffee from Styrofoam cups as they waited for the prime minister to arrive. He was already fifteen minutes late. When he did arrive he would take his seat under a great gilt-framed portrait of Sir John A. Macdonald, the first to hold the office. It was Macdonald who—as much in frustration as in humor—once listed his occupation as "cabinet maker". As his successors would discover, building a cabinet from a patchwork of often ill-fitting pieces was no easy task. All regions and major ethnic groups need be represented whether they could provide anyone of cabinet-level competence or not. David Osgood was a case in point. His primary talent seemed to be finding a strategic spot between the prime minister's elbow and the nearest TV camera...that and ingratiating himself on Bay Street which enabled him to steer financial backing to a number of the party faithful, including several now hovering around him.

"...some information has come to my attention which may affect the investigation," he was telling them. Allowing a dramatic pause to assure their attention, he continued in a louder voice. "As I advised the prime minister, I have learned that a number of Québec stocks were heavily shorted in the weeks prior to the bombings and those shorts were covered within 24 hours after the bombings." Other conversation in the room suspended. Osgood had their attention.

"How heavily?" someone asked.

"Very," Osgood replied, "...nine figures—possibly more."

"Do we know who initiated the shorts?"

"Yes and no," Osgood replied. "We know which brokers placed the orders."

"But?"

"But they were for off-shore accounts. Meaning we don't know the identity of the ultimate investors. This is something I would remind you that I recommended we..."

Andrew cut short the start of what had the makings of a self-serving speech. "How many off-shore accounts are we talking about?"

"Not many; perhaps a half dozen, but maybe only one spreading his business around...probably more though."

"Do I understand correctly," Andrew asked, a skeptical edge to his voice, "that you are suggesting the bombings may not have had anything to do with the referendum but rather with gaming the markets?"

"Possibly so," Osgood replied. "The timing certainly could support such a conclusion."

"So could common sense." Marcel Gigiere jumped into the conversation. "It wouldn't take much of a financial whiz to bet that a separatist win would depress the market and nowhere more so than among Québec-based companies. In such a scenario, short-selling not only makes sense, it's virtually compelling."

"But at that point the referendum was still nearly four months away. And they didn't stay short," Osgood pointed out with a triumphal edge to his voice.

"There was no need to wait once the bombs went off," Marcel replied. "From an investor's standpoint, the bombs only advanced their timetable. Holding on to the shorts served no purpose and, indeed, if they were on margin, it could only cost them."

"That is, of course, a possibility," Osgood conceded, "but given the timing and degree of anonymity, it still strikes me as very curious." He might have been surprised to discover how many others in the room, including critics, shared his doubts.

The exchange between Osgood and Marcel was followed by a lull in conversation in which eyes again shifted to the inner door, wondering what was delaying the PM. It was most unlike McKinley Marston to keep anyone waiting. Indeed, more than one cabinet minister had learned to his chagrin that the prime minister considered punctuality an essential constituent of good manners.

As they waited, their conversation drifted back to more mundane matters...vacation plans, the outlook for the Blue Jays, the cost of real estate in the pricy capital region...as though by ignoring the issue that most worried them they could buy a few minutes peace. But that escape route was abruptly closed when the prime minister at last entered the room followed by Jean Duqua, the foreign minister. That was the first sign something might be amiss. Duqua was not a member of the committee. A subsequent look at the prime minister confirmed something indeed was wrong. Andrew's first thought was that the PM was ill. His cheeks were flushed and he seemed agitated.

Foregoing his usual elaborate courtesies he ordered everyone to take their seats; not suggested or even asked—ordered.

"I must apologize for keeping you waiting but it was not without cause," he began. Unfolding a piece of paper he carefully smoothed it out on the table in front of him. His hands trembled as he did so. Every eye in the room was on the document. Whatever it contained, clearly it was not good news. Almost as an afterthought he added, "I have asked the foreign minister to join us as certain developments directly concern his brief." He cleared his throat. "I have here a dispatch from the Canadian Press newswire which was received a few minutes before we were to meet. I delayed joining you while we sought confirmation. It reads as follows:

Québec separatist leader Lucien Renard made a dramatic flight by helicopter from the port of Sept Iles Friday morning to the deck of the French nuclear-powered aircraft carrier 'Charles de Gaulle' which is presently in the Gulf of St. Lawrence. An announcement from the premier's office in Québec City says he is to lunch with the ship's officers before returning to shore. His surprise visit to the flagship of the French navy follows weeks of speculation about Renard's frequent suggestions in the wake of the June 25th Montréal bombings that Québec might need to look elsewhere for its defense if Ottawa cannot adequately provide it."

The prime minister read the dispatch in a tight but controlled tone. When done, he methodically proceeded to remove his reading glasses, fold them, and deliberately tuck them in his breast pocket. Without looking directly at his colleagues he quietly added by way of explanation, "the *de Gaulle* was supposedly on a routine cruise that was to have stopped at St. Pierre and Miquelon, as it is free to do so under an agreement of some years standing. The islands are, after all, French territory. However, the *de Gaulle* did not stop there."

He paused, seemingly to collect himself, but then erupted with quiet fury. "The insolence of it! For the French to send their navy to entertain the premier of Québec! The premier of Québec! As though the damned referendum had already been decided!" He spit out the words with a venom few had ever witnessed in the PM. Andrew was not alone in worrying the old man would have a stroke.

"Perhaps they were invited, prime minister," someone said in a quiet voice, perhaps hoping to calm the storm. It did not.

"Invited? By what *country*? They were not invited by Canada! Countries treat with countries. Provinces do not." His open palm slapped the table top giving his angry words added emphasis.

"Then tell that bastard Renard to get off the bloody boat." The agriculture minister was a plain-spoken prairie politician whose blunt language often made his colleagues cringe but endeared him to the voters of his riding.

The foreign minister replied. "May I suggest it's probably a little late for that?"

"Then how about telling the French to turn around and go home and take the little prick with them?" There were several nods of agreement at his words.

"We have issued a reminder to the Quai d'Orsay and the United States has done the same pointing out the demilitarized nature of the St. Lawrence Seaway," Duqua quietly responded. "But, in point of fact, the *de Gaulle* has not entered the Seaway but is some distance off-shore in international waters. Whatever we determine to do next, I urge that we not elevate or prolong the matter. I fear that would be playing into Renard's hands."

"Maybe we should bypass the French foreign office," Andrew suggested so quietly that those at the far end of the table asked him to say again. "Maybe we should get someone to drop a word in Legrande's ear advising him that he's unwisely intruding in an internal Canadian matter and that it's unhelpful not only to us but, potentially, to NATO unity."

"Why should we ask someone else to do our job for us? What if they cock it up?" the agriculture minister asked.

Before Andrew could reply Duqua stepped in: "Because it gives us deniability. If the French do go running to the press it will be in response to someone else's request. We can say something about welcoming opportunities to strengthen relations with an old and valued ally although this may not have been a particularly opportune moment to do so."

"The usual bullshit."

"Precisely so," the foreign minister replied, inclining his head in apparent agreement with the premise if not the phraseology, "but useful all the same."

"Who did you have in mind Andrew?" The prime minister seemed to have regained his composure. His voice betrayed no more emotion than if he were inquiring about filling a minor government post.

Osgood saw an opening in the discussion and jumped in before Andrew could reply. "The British might do it."

"No," the foreign minister interjected. "That would be seen as English versus French. Hardly helpful in the present circumstance."

"What about the Germans?" someone asked. "They've got a special relationship with France."

"Yeah, they conquered it, twice." Several seated near the agriculture minister chortled. The prime minister shot a look their way and they fell silent.

"What about asking the Germans?" The PM looked toward his foreign minister as he repeated the question.

"It's possible sir, but if I were Legrande I'd ask them 'why do you care?' They might find that difficult to answer without admitting to our prompting."

Andrew spoke up. "What about Washington? They've already weighed in publicly and they can rightly say they care what happens on their border."

The prime minister didn't say "yes" or "no" but looked thoughtful. "I think we might consider your suggestion."

After a lengthy discussion in which multiple views were advanced, some on topic, others less so, the prime minister glanced at the wall clock. "No doubt you all have other obligations; therefore, I think we should adjourn having taken your advice. Looking toward Duqua he added, "Perhaps you and the defense minister could join me for a few minutes." To the others he said, "I think, if asked, we had best say it was a routine, if lengthy, meeting. And, if pressed as to why lengthy, you can always say that we spent part of the morning listening to the agriculture minister. I'm sure the press will take your meaning." And with that he stood, amid general laughter, signaling an end to the session.

Friday, August 7th
12:30pm EDT

Jean Duqua was something of an anomaly in Canadian politics. Although he was French, he was not from Québec nor was he Catholic. Four hundred years ago one of his ancestors, a Huguenot from Royan, travelled to present-day New Brunswick with a cartographer named Samuel de Champlain. Champlain eventually returned home, his travelling companion did not. In building his cabinet, McKinley Marston had looked upon Jean Duqua as a political trifecta: New Brunswick, French and Protestant—a virtual one man balancing act. That he had turned out to be a steady, capable foreign minister was all to the good. Now he sat in one of two chairs facing the prime minister using a corner of his desk to rest his coffee cup.

"I must apologize for allowing my displeasure at the French to show," the PM began, "but they're effectively recognizing Québec as a separate country. The *de Gaulle* after all is a flag ship, not just some ordinary steamer. It is arrogant and insolent."

"But probably not capricious," Duqua suggested.

"I can understand why Renard would welcome 'recognition' as you say sir," Andrew addressed the prime minister from the other corner of the desk, "but what's in it for France? They surely can't think we'd appreciate it."

"Frankly, I doubt they very much care what we think," the prime minister replied, "They have a history of meddling in Québec affairs. I would remind you of deGaulle and his '*Québec libre*' speech."

"With all due respect sir," Duqua interjected, "what we have to do now is decide how to respond to this present matter. The only plausible suggestion I heard was yours Andrew…ask Washington to have a quiet word with Legrande suggesting he not further involve himself in an internal Canadian matter."

"Before we do that," Andrew replied, "you mentioned a wire service story about Renard's visit, sir. Would you by any chance have that available?"

The prime minister looked about his desk top for a moment before locating the sheet of paper he had brought with him to the meeting. "Here's the full dispatch; the usual preening from Renard's office plus the usual diplomatic blather." Catching himself he looked across the desk at Duqua with an embarrassed smile, "Present diplomats excepted, of course."

Andrew quickly scanned the story before handing it back. It added little to what the prime minister had already read aloud. Mostly boilerplate—some details of the *de Gaulle*—her size, how many planes in her air wing, a mention that a sister carrier had long been planned but not built, and a bland remark by the French foreign minister that what he termed "a goodwill journey" was intended "to further French economic, cultural and political interests and open new frontiers." He apparently did not see any inherent contradiction in using a nuclear-powered aircraft carrier to spread goodwill. "If you don't mind Prime Minister, I'd like to make a phone call to see if I can get a little more information."

"Certainly. Just ask my secretary to show you to an empty office. Anything you can learn will no doubt be helpful. Meanwhile Jean and I will try our hand at outlining the statement."

Moments later, seated in a borrowed office, Andrew entered a number in his cell phone. It only rang twice before it was answered. He asked that his call be transferred.

"Hey, Andy. What's up?" In a few well-chosen words he told Mark of Renard's helicopter ride.

"Yeah, I saw that. For an ally the French sure can be a pain in the ass."

Andrew let that pass without a response, although he was tempted to add "they're not the only ones." What he said instead was, "I must admit this caught us by surprise. The only information we have is a newswire story. Apparently there's a small press pool with Renard but so far they haven't filed. I was wondering if you guys knew anything more."

"No," Mark replied, "As a matter of routine I looked when the story came in this morning to see what we had on it—nothing secret—just the usual crap the analysts feed me. The only additional info I came up with was a week old press release announcing port calls by the *de Gaulle* in Tokyo, Osaka and Pusan later this month. While they didn't say so, I'd expect they'll also try to make one or two Chinese stops before doing their usual round of Gulf ports on the way home."

"But no mention of Québec?"

His question was met by silence on the line. After a moment Andrew asked, "You still there?"

"Yeah," Mark replied, he sounded as though his attention had been distracted by something. When he continued speaking his tone was more deliberate, softer. "Without mentioning your source—certainly not me, certainly not the people I work for—I would *strongly* suggest you think about what I just told you and then very carefully re-read the wire story you've got about Renard going to lunch on the *de Gaulle*, especially the comments from the French foreign office." After a further pause in which he seemed to be debating whether to say something more, he suddenly ended the conversation. "Do that Andy and if I pick up anything else I'll give you a holler."

Andrew's bewilderment sounded in his voice. "Yeah. Well, thanks for whatever you just gave me. Talk to you later." He thumbed his cell phone, breaking the connection, scowling as he did. He apparently had been given a message but he didn't have a clue what it was. He stood silently in the office for a long moment, then shook his head; time to get back into the meeting which, hopefully, wouldn't run much longer.

As he re-entered the prime minister's office Duqua was explaining why it was better to basically ignore Renard's luncheon on the carrier and act as though this was little more than a routine visit of a NATO ally, downplaying the whole thing. Keep all public comments short and sweet.

The prime minister paused and looked expectantly at Andrew as he took his seat.

"Anything you'd care to add to our discussion?"

"I must admit I'm not entirely sure sir. I have learned that the *de Gaulle* will be making Asian and probably Gulf stops later this month on her way home which means she doesn't intend to take up residence here..." His voice trailed off mid-sentence.

"In that case they'll probably also make some stops in the Caribbean enroute to Panama," the prime minister suggested. "They've still got a few islands there." Turning to Duqua he said, "That might actually be useful in underscoring your point about it just being a routine visit to friendly countries and French overseas territories if you mention the Caribbean ones along with St. Pierre and Miquelon."

"No..." Andrew said aloud, only half listening to the prime minister. "No sir... they won't be going through the Panama Canal." Shaking his head as he spoke, he added, "The *de Gaulle's* too wide to fit through the locks." Something Mark had said was roiling just below the threshold of his consciousness, just out of reach. "Sir, may I take another look at that news story." For a second time he read it very carefully as Mark had suggested, paying special attention to the French foreign office statement that the voyage was intended to "...further French economic, cultural and political interests *and open new frontiers.*"

"Sir," he addressed the prime minister. "I don't think they're going south. I think they intend to go through the Northwest Passage."

4861 Chemin de la Côte-des-Neiges, Montréal
Friday, August 7th
10:30pm EDT

It had been a long day and now home he debated whether to call Mark to let him know he'd deciphered his message. Before he could make up his mind the phone rang, making the decision for him. His neutral "hello" was greeted with a breezy "Hey Andy, how goes it?"

"Don't you ever go home?"

"Not if I can help it. This place is better furnished. Hey," he added, the banter gone from his voice, "I'm sorry I had to play games with you this noon but I wasn't sure how far my brief extended. I hope you figured out where I was heading."

"I did although I must admit it took me a few minutes. But, between Tokyo and that foreign office line about 'new frontiers' I finally got it."

"You think you got it," Mark cautioned. "We won't know for sure until we see which way they actually head. They can always change plans. The French are nothing if not flexible."

"That's one way of putting it. I can think of a couple of other ways."

"If I were sitting where you are I'd probably rephrase that myself. Did you find the rest of the *de Gaulle*'s battle group?"

"Yeah. They're sitting about 200 miles south of St. Pierre and Miquelon, apparently waiting for her. She's supposed to make a stop at the islands tomorrow."

"So what are you going to do if they do head north?"

"Probably issue a statement reiterating our position that the Northwest Passage is an internal Canadian waterway and threaten some sort of legal action, maybe take it to the Law of the Sea tribunal in Hamburg."

"For the record I have to officially dissent; off the record, I feel for you. You're in a tough spot."

"Yeah and the French aren't making it any easier by flipping us the bird."

"In politer company I think it's called hedging your bets," Mark laughed. "It doesn't take too many smarts to see that an independent Québec will need friends and who better than someone who already speaks the language?"

"Speaking of friends, have Renard's people been to see you guys?" Andrew asked.

"Not that I'm aware of but we don't speak French. Since the separatists see everything in terms of language, they probably assume we'll go with English Canada."

"Are they right?"

"I suppose so. It's Canada that's in NAFTA and NATO, not Québec."

"Has anyone down there pointed that out to Renard?"

"I don't know that anyone down here has ever spoken to Renard."

"Maybe it's time you did."

"Maybe but I don't see it happening. I understand State said 'no' to your foreign minister's request this afternoon that they put a word in Legrande's ear suggesting he not interfere in Canadian affairs."

"They said 'no'? Why?"

"I wasn't in on the discussions but I suppose they decided it's between Canada and France, both U.S. allies. There's no advantage for us in taking sides between two allies."

Andrew wanted to note there was a substantial difference in reliability between the two allies but contented himself with a simple statement of fact. "You're a joint guarantor of a demilitarized St. Lawrence."

"They haven't entered the river and promise they won't. So far they've stayed in what we consider international waters. That's a no-brainer for us. We have to take a consistent stand on freedom of navigation. There are too many places where failure to do so could pose real problems starting with Panama, Suez, the Bosporus, the Taiwan Straits, the Cuba Straits…it's a long list."

"And the Northwest Passage?"

"That, too. I know you consider it an inland passage, but we don't."

"You guys really are pricks, just like everybody says." His laugh took some of the edge off his words, but not entirely.

"Hey, who was it, Machiavelli, who said 'politics ain't beanbag?'" They talked for another ten minutes, one gently probing, trying to find out what Washington's reaction would be if Renard won the referendum; the other trying to get some inkling whether that was likely.

"You know," Andrew finally said, "I've got the strongest feeling there's something more going on that we aren't aware of—some force at work that we aren't seeing."

"What's that, Defense-Minister-Speak? You sound like Rumsfeld. Remember him?"

"How so?"

"He had a saying when he was running the Pentagon: 'There are things we know and there are things we don't know. And there are things we know we don't know. But the worrisome things are the things we don't know we don't know.'"

"Believe it or not, I understand what you just said and, worse yet, I agree. We've been busy looking for ties between the bombings and the referendum. But what if they're not connected? "

"You mean some non-political nut case?" Mark asked.

"No, I mean some diabolically clever chess master who's looking beyond the present state of play. What if this person or persons wasn't just trying to scare a few votes one way or the other but was laying the groundwork for moves much later in the game, after the referendum?"

"To what end?"

"I don't know…initially maybe just chaos to clear the ground for whatever comes next, make it impossible for Renard to govern if he does win." Andrew suddenly sounded deflated. "But maybe I just so don't want to see my country torn apart that I'm starting to look for boogey men where they don't exist. Maybe it's really as simple as Renard says—they're French, we're English, we can live on the same street but not in the same house."

"If I can make a suggestion mate, I'd suggest you find a cold beer. The Jays are on a west coast swing. Take a break. Watch somebody else bat the ball around for a while. Then, after a good night's sleep you'll be ready to resume play. And—not that as a bachelor I'm anyone to give marital advice—I'd suggest you do your playing down at the lake with that lovely lady of yours."

As he put the phone back in its cradle, Andrew knew he had been given good advice but how could he sit around sipping beer and watching TV, much less sleep, when his country was under assault... even if he didn't know the identity of the assailants? Besides, it wasn't as if Marie-Paule wanted to play anymore. Since he'd been campaigning against the referendum she'd been even more remote. Hell, he didn't even know how she intended to vote in the referendum, if at all.

For a time he sat looking out at the lights of the still busy city and the long dark strip that marked the river's course. Some of those lights were in newspaper offices where tomorrow's editorials were being written. The pro-federalist papers would no doubt slam the government for a weak response to France's intrusion into Canadian affairs. The pro-separatist papers would probably suggest this was a preview of what the foreign policy of an independent Québec might look like: bold, reaching out to ancient friends, unbound by custom or convention. And yet neither side knew the half of it. Just wait until the French slapped Ottawa's face with the other hand, sending the *de Gaulle* through the Northwest Passage. If only the damned ship would get stuck in the ice! But in August the chances of that were somewhere between slim and none. The channel was basically clear...basically...but not entirely.

With a glance at the clock he pulled his Rolodex to him. It took only a moment to find the number he needed and dial it. Despite the lateness of the hour the phone was answered immediately. "This is Defense Minister Andrew Fraser. I need to speak with the prime minister." There was no need to say the matter was urgent. Calls to this number at this time of night were understood to be urgent. The wait was surprisingly brief. The PM must not have gone to bed yet. "Prime Minister, I'm sorry to bother you at this hour but I think I've got an answer to the problem we discussed this afternoon. However, to do it, we will to have to move fast. Tonight. And I will need full authority from you to do so."

It took only a few minutes to describe what he wanted to do and get the prime minister's go-ahead. With that authority in hand, he returned to his Rolodex. Over the next half hour he dialed a dozen numbers beginning with the chief of the Canadian Forces Maritime Staff and the Minister of Fisheries and, on instruction of the prime minister, concluded with the PM's press secretary, who had to be tracked down at a movie theater in a suburban shopping mall.

By midnight, lights were beginning to blink on in offices across Ottawa. By dawn the wake of the frigate HMCS Halifax and three other ships of Maritime Forces Atlantic would be roiling the ocean as they proceeded at flank speed toward a point approximately 200 miles south of St. Pierre and Miquelon. Meanwhile, far to the north, the icebreaker St. Laurent reversed course in the night as it threaded its way through the channels of the Queen Elizabeth Islands and headed toward a point north and west of Baffin Island. It was well after three in the morning when he at last kicked off his shoes and sagged onto the couch to quickly fall into a deep sleep but not before resolving that when he awoke he would head down to the lake to spend the rest of the weekend with Marie-Paule. There was nothing more he could do here while the pieces he was playing moved into position on a chess board that covered two million square miles.

Chapter Nine

Chateau Cher
Sunday, August 23rd
11:00am CEDT

The news was not displeasing although events hadn't unfolded quite as planned. The newspapers the president perused over a belated breakfast on the terrace all carried similar headlines in varying sizes of bold type: "French flagship transits Northwest Passage. Arctic course cuts time between Europe and Asia."

Those papers that usually found something to criticize about his government took pains to note that the voyage had taken place in summer, not winter and one obnoxiously noted that a German cruise line sends a couple of ships through the Northwest Passage every summer, thus implying it wasn't such a feat. What they didn't say was that the smaller, more maneuverable German ships routinely took 19 days to transit the passage. The *de Gaulle* did it in 14 and could have done it in less if the Canadians hadn't been in the way.

Indeed, *Le Monde* mentioned there was some debate in Canada about its government providing an "escort" for the French carrier. The Canadian prime minister told an interviewer, "It was the courteous thing to do. One should always make sure one's guests do not get lost while visiting your home." That was, of course, a double slap—the *de Gaulle* was hardly a "guest" and it most assuredly did not consider the passage, much less the rest of the Arctic, Canada's "home." But nothing could diminish the larger story of a "voyage across the top of the world" as one pro-government paper grandly proclaimed it.

Asked why the voyage had been kept secret until it was over, the Canadian prime minister noted that the movement of military ships is traditionally classified, especially when there is risk involved as obviously there was in this case. André wouldn't dispute that, albeit for different reasons. The *de Gaulle* was never in any physical danger. As it turned out there was more ice in its galley than beneath its bow but politically it was undoubtedly better to be discrete than disgraced. Tomorrow he would hold a satellite news conference with the carrier's captain. It could have been held today—the uplink on board the ship had been tested and was working perfectly—but holding off 24 hours meant a second day of favorable news coverage. Of course there would be a third such day when the ship returned to Toulon next month. He would personally welcome it home and award the captain the *Légion d'honneur*. But that wasn't the welcome he most anticipated extending.

How fortunate, he thought, *that the economic summit is to be held here this fall*. It would provide opportunity to be condescendingly charming to McKinley Marston, especially if the Québec referendum went against him. As Churchill said, "In victory, magnanimity." Of course, not too much magnanimity. Philippe would make sure the Canadian PM was at the far end of the row in the traditional group photograph. As host he, of course, would be in the center with the U.S. president on one side. He had not yet decided who would be on his other side, probably the German chancellor. But that might be carrying Euro goodwill a bit further than necessary. He must discuss it with the Cardinal.

As if on cue, the butler appeared. "M. le Président," he announced, "M. Dumont is here."

"Ah, wonderful. Do show him in and see if he'll have a bit of breakfast."

"Not breakfast, thank you, but perhaps a cup of coffee if it would not be too much trouble." The Cardinal, as it turned out, needed no showing in having followed hard on the heels of the butler.

"No trouble at all Jean-Pierre. Delighted." And so saying André nodded to the butler whose task it was to make sure that, indeed, the President of the Republic was not put to any trouble.

"I have just been reading about the *de Gaulle*," the president said to the Cardinal. Noticing his advisor's expression he added with a broad smile, "What a pity they ever changed the ship's name. *Richelieu* was so much more appropriate. After all, it was he who returned Québec to French rule after a British interlude."

"Ah yes," the Cardinal responded, fully aware that he had been challenged, "The Treaty of Saint-Germain-en-Laye; a place the English have more than one reason to remember with a bit of regret."

The president surrendered gracefully. "Do tell."

"It was about fifty years after the treaty that their King James II took up residence at Saint-Germain during the so-called 'glorious revolution' which may be one of the great misnomers of history. After all, they exiled a Francophile and got a Dutchman in return. What, pray tell, could be so glorious about that?"

André threw his head back and laughed aloud. His challenge had not only been met but he'd been utterly routed. "Tell me," he grinned at the Cardinal, "what sort of 'king' do you expect our friends in Québec will get out of their revolution?"

"Well, they haven't actually had the revolution yet," the Cardinal cautioned, "but assuming they do—and that seems plausible if the public opinion polls are to be believed—I doubt it will be Lucien the First. I don't think he has any idea what forces are at play in his 'kingdom'. He may win the revolution but I doubt he will win the peace."

"Are you suggesting opposition from Marston? If I read the man correctly, I don't see him as having the ingenuity to wage the sort of campaign that would be necessary to hold, much less retake, Québec. His efforts so far in the referendum certainly haven't suggested he has the necessary...shall we say...skill set."

"True enough. But there's someone in his government who does. Escorting the *de Gaulle* to and through the Northwest Passage was brilliant. They knew they had no grounds—and certainly no power—to stop us. So they cut their inevitable losses and co-opted our effort. I must say someone played a very bad hand brilliantly."

André Legrande looked thoughtful. "You suggest it was someone at Marston's elbow. Could it not have been his neighbors?"

The Cardinal shook his head. "No, I don't think so. When I spoke with the American security advisor back in June I got the impression he was only vaguely aware anything was happening in Canada. The Americans are rarely pro-active. They're reactive…usually over-reactive. Besides, as I say, they like the idea of us transiting the Northwest Passage. They've done it themselves. It's only the Canadians who don't like it. And if the Americans assume we're going to join them in challenging the Russian claims to the Arctic—which we may—then we've accomplished what we set out to do: divert their attention from Québec and, when they get around to reacting, as they will, they'll find themselves with a choice between a Canada that contests a basic principle of unimpeded navigation which affects American interests around the world, and a France that has demonstrated its determination to keep the sea lanes open."

The president pretended to be engrossed in a bit of toast. "It is interesting is it not, that no one has questioned our choice of instrument for the demonstration. It was not a commercial freighter that made the voyage but a warship; a very big warship. Do you not think anyone noticed?"

The Cardinal deconstructed the question and its premise and, despite finding multiple negatives embedded in it, decided to answer anyway. "I suspect they did. At least whoever devised the Canadian response probably noticed. Of course it had to be a warship for Renard's visit to carry the intended message. Had he had lunch aboard a freighter the message taken would have been something to do with trade. As I said, in the circumstances, the Canadian response was quite good, quite ingenious."

André still seemed dubious. "And the Americans...they will not object to a symbol of French military power rather than commercial power having been used?"

"I doubt it. As I noted, in my conversation with Hamilton it did not come up but the Russian claim to the Arctic did. In fact, I brought it up and reminded him that under the Law of the Sea treaty we have been awarded a seabed mining concession in the Pacific. Although the Americans have never ratified the treaty I am quite confident he took that as an inference that we have similar aspirations in the Arctic and from there it would require only the smallest of leaps to infer that our sending the *de Gaulle* was a warning to the Russians not to assume their quite preposterous claims will go uncontested. In short, with one voyage we have demonstrated our resolve on two issues the United States cares strongly about: defending freedom of navigation and off-shore economic zones. Not a bad week's work."

"And what of M. Renard? Has he had anything more to say since his 'thank you' call for an agreeable luncheon on the *de Gaulle*?"

"Indeed he has. He rang up Friday to inquire what your response might be were he to invite you to be guest of honor at the annual winter carnival in Québec City. It's not until January but I gather he'd like to be able to issue the invitation now and have an acceptance to flaunt before the referendum. Though he did not term it as such, it would, in effect, amount to a state visit although he assured me the public obligations would be modest...deliver some remarks at the opening dinner, cut the ribbon at the snow sculpture exhibit, that sort of thing."

"And the private obligations?" André asked.

"They might prove more substantial. I gather that money is fleeing Québec in advance of the referendum."

"That was to be expected, was it not?"

"But of course. Uncertainty is the enemy of economics."

"Indeed, it is. But surely he anticipated that when he called the referendum?"

"I don't doubt but what he did. What I don't think he anticipated was the violence which undoubtedly increased the outflow of capital. In response to my casual inquiry as to how the referendum was going—it would have looked odd for me not to ask—he admitted his campaign was thrown off stride by the bombings and hasn't fully regained its footing although he expressed confidence he will win."

"No doubt he did. Don't we always?"

The Cardinal took the president's "we" to mean "politicians"—a famously optimistic breed, but he tactfully avoided comment. "He said the bombings focused press attention on the most outspoken but least responsible elements in the separatist movement rather than on him and his message which was calculated as he put it 'not to enflame but to empower'. The result was to scare money away. He said there had been a lot of short-selling of Québec-based stocks. He also said the violence had dried up donations to his campaign. I gather there was a business element that was hedging its bets with some financial support."

André raised a cautionary hand. "Lest you ask, the answer is 'no'. Money leaves a trail. Not a sou."

"I quite agree."

"And you told him so?"

"Not in so many words. I told him that while we are receptive to the peaceful efforts of a French-speaking people to achieve their national aspirations, given our international obligations we could not be seen to be meddling in the internal affairs of an allied country. I am quite certain he took the point. He is not a dumb fellow."

"However?" the president was listening intently.

"However, perhaps the timely announcement of an intended investment in Québec by one of our companies might be useful..." The Cardinal's voice trailed off.

"And..." André prompted.

"....and I suspect he is right to worry about capital flight; I would not be surprised if a certain banker has not flown off with some."

"The short-selling you mentioned?"

"Possibly. In fact, probably. I would not be at all surprised to see him eventually emerge as a significant player in Québec's economic life."

"Despite the socialism of the separatists?"

"Actually, because of it. They were already scaring away existing investors even before the bombs. So where is new investment to come from? Not from the capitalists on Bay Street or Wall Street."

The president picked up his advisor's point. "It will have to come from someone who can see opportunities around the corner."

"Precisely."

André thought about that for a long moment, picturing the rotund little man with the flowery speech who had strolled through the gardens with him and later spun his extraordinary idea of reclaiming Québec for France. He thought at the time that—like a chess master—the banker was looking several steps ahead and positioning his assets to meet opportunities when they arrived. After all, the fellow had as much as admitted he would profit from his scheme. "What was it again that he said about his interest in Québec, something about caravans?"

"He spoke rather poetically of the opportunity for merchant caravans to follow the French flag and to prosper in its shade."

"I wonder how camels do in the snow?" The president chuckled softly. "So, M. Renard would like me to visit. What did you tell him?"

"I told him I would bring his gracious invitation to your attention—which I have now done—and that your January calendar would be carefully reviewed although, as he no doubt could appreciate, many dates have already been committed even at this distance."

"And if I cannot go because of that calendar—which actually does have some dates filled in—or because of other unforeseen circumstances here or there?"

"Then the culture ministry might be persuaded to send an art exhibit or a handful of musicians in your place."

The president, having finally resolved to finish off the toast, turned his attention to the several pâtés available to assist the job. "That 'least responsible element' Renard mentioned…was he suggesting they might be the ones doing the bombing?" André asked.

"Perhaps."

"Who else?"

The Cardinal shrugged. "I'd rather not speculate."

The president paused with the toast halfway to his mouth. "Surely you don't think our banker friend was involved?"

"To be quite frank, I don't know just what I think about M. Khashan. His idea is audacious and could possibly work to our benefit. But I must admit I have concerns, although, I must hasten to add, based on nothing more than perhaps an abundance of caution. Still, I do recall when I asked him how he saw his ideas unfolding he said something about interests with which he was familiar being prepared to act as 'precipitators'. At the time I thought it an odd choice of word but put it down to vocabulary considering French is his second or perhaps third language."

"And now?" André inquired.

"And now I'm of the opinion we ought to continue as we are but keep some distance from M. Khashan which, by the way, should not be difficult. Apart from a couple of telephone calls and a note a day or so after our initial meeting thanking me for taking time to listen to his 'investment strategies' I've heard little from him. Between M. Renard's luncheon and the 'voyage across the top of the world', as I see one of the papers describes it, we've played a rather good hand so far. I suggest we should now be patient and await events in Québec."

M. Legrande inclined his head in agreement as he popped the last bit of toast into his mouth.

SEPTEMBER/
SEPTEMBRE

Chapter Ten

Compton, Québec
Labor Day, September 7th
2:00pm EDT

The volunteer committee had done its best and many of the lawn chairs in front of the bandstand were filled an hour before the rally was to begin. It was a genteel crowd, mostly middle aged to elderly. The women tended to colorful dresses; the men to short sleeves and slacks as summer made what would probably be its last stand of the year. More than a few of the men wore souvenir straw boaters with a bilingual hatband proclaiming "Quebec in Canada— Québec en Canada".

A large maple leaf flag, stretched from one side of the bandstand to the other, occasionally fluttered in a welcome breeze. Many of those waiting fanned themselves with leaflets they had been handed by teenaged volunteers who now stood in little knots on the sidewalks leading to the bandstand laughing self-consciously among themselves while their younger brothers and sisters noisily scampered up and down the grassy banking that separated the park from the homes and streets beyond.

A large, metal trash can—set where the several walkways converged in front of the bandstand—bore witness to the number of people who had made a picnic out of the rally. Empty cardboard buckets and boxes from nearby food shops filled the barrel to near overflowing. A couple of yellow jackets buzzed about its lip, attracted by the scent of the scraps.

Recorded music blared from large speakers on either side of the bandstand. By now it was a familiar sight to Andrew as he waited behind the bandstand with a half dozen of the organizers and their wives. One of his guardians stood a few feet away, close enough to be useful, not so close as to be intrusive; the other was out front watching the crowd. Over the past three months, he had spoken in similar venues across Québec beginning with breakfast meetings with Rotary and Kiwanis clubs, mid-morning interviews with local newspapers and radio stations, then luncheons with ladies clubs before moving on to the next town for more interviews followed by backyard suppers with neighborhood groups and evening rallies in church halls, fire stations and once on a cruise ship tied up in the St. Lawrence. But he tried to keep Sundays clear and, weather permitting, retreat to the cottage and club where Marie-Paule had taken up semi-permanent residence for the summer.

Night after night he went to bed with a raw throat and the knowledge that in a few hours he would get up and do it all over again in some other place. But it was having an impact. The separatist advantage in the polls had narrowed over the summer to statistically "too close to call" as the "undecideds" began to choose sides between the largely emotional appeal of the separatists and his appeal to economic and cultural self interest.

"Will you be richer in a Québec that's isolated from the economy of the rest of the continent where you live?" he would ask. "What will replace Québec's share of the 50% increase the Canadian economy got from the North American Free Trade Agreement? When you sit down at the kitchen table to pay your bills, can you do it with half as much in your paycheck?" Can you afford the taxes it will take to raise an army and navy to protect you? Will your French language survive in English-speaking North America without the protection of Canada with its official bilingualism, albeit often imperfectly recognized?

Did you try speaking French the last time you went to the States?" Andrew would end his barrage of questions with the declaration "It is Canada that allows you to be Québecers, not Québec that allows you to be Canadian."

It had proven effective and should be especially so today as Compton was the birthplace of Louis St. Laurent, the popular post-war prime minister. St. Laurent's father was French, his mother Irish and he was bilingual to such an extent that his English was flavored with a brogue. There could hardly be a better place to make the case for national unity.

With a last hurried glance at his watch and nervous read-through of his introductory remarks, the committee chairman finally suggested "It's time sir, perhaps we should be getting started." With Andrew's agreement they mounted the two or three steps to the bandstand and, ducking around the end of the flag, took their seats on a row of folding metal chairs facing the crowd. Someone abruptly stopped the music. An officious-looking man stepped up to the heavy oak lectern and tapped the microphone. A series of loud "thunks" could be heard through the speakers followed by the faintest of high-pitched squeals. He muttered something about "feed-back" and scurried off to the side of the bandstand to adjust his equipment. The chairman took that as the signal to begin. With a final look at his notes he nervously cleared his throat and advanced on the microphone.

There were innumerable people to be thanked for their efforts in organizing the rally and he apparently did not leave a name unmentioned. The audience began to fidget. He was not the one they had come to hear. Finally realizing that, he proceeded to introduce Andrew noting his academic and political achievements and concluding with the words he had practiced for days: "My fellow Canadians, I am very pleased and indeed honored to introduce to you the Honorable Andrew Fraser, Member of Parliament for Westmount-Ville Marie and Minister of Defense of the Government of Canada." This time there was sustained applause, even a few cheers.

Andrew, who had only been half listening to his introduction, glanced at the program to make sure of his host's name, then stood and shook hands with him before stepping behind the lectern where he raised his arms in acknowledgement of the several hundred people who were standing to welcome him. A lady in a bright print dress took advantage of the moment to make a quick trip to the trash barrel with one more empty container. She did not make it back to her seat.

The flash was incredibly bright. People would later tell reporters it was like a giant flashbulb. To Andrew everything seemed to occur in slow motion although in reality it was over in a split second. A jagged piece of metal made a high-pitched scream as it tore past his head, shredding the flag behind him. He tried to react to what was happening but his brain was so overwhelmed with incoming data it couldn't process everything it was receiving. He felt trapped as in a nightmare where you know you ought to run but can't. The lectern was jammed so tightly atop him that although his left shoulder hurt very badly he couldn't reach across to rub it.

He could see others bent in odd postures. He sensed they were screaming but he couldn't hear them. His ears were filled with a soft rushing sound like tap water through an aerator. It wasn't an unpleasant sound but distant. Indeed, he didn't seem in any way connected to where he was or what was going on around him. He stared at the sky. It was remarkably blue. He thought it must be a beautiful day. It was a shame Marie-Paule had not come with him. She would have looked so lovely in one of her silk sheaths, perfectly balanced on heels that would stress the shapeliness of her legs. Perhaps she would be wearing one of those big, floppy, white hats that framed the oval of her face with its almond-shaped eyes, high cheekbones and pouting red lips. And then it all faded away. The bandstand…the blue sky… Marie-Paule.

Hatley, Québec
Labor Day, September 7th
2:20pm EDT

The first inkling of what had happened was a trail of bold letters crawling across the bottom of the TV screen during the second quarter of the game: "Breaking News: Bomb explodes in Québec. Police report casualties." The crawl recycled its message several more times before new information was added. "Seven dead in bombing at confederation rally in Compton, Québec. Many injuries. Defense Minister Andrew Fraser among casualties."

For the small knot of men who had been watching in the clubhouse the game was forgotten.

"Is she here?"

"She was. Down by the dock."

One man detached himself from the group. "I'd better get her."

The crawl continued to cycle across the bottom of the screen but the men turned away to watch as their colleague strode purposefully across the lawn toward a vivacious young woman who seemed to be holding court in the midst of an admiring circle of men, some younger, most older. On reaching her he leaned close and spoke quietly in her ear. "Mrs. Fraser. You had better come. It's your husband." She looked up, startled.

"Here? No. He has a speech this afternoon. He won't be here until the barbeque."

"No ma'am. I think he's been hurt. It's on television." She turned so pale so quickly that even her lips seemed to lose color. She looked as though she were about to faint. He instinctively took her arm and helped steady her. Together they walked slowly at first and then more quickly toward the clubhouse. A few feet from the porch she broke free of him and ran up the steps.

The game was gone. In its place was a news anchor. He spoke evenly without feigned emotion, his words projecting their own drama. "Shortly after two o'clock this afternoon a powerful bomb exploded in a park in Compton in the eastern townships region of Québec killing at least eight people and injuring many more. The bomb's intended target may have been Defense Minister Andrew Fraser who was about to address the gathering. Mr. Fraser was injured but the extent of his injuries is not yet known. One of the members of his RCMP protection team was among those killed.

"Paul Saint Claire, the chairman of the committee that organized the rally and who had just introduced Mr. Fraser, was also killed as was the mayor of Compton, Estelle Hartley, and her husband Edward who were seated on the stage. Most of the other casualties appear to have been among the audience which had gathered to hear the defense minister speak in opposition to the separatist referendum in Québec. Several of the injured were teenagers. The deaths and injuries appear to have been caused when a metal trash can in which a bomb apparently had been hidden was turned into shrapnel by the force of the explosion. Police have cordoned off much of Compton. The RCMP will assume jurisdiction over the crime scene as a federal cabinet minister is involved. If indeed it is determined that Mr. Fraser was the intended target, this would be the first attack on a minister of the Crown in more than 50 years."

The newscaster looked down at his notes. "For those of you just joining us, a bomb has exploded in the Québec town of..." All eyes in the room turned as one from the TV set to Marie-Paule. Her ghostly pallor had been replaced by a flush.

Sherbrooke, Québec
Labor Day, September 7th
5:00pm EDT

He looked peaceful. Many a summer afternoon she had seen him dozing like that on the couch at the cottage blissfully unaware they were supposed to be somewhere for something. She hated to awaken him then but now she wished she could. The wires and tubes coupled to him were frightening; the insistent low chirp of the cardiovascular monitor threatening. She found herself holding her breath, willing the machine to beep, terrified it would not. The doctor who came to see her said sleep was the best treatment for what he called a grade-three concussion; sleep and watchful waiting. "In terms of overall severity," he told her, "we rate it a 13 on the Glasgow scale," explaining that by the international standard for measuring the severity of a concussion Andrew was on the border line between mild and moderate.

The doctor theorized that he had been knocked unconscious by the concussive power of the blast rather than by any object as an MRI had revealed no cranial injuries. In any event, he had regained consciousness enroute to the hospital which was a good sign. And, in the emergency room, he had been observed trying to rub his badly bruised shoulder, which was another good sign. Response to pain suggested the brain was responding to stimuli as it should. His hearing apparently was giving him problems, he had complained of a rushing sound and said the voices of the doctors sounded distant and hollow as if they were speaking from the bottom of a barrel. Perhaps as a consequence his answers to their questions were uncertain and hesitant. He had no memory of the blast or of the trip to the hospital and had asked where he was and why he was there. "He may never remember the actual event," the doctor advised, adding "That may be one of nature's ways of helping us cope with trauma."

He had explained to Marie-Paule that for the next week Andrew would probably sleep a lot and should. He might feel nauseous, his head would probably hurt—for which he would give him a prescription that would ease the pain without risking sub-cranial bleeding. Indeed, for that reason they were listing his condition as "guarded" and would keep him overnight so he could be monitored. But, as a steady stream of emergency vehicles began unloading the victims of the bombing, it was clear Andrew was one of the fortunate ones.

Some were carried on stretchers, others walked with assistance, a few hobbled painfully on their own into an emergency room that had become a triage center sorting among bloody gashes, hideously broken bones and empty, staring eyes to determine who needed immediate aid, who could wait a bit and who was beyond human help. The only preference shown was that demanded by the nature and severity of the wounds. Every few minutes the roar of a helicopter engine and the thump of its blades signaled an air ambulance was carrying another casualty to one of the Montréal hospitals where further, specialized care could be had now that the patient had been stabilized.

Andrew had been the first to arrive only because he didn't have to wait for an ambulance. The surviving RCMP constable charged with his protection had wrested the oak lectern off him and carried him to the SUV. He had wasted no time, not even to run to the front of the bandstand and help sort through the rubble for his colleague. That wasn't what the manual said to do. It said to protect the person in your charge, get him out of danger and to help. Everything else came second. Who was to say there would only be a single blast? The imperative was to go—*now*. And so, with the SUV's usually inconspicuous red and blue emergency lights flashing and its siren climbing from a moan to a scream, he began a dash for the nearest hospital, scattering holiday traffic from their path. Now and again an emergency vehicle would flash past, heading the opposite way as a widening call for help was answered.

Labor Day, September 7th
7:00pm EDT

It had been nearly five hours since the bomb exploded. In the interval several TV vans had taken up position in the street near the hospital's emergency room dock. Reporters who were linked to the vans by an electronic umbilical cord stood impatiently behind a yellow tape line police had strung to keep the way clear. On the monitors inside the TV vans a similar scene was visible from Compton where powerful emergency lights cast long, eerie shadows as forensic teams sifted through the rubble that had been the bandstand. Now and again one of the searchers would straighten up and the bright yellow letters "RCMP" or "Sûreté" could be seen stenciled across the back of their jackets. There had been no skirmishing over jurisdiction. While it might not prove true further up the bureaucratic chain, at street level the issue was simple: there was a job to be done. Who could help do it?

From time to time a smaller pool of light would encircle one of the reporters outside the hospital or on the bluff overlooking the ruins of the bandstand and they would tell as much of the story as they knew to anchors seated in studios in Montréal, Toronto, New York or even distant London and Paris. On an otherwise slow news weekend this was the lead story. When the available facts proved insufficient to fill the allotted time, experts provided speculation. Someone in the audience at Compton, thinking to record the opening of the rally, had caught the moment of the blast on a cell phone camera. It was jerky and in the immediate aftermath of the explosion aimed not at the bandstand but the sky, still it was run repeatedly on the networks along with pictures of ambulances arriving at the hospital.

All the while Andrew lay asleep unaware his name was being repeated around the world and that countless unknown people were quietly praying for him. But, of course, there were some who were not and it was they who worried his friends and guardians.

Chapter Eleven

4861 Chemin de la Côte-des-Neiges, Montréal
Saturday, September 26th
12:00 noon EDT

The doctors had needlessly insisted he rest. In point of fact when the RCMP brought him home from the hospital almost three weeks ago he hadn't felt like doing anything else. It took a couple of days before he could walk about the apartment without losing his balance and only now could he move his left arm—up to a point—without his shoulder hurting. The ugly yellow and purple bruises were slow in fading but his hearing had quickly cleared to the point that he could make telephone calls. One of the first was to return those from Mark, his old college roommate.

He didn't presently have a roommate. After hovering for several days Marie-Paule finally accepted that sleep was really what he most needed. So she had started going to the gallery for a few hours each afternoon while he napped. More than once he reflected that maybe it was true that some good did come out of misfortune. She had fussed about him, bringing his meals on a tray to his room—still the guest room—but perhaps not for long. After all, it was his own doing that had landed him back there. The RCMP officers who brought him home had asked where his bedroom was and out of habit he had directed them to the guest room.

In a further sign that their estrangement might be ended, she had curled up beside him that first night back, cradling him in her arms as if to ward off any further harm. Of course she was not his only guardian. A constable sat at a table in the hallway by the elevator and two more were in an unmarked car parked on the drive, midway between the front door of the building and the entrance to the parking garage.

At first her attempts at conversation met with a less than equal response from him. He found that even talking took more energy than he could easily muster and he would drift off as she was speaking. But after a few days he began taking an interest in her chatter which was mostly about the gallery. It seemed she had found some backing thus easing the parlous state of its finances. However, given the testy history surrounding her earlier, unsuccessful efforts to get him to intercede with the Arts Council, he thought it best not to inquire too deeply into her sources. The key thing was that she still loved him, even if he nearly had to die to find it out. And while she had now returned to "her" room it was premised on his need for sleep, nothing more.

As his recovery progressed at a quickening pace he was able to spend some time each morning on the contents of his dispatch box—reading reports, making notes in the margins, signing letters. The routine was undemanding but reassuring; one more grip on reality. But he missed human contact. He couldn't fathom how people could willingly telecommute. At last his doctors had given in to his restlessness and pronounced him fit enough to leave the apartment for a few hours each day so long as he didn't overly exert himself and rested on his return. Consequently, he actually found himself looking forward to tonight's Chamber of Commerce dinner, an event he previously had regarded as one of the necessary burdens of office. He would make an appearance but not speak and would leave early. Marie-Paule said she would be back by five and would accompany him. He suspected she had an ulterior motive in doing so but that was no problem. If she could talk a few of the other attendees into backing the gallery, it was fine by him. It would show her that government grants weren't the only way to fund the arts.

He wished she were here now. His tuxedo, formal shirt, tie and cummerbund were hanging in the closet, still in the cleaner's bag, but the cuff links and studs were nowhere to be found. That could mean they were in what was still officially "their" room, put there by the twice a week housekeeper who had more trouble than he adjusting to the fact that he slept in the guest room.

He crossed the hall to the master bedroom and was surprised how much he felt like an intruder going into what was, by definition if not by usage, as much his room as hers. The big double bed was neatly made up with two sets of pillows even though only one got used. The night table on what had been his side of the bed had a book lying on it as if it were only last night that he had set it aside for sleep. His bureau still contained some shirts and socks he didn't like; those that he actually wore having migrated some time ago to the guest room. Still on top of the bureau was the old leather jewelry box that had belonged to his father. Working from the unlikely premise that the housekeeper might actually have put things where they belonged he began poking through its contents: a collection of old campaign buttons, a cheap watch whose strap had broken years ago, an out-of-date gasoline credit card and a pack of matches from a long defunct restaurant whose principle attraction had been its view of the city. A building boom had put an end to the view and an exceedingly modest menu and over-priced drinks couldn't sustain it. But back when he and Marie-Paule were first dating it was *the* place to go. Indeed, that was where he took her the evening he proposed.

All those memories were in the old jewelry box but not the cuff links and studs.

He straightened up and looked around the room. It was any-one's guess what the housekeeper might have done with them. Could it be that in whatever mental process she applied to her work she had categorized them not as "his" but simply as "jewelry" and thus co-mingled them with Marie-Paule's? Since his tooth brush regularly showed up alongside his hair brush it was not beyond the realm of possibility.

Marie-Paule kept her jewelry in a lacquer box he had brought home from Japan on a long ago "fact-finding" mission. The only "fact" he had found was that it was a hell of a long flight from Vancouver to Tokyo. The most remarkable thing about the jewelry box and the strand of Mikimoto pearls he had placed inside was that after four days of over-the-top Japanese hospitality he still had the presence of mind to get her a gift even if it had been acquired at the last minute from the duty-free shop at the airport.

When you lifted the lid a little Japanese tune was supposed to play—*Sukiyaki* or something like that—but the box hadn't been wound for a long time and so opened silently. He thought for half a moment of winding it but then she'd know he'd been in her things and would demand to know why and. . .the hell with it. Beneath the open lid was a tray with two compartments each topped with its own little red cushion. He lifted each in turn. Amid various pieces were the earrings he had given her on their fifth anniversary plus two brooches she'd inherited from an aunt. But no cuff links. It was most unlikely they would be in the larger, bottom compartment but, grasping the tabs of the tray, he lifted it out anyway. There were several more bracelets and necklaces, again, presents from him or hand-me-downs from relatives. The Mikimoto pearls were there, too, in their original red velvet box. There was also a small manila envelope with "Royal Bank" printed on it. He picked it up. It wasn't sealed. It contained their old bank book from newly-wed days when she still worked in one of the bank's branches. In an abundance of caution to avoid any hint of conflict of interest he had opened a new account at the Bank of Montréal when he was elected to parliament. His paychecks went there while hers continued to be deposited in the old account. It was rather sweet that she had held onto the bank book, a memory of their early days when each month was a close run contest between income and outgo. With a bit of a grin he tugged the book from its sleeve.

The title page had their names and their old address as well as the account number. The next half dozen pages were filled with single spaced entries that were now just numbers but then had been milestones as they built their lives together. The deposits were modest but regular and there was just one big withdrawal—for the down payment on this apartment. But then there came a time when the deposits ceased and a series of small withdrawals began, marking the date when Marie-Paule stopped working at the bank. It was funny how the story of their lives could be traced from such numbers. If she were here she could probably identify each withdrawal as a gift to a niece or nephew or something for him. Now she simply used a debit card tied to their joint checking account. It was undoubtedly more efficient but also more impersonal. He idly flipped to the last page to see whether there was anything left in what, in effect, had become her account. He looked, then, disbelieving, looked again before slumping heavily on the edge of the bed staring at the bank book. It showed a current balance of $45,449.87.

He thumbed back a page. The last small withdrawal had been almost two years ago and was for $100.00 leaving a balance of $260.67 cents. With several entries for interest it had grown to $279.23 when on July 15th, barely two months ago, a deposit of $50,000 had been made. There were also interest payments of $57.84 in July and $112.80 in August. Offsetting that were withdrawals of $2000.00 on July 27th and August 24th and another $1000.00 just this week. His hand trembled as he reassembled the booklet and sleeve and tucked them back in the envelope which he returned to its hiding place. He then refitted the tray and set the jewelry box back on her vanity table. As he did, its spring found one last reserve of strength to chime a single plaintive note.

Hatley, Québec
Saturday, September 26th
12:00 noon EDT

Mist collected on the nearly bare branches until a gust of wind sent a drum roll of droplets dancing across the porch roof. Only a few weeks ago summer had flirted with autumn but now brown piles of leaves lay against the side of the clubhouse. The shoreline, visible only as far as the rocky outcropping where he used to swim to her was—like everything else—wrapped in gray. The raft where she flirted had been dragged from the water and, listing to one side, lay beached for the winter. The clubhouse was shuttered and locked, the white rockers that lined the porch in summer, now snuggly stowed inside. Fernand shivered and wished she would come. He belatedly wondered about the burglar alarm. Perhaps by walking on the porch he had already triggered it and the police would soon arrive to ask what a summer employee was doing here now. When Marie-Paule telephoned Thursday to say she had a problem and needed to see him, he had agreed without thinking. "Oh good," she'd said. "Do you remember the clubhouse? Let's meet there Saturday noon."

He now realized he should have invited her to his place which at least was warm and dry. He could have offered her a cup of coffee and a croissant from the café in the village. But her call had been as brief as it was surprising and before he could collect his thoughts she had rung off having received his promise to meet her here. He didn't know her telephone number so he couldn't ring her back and wouldn't have anyhow for fear her husband might answer. Maybe she wouldn't come on a day like this. He pulled his father's big silver watch from his pocket and checked it for the third or fourth time since he'd arrived a half hour ago. It was barely past noon.

The sudden crunch of tires in the parking lot made him start. *What if it were the police? Best he get off the porch.* He descended the two or three steps to stand on the lawn looking out at the fog-shrouded lake.

"Ah, Fernand, you *are* here!" She sounded relieved to see him. She was dressed in a smartly tailored beige jacket and dark slacks. A maroon turtle-neck sweater showed at her throat. She was wearing brown leather gloves and boots. Her hair was tucked into a toque that partially covered her ears. She looked like one of those models he used to see in the Eaton's catalogue. So many emotions swept through him so rapidly that he could think of nothing to say in reply.

"I'm so glad to see you," she continued, apparently not noticing his discomfort. "You have been well?" He nodded. "Brrr," she shivered. "How gray it looks." He looked where she indicated, toward the mist-shrouded lake. "There's the raft," she said in a very matter-of-fact voice as though inventorying the summer properties. "What did they do with all the chairs?" she asked.

"They're inside."

"I don't suppose we can get in, though?" She started to mount the steps as if to test the door.

"No," he said, quickly adding, " the door may be alarmed."

She pulled her hand back without touching the handle. Then, taking a deep breath, she turned to him, "Well, can we talk?" That seemed to be a cue for him to join her on the porch. He retraced his steps and stopped, uncertain what to do next.

She smiled at him. "I'm so glad you agreed to meet me. I suppose you're wondering why I asked."

He nodded silently—almost afraid to look at her.

"I..." She caught herself and began again. "Some friends of mine have a problem that I thought you might be able to help us... them...with." She paused as if uncertain how to proceed. When she did her tone was a little sharper, a little more confident as if a momentary doubt had been resolved. It was the sunbather who wanted a service from a club employee rather than the coquette trying to amuse her courtiers.

"You didn't tell anyone you were going to meet me, did you?" she asked.

"No," he answered, "you said not to." He didn't know who he could have told anyway. His brother would have said he shouldn't meet her and would have asked a hundred questions he could not and would not have answered.

"You do still take hay down to the States, don't you?" He nodded. "When is your next trip?

"Monday." He was surprised she remembered and wondered why.

"Well, Fernand," she said in a tone that suggested he was in her confidence, "I have a very big favor to ask of you. A man who has been very helpful to me has two guests visiting Montréal. They hadn't planned to go to the States on this trip but a friend of theirs in New York begged them to come. The problem is they don't have U.S. visas." She looked down at the ground as if embarrassed about something. "So I did a very foolish thing. I said I was sure my husband could take care of it but, as you know, he was hurt and I don't want to bother him with it. And ..." her voice faltered, "...they made plans based on my assurances."

He said nothing but he felt sorry for her. It was hardly her fault her husband had been hurt. They ought to understand that and not press her.

She paused for a long moment as if hesitating to go on, "And then I thought of you." Fernand looked baffled.

"Me? What can I do?"

"I thought maybe you could give them a ride when you go to deliver your hay." She rushed on to explain, "Not all the way to New York of course...you really couldn't drive a load of hay into the city." She gave a little laugh at the idea and Fernand smiled weakly in reply. "Just to some place where their friend could meet you and take them the rest of the way." She paused, "They told me to tell you they would be happy to pay you what they had would have paid for airplane tickets; a thousand dollars."

"But they will still need papers even if they ride with me," Fernand protested. "I have to go through customs."

"But surely the customs people all know you by now."

"Some do, but they only know me. I never have anybody with me."

"Couldn't you tell them they're your helpers? They'd understand that you need help to unload the hay. Tell them you hurt your back and you can't do it by yourself."

"They would still want to see their papers. They ask everybody for papers now. They ask a lot of questions, even if they know you. And they want papers."

Marie Paule paced up and down the porch as he spoke, clearly upset. He wanted to help but he knew the routine. U.S. customs used to just ask where you were born, how long you planned to stay in the States and if you had anything to declare. Since 9-11 it was different: more questions... and papers.

Halfway down the porch she suddenly stopped pacing and spun toward him. "Couldn't they ride in back under the hay?" she asked. "Not the whole way, of course, just while you cross the border?" Warming to the idea she laughed, "It would be like a hayride!"

He shook his head. "It's not loose hay. It's big bales. They're heavy."

She looked deflated and turned away toward the lake before wheeling on Fernand again. "Couldn't you leave some bales out and let them ride there?"

He didn't like the sound of that at all. If he were caught he'd be in very serious trouble. But all he said to Marie Paule was "How would they get back? I won't have any hay on the way back."

"That will be up to their friend in New York. I only said I would help them get there. I don't even know if they are planning on coming back this way. Maybe they'll just go home from New York." She had paused her pacing directly in front of him, her lips gathered in a pout. "You won't say 'no' will you? You will help me Fernand, won't you?"

He didn't answer. As much as he wanted to please her, he didn't want to get into trouble. And this sounded like trouble. But she took his silence for assent.

"I knew you would help me," she said, her eyes suddenly sparkling. "I knew you wouldn't let me down." She stood on her tiptoes and kissed him ever so lightly on his cheek. He instinctively reached up and rubbed it.

Then she was back to business: "When do you leave Monday?"

"Early," he said. "Around 6:00 o'clock but..."

She cut off his hesitation. "Then they better come down tomorrow. You can find a place for them to stay, can't you?" He nodded. She pulled a leather note book from her jacket pocket and tugged its little pencil loose. "Tell me how to get to your farm." With his doubts increasing by the moment he nonetheless complied. It was simple. There was only one numbered highway in Ste. Herménégilde and he lived beside it. The St. Germaine Freres sign with the drawing of a Guernsey cow his father had put up years ago still hung from a post by the driveway. But ...

She left him no time to voice his doubts. Her eyes bright with excitement she pocketed the note book and turned as if to head back to her car. But on the second step she turned and sprang back up on the porch and. again standing on tiptoes, kissed him on the check a second time and whispered in his ear, "You are a dear." She smelled like some sort of flowers.

And with that she was gone. Moments later he heard her car start, its tires again crunching on the gravel. He looked about him half expecting someone had seen their meeting and the kisses. But as he looked across the lawn to the lake, which was disappearing into the mist, his thoughts were of her rather than of the treacherous task she had given him.

As he thought of it on his way back to the farm he had a moment of cold panic. *What had he done? There was no way he could take two men across the border without papers. And he certainly couldn't smuggle them in the hay. They would put you in jail for that. He had to tell her "no" but how? He didn't have her telephone number and didn't know her address, except that it was somewhere in Montréal. He would just have to tell them when they came Sunday that he couldn't do it. They undoubtedly would be angry at having travelled all the way from Montréal for nothing and she might never speak to him again. Maybe he wouldn't be able to continue working at the club which would mean he'd never see her again.* A jumble of thoughts churned through his mind. He didn't want to get into trouble but neither did he want to never see her again. He wished he could talk to Raymond, but of course, he couldn't and besides he knew what he would say.

Yet, at that moment, without speaking, his brother provided the answer he was seeking. Stretching from the road beside a four board fence was a rutted track that brought to mind the one they had followed the day they went hunting across the border. He tried to remember details. Raymond had said it came out on a paved road in Vermont. And it was supposed to be wide enough for a fire truck so it would probably be wide enough for him although with a load of hay he would be taller than a fire truck. His center of gravity would also be higher meaning crossing the stream could be risky. Still...

Back at the farmhouse he went down to the barn where the truck waited. It was hard to tell from looking at the sky what to expect in the way of weather. Everything was a uniform gray. He didn't want to get the truck loaded and then have it sit in the rain. He would compromise: do only as much as would still allow him to put it into the barn for the night and then top up the load Sunday afternoon.

He climbed onto the step on the passenger side and tugged the door open. In the glove compartment was a roadmap of the New England states and adjacent New York which he had bought on his first trip south three years ago. He hadn't looked at it in a while since he usually took the same routes to the same places but he pulled it out now and, climbing down, spread the map on the hood. It took a moment or two to locate where he was. The provincial highway showed as a thin black line with the sharp turn where his farm sat clearly visible on it. The track was not marked but he figured it was somewhere on the big curve where the highway nearly brushed the border. On the Vermont side there was a fine blue line. That had to be the paved road Raymond had mentioned.

It, in turn, ran into a darker line—a numbered highway—that continued west until it met the red of the interstate an inch or so below the border. The track through the woods wouldn't be very long but if it rained the stream might not be passable. Fire roads didn't need to be passable in rain. Ideally he should go down there and walk through to the blue line on the map but the hay had to be loaded and if he didn't start now he wouldn't be able to finish even a half load before dark. With a deep sigh he refolded the map, uncertain whether he could go through with what she asked, but fearful she would never speak to him again if he didn't. Unconsciously he ran his hand across his cheek.

Chapter Twelve

Ferme St. Germaine Freres
Sunday, September 27th
4:30pm EDT

It was disappointing. She had not come with her friends. Someone else drove them. Someone who rolled down the window and with a sneer asked "You St. Germaine?" Receiving a nod in reply, he rolled the window back up, said something to the two men who were with him, one in the passenger's seat, one in back. Then they all got out. The driver popped the trunk lid. He didn't introduce himself. Fernand wanted to ask why Marie-Paule didn't bring them but she probably had other things to do. It was Sunday.

The two passengers each had a canvas tote bag as well as a brown fiberboard suitcase they apparently shared. They put them on the ground and stepped back. Fernand didn't say anything but he must have looked curious. "Presents," the driver volunteered.

One of the men grinned broadly. "Yeah, we bring presents," he laughed, pointing at the suitcase. The driver joined in. The other man apparently didn't see the humor because he didn't laugh.

They looked around, surveying the farm yard. "What's in there?" The bigger of the two men, the one who had laughed, pointed toward the barn.

Fernand shrugged. "Hay."

"Where are the cows?"

"Don't have any."

"There's a picture of one on your sign." The man gestured with his thumb down the driveway toward the road.

"It's an old sign."

The man grunted. "Who else is here?" He looked toward the house.

"No one. Just me."

"You're not married?"

"No."

The man seemed to relax. "Why not? A fine looking bull like you with a big barn to play in? You need a cow." He laughed hard at his crudity. The driver joined in. Fernand managed a polite smile. The other, smaller, man had his back turned, gazing out toward the road. He gave no sign he had heard them.

The comedian continued, pointing at the truck with its load of hay. "That's our taxi?" he asked, laughing at his own wit. His French had a strange accent. "Maybe we should put our suitcase on board, no?" the man asked.

"Won't you need it tonight?" Fernand asked.

"No, just these." The man indicated the tote bags. "We travel light," he laughed, "except for our presents" he added, eyeing the suitcase. For some reason that struck him as very funny. Fernand noticed the other, smaller man still didn't laugh or give any sign he heard his companion. His eyes continued to scan the fields. He appeared to be watching for someone or something.

**Sunday, September 27th
7:00pm EDT**

It had been easy enough getting their suitcase onto the truck. For its size it wasn't particularly heavy. He had suggested they stuff it behind the seat in the cab where it would stay dry but they said it should ride in back, in the hay. Fernand shrugged and offered to help load it but they said no. He couldn't tell whether they were being polite or were afraid he'd drop it and break the presents.

He removed one of the top bales of hay and they put the suitcase in the hollow it created. It seemed like a good idea since the hay would act as a cushion if they hit a bump and it was almost certain they would on the old fire road. He tied the displaced bale on top of the fuel tank. That way his customers would get all the hay they had ordered and he wouldn't have to explain why he was a bale short. With the tarpaulin roped down, the load looked just as it always did.

He suggested they go into the village for supper but they said no. He offered to run up to the IGA and get some steaks but the smaller one barked "non" adding "you stay here." His voice was harsh with more of an accent than his companion. There was an uncomfortable moment of silence and then the big man laughed and said they just didn't want him to go to any trouble, they had had a late lunch and just something simple, whatever he had on hand, would be fine.

That proved to be scrambled eggs, several thick slices of ham, and a plate of toast accompanied by a crock of deep yellow butter and a pot of homemade strawberry jam, a thank you from the wife of a farmer he'd helped. The two men ate hungrily of the eggs and toast.

The big fellow asked him about the States and what it was like there. "Mostly like here I guess," Fernand replied. "I haven't seen a lot of it. Just what's a few hours south of here...except for Hampton Beach." He told them about going there one summer with his aunt and uncle and their kids. Again, the big fellow seemed interested. The smaller one didn't. But it was he who, at the end of the meal, pulled a white envelope from his pocket and gave it to Fernand saying only "For you," then adding "for taking us." Fernand took it, said thank you and set it on the table. He didn't open it. Not right then. Later, after they had gone upstairs to the bedrooms he'd readied for them, he did. There were ten crisp, new-looking hundred dollar bills inside. He put the envelope in the top drawer of the little chest under the clock and then, having crossed the kitchen he retraced his steps, pulled the drawer open again and this time tucked the envelope under the ledger. It was a lot of money. One should be careful.

In the course of supper he had asked them how they knew Marie-Paule. The big fellow's answer came as a surprise: "Who?" Fernand repeated her name. He appeared to draw a blank.

The smaller, quiet one spoke up for one of the few times in the evening. Even so he didn't address Fernand but his companion. "We have a friend who arranged everything. We do not know his other friends." Fernand didn't ask any more questions. Following supper they watched TV for a while and then, after inquiring what time they would leave in the morning, the two headed upstairs where he heard water running in the bathroom before everything fell silent. Fernand cleaned up the supper dishes. The eggs and toast were gone but they hadn't touched the ham. That was a shame. It was a very good ham, not overly salty. He probably should have told them. Oh well, it would keep. Maybe they'd like some at breakfast. For now, it was time for him to get some sleep, too. Tomorrow would have been a long day in any event. Now, who knows? He was half frightened at what he was about to do, half excited. But before he fell asleep he brushed the back of his hand across his cheek and smiled.

Chapter Thirteen

White River Junction, Vermont
Monday, September 28th
6:00pm EDT

Just a mile off the interstate, he found himself in another world. People who lived here weren't going far and were in no particular hurry to get there…SUVs stuffed with kids on their way home from soccer practice, panel trucks returning from a day's work, one-size-too-big sedans driven by couples made small by age enroute to a familiar restaurant. Most cars already had their headlights on even though it was not quite dark.

You had to exit the Interstate to get food or fuel and he needed both. On one of his earlier trips he'd discovered a 24 hour discount gas station next door to a diner that served generous portions of meat loaf, big wedges of pie and steaming mugs of coffee delivered by a waitress who addressed all her customers as "sweetheart" or "darling". One stop to fill truck and driver and, in a few hours, they'd both be home, richer for their efforts.

Seated in the warmth of the diner, its windows fogged, he finally began to relax. This bizarre, sometimes frightening day was almost over. With one exception, it had gone surprisingly well. Even the exception—when a low-hanging branch on the fire road scraped off several bales and the suitcase with them—apparently had done no serious harm. The tarp had a rip in it but restringing the rope through nearby eye sockets had kept it from flapping and ripping further. Even the suitcase wasn't badly damaged, although one of its corners was crumpled and when he lifted it onto the truck bed, a grayish-white powder had trickled out. The smaller of the two men swore at that in some strange language. There's something universal about swearing. You may not recognize the words employed but you instantly recognize them for what they are.

"Put it down," he barked, signaling Fernand to set the suitcase back on the ground. He did as ordered all the while apologizing for the accident. His apology was ignored. "Go get your hay," he was told, even as he waved him away from the suitcase. Obeying orders he had backed toward the nearest hay bale five or six feet away while the man tugged some keys from his pocket and opened the suitcase. Inside were a number of foil-wrapped packages. One had broken open spilling some of its contents.

That's when he had made matters worse. On seeing the contents of the suitcase he'd blurted out "drugs" and backed further away. He didn't know what sort of drugs they might be but he'd seen enough TV shows to know what illegal drugs looked like. "I'm not carrying drugs," he told them. "I'll take you back to the farm and you can have someone come get you but I'm not going to get involved in drugs."

His protest was first met by stony silence from the little man and then tension-breaking whoops of laughter from the big one. "Drugs? You think these are drugs?" he had asked. "My friend you could not get high on this stuff. Fat maybe but not high. This is flour, very fine Lebanese flour. You can't buy it in the States. It's a special gift for our friend."

Even now, the trip essentially behind him, Fernand still felt foolish. He should have known Marie-Paule would not be friends with anyone involved with drugs. He hoped they wouldn't tell her what he'd said. He'd repeatedly apologized and they seemed okay about it. Indeed, as if to disprove his suspicions, the big fellow had picked up the broken packet with the pitchfork stowed on the truck and, holding it out in front of him, strutted down to the stream ludicrously humming a march tune and tossed it in. "If that was drugs," he laughed to Fernand, "you think I would throw all that money away?" He then carefully removed the other packages, set them aside and, slipping the tines of the pitchfork through the handle of the now empty suitcase, dragged it to the edge of the stream where he upended it and tapped several times to dislodge the remaining flour. He then repacked the suitcase, snapped its locks shut and handed it up to his companion who rearranged the hay bales around it.

That aside, everything else had gone smoothly. There were only a few inches of water where the road crossed the stream and the truck easily splashed through on what proved to be a firm bed. Within a half mile they'd topped a little rise and emerged onto the paved road he'd seen on the map. If they had tripped any hidden alarm there was no sign anyone knew or cared. A few minutes later they passed through a small Vermont village but the handful of people about at that hour paid no attention to a farm truck. And so it was a little before noon when he'd pulled into the back of a supermarket parking lot near Saratoga Springs where his passengers' friend was waiting for them. He'd worried how they could get the suitcase down and the replacement hay bale up without attracting attention but, in the end, no one seemed to notice.

I-91 Vermont
Monday, September 28th
9:00pm EDT

As he drove north Fernand continued to mull over his day, a little proud and—if truth be known—surprised that he had been able to carry it off so well although he could still feel the tension between his shoulder blades. The little guy may have been just as tense although he said almost nothing but twice when they'd passed police cars idling at the curb he had sat very still, almost rigid, as if he were holding his breath. Since he was in the middle, straddling the gear shift, his silence had discouraged conversation between Fernand and the big guy who eventually leaned back and napped. But, for all that, the day had gone reasonably well and certainly had been very profitable.

Not only did he have the hay money but there was that thousand dollars in the envelope in the kitchen drawer which, however, presented a problem of its own.

His initial impulse was to put the money in the bank along with the hay check but he realized it would look odd to give the teller a U.S. check with one hand and ten crisp Canadian hundred dollar bills with the other. People who banked at the Caisse Populaire didn't carry a thousand dollars cash around with them. What would he say if they asked where he got it?

He turned the matter over in his mind, rejecting several options before deciding to keep the cash at home and just draw on it as needed for living expenses. But that raised another problem. If the money were in tens or twenties he could use it to buy groceries, but hundreds? Anyplace he shopped they'd say something, joke whether it was real, want to know if he didn't have something smaller, thus drawing attention to him, especially if he did it more than once.

The glare of lights on the road ahead abruptly interrupted his thoughts. Dear God! He was coming up on the border! Lost in thought, he'd driven past the exit for the old highway that crossed through a Vermont village that melded into an adjoining one in Québec. Some homes actually straddled the border so meals cooked in one country were eaten in the other without ever leaving the house. In such a setting the customs post on the main street was more a formality than a barrier with locals casually waved through. An empty farm truck like his would be considered "local" and barely given a second glance. The border station on the Interstate was something else. At this hour of the night it would be busy, which meant a wait, perhaps a long one, and they asked questions. He suddenly felt queasy. His nerves had been stretched as far as they could go for one day. He didn't want to wait. He didn't want to answer questions. He just wanted to get home and go to bed.

For a moment he considered turning around and heading back to the missed exit but the only place to turn around was in the plaza immediately before the border station which would surely attract attention and then he'd have to go through U.S. customs a quarter mile south. He rolled down the window to let in some cool air and tried to think. *Going south you go through U.S. customs. Going north you go through Canadian customs. Are they hooked together? Could the Canadian customs agents look in a computer and see that he hadn't gone through U.S. customs on the way south this morning?* Despite the coolness of the night he unbuttoned his jacket.

Only two of the three truck lanes were open. He pulled into the shorter line behind a *Bergeron Exprés* out of Quebec City. Lights glared in his mirrors as a semi lined-up behind him. At least the agents could see he was empty. There was nothing for them to search.

Every couple of minutes a collective growl rose from the line as the trucks ground into gear, belched exhaust and crept a few feet ahead as one-by-one they cleared customs. Twenty minutes passed and now there were just two tractor-trailers ahead of him. Beyond the brightly lit island of the border post the countryside was black and vaguely hostile. And yet he knew the danger wasn't out there in the dark. It was here in the light.

He wiped his sleeve across his brow to blot the perspiration. The tension was stabbing between his shoulder blades. He needed to pee. In an effort to calm himself he took long, deep breaths of the diesel-tainted air. Logic told him there was no reason why he should have any problem but something else—maybe his nerves, maybe something he wasn't remembering—suggested otherwise. As he waited he watched moths pirouette dangerously near the lights, unaware how close to danger they were or, perhaps, uncaring in their infatuation with the glow.

Now only the Bergeron truck remained ahead of him. He could see the driver open his door to hand some papers down to the customs agent who at first reached for them but then suddenly jumped back. A bottle tumbled from the cab shattering on the pavement at her feet. He couldn't hear what was said but the agent looked peeved as she took the papers and stepped into a little glass-walled kiosk to examine them. She stamped some, scribbled on others, then re-attached them to the clipboard and handed it back. She spoke with the driver for a moment before waving him through. Whatever she said the big truck eased to the right, away from the broken glass before slowly moving out. As he did she pulled a walkie-talkie from her belt and spoke into it while holding up a hand signaling Fernand to wait where he was. A minute later a second agent, carrying a push broom, stepped in front of his truck while the one with the clipboard walked toward him jotting down his license number as she approached.

"Name?" she asked. Fernand told her.

"Where are you going?"

"Home."

"Where is that?" She sounded cross.

Without thinking he replied, "St. H." The French "H" made it sound like "sane–tash".

"Where?"

"St. Herménégilde. Near Coaticook." She nodded.

"What was the purpose of your visit to the United States?"

"I had to deliver a load of hay."

"How long were you there?"

"Just today."

"Are you bringing anything back with you?"

"No ma'am," Fernand replied. She glanced at the empty truck bed.

For customs agent Marcelle Pelletier her workday still had a couple of hours to go. From this point—almost half past nine—until she got off at midnight, it would be mostly 18-wheelers coming through, tourists and business travelers likely having reached their destinations or stopped somewhere for the night. Every three months she drew this shift. Some of the agents actually liked it. She didn't, especially in winter, although the night differential looked good on her paycheck. The real challenge was not to breathe...or get splattered, although it probably didn't much matter. Her clothes were headed for the wash anyway as they reeked of exhaust by the time she got home. At least she didn't have to be outside all evening. There were breaks when she could retreat to the office and a cup of coffee and whatever pastry someone had brought in. Of course, if anybody was off or if there was a lot of traffic, there might not be a break. For all the talk about security, border crossings were still notoriously understaffed, especially at night. The previous year when the U.S. and Canadian national holidays bracketed the same long weekend the backup stretched nearly a mile. That, of course, wasn't true everywhere. Some crossings only had a single lane and a single agent. Some weren't even staffed at night. They just hung out a sign saying they were closed and instructing travelers to report to the nearest open customs station. Some did. Some didn't. As congressional and parliamentary investigators on both sides of the border had discovered, security was more an objective than a *fait accompli*. It was also an expense in a time of tight budgets.

As she knew, a customs agent's primary job was to ask questions; not just for the answers but for the way the answers were given. A certain degree of nervousness was to be expected, especially from tourists and other casual travelers, but answers that were too nervous or—conversely—too smooth might invite a closer look. In any event, licenses and registrations—and, for commercial drivers, travel logs—had to be checked to make sure names, addresses and dates matched and that some trucker wasn't on his fourteenth or fifteenth hour behind the wheel, loaded up on pills that worked until they stopped working sending him bleary-eyed into whatever was in his path. In addition, there were multi-colored forms that had to be filed—bills of lading, insurance, NAFTA certificates—a sheaf of paper for almost every truck that passed through.

Almost every truck…but not this one…it had farm plates. He wouldn't have much in the way of papers beyond his license and registration. Still she checked them to make sure they agreed: "Fernand St. Germaine. Ferme St. Germaine Freres. St. Herménégilde, Québec." A big name for what had to be a very small place.

"Once he's done cleaning up that mess you can go through," she said. She then turned to tell the yellow moving van that was nearly perched on the farmer's tail to follow him and stop under the portico.

Fernand felt some of the tension drain away. Another hour and he'd be home, this incredible day over.

Dumping the swept-up glass into a trash barrel, the agent with the broom turned and waved him through. But before he could get his truck in gear the big van that was waiting behind him released its air brakes with an earsplitting blast while revving its diesel engine. Marcelle turned away, covering her ears against the noise. The empty farm truck moved through the customs portal closely followed by the van which came to a halt under the roof, its noise temporarily drowning out all other sound. More than once Marcelle had grimly joked it would be a close call whether her lungs or her hearing would go first.

It wasn't until he was a few hundred meters from the border, safely into Québec, that Fernand began to breathe normally, relieved but exhausted. He would stop in a moment to take a leak but after that it would be one of those open-windows, face-slapping, talking-aloud rides. If he were much more than an hour from home he might have pulled over and taken a nap but not this close to his own bed and not tonight. He switched his headlights to high-beam and peered ahead into the tunnel they created in the darkness, not looking back. Had he done so, he might have wondered at the scene that was unfolding in his wake.

Stanstead, Québec
Monday, September 28th
9:25pm EDT

As the van's noise subsided, Marcelle suddenly became aware of another, frightening sound; an insistent, rasping squawk that seemed to claw at the night. A red strobe light in the ceiling of the portal added urgent flashes to the cry of the klaxon. For just an instant she stood frozen, disbelieving, then keyed her walkie-talkie barking as she did: "Lane One! Radiation!"

Someone slapped the reset button silencing the klaxon and darkening the strobe as she moved to the driver's side of the van's cab; her voice calm but firm. "Sir, please pull over there." She indicated the vacant parking area just beyond the customs post. The driver looked bewildered.

"What's the matter?" he asked.

She ignored his question. "Right now, sir." There was a steely edge to her voice. Her "cop voice" as her husband called it. It got the kids moving when she used it at home. It also got the driver of the van moving.

This time she did not turn away. Indeed, her eyes never left the driver as the big rig began to creep out of the portal. As it did, she could see another agent standing on the far side of the van holding something about the size of a school lunchbox. As the van slowly turned toward the parking lot, she noticed the cruiser stationed at the post was blocking the exit onto the highway.

"You okay?" Alain Proust was the nighttime agent-in-charge of the border station.

"Yeah. Fine." *True enough*, she thought, *if you didn't count nerves.*

"Okay. You know the procedure. Let's get rolling." While she turned to follow the van at a slow jog across the parking lot, Proust entered the kiosk where he leaned over a computer terminal and typed something on its keyboard. In a moment a series of numbers scrolled down the screen. The computer showed no radiation signature now but a minute ago there had been enough to trigger the alarm. That was logical. The van had moved out of the portal, away from the sensors imbedded in the roof. Looking across the parking lot he could see Marcelle standing beside the van. The cold bluish glare from the light towers made it look like a scene out of a sci-fi movie. He left the computer and headed outside to join her.

Swinging his door open and looking down the driver of the van again asked "What's the matter?" and again she ignored his question. Sharing information, even if only to answer a simple question, would reduce the psychological distance between them, subconsciously equalizing them. Right now the driver needed to feel isolated, vulnerable and unequal.

"Sir, please turn off your engine and get down." He said something under his breath but did as she requested and, with a sheaf of papers in one hand, climbed from the cab; a small, wiry man in need of a shave.

"So what's the matter?" he repeated.

This time his question was met with a question. "Do you have a cell phone?"

"Yeah. Why?"

"Please give it to me, sir. Do not activate it. Do not turn it on or off." Her voice brooked no argument. Her flat, even tones made her sound as though she were reciting from a book. In a sense she was. The training manual explained how cell phones could be used to trigger explosives.

The driver handed it over complaining as he did so. "I should call in if this is going to take long. I've got a schedule. They're expecting me."

Proust joined them. "Please put your hands on the side of the truck and spread your legs."

"What is this? What the hell is going on?"

"Do it," he snapped. The driver turned and did as he was told. Proust quickly frisked him. Nothing. "Thank you, sir. You may stand up."

The driver pushed back from the fender and turned toward Proust. "Who are you?"

"I'm the agent in charge of this post, Alain Proust."

"Then maybe *you* can tell me what's going on and why I can't call my dispatcher." He put a lot of emphasis on the "you".

"Your truck has set off an alarm. We need to check it and you."

"What kind of alarm?"

"Radiation," Proust replied.

In an instant fear chased irritation from the driver's face. "Radiation? You gotta be kidding!" He looked apprehensively at his van. "There's just furniture and stuff in there." The tremor in his voice belied the assurance of his words.

"Do you know that for a fact? Did you personally load the truck?" Proust asked quietly.

"No..." The driver hesitated. "It's loaded when I get it. Always is...except for some stuff I picked up on the way in Hartford. The local warehouse crew loaded that. Union rules don't..." He interrupted himself as a sudden thought occurred. "You don't think I..."

"Let's find out." Proust extracted a thin wand from the device he was carrying. Below the handle there was a dial, several switches and an LED display. "Stand still and raise your arms away from your sides."

The driver looked frightened. If something in his load was radioactive and he'd been driving it for the last eight hours... The agent passed the wand up and down the driver's front, back and sides, watching the LED display as he did. At last, satisfied, he collapsed the wand back into the handle. "You're clean," he told the driver. "Now would you please open the rear doors and then accompany agent Pelletier to the office." The driver tugged a key ring from his pocket, selected one and undid the padlock that secured the doors. As he pulled them open the two agents could see cardboard cartons piled high, each labeled with a plastic pouch that contained a list of its contents. Several large pieces of furniture were draped with thick cloth mats and secured to the sides of the van. As he swung the doors open the driver backed away.

Marcelle put out her hand. "Your papers, please, sir." The use of "sir" was not a matter of politeness. It was a signal of formality. It reminded the subject that this was an official matter, to be taken seriously. He handed the papers to her. "Would you please follow me, sir." It wasn't a request and it didn't sound like one. He followed as she walked toward the office. Behind them Proust began sweeping the van with the wand.

Someone had pulled a sawhorse across Lane One closing it to further traffic even though that meant increasing the wait at the single truck lane that remained open. Marcelle held the door open for the driver to enter the office. "Please go inside and take a seat, sir." The wall clock read twenty minutes to ten as she followed him in.

"Mr...?" Marcelle paused with a question in her voice even though she had his driver's license and the trip log with his name in her hand. But they were just words on a piece of paper. She wanted to hear him say them.

"D'Annunzio."

"Your first name Mr. D'Annunzio?"

The driver looked toward the papers Marcelle was holding as if he wanted to point out the obvious but answered anyway. "Joe. Joseph."

"Where do you live, Mr. D'Annunzio?"

"6603 Avenue D, Bayside, Queens, New York."

That agreed with what it said on his driver's license. Maybe it was true. Maybe not.

"Where is your place of employment, Mr. D'Annunzio?"

"44-400 Kew Gardens Parkway."

"And where is that?"

"Brooklyn."

"To whom is the truck registered?"

"Allied Van Lines. That's the Kew Gardens address." He looked through the glass wall of the office toward his van with its name emblazoned across the sides but said nothing. The agent with the radiation detector was moving slowly around it.

"Why are you seeking entry to Canada, Mr. D'Annunzio?" Her tone implied entry was not a sure thing. The subtlety wasn't lost on him.

"I'm hauling a load."

"To where?"

"Montréal. We've got a warehouse there. I don't know where the stuff goes after that. That's up to the locals."

"Wouldn't it have been shorter to take 87?" That was the Interstate that ran from New York to Albany and on north to Montréal.

"Yeah, but like I told the other guy I had to pick up a partial in Connecticut. From there 91 is faster. It's all in there," he said, pointing to the papers she was holding. Indeed, it was and like his ID and travel log the words on the papers wouldn't change. Her questions were intended to find out if his story would.

"What is in your load, Mr. D'Annunzio?"

"Furniture and stuff. Like I told you. Like you saw."

"Are you traveling alone?"

"Yeah." He pulled a pack of cigarettes from his windbreaker. "Is it okay if I smoke?"

"I would prefer that you didn't." He grunted and stuffed the cigarette pack back in his pocket. Almost ten; he'd wanted to be in Montréal by midnight, drop off the trailer at the warehouse, have a beer and get some sleep. Instead, here he was, still more than two hours away with what may be a hot load. He must have crossed the border a half dozen times this year alone—although not here—and except for one time when it turned out the company had given him a wrong bill of lading, he'd never had any trouble. Even then it had only taken a phone call and a fax to straighten it out.

"Can I call my dispatcher?" he asked again.

"Not yet sir, there are a couple of things we need to clarify."

She could see he was nervous. What she couldn't see was why. Was it just the stress of the situation or something more?

She continued her questions, asking for details of his trip, which weigh stations he stopped at, when and where he stopped for supper, checking each of his answers against his travel log. They matched.

After a few minutes she could think of no more questions to ask and, taking a seat behind the desk, pretended to study his documents while she waited for Proust. When he arrived a few minutes later it was to tell them there was no radiation coming from the truck or its load. He then took D'Annunzio's clipboard from Marcelle, initialed a couple of pages, detached copies for the files and handed the rest back to the driver. "Thank you for your cooperation, sir. You can close up the truck and, unless agent Pelletier has any further questions, you are free to go. Welcome to Canada. I hope you enjoy the rest of your stay." D'Annunzio looked at Marcelle who was fighting to keep a straight face.

"I presume we can reach you at this number Mr. D'Annunzio should we need to?" She held out his cell phone.

"Yeah, sure," he said. He sounded a little confused but climbed to his feet and headed toward the door. This would be one to tell the guys when he got home.

The two border agents watched from the office as D'Annunzio slammed the big doors shut and re-fastened the padlock before climbing into the cab and starting the engine. A minute or two later the van began to curve out of the parking lot heading north. The cruiser that had been blocking the exit was nowhere to be seen.

Proust pulled an old Alouette's mug from a drawer. "You want some coffee?"

There was a little over two cups left in the pot. It looked lethal. "No, I ought to get back out there. They're stacked up."

"In a minute," Proust replied. "First run me through what happened from the first time you saw the van. Step by step. Don't leave anything out. I'm going to have to write up a report."

"In that case, I'll take a half a cup," she said.

He fixed it; she took it and then sat down in the seat vacated by D'Annunzio. Proust leaned against the counter, took a tentative sip from his mug and grimaced. Marcelle noticed the look on his face. "If that's no good," she said, "I can put on some fresh. It's been there a while." Outside trucks hissed and growled. Proust took another sip and said it was fine but she noticed he put it down without drinking any more.

"So, what happened?" he asked.

"There isn't a whole lot to tell…pretty much routine…a well-known carrier…papers in order. We probably ought to get the monitor checked."

"Where precisely were you when the van pulled in?" he asked.

"Just about there." She pointed to a spot a few feet in front of the portal.

"Why there? Why not in front of the kiosk? "

"A bottle fell out of a truck." She glanced down at her pants. "It broke, made a mess. Rudy was sweeping it up. To keep things moving, I walked back to start on the next truck."

"At what point did the alarm go off?" The question jolted Marcelle's memory. It must have shown in her face. "What did you see?" Proust asked.

"I…" she hesitated. "I didn't actually see anything. The van was revving his engine and bleeding his air brakes. I turned away from the noise and put my hands over my ears."

"You were facing away?"

"Yes, sir." She was surprised to hear herself say "sir". Although their shifts didn't always correspond, she and Proust had worked together off and on for probably ten years, long before he was promoted. The tension of the past hour must be getting to her.

"When did you look up?"

"Almost immediately; just as soon as the noise stopped. The other truck had gone by then and the van had pulled under the roof."

"The other truck? The one that broke the bottle?"

"No. After that. There was an empty flat bed in-between the bottle truck and the moving van. Farm plates. A local. I'd already cleared him and he was just waiting for Rudy to clean up the glass."

"What was he carrying?"

"Nothing. As I said, he was empty. He said he was coming back from delivering hay down in the States."

"What else?"

She shrugged. "There's not much else, just a farmer on his way home. His license and registration checked."

"Tell me about the driver."

"Again, not much to tell...sort of nice looking guy...30s...wearing a work jacket...flannel shirt...no hat....dark hair, kind of long but not hippy, just needed a haircut....no glasses."

"Nervous? In a hurry?"

"No. Not especially. Maybe a little impatient. He'd been waiting a while. We were backed up. And then he had to wait while the glass was being swept up."

"What happened next?

"Nothing, really. As soon as Rudy was done he waved him through and the moving van pulled in and then I heard the alarm."

"Do you have any paperwork on the farmer?" They didn't fill out forms on every vehicle that came through. Some of the big trucks had loads that required it but mostly it was a matter of checking to make sure papers agreed and no one and nothing got through that shouldn't.

"Actually, I do," she replied. "I write down the plates as they pull in. That way I don't have to walk around front again to compare them to the paperwork. It speeds things up a little." She consulted the list of numbers on her clipboard. The farm truck's license number would be the next to last one, immediately before the moving van. She read it off to Proust who wrote it down in his notebook. "Excuse me," Marcelle said, "but you're not suggesting the flat bed set off the alarm? He was empty."

"I'm not suggesting anything," Proust replied. "Just trying to get a complete picture of what happened. I'll buck it up to headquarters and let them decide what they want to do. But the farmer was there in line and maybe he saw something you didn't and," he hastened to add, "that's not being critical of you, I've done the same thing." He snapped his notebook shut and stood up. "It'll probably turn out to be something screwed-up with the alarm. I'll have them send somebody down to check it out." Then, in a tone that told her the evening's excitement was over, he added, "I should have taken up your offer on the coffee. Gawd, this stuff is poisonous."

As Marcelle left, Proust sat down at the computer and brought up the page he had scanned earlier. This time he studied it. The alarm had gone off at 9:24 pm. Low level; barely enough to trip the sensors. But they had tripped, whether because of an anomaly in their electronics or something else would be a judgment call made several pay grades above his. His job was to file an incident report to Border Services including whatever information he had and let them forward it or not to whomever they chose inside the Public Safety ministry and maybe even to the Americans. With that potential audience in mind, he was very careful how he worded his report, especially the part about Marcelle not actually seeing who was positioned where when the alarm went off. He didn't want to get her in trouble so he just wrote "the coincidence of the alarm with the movement of vehicles was not observable by the agent on duty." He wasn't sure whether there was such a word as "observable" but to say it wasn't observed might provoke someone to ask why not. "Not observable" tended to suggest a problem with the line of sight rather than with an agent not looking. Then he added, "Another vehicle in transit through the facility may have observed the movement of traffic in the lane at the moment the alarm went off." He put in Fernand's license number and noted that it belonged to an empty flatbed farm truck. Then, having read his work through twice and fixed a couple of typos, he took a deep breath and hit "send". Whatever had happened tonight was now someone else's problem.

Chapter Fourteen

RCMP Division Headquarters, Montréal
Tuesday, September 29th
8:30am EDT

Inspector Paul Gautier got to the office first. He usually did. Maybe
it was an overly acute sense of responsibility or maybe with his
wife at work there was nothing to do at home. That's why they both
dreaded the thought of his retirement. He had absolutely no idea
what he would do to fill his days and she had no idea how she would
get anything done with him underfoot. Weekends were one thing,
but seven days a week? Unthinkable. His wife regularly pointed out
that the only people he knew were the people he worked with. He
routinely replied that he knew the neighbors. "On that side," she'd
answer, "and why not? They've lived there for twenty years." But the
identity of the "new neighbors" who had moved in on the other side
three years ago was still a mystery to him. "And you're a police inspector!" she'd snort, only half in jest.

The much younger and still unmarried Sergeant David McNeill
arrived a few minutes later with two cups of coffee from a Horton's
he passed on his way in. "No donuts?" Gautier asked as he accepted
one of the cups.

"I want to see you walk out of here when you retire, not get carried out," McNeill teased. "Anything going on?"

Gautier picked up a small stack of incident reports. "Not much. The guy we busted last week on the drug thing has started to talk, thankfully not to us. I hate that stuff." He shuffled through a couple more sheets of paper. "We've got a request from the FBI to run background on some guy who's up for a big job in Washington."

"Why us?"

"They want to know what he did when he was in college. He went to Bishops."

"When was that?"

Gautier squinted at the paper. "Twenty-five years ago."

"Good luck. I don't remember what I did last Saturday night."

The inspector tugged a sheet lose from his stack. "We could combine it with this one. They're both in the same direction. Something tripped the radiation alarm at Stanstead last night. They don't know what did it but there was a farm truck that might have been in position to see something."

"Maybe that was what did it."

"No, it was empty."

"Then it sounds to me like they ought to start by checking the alarm," McNeill said.

"They're doing that. But because he wasn't carrying anything doesn't mean he didn't see anything," Gautier replied. "Besides, he lives in Ste. H." He used the French pronunciation.

"Saint what?"

"Ste. Herménégilde. It's a bump in a not entirely paved road but a pretty bump; sits up high. On a day like this you can see forever."

"Where is it?"

"Down in the Townships."

"That's where the truck comes from?"

"Yeah. They ran the plates." Gautier picked up another sheet of paper from his desk, "Ferme St. Germaine Freres. Route 141. Saint Herménégilde."

"Why don't they send Sherbrooke? They're closer."

"They're still tied up with the Labor Day bombing."

"So we're supposed to drive all the way down there to talk to this farmer?"

"That and perhaps to look in on *Au Pied de la Montagne*."

"What's that?" McNeill asked.

"The home of the finest *torte au viande* in the world, or at least any part of it I'd ever care to visit. A light flaky golden crust, tender savory beef, vegetables simmering in rich brown gravy. It is to live for. Add a little glass of the house red and perhaps a baked apple with a touch of caramel..." Gautier's voice trailed off as he pictured himself, napkin tucked beneath his lower chin to protect his vest from the gravy, sunlight streaming in the café windows and slanting across red checkered table cloths, perhaps a little music in the background...

The look on the inspector's face actually made McNeill envious. He liked a decent meal as much as the next man but he could never muster the passion the inspector brought to the table. Nonetheless he broke in on his reverie. "What if the farmer's not there?"

"In that case we have lunch and go check out the guy at Bishops."

"Apart from lunch, why not just call him?"

Gautier shook his head. "For some things that's okay...check a name, a date, a number. We want someone to sketch a scene for us, fill in the blanks. That's best done in person, where you can spot the blanks and get a feel for how good the information is. Is it coming from a guy who's alert, sharp or something else? Besides, this isn't about just any problematic border crossing. It was a radiation alarm that went off and this guy may have seen something that he doesn't even realize he saw. That's why we have to talk to him in person.

Ferme St. Germaine Freres
Tuesday, September 29th
11:15am EDT

He didn't notice anything out of the ordinary when he opened the door of the loft to let in some daylight. It would have been nice to have electricity in the loft but unless you were prepared to pay the cost of metal conduit you were just inviting mice to chew their way to a fire. As he rested, one hand on the jutting ridge pole with its old but workable rope and pulley assembly to transfer hay from the baler to the barn, he could look far down the road that bent around the fields of the neighboring farms, sometimes at a ninety degree angle. His father used to say if you grabbed both ends of the road and pulled it taut you'd have a couple of miles extra pavement. You'd also have a rebellion at the next election. The choice between going a little faster or cutting through land that represented a farmer's wealth and patrimony was no contest. So the road retained its sharp turns as it snaked between the fields of the townships.

Fernand gazed on the familiar scene for a while but at last shrugged and returned to his work. Hay might not be the most demanding crop but it still took work, especially if you hoped to get a decent price. It wasn't just a matter of letting the grass grow. And it certainly wasn't a matter of letting the bales sit stacked in the same place for too long. That was another ticket to a fire, especially when the hay was green. So his chore this morning was to shift the bales allowing air to get to them and, in the process, move some closer to the open loft door ready for his next trip south.

Sometimes working alone in the empty barn he thought about restocking the herd and getting back into the milk business. But the numbers just weren't there. Apart from a couple of weeks of haying he could pretty much run the farm by himself. With cows you had to be there twice a day every day for hours on end. That meant help and that cost money. Even with the provincial subsidies it was a losing proposition unless you were very big. And *Ferme St. Germaine Freres* wasn't.

The other advantage to hay was that it left him time for his summer job at the swim club. Originally that had been an economic necessity. Now, while the income was still welcome, the opportunity to see Marie-Paule was as much if not more of a reason for continuing.

After an hour of moving bales and sweeping-up, he put the broom back in the corner and turned to close the loft door. It was then that he saw the car, a black SUV stopped in a wide spot by the culvert a quarter mile up the road as if uncertain of which way to go. As he watched it pulled out and slowly drove down the road to his driveway and turned in. As it did he noticed it had a searchlight beside the driver's side mirror modestly facing downward and its roof bristled with antennas

He stared in disbelief. Police! Dear God! They must know! Those guys he took across the border must have been caught and talked. Fear gripped him. His hand trembled as he closed the loft door and latched it. He looked back at the shadows behind him. Maybe he could stay up here and they would leave. Car doors thudded. He could hear voices but couldn't make out what they were saying. A long moment passed in silence. Then he heard footsteps on the wooden planks of the barn floor below. Someone called "Hello." Fernand swallowed hard but didn't answer. Again the voice called "Hello." He heard the storm door on the back of the house slam, tugged shut by its spring. A different voice said "No one answering."

"Are you sure you saw him?" the first voice asked.

"Someone was up there. The door to the loft was open and someone was standing in it."

"It's closed now." Whoever noted that called again louder. "Hello. Anybody home?"

Fernand needed to take a leak. Badly. That made up his mind. "I'm up here. Who is it?"

He expected to hear "police" but the voice said something different that he didn't catch before adding "Would you please come down?"

He hesitated. "Yeah. Just a minute. I'll be right there." Fernand moved toward the far end of the loft and the steep flight of stairs that led down to the main floor and the back door. He really had to go. "I'll be right there. I gotta take a leak."

Gautier and McNeill looked at each other as they waited just inside the wide barn doors. A big flat bed truck stood in the middle of the aisle, empty cow stanchions to either side. They didn't look as though they'd been occupied in some time. McNeill said quietly, "I'll go see."

Fernand was just zipping up when McNeill reached the foot of the stairs to the loft. An open door led out behind the barn. "Sorry," Fernand said. He started to extend his hand but realized the neatly dressed man probably wouldn't want to shake it. He dropped his hands to his sides and surreptitiously rubbed them a bit on his coveralls.

"Are you Fernand St. Germaine?"

"Yeah," Fernand replied, his voice sounded steadier than he felt. The man pulled a little wallet from his breast pocket and snapped it open. There was a badge on one side and a picture I.D. card on the other side behind a little plastic window.

"Sergeant David McNeill, RCMP." Fernand felt pure terror well up in him. He'd seen the RCMP on television and once had attended a parade in Sherbrooke where a detachment in those red uniforms and big hats rode beautiful chestnut bays. This man, who had arrived in a black SUV, was dressed in a brown suit, white shirt and paisley tie. No hat. No horse.

"If you could step this way sir we'd like to speak with you." It was a polite request but not the sort you felt you could refuse. McNeill gestured toward the other end of the barn where sunlight was streaming in through the open doors.

"What about?" Fernand asked as he began moving in the direction the officer had indicated. There was no reply. He wanted to add,

"I haven't done anything wrong," but immediately thought better of it. It wasn't true and they probably knew it. He was too old to cry but, damn it, he felt like it.

"Mr. St. Germaine?" Another man, who had been standing in the shadows watching his partner advance with the farmer, pulled out his I.D. wallet and flashed a similar picture. "Inspector Paul Gautier. We'd like to ask you a few questions." Fernand nodded in response. "Would you like to go inside or would you prefer to sit in the car?" Gautier knew in advance what the answer would be. No one wants to sit in the back of a police car when they could be in the security of their own home. But for Gautier to get inside the house and take a look around he would either have to have a search warrant or be invited in and he didn't have a warrant.

"Go inside," Fernand replied, still nodding his head. "We can go inside." He thought he might have to pee again.

He led the way toward the steps that climbed to the stoop and pulled open the aluminum door giving entrance to a narrow lino-leum-floored porch that in summer had screens, but now already had its storm windows in place. A few feet further on there was a second, heavy wooden door that led into the kitchen, a large room with a yellowing tin ceiling with a big three bladed fan hanging from its center. A black, wood-burning stove sat along the far wall on a brick hearth, its flue pipe rising almost to the ceiling before bending into the chimney. To the right of the stove sat a sturdy-looking wood and leather rocking chair. To the left was a door leading to the pantry. A white enamel sink with a large drain board stood along one of the walls beneath a half-curtained window overlooking the driveway. On the opposite wall an old refrigerator hummed beside a doorway that opened into the front of the house. A small TV set with a rabbit-ears antenna sat atop the refrigerator.

On the far side of the kitchen a narrow flight of stairs, its treads hollowed by years of use, led to the second floor. Most of the family's living had been done here in the kitchen. Now, alone in the farmhouse, it was the only room apart from his bedroom that Fernand ever used. Indeed, sometimes he fell asleep in the big rocker while watching TV only to awaken in the night, stiff and a bit disoriented.

In the middle of the kitchen was a sturdy oak table worn smooth by generations of hot casseroles slid along its surface. There were simple chairs at the ends and benches along the sides. Salt and pepper shakers, a sugar bowl and a jam pot sat in a little cluster in the middle. Underneath, a braided rug flowed out across the broad oak planks that formed the floor. The porch robbed the room of some of its natural light but that didn't matter at night and was welcome on hot summer days. In any event, Fernand didn't sit around much during daylight hours. There was a farm to run, deliveries to make and, part of the year, clubhouse grounds to maintain.

The older RCMP officer who had identified himself as Gautier took a seat on one of the benches facing the barn yard. Out of force of habit Fernand took a chair at one end of the table. The other officer stayed outside.

The inspector produced a notepad and opened it to a blank page. He then pulled a pen from an inside pocket and clicked its point into readiness. A wall clock ticked back, its pendulum swinging in a broad arc behind a little window. "Mr. St. Germaine." Gautier cleared his throat. "We are inquiring about an event that occurred at the Stanstead border station about 9:30 last night. I understand you passed through at about that time. We thought you might be able to help us."

"Sure," Fernand replied, almost too eagerly. Maybe this wasn't about his passengers.

"In point of fact, did you cross the border at Stanstead on or about that hour?" The formality of the wording was not lost on him. This might not be just "a few questions" as the inspector had said in the barn. It sounded like something more.

For the next several minutes Gautier had Fernand retrace in min-ute detail everything he did and saw at the border station. He noted the Bergeron truck that had preceded him, the bottle that fell out and broke when the driver opened his door, the delay while that was cleaned up, the impatient van inches behind him. At first he was very nervous and had to be prodded for more detail but as the inspector didn't seem particularly interested in him but only in what he'd seen he began to relax. At length Gautier snapped his ballpoint pen shut, closed his notebook and leaned forward as if to rise when he apparently thought of another question. "Mr. St. Germaine, when and where did you cross into the United States with your load of hay?"

He could feel his stomach tighten. He suddenly needed to take another leak. "I uhhh went down about six o'clock."

"Yesterday morning?"

Fernand nodded. "I need to use the bathroom." It was a statement of fact but the way he said it made clear he was also asking permission. Gautier looked long and hard at him before nodding his okay.

Fernand hurried to the stairs and loudly clomped his way to the second floor. Gautier took the opportunity to look outside. McNeill was just climbing down from the cab of the truck.

Gautier heard the toilet flush and wondered if hitting the head twice inside a half hour signified nerves, a medical issue or maybe a Labatt's problem. Fernand's heavy boots sounded on the back stairs. As he reached the landing to turn toward the last three steps leading into the kitchen he saw Gautier looking at him. "I'm sorry," he stammered, "I dunno. Maybe something I ate. I dunno..." His voice trailed off.

"No problem, Mr. St. Germaine. We only have a couple of points to clear up." Fernand resumed his seat at the end of the table. Gautier again sat on the bench facing the barnyard which meant that in order to talk to him Fernand had to face the other way.

"How many hours were you behind the wheel yesterday?" Fernand suddenly realized he'd opened himself to a new problem. By law you could only drive a truck so many hours a day. Professional drivers had to keep a log book with their hours in it. Some fleets equipped their trucks with trip recorders like an airplane's black box to make sure their drivers didn't go over the limit. He didn't know how many hours were legal but it was likely he exceeded it on most every trip. As usual when confronted with a question to which he didn't know the answer, he shrugged.

"Well, Mr. St. Germaine you said you started out about six a.m. and you didn't re-cross the border into Canada until nearly 10pm. By my reckoning that would come to about 16 hours less whatever time you took for meals and unloading and such." So now he wanted details of Fernand's route, where he crossed the border going south into Vermont, where he dropped off his load, where he stopped for meals and gas and did he have credit card receipts for any of the stops? Fernand didn't. He paid cash. But he did have an answer to where he'd crossed into the States. It had occurred to him when he'd been upstairs. It was where his aunt and uncle had crossed on that long ago trip to Hampden Beach.

"Philon. I crossed at Philon."

"Why?" Gautier asked, his voice indicating no particular interest, suggesting that the question had been asked merely for form's sake. "That's not the nearest point."

"Loaded I drive too slow for the main road. People get mad at me. So I take back roads when I'm loaded. I take the highway coming back when I'm empty." It made sense. He probably couldn't do much over 40 miles an hour with a loose load like hay bales on an old truck that likely didn't have much in the way of springs.

"What time did you cross at Philon?"

Fernand shrugged again. "I dunno. It takes about a half hour from here...maybe 6:30."

Gautier seemed to debate whether to pursue the point, sighed and did not. Most people around here had long regarded the border as little more than a speed bump, only intended to slow you, not stop you. He closed his notebook and stood up. "Thank you for your time Mr. St. Germaine. But as he reached the door and had his hand on the knob he turned to ask a last question. "Oh, by the way, there wasn't anyone else traveling with you was there Mr. St. Germaine." Fernand couldn't help but look startled.

"No," he lied. "No. I do not have any help. I work alone. I live here alone. Just me." The protests tumbled out in a rush of anxiety to cover all possibilities. "The lady at the border. She saw me. I was alone."

"Coming back," Gautier pointed out. "Apparently no one saw you going down."

"Going down, too. Just me." Fernand bobbed his head as he spoke, trying to physically add emphasis to his words.

Gautier said nothing but stood for a long moment with his hand resting lightly on the door knob looking at Fernand as if uncertain whether to turn back or not. At last he spoke in a very soft, very even tone. "So you say, Mr. St. Germaine. So you say." Fernand found it hard to breath. He prayed the inspector would leave. He couldn't think coherently. He couldn't remember what he had told him. Had he accidentally said "we" or "they" when recounting the details of his trip?

Gautier held out a small white business card. "If you think of something you forgot to tell me, you can reach me at that number. Thank you for your time, Mr. St. Germaine." With that Gautier swung the door open and crossed the porch to the steps.

Fernand at first remained seated and then moved to the window by the sink where he could see the inspector walk over to the sergeant who was standing by the black SUV. They spoke for a minute. At one point they both looked up at the house. Fernand instinctively leaned back from the window and averted his eyes as though if he couldn't see them, they couldn't see him. Another minute passed and then he heard the engine start and the SUV head down the driveway to the road. A troubled silence slipped in behind it.

He had to take another leak. He wondered what was wrong with him. But this time, instead of coming back downstairs he walked to the front of the house, to the hall window which looked out toward the road. There was no sign of the SUV. The road was empty and somehow made all the more ominous for it.

Once he returned to the kitchen he again sat at the table trying to reconstruct what had been asked of him and what he had answered. But in his mind he began to edit his answers until he was no longer sure what he had actually said. Fear began to grow like shadows creeping across the barnyard. At last, with an effort, he got up and went outside. He needed to do something, to work, be active, even as he needed to think what to do.

Ste. Herménégilde, Québec
Tuesday, September 29th
12:30pm EDT

"Well. What did you find?" Gautier asked as McNeill steered the SUV around a dead something in the road. "

"Nothing out of the ordinary. I checked out the truck. It's old but seems to be well cared for."

"What about the barn?"

"Nothing again. I even climbed up to the loft where you saw him. Hard to see up there. No lights. How about you? He have anything to say?"

"Probably more than he realized, although he was very nervous. At first I wanted to believe him, but then I asked if he had anyone with him on the downward trip. He looked like he'd been shot."

"You figure he had someone with him on the trip south?"

"I don't know about that. What I do know is that he didn't cross at Philon as he claimed."

"How so?"

"It hasn't been open for three, maybe four years. Even before that it was only a part-time crossing which is why they closed it. Not enough traffic."

"So he was lying."

"About where he crossed anyway."

McNeill slowed as the road took a ninety degree turn around the end of a field crowded with the dry stalks of the summer corn crop. "So what's the next step?"

Gautier shook his head in disbelief. "You really are a slow learner, aren't you? We file a report. You always file a report. If we didn't file a report there would be nothing for the people who sit behind desks all day to read; nothing for their secretaries to catalogue; nothing for the bean counters to count. You'd start a recession. So we'll file a report." He paused in his peroration and laughed, "Right after we eat."

Au Pied de la Montagne was nearly empty when they arrived giving them a choice of tables. Gautier picked one beside a sun-filled window that looked out toward the southwest and the hills around Villette. He didn't consult the menu, but as promised, ordered the *torte au viande*. McNeill knew when to lead and when to follow. *"La même chose pour moi, s'il vous plaît."*

With a basket of freshly baked bread and a carafe of a very acceptable local red placed midway between them, it was time to talk. "After you file your report..." McNeill began, hoping to establish authorship.

"*My* report?" Gautier looked up from buttering a thick slice of bread.

"You did the questioning. I was outside."

He had a point. But Gautier returned to the bread without conceding it. McNeill pressed his advantage. "Once you've done your report, what's next?"

"We wait for orders from whoever reads the report."

"You think there's more to be done here?"

"I do. That farmer may be dumb as dirt but something isn't right. Even accepting his story as he told it, why would he go 20 kilometers out of his way to take a winding back road when he could have gone straight down 141? Forget his argument about not wanting to hold up traffic…there can't be much traffic around here at six o'clock in the morning. Plus, as I said, he couldn't have used the Philon crossing." Gautier paused to sniff then sip his wine. A pleased smile played across his face.

"Why don't we just go back now and confront him?" McNeill asked.

"Because we don't have a warrant. We were only sent down here to ask him what he saw at the border crossing…a possible material witness, not a suspect. I can't even mention your sniffing around in the barn in the report."

"Wouldn't the third floor be willing to overlook that?"

"They might but a defense attorney wouldn't. So we'll just have to say that on the basis of some apparent holes in St. Germaine's story we think his truck, house and barn ought to be checked. We don't have to say we already gave it a quick sniff. "

"Reasonable and probable grounds to believe an offense has been committed." McNeill quoted from the manual.

"Precisely. In any event, I'd be interested to know why he sat there and lied to me although he was so nervous that he had to go take another leak while we were talking."

The arrival of the meat pies redirected their attention for several minutes with McNeill having to agree they were all that Gautier had promised. When their conversation eventually returned to work, Gautier set out the agenda for the rest of the day. "After we stop by Bishop's to find out if anyone remembers what Mr. Big did when he was on campus we need to do some research on Fernand St. Germaine. See what we can learn about him."

Ferme St. Germaine Freres
Tuesday, September 29th
7:00pm EDT

Apart from the glow of the little lamp over the telephone, the kitchen was in shadow. Supper had consisted of baked beans, which he ate cold from the can, a couple of thick slices of bread he had cut from the bakery loaf and a glass of creamy milk. As Fernand ate he made a conscious effort to fight back the fears that threatened to engulf him. At one point he picked up the card the inspector gave him and debated calling and telling him everything. But, then, when he started to run through what "everything" was he put the card back on the table. Not only had he illegally crossed the border with two men he didn't know but had lied about it to the RCMP. He knew little of the law but he was sure what he had done was outside it.

And if he did call, how would he explain his passengers? He toyed with the idea of saying they were hitchhikers...but at six o'clock in the morning on a back road? Then he thought of saying he'd met them in town and, on learning they were heading to the States, offered them a ride. As for the pre-dawn start, he could say they spent the night here. But the RCMP would want details. What were their names? Where did they come from? Where were they going? If he said he didn't know, they wouldn't believe him. They would ask how could he take two strangers into his home overnight and drive a couple of hundred kilometers with them and still not even know their names? He stirred uncomfortably. They might think he was queer.

As for telling the truth, that was impossible. When Marie-Paule kissed his cheek in thanks Saturday afternoon on the porch of the club she'd said "I just knew I could count on you." He couldn't betray her trust. They shared a secret. It bound them together. Tell the secret and the bond would be broken.

But what might the bond be tying him to? His uncertainty offered no limit to his imaginings. If only she knew what he was doing to

protect her. His thoughts paused there. *If she did know, then, maybe...*
His mind wandered over highly improbable terrain. It was only the
splash of a tear on his wrist that brought him back from the summer
sunshine, where she always lived in his mind, to the empty darkness
of the kitchen. It was then that he began to think he should tell her
what had happened. Warn her.

He began to frame the conversation in his mind; how she would
sound when she answered the telephone, that warm, husky voice that
always seemed a little bemused by him. But what would he say to her?
It would probably be best not to begin by saying the RCMP had been
here. That might scare her or make her think he was scared. Better
that he begin by telling her everything had gone smoothly, that he had
taken her two friends to the supermarket parking lot as agreed. He
tried to imagine her reply. She'd say something nice; friendly. Again
his thoughts wandered until he realized he still hadn't figured out how
to tell her about the Mounties.

He couldn't say "everything went fine except that the RCMP
came and asked me lots of questions about the trip and what should
I do now?" For more than an hour he tried to think through how he
could tell her. Maybe he shouldn't tell her after all. The inspector
hadn't said they were investigating *him*. He had said they were investigating something that had happened at the border station last night.
Indeed, he had asked lots of questions about the Bergeron truck that
was ahead of him and the van that sat on his tail. His fear began to
fade. One of those trucks must have done something and they just
wanted to know what he'd seen. And he had told them everything he'd
seen. Maybe he didn't need to call her at all. Maybe it was nothing.

But then why had the inspector asked had there been anyone with
him? Fernand could feel his stomach tighten again. Was that just a
routine question or something more? He really had to call her. He
had to talk to somebody who could assure him everything was alright.
Maybe she'd say "oh go ahead and tell them. My husband will make

it right." After all, he was a big shot in the government. He'd been on TV with his name printed across the bottom of the screen.

And what if there was something wrong; something really wrong? She ought to know shouldn't she? A few more agonizing minutes of weighing pros and cons and finally Fernand decided he should tell her and, besides, he wanted to tell her, to hear her voice, to share their secret. But how? She hadn't given him a telephone number. Perhaps he could get it from the operator.

He stood up, still uncertain, but went over to the telephone which waited on the chest at the foot of the stairs. He fished a pencil and a scrap of paper from the top drawer, lifted the receiver and dialed the three digits for information.

Two rings and an operator asked what city he was calling. "Montréal."

"What name?" He started to say Marie-Paule but caught himself. The phone would probably be in her husband's name, Andrew Fraser. He told the operator.

"One moment please."

A few tense seconds went by and then a mechanical voice came on the line: "The number you requested is not listed. Please check your information and try again."

Fernand quickly put the receiver back in its cradle. The courage he had summoned to make the call evaporated. She was beyond reach, as she had always been apart from those now distant interludes on the raft and the few minutes on the deserted club house porch. He could only summon her in his memory and in his imagination. In real life she inhabited another world, one he couldn't enter. It was early yet but he banked the fire in the stove, checked the lock on the door and slowly began the climb to his room, thoroughly exhausted, drained even of his fear. Only sadness remained.

He had no idea how long he'd been asleep or if he had actually fallen asleep but suddenly the answer he had been seeking was there. The boat club! They would have telephone numbers for their members. He'd seen file cabinets when he'd gone into the office to collect the trash. Her number must be in one of them. He fell back asleep thinking how he could gain access to the clubhouse and, ultimately, to her.

Chapter Fifteen

Ferme St. Germaine Freres
Wednesday, September 30th
6:00am EDT

Fog had crept in during the night and consequently the day was dawning cold and gray. *Not much of a start for a birthday.* In any event it wouldn't be the first he'd celebrated alone. For a time he snuggled down in the warm hollow of his bed, postponing its start. Finally, flinging the covers back, he pushed his legs over the side, forcing himself to sit up. Then, as the damp chill fully awakened him, he lumbered into the bathroom. His needs resolved, his teeth brushed and cold water splashed on his face, he rearranged his hair with the brush and returned to his room to don his workaday clothes: a plaid shirt, a worn pair of overalls and a coarse green wool sweater. With thick socks covering his feet he headed downstairs. His work boots sat by the door but he wouldn't put them on until he was ready to go outside.

For the next several minutes he busied himself with stoking the fire in the stove and putting the coffee pot on to boil. After cooking a few strips of bacon he poured off most of the grease and cracked a couple of eggs in what remained. Two slices of toast emerged from the toaster. He moved the coffee pot back from the heat and sprinkled a little salt in the water to settle the grounds. Breakfast was ready.

As he ate he thought of what he had to do. By the time he'd washed his dishes and tugged on his boots he had a plan in mind.

Exiting the driveway Fernand glanced up the road to where he'd seen the SUV stopped yesterday. There was no one there nor did he see anyone during the familiar ride to the club. The road around the lake was as deserted as the cottages it served. There were a few year-round residents near the village but none down here.

He parked his pickup behind the groundskeeper's shed, out of sight of the road. He had a key to the padlock on the shed but not to the clubhouse. No matter. From beneath the seat he fished out a ragged towel and tossed it over his shoulder. Then, unlocking the shed he stepped inside. A moment of rummaging in a tool box and he emerged with a large bladed putty knife, a hammer and a small crowbar. A stepladder leaned against the wall. He took it, too.

The office window behind the bushes that fronted the club house had been painted shut years before and had no opening that would permit entry of even the blade of the putty knife. That was a shame because the bushes would have provided cover had anyone happened by. In any event, they hid the step ladder as he climbed to stuff the towel in the alarm bell.

As he worked he could hear the side window of the office rattle in the occasional gust of wind off the lake. Once the alarm was muffled he moved around the corner and easily slid the blade of the putty knife between the upper and lower sashes of the window. A gentle tap with the hammer on the side of the putty knife was all that was needed to snap the catch back. He knew that when he raised the window the burglar alarm would probably go off but with the towel in place it wouldn't be heard more than a few feet away, and certainly not by anyone driving by on the road. Sure enough, as he raised the window he heard the muffled protest of the bell.

An old desk with a slat-backed wooden arm chair sat in the middle of the small office with two straight-backed chairs along a wall where a collection of photographs of long ago awards nights hung.

Two beige file cabinets stood beside the door to the front hall. One had a lock, one didn't. That saved time. Membership records would almost certainly be considered important enough to be in the locked cabinet. Inserting the splayed tip of the crowbar under the arch of the padlock, he gave a sharp rap with the hammer on the other end. The lock popped open.

The top drawer held the club accounts—grocer, light company, lawn mower repair shop. The membership files were in the second and third drawers. It took only a moment to locate "Fraser, Andrew". Inside were perhaps a dozen sheets of paper. The one Fernand sought was last, the club membership form. Across the top it listed name, address, phone number and who to call in case of emergency. Fernand fished a pencil stub from his shirt pocket and looked around for a piece of paper. Everything had been put away for the winter. The muffled whir of the alarm bell seemed louder. Maybe the towel was working loose. He needed to hurry. He pulled one of the other sheets of paper from the Fraser file and without bothering to look at it, copied the address and phone number on the back.

The sudden shrill of the telephone so startled him that he yelped in fright. For a moment he stood frozen in place and then, moving quickly, returned the Fraser file to its place and ran his hand across the top of all the files to smooth them and thus disguise which one he'd withdrawn. The ringing of the phone was insistent, nerve jarring. He closed the drawer and slipped the padlock back in place. It wouldn't snap shut but at a casual glance no one would notice. He looked quickly around the office. Everything was as he had found it. His eye chanced upon a newer picture in the gallery along the wall. There were a half dozen men and women in tennis whites smiling at the camera. She was among them. He thought for a moment of taking the picture but the shrill of the phone urged him to hurry. If the security company didn't get an answer to their call they would surely notify the police. What happened then would depend on how close a patrol car happened to be. Probably not very close at this hour of the morning but he couldn't take the chance. With the precious paper stuffed in his pocket along with the pencil stub he gathered up his tools and returned to the window. There was no one to be seen. Halfway through the window, as if aware that the intruder was leaving, the phone suddenly fell silent.

Fernand pulled the sash down. There was no way of locking it from the outside but, again, you'd have to go inside the office and specifically look to see that it wasn't locked. He set the tools down on the ground and carried the step ladder around the corner. Taking one last look up and down the road he climbed halfway up and yanked the towel from the bell which, now freed, produced an ear-shattering din. Quickly dismounting, he re-folded the ladder and—only pausing long enough to pick up the tools—ran down the slope to the shed. It took no time to put everything back and replace the padlock. He hurried around the front of his pickup and climbed in. For one awful moment he thought *what if it won't start?* He tromped on the gas and turned the key. His breath caught in his throat. The truck, knowing nothing of its owner's panic, let its starter grind for what seemed an eternity before its engine caught with a sputtering cough. Fernand's leg was trembling so much that his foot slipped off the clutch causing the truck to buck forward and nearly stall. He took a very deep breath and, hands shaking, steered toward the road. The alarm bell continued to shrill. He glanced in the rear view mirror. Nothing...or was that someone far behind him? A figure by the side of the road...or a tree trunk? Whoever it was, whatever it was, it didn't move.

As the frantic sound of the alarm bell faded to be replaced by the familiar drone of the engine he began to relax although his breath still came in deep gulps. He lifted one hand from the steering wheel and looked at it. There was a tremor but it wasn't shaking wildly anymore. A fine mist clouded the windshield. It wouldn't last. It never did at this time of year. Probably burn off by noon. He turned the wipers on getting a smear at first. There was a man up ahead, walking this way. A large black dog bounded in and out of the bushes beside the road. Fernand slowed, uncertain where the dog might run next. He wanted to turn his head away so the man wouldn't see him but at that moment the dog scampered back into the road and the man turned to call it out of danger. His concern was for the dog, not the nondescript pickup truck. Looking in the rearview mirror Fernand could see the man bending over the dog patting it. He wasn't looking his way and he was too far from the club to hear the alarm bell.

For the next ten minutes only the intermittent slap of the windshield wipers and the whirr of the tires on the road could be heard apart from the engine. He began to relax. When he lifted his hand from the wheel it was no longer trembling. But he did need to pee. He debated whether to stop by the side of the road or hold it until he was home. The sight of an approaching police car, its blue lights flashing, decided him. He held tightly to the wheel as it rushed past, then watched in the rear view mirror as it disappeared down the road in the direction of the club.

Wednesday, September 30th
8:10am EDT

Safely home Fernand sat at the kitchen table, a mug of warmed-up coffee in hand. Now he had to decide how to use the information he had retrieved. When should he call her and what should he say? What if her husband answered? Slowly, carefully, he thought through each possibility, composing a scenario only to put it aside in favor of a better version. The best time to call probably would be now. Her husband would have gone to work. She would be home alone.

In any event, whether he used it now or later, he had the prize he sought: her phone number. For a moment he worried that perhaps he hadn't copied it correctly. That damn telephone in the office had made him rush. There hadn't even been time to find a blank sheet of paper. He'd had to snatch one of the pages from the file. Idly he turned it over. It was a three year old letter from her husband, something about guest privileges at the club. The return address was in Montréal—4861 Côte-des-Neiges. It sounded grand. He wondered what it looked like. It was with effort that he pulled his attention back to the task at hand. Wherever she lived, it was time to speak to her, to tell her what had happened and see what, if anything, she wanted him to do.

He stood up and, clutching the paper, advanced toward the telephone. He carefully dialed the 514 area code and then the number. A burst of musical tones suddenly interrupted followed by a mechanical voice telling him that "you must first dial one before the area code." He quickly replaced the phone in its cradle, his hand shaking as he did so. He hadn't yet said a word to her and already it was going badly. Maybe it was a sign that he shouldn't call her. He retreated to the table to rethink the situation. What if the RCMP came back? What if they arrested him for crossing the border? He wouldn't know what to do. He didn't know any lawyers. Raymond might but she surely would. Yet, if he were in jail he wouldn't be able to let her know what had happened to him because of her...for her. The moment of panic passed and he returned to the phone. This time he began dialing with a one.

There was a pause and then a couple of mechanical clicks followed by the purr of the ring tone. Once. Twice. Three times. She wasn't home. His reaction was somewhere between disappointment and relief. He was about to hang up when suddenly the ringing broke off and a voice came on the line, a man's voice. He hadn't expected that. He had rehearsed what he would say when she answered, not if her husband answered. All he could think to say was *excuse* but when he opened his mouth he discovered he couldn't even get that out. He hung up in panic having said nothing at all.

4861 Chemin de la Côte-des-Neiges, Montréal
Wednesday, September 30th
8:45am EDT

There were at least a half dozen fat manila files in the dispatch box the attaché had brought down from Ottawa along with two books of minutes from meetings he hadn't been able to attend. As much as he urged single page summaries of the key points of meetings, junior ministers inevitably felt all points were important with the ones they'd made especially so. A second cup of coffee would be in order before beginning the read. Hopefully this would be his last week away from the ministry. He would visit his constituency office for an hour or two today to start getting used to getting out.

He had only just left the study enroute to the kitchen when the phone rang again. He started to turn back to answer it but, even as he did, he heard Marie-Paule pick up in the kitchen. As always she used the linguistically neutral "hello" on answering but then continued in French. Fine. Some friend or relative of hers.

It was not so much her words but her tone that made him pause before pushing open the louvered door to the kitchen. "How did you get this number?" she asked, her voice low, intense and rather cross. Whatever the answer she was silent for a long moment before asking "When? What did they want to know?" Whoever was on the other end must have been upset for she suddenly changed her tone from inquisitor sharp to comforter soft. "No, no, no, you did just fine. You handled it very well. There's absolutely nothing to worry about. You were quite right to call me. Now just run through it one more time as best you can remember. Try not to leave anything out."

For the next minute or so her end of the conversation consisted mostly of soft murmurs of encouragement for the caller to continue whatever tale was being told. Andrew was again about to push open the kitchen door when her next words made him stop. "I knew I could count on you. I won't forget what you've done for me. You are a love. Don't worry about a thing. I'll see you soon."

With that she hung up. He thought for a moment whether to go into the kitchen and casually ask who had called. But, from experience, he knew she probably wouldn't tell him and likely would demand to know how long he'd been listening. She'd then accuse him of acting like her jailer, not her husband. He'd brushed up against Marie-Paule's bristles before. The hell with the coffee; discretion being the better course he turned and walked quietly back to the study where, closing the door, he sat in silence. *Was this another of her flirtations or something more? Was he being naïve or just ducking a confrontation he didn't want to have because he suspected he knew how it would end?* Not for the first time he wondered if their lives had become so distinct and separate that they couldn't cross the boundaries.

He also wondered about his reaction. Shouldn't he be hollering and shouting, demanding to know the identity of the caller and was the caller a competitor? Was being more sad than angry a mark of civilization or cowardice…or emotional exhaustion? Maybe too many strained moments and too many nights alone in the guest room had taken their toll. Maybe he was all burned out, unable or unwilling to fight for her anymore, ready to see her go and to welcome peace in her place. He slowly turned his head from side to side finding something oddly comforting in doing so. He slumped in his chair, staring at nothing, wanting to see nothing. Lost in thought, the tap at the door startled him. Marie-Paule entered wearing a matching beige hat and coat that emphasized her green eyes which flashed above her high cheekbones. God she was beautiful.

"I'm going out for a while," she told him, her tone factual, disinterested. She could have been telling the housekeeper.

With an effort he tried to match the insouciance of her tone he replied. "I'm going out, too." She looked sharply at him.

"Are you alright?"

"Yeah, just a little tired."

She glanced at her watch. "It's only just nine. Maybe you should lie down for a few minutes." Her words could have been construed as connoting concern. But the tone in which they were delivered made them seem neutral, distant, almost clinical.

"No, I'm okay. I'll just get a cup of coffee." He motioned toward the stack of files. "I've got to get some work done before I go."

"When will you be back?"

He shook his head. "I don't know. It won't be late but I don't know. I'll call you." She didn't respond but looked hard at him as though trying to see through his words.

"Okay." She exhaled the word. "I'll see you when you get here I guess." With that she turned and left, the door remaining partially open behind her. A moment later he heard the tattoo of her heels on the foyer floor and then the hall door close. Suddenly the apartment seemed very empty. Andrew took a long, deep breath and heaved himself out of his chair. That cup of coffee was probably a good idea.

The pot was still a quarter full but not very hot. He poured some into a mug and put it in the microwave. As he waited his eyes drifted toward the telephone. He'd love to know who it was that had called her. *Was it someone they both knew? Or had her constant flirting with waiters, bartenders, musicians and other hired help somewhere crossed the line?* Faces to which he could attach no names flashed through his memory; that bartender at the PM's reception; the trumpet player at the election night party. He was surprised how clearly he remembered them. Some of his colleagues had noticed, too. David Osgood had once remarked with a little more enthusiasm than the situation called for how "catholic" Marie-Paule was. He had thought at the time what an odd choice of adjective. Did David mean it in its broadest sense or more narrowly? Knowing Osgood, either was possible.

The microwave beeped. The coffee was not only heated but, when he tried to sip it, scalding. As he turned to head back to the study his eye again fell on the telephone. After a moment's hesitation he put down the mug and, pulling a piece of paper and a pencil from the basket beside the phone, accessed its call log. A number began to scroll through the window…" 8-1-9…" It continued for seven more digits as he made note of each in turn.

8-1-9. It wasn't local but he knew it well. It was in the Eastern Townships. He let out his breath with a sigh, feeling the tension that came with suspicion starting to drain away. It must have been some member of her family. He picked up the coffee mug and headed back to the study feeling relieved and, if truth be known, a little ashamed. Maybe he was too jealous, too possessive as she had more than once charged. "You think you own me but I am not an English colony" she had stormed after an election celebration that she had ended with a flamboyant, barefoot dance in front of the bandstand with the trumpeter. The men in attendance had been amused, maybe even envious; their wives were decidedly not. That would have been it except that a photographer who had stayed after the speeches to forage in the buffet was watching, too. The resulting picture of Marie-Paule in the morning paper was captioned "Playing Defense."

The Chief Whip was not amused. As he said with jowl-wagging emphasis, it suggested a lack of sobriety for a government minister with a serious portfolio. No matter that it was not he but his wife who was dancing. He permitted himself a wry smile as he put the coffee mug down on his desk. There was no question Marie-Paule was a free spirit and, although she could make him jealous and sometimes probably did so on purpose, she had never actually given him cause to doubt her fidelity.

He sighed again, but this time with contentment, and tapped the computer keyboard to re-light the screen which had gone dark waiting for him. Out of habit he hit the Internet key and checked the Canadian Press website to see if anything was happening. There was a rehash of the previous night's parliamentary debate which had seen the government on the defensive over the slow pace of the economy and a couple of puff pieces about members of the opposition's front bench, the sort of thing that starts to appear when reporters sense a government might be nearing its end. He checked his e-mail. Nothing he had to answer now. He was about to log off and return to the contents of the dispatch box when on impulse he typed "white pages" into his search engine. He used it on occasion to check an address or get a phone number. Still, he hesitated for a moment before he hit "reverse search" and typed in the 8-1-9 phone number feeling a little sneaky as he did so. An hour glass appeared briefly, then an address block:

> Fernand St. Germaine
> Route 141
> Ste. Herménégilde, Québec.

That was odd. Marie-Paule had a big family but he knew most of them and couldn't recall any one named St. Germaine. Maybe an in-law or maybe not a relative at all, maybe just someone she knew? But her parting words on the phone argued against that: "I knew I could count on you. I won't forget what you've done for me. You are a love. I'll see you soon." It wasn't intimate but neither was it distant.

Clearing the computer screen he typed in Ste. Herménégilde, Québec. The single paragraph that appeared said it had the distinction of being the highest village in the Eastern Townships and was named for a sixth century Visigoth saint who was persecuted by his heathen father for his Catholic faith. An accompanying map showed it as a dot an inch or so above the Vermont border. *Who would she know there?* That question inevitably led to others and not for the first time he sat slumped in his chair letting them play through his mind in hopes of at least finding the right question if not the right answer.

At length he shut down the computer. Saint Herménégilde would have to wait. Maybe she'd tell him about the call this evening. Sometimes she did when one of her relatives rang up to say they were pregnant or a child was having a first communion or graduating from high school. Frankly, he didn't pay much attention which is probably why he didn't recognize the name attached to the phone number. Dealing with her family was her department. In any event, some relative in Saint Wherever was among the least of his concerns.

RCMP Division Headquarters, Montréal
Wednesday, September 30th
9:00am EDT

Gautier sipped gently at the coffee. Perhaps in return for Tuesday's *torte au viande*, there were donuts this morning; plain ones, but donuts nonetheless. McNeill, who had provided both the coffee and the donuts, was sifting through his in-box. "Upstairs say anything about our farmer?"

"Haven't heard anything," Gautier answered as he considered which of the donuts to appropriate.

"What did you tell them?"

"I just pointed out the holes in his story while recalling the border post's observation that his truck was close to the sensors when the alarm went off. I trust they're smart enough to put two and two together."

"What do you think they'll do when they see it doesn't add up?"

"What do I *think* they'll do or what do I think they *ought* to do?"

"Both."

"I think they'll stamp our report "classified", staple it to the report from the Agent-in-Charge at Stanstead and forward them up the chain with a copy to IBET." The Integrated Border Enforcement Teams brought five U.S. and Canadian agencies together. Enforcement was up to the RCMP and the Border Services Agency on the Canadian side and three agencies on the U.S. side ranging from the Border Patrol to the Coast Guard. The object was coordination. Sometimes it happened, sometimes it didn't.

"C.Y.A."

"Precisely."

"And what do you think they *ought* to do?" McNeill kept his tone conversational but he really wanted to know. He genuinely respected the older man's feel for his work. Gautier could walk into a room and see things others missed. And he had a well-honed instinct for what was important and what wasn't.

"I think they ought to turn that farm upside down, make sure he wasn't carrying anything that could have tripped the alarm, and find out how come he sat there and lied to my face even though he was scared to death. There may be a perfectly innocent explanation and, if so, let's find out what it is." The telephone suddenly shrilled. The inspector picked up. "Gautier." He listened intently for a moment, said "Yes sir" twice and hung up. "We're wanted upstairs."

The meeting was in the deputy commissioner's office. He was one of seven deputies who headed RCMP divisions. His was "C" Division which covered Québec. Apart from Ottawa, "C" Division most demanded a diplomat. The Sûreté jealously guarded its turf against federal encroachment. The deputy commissioner's job was to avoid conflict and achieve as much inter-force cooperation as possible.

In addition to the deputy commissioner, who was standing behind his desk, there was the superintendent, one of those rare managers who didn't pretend he was born with all the answers. He actually sought and often took guidance from the ranks. He too was standing. A sure sign they intended it to be a short meeting.

The deputy commissioner spoke first. "Gentlemen, I've read your report on the Stanstead incident. The next question is where do we go from here? Your thoughts inspector?"

"Back to Ste. Herménégilde."

"To what end?"

"We went down there yesterday to see what, if anything, that farmer could tell us about what happened when the Stanstead radiation alarm went off. It wasn't a hostile inquiry but what we got were untruthful answers. I think we ought to get a search warrant and turn the place upside down … take a tech and a spectrometer with us and see if that truck is as innocent as it looks. If St. Germaine didn't tell the truth about his trip to the States, what else might he not be telling? We need to fill in the blanks; maybe take him over to the Sherbrooke barracks and question him in a less friendly setting."

"I agree," the superintendent said, "Maybe there's nothing there, but we better find out."

That agreed, the deputy commissioner sought to bring the meeting to a quick close. "Unless there's anything else…" He looked around for follow-up questions.

McNeill cleared his throat. "Sir, do we know whether the radiation detector at the border station was working properly?"

"Apparently it was. A test in place was run on it yesterday and it seemed to be fine. But just to be on the safe side they replaced the unit and will have the manufacturer take a look at it."

No one else had anything to add. "Well then, I suggest we get on with it." Turning to the superintendant he asked "You'll take care of the warrant and technician?" It was phrased as a question, but it wasn't. "Keep me informed."

As Gautier and McNeill headed downstairs the superintendant caught up with them and draped one arm across Gautier's shoulders. "How in the world did you ever find Ste. Hermé…" His voice faltered. "How do you say that again?"

"Herménégilde," Gautier replied.

"That's a new one on me. How in the world did you ever find it?"

"It was in the food section of *La Presse.*" Gautier replied to the super's bewilderment.

Chapter Sixteen

Ferme St. Germaine Freres
Wednesday, September 30th
12:00 Noon EDT

Considering all that was on his mind, Fernand had to admit he
actually had a fairly productive morning. He'd done some household chores and put the plow on the tractor to be ready for the first
snow which, although it usually didn't come until November, had
some years arrived as early as October. Then a phone call brought
another order for hay. They wanted eight tons which would mean 200
bales, a very full load. So now, with lunch over, he began moving the
bales nearer the loft door in preparation for loading the truck which
he had pulled into place below the jutting ridge pole. As he worked
he thought about the events of the past 72 hours. He knew he had
done a foolish thing in agreeing to give those two a ride but there
was no doubt he had done the right thing in calling Marie-Paule this
morning. Although he'd been nervous when he started talking to her
and perhaps had scared her a little by blurting out that the RCMP
had been here asking questions, once she realized he hadn't told them
anything she was very nice and even called him "a love" and said she
wouldn't forget what he had done for her. He wasn't sure just what, if
anything, that meant but he liked the sound of it. She hadn't specifically asked him not to say anything more to the RCMP but he didn't
intend to anyway...although he didn't expect to have his intentions

put to the test so soon.

As he lifted a bale onto the stack by the door he saw a black SUV turn off the road into his driveway. He watched as it rounded the corner of the house and came to a stop in the barnyard. He tried to remember the names of the two officers. One was French, the other English. It was the French one who had asked all the questions, including whether he had traveled alone. He'd have to be careful with him but he wouldn't tell them anything. She was counting on him.

As it turned out, it didn't matter whether he could remember their names. These were two different ones. He watched as they approached the barn. One of them looked up and spotted him standing in the door of the loft. "M. St. Germaine?" he called. Fernand nodded. "We'd like to talk with you for a minute if you don't mind." Fernand shrugged. What did he care. They could talk but he wasn't going to.

"I'll come down," he said.

"No, that's alright," the man answered, "we'll come up. Where's the ladder?"

"There are stairs back there." Fernand pointed to the back corner of the loft. Interesting they were willing to climb up here in their good suits. They obviously wanted to get a look around the loft. Well, they could look around all they wanted. There was nothing to see except hay and once he got these bales onto the truck there wouldn't even be much of that. The loft would be half empty while his bank account would be fatter than it had ever been. Plus there was the thousand dollars in the chest in the kitchen.

"Be right with you" the man answered. Fernand nodded and turned to wait for them. They might have scared him the other day but not today, although he did feel as though he needed to take a pee. Well, today he could hold it. They wouldn't be here long once they discovered he had nothing more to tell them.

Wednesday, September 30th
2:00 pm EDT

By the time the warrant had arrived it was nearly eleven o'clock making it a little after one when Gautier, McNeill and the tech finally got to Coaticook with the farm still some twenty minutes away. After a brief discussion they stopped at a diner and a half hour later had boosted their cholesterol levels a few points. Now, as they pulled around the corner of the house into the barnyard of *Ferme St. Germaine Freres*, McNeill stated the obvious: "We're not alone."

In addition to two provincial police cruisers, a couple of private cars, and a pickup truck there was an ambulance. A small knot of men stared as they drove in. One, a stocky man in a dark blue suit, was obviously in charge. He stood, feet slightly apart, like a bulldog waiting for a suspicious move before deciding whether to attack. He watched warily as Gautier, McNeill and the technician approached.

Gautier flashed his ID. "RCMP" he said.

"Oh shit," Blue Suit replied. "What do you want?"

Gautier answered the question with a question. "What's going on?"

Blue Suit looked at him a long moment, probably trying to decide whether to answer Gautier's question or wait for an answer to his own. At length he stepped aside, clearing their line of sight to a white sheet draped over a figure on the ground. A pair of heavy work boots protruded from one end of the sheet. "Suicide," he said, pointing up at the hoist that extended from above the hay loft door. Its rope had been cut partway up. "What's the RCMP's interest here?"

Gautier's answer was another question: "Fernand St. Germaine?" Blue Suit nodded yes. "We have a warrant to take a look around and ask him a few questions about a possible illegal border crossing he made earlier this week."

"Well, he isn't going to answer," Blue Suit replied. Seeing the pained look on one of the men's faces, he apparently felt compelled to change his tone. He put out a large, beefy hand, "Detective Sergeant Paul Charbonneau, Sûreté."

Gautier responded by perfunctorily shaking his hand and introducing himself, McNeill and the tech. "When did it happen?"

"The doc says a couple of hours ago, maybe noon, perhaps a little after." Charbonneau indicated an older, slight, bespectacled man whom he introduced as the medical examiner. The doctor acknowledged the introduction with a nod. Turning to the other civilian he said "This is Raymond St. Germaine, the deceased's brother. He found the body." There was no doubt as to Raymond's identity. He was a near copy of Fernand even down to similar Bib overalls, plaid shirt and heavy boots. He was the one who had reacted when Charbonneau said the RCMP wouldn't get any answers from his brother. He looked shaken.

The detective answered the obvious next question without being asked. "He hung himself from up there," indicating the beam that extended like the prow of a sailing ship from above the loft door. A pulley hung on its far end. The rope that ran through the pulley was sliced clean, dangling a few feet above the truck bed. The other end disappeared into the loft. "Raymond got a knife from the kitchen, climbed up on the back of the truck and cut him down."

"When was that?"

Charbonneau answered for Raymond. "About an hour ago," needlessly adding, "too late. He then called us. Officer Lemoyne responded." One of the uniformed officers nodded his head in acknowledgement.

Gautier turned to Raymond. "I'm very sorry. Do you have any idea why he would have done it?"

Raymond slowly shook his head no but his answer amounted to a yes. "I think maybe he was having a tough time. I tried to get him to sell the farm and come work with me but Fernand, he had his pride and..." His voice broke and he gulped several times in an effort to stifle a sob. Charbonneau picked up the story, apparently having asked the same question.

"This was the family farm. It was okay when there was family to work it. But you can't do dairy farming alone and it wasn't profitable enough to hire help. So when his uncle and his father died and his brother got married and moved out he got rid of the cows and just grew hay which he sold, mostly down in the States."

Raymond, who had been listening, added "And he worked during the summer for a camp on the lake. Fernand worked hard, he…" His voice trailed off.

"Camp?" Gautier asked.

"Not really a camp," Charbonneau corrected him. "A boat club on Massawippi. Bunch of Montréalers. Mostly English. Maybe all English. I don't know. "

"What did he do there?"

"Handyman. Cut the grass, trimmed the shrubs, that kind of stuff."

"So that and selling hay was it?"

"Apparently," Charbonneau shrugged "…and apparently not enough."

Gautier directed his next question to Raymond. "He lived alone?"

Raymond nodded. "Yes." His eyes welled with tears at the thought of his brother living alone.

"Girl friend?"

Raymond shook his head. "No. I don't think so".

"Where do you live?" Gautier asked in a gentle voice.

"Near Coaticook. I have a farm there. It was my wife's father's place."

"Did you see your brother often?"

Raymond half shrugged. "Sometimes we went hunting."

"Why did you come today?"

"It was his birthday. He was going to come to our house but he called up and said he couldn't. Said he was busy. My wife had made him a cake and we'd got him a present. So after lunch I brought them over. I thought maybe we'd have a piece of cake together." He paused for a long moment, trying hard to pull himself together. "They're in the car." He looked toward a grey Chevy left where he'd jammed the brakes on after seeing his brother hanging from the beam. "Just a shirt and a bottle of wine." The thought of the modest gifts was too much for Raymond who turned and sobbed out loud. The uniformed officer standing next to him looked uncertain whether to comfort him or keep a professional distance. It was the doctor who went over and put his arm around Raymond's shoulders and led him out of earshot toward the clothes line where five sheets hung limply, their irregular spacing indicating there had been one more.

Gautier turned to Charbonneau. "Cause of death?"

"Broken neck. He tied a pretty good knot. It snapped that bone at the back. Most of the time suicides suffocate themselves. He didn't. It was quick and clean. Pretty painless. You want to take a look?" Gautier nodded. At a word from Charbonneau the second uniformed policeman, who had been standing by the body, pulled back the sheet. The doctor tactfully kept Raymond facing the other way. The odd way the head lay in relation to the rest of the body confirmed the cause of death. He was dressed in a plaid shirt and stained overalls.

"What's the stain?"

"Wet himself. The doc says it's a natural reaction when the nervous system is stressed."

"Anything in his pockets?"

"Dirty handkerchief. Couple of screws and a washer. No money."

"No note or anything?"

"Nope."

"Watch?"

"Nope."

"Rings?"

"Nope."

"Billfold?"

"Not on him. There's one on the kitchen table…about sixty dollars in it, two gas cards, driver's license, national health card and a rosary card."

Gautier looked back at the body. "Where's the rope?"

"The doc took it off. I've got it in case the coroner's inquest wants it."

"Coroner's inquest?"

"Routine."

"Mind if we have a look around as long as we're here?"

"You've got a warrant. Go ahead. What did he do anyway?"

McNeill spoke up for the first time. "Apparently crossed the border without going through customs; maybe more than once."

"And they sent three of you all the way down here from where, Montréal, for that? You don't come from Sherbrooke. I know the people there."

"Montréal," McNeill confirmed.

Charbonneau's voice and eyebrows went up in disbelief. He looked hard at McNeill as if he were an alien species. "All the way from Montréal because some poor bastard who can't pay his bills slips across the border to fill his tank to save a buck," the detective shook his head. "I dunno. I don't get it. Hell, when I was a kid we used to go down to Vermont all the time to get cheap gas. We never bothered with customs. Nobody around here ever did. This area's full of old logging trails that cross the border, a lot of them probably not passable now but back then they were." He cocked his head to one side in disbelief. Gautier thought it an ironic touch with St. Germaine lying there with his neck bent at much the same angle. "Go ahead; take a look around if you want. I've gotta get this wrapped up." He turned to address the ambulance driver while pointing to one of the uniformed officers. "He'll give you a hand. Better get him out of here." And looking over to the medical examiner who was talking quietly with Raymond, he called "Usual place doc?" The doctor nodded.

He'd explain to Raymond that the local funeral home would collect the body from the morgue in Sherbrooke.

Gautier started to turn away but paused, "One thing, what was the name of that club?"

Charbonneau consulted his notes. "Fair Haven. Fairhaven. I don't know if that's one word or two. On Massawippi, about a half hour from here. But there won't be anyone there this time of year. They close up after Labor Day. Just open in the summer."

Gautier thanked him and, turning to McNeill and the technician, led them a short distance away from the others. "You," he said quietly to McNeill, "take a look around in the barn, especially the loft. I'm going to take a look in the house. You," he said to the tech, "come with me."

The door to the porch was shut but the inner door to the kitchen was standing open. The place was generally as he remembered it. Yesterday's *La Tribune* was on the table, sports section on top. The wallet Charbonneau mentioned was beside the sugar bowl and salt and pepper shakers. A few dishes were sitting on the sideboard where they'd been put to dry. "What are we looking for?" the technician asked.

"I don't know. Something out of the ordinary. Something that doesn't fit. Why don't you start upstairs and work down. I'll start here and work through to the front of the house."

Gautier began his search by just standing in the center of the room and letting his eyes drift across its surfaces, not so much looking as feeling the space. Nothing stood out. It seemed unchanged from yesterday. He checked the pantry, looked inside some canisters which proved to be empty, rifled through the drawers by the sink; lots of stuff but nothing unusual. Just what you'd expect to be there. The only sound in the kitchen apart from the tech's footsteps upstairs was an old wall clock, its pendulum marking off the minutes.

A little chest sat beside the back stairs, a small wall lamp above it. A telephone, some letters and an empty flower vase waited on top of the chest. The envelopes had been opened—a light bill, a telephone bill and a thank you for a $20.00 contribution to the Holy Name Children's Charity with an envelope in case you wanted to give more. He noticed both the bills had been paid in full the previous month; nothing past due, no balance carried forward. There was also a letter without any envelope. It was addressed to a Boyden Mann at the Fairhaven Boat Club. Curiously it was dated four years ago. Something about guest privileges. It had a return address in Montréal and was signed "Andrew". Gautier copied the name and address in his notebook as well the phone number scrawled on the back before replacing it and the three envelopes where he had found them. He then pulled open the top drawer of the chest.

It contained a grayish-blue ledger, a tray with pencils and paper clips, and two bundles of envelopes fastened with rubber bands. The business card he'd given St. Germaine yesterday was tucked under one of the bands. A check book was tucked under the other. The ledger listed perhaps a dozen places, mostly in Vermont and the Hudson Valley of eastern New York—presumably his hay clients. The entries were neat. One column had the date. The next had a number which Gautier guessed was the number of bales of hay. The third had a dollar figure. Once it went as high as $2200. There wasn't any indication that St. Germaine extended credit to anyone. No running totals or past due balances. The age of the entries varied. One client had no entry for almost two years. A couple had some last year but none this year. Most of the rest had one or two entries for this year, the most recent being this past Monday—some place called Saratoga Feed & Grain in Saratoga Springs, New York: $1560. Gautier made a note of the name then picked up the check book. The last entry was a deposit dated September 29th—yesterday. Allowing for the exchange rate it seemed to match what the feed store in New York had paid. The total bank balance was just shy of $6,500.

Next he thumbed through the envelopes. One held deposit slips from the *Caisse Populaire* with yesterday's on top. The rest held routine bills; again, none indicated any outstanding balance. He was about to return the records to the drawer when he noticed a white envelope that had been underneath the ledger. He picked it up, looked inside and whistled softly.

The sudden whine of the spring on the porch door startled him. Charbonneau and Raymond St. Germaine entered the kitchen. "He needs to use the phone," Charbonneau said. Gautier put the envelope and ledger back in the drawer and, closing it, stepped aside. While Raymond spoke with his wife—apparently not the first time since his grisly discovery as he asked about her efforts to reach the parish priest—Charbonneau motioned Gautier onto the porch, closing the kitchen door behind him.

"How long do you expect to be?" he asked. "Since he's dead I guess you'll be closing the book on this one, no?"

"I don't know," Gautier replied, "Like you, I file reports and wait for orders."

Charbonneau raised his eyebrows indicating his agreement. "Look, I don't want to hurry you, I know you're going to have to do a bunch of paperwork when you get back and you need to be able to say you did whatever you needed to do but I've got to secure the place before I leave and I was kind of hoping not to spend all day here."

"I understand," Gautier replied. "I think we'll probably need forty-five minutes, maybe an hour, to wrap it up." Charbonneau eyed him curiously. It seemed odd given that whatever they found they wouldn't be able to bring any charges. But, they had a warrant, so some judge thought there was a reasonable chance the poor bastard had broken some law.

"Okay," Charbonneau said, "I'll tell you what. I was on my way to lunch when I got called over here. So I'm going to get a bite to eat. That should give you enough time."

Gautier had just agreed when the kitchen door opened and Raymond stepped onto the porch. He looked shaken. "What's the matter?" Charbonneau asked, thinking as he did what a stupid question it was given what this guy's day had been like so far.

"The priest says Fernand cannot be buried in the cemetery because he committed suicide. That's a cardinal sin for which there can't be absolution because he can't..." He couldn't bring himself to finish the sentence but both men, themselves Catholics, understood. Since you had taken your own life there was no way you could repent for what you had done and therefore no way you could receive absolution for the sin of taking a life, even if it was your own, and no one who died in sin could be buried in consecrated ground. In an odd sort of a way it all made sense. Neither policeman quite knew what to say so they said nothing. Charbonneau opened the porch door and Raymond followed him outside.

Gautier could see McNeill standing in the door of the loft, looking down as if trying to picture what had happened. The sound of the technician's steps on the stairs turned him back toward the kitchen. "I don't know, inspector. Everything looks normal to me, given that I don't have anything to compare it with. Two of the rooms don't look lived in. The other one was obviously his bedroom. Everything is neat and clean. He even has fresh sheets on his bed. I gave everything in there a toss—the mattress, closet shelves, bureau drawers, even checked the floorboards and went through the pockets of his clothes—nothing. Same with the bathroom. No sign of any women."

Gautier, who seemed to be only half listening, nodded his acceptance of the technician's report. He hadn't really expected anything else. Sunlight, reflected from the windshields of the departing cars, flashed across the ceiling. "Look," he told the technician, "the brother is going home and the detective is going to lunch. Why don't you get your stuff and give the truck a sweep and then, as time permits, check the barn. Just have your gear out of sight before Charbonneau gets back. I don't want to have to explain what I'm doing since I don't know myself." As the technician headed to the van to carry out his instructions, Gautier started to return to the chest but thought better of it. Instead, he turned on his heel and followed the technician outside.

McNeill was just emerging from the barn. He had a perplexed look on his face.

"Inspector, something doesn't add up."

"Tell me about it."

"Well, this guy's getting ready to load hay onto his truck, presumably to haul it somewhere to sell it. Halfway through the job he stops and hangs himself because he's broke? That hay was money just waiting for him." McNeill paused. "Am I making any sense?"

"You are," Gautier replied, "go on."

"Well, from what we saw of him yesterday, I didn't figure him for a suicide. He was nervous but we tend to have that effect on people. But he was also holding something back. That's an act of defiance, not depression. And..." McNeill's voice trailed off.

"And?" Gautier prompted him.

McNeill sighed. "And it was so neat. I mean how many suicides manage to tie the knot just right and place it so perfectly that it breaks the neck and doesn't leave them hanging there turning purple? He was a farmer. He was used to tying bales of hay, not positioning slip knots."

"So what are you suggesting?"

"I'm not suggesting anything. I'm just not able to make it add up in my own mind but maybe that's just me. Maybe I feel a little guilty at missing some sign yesterday."

"Anything else?"

"Not really, it's just that..."

"Just what?"

"Well, like him being broke. The place looks okay to me. It's not fancy but it's not falling down. The house is neat. The barn is neat. Fences are all up. Hell, he just made a hay run and that must mean he was flush for the moment anyway. And he has an apparently prosperous brother living nearby. If he were in a tight spot you'd think he'd tap his brother for some help, wouldn't you?"

"Not necessarily. People have their pride. Besides," Gautier added after a pause, "he wasn't broke."

McNeill looked surprised. "What do you mean?"

Gautier beckoned for the sergeant to follow him back into the house. "I mean he had some money in the bank—several thousand dollars—his bills were all current, no past due balances, no delinquency notices that I could find. He had a mortgage but he was current on that, too. He didn't have a lot of money but he apparently didn't spend much, either." Their footfalls on the wooden steps echoed eerily between the house and the barn.

Once inside Gautier walked over to the chest and, tugging open the top drawer, rummaged about for a moment before pulling out the white envelope which he handed to McNeill. "And then there's this." McNeill looked inside the envelope. There was a wad of crisp, new $100 bills. He looked at Gautier, mouth open in surprise, and counted it.

"A thousand dollars? They paid him in cash? That's risky keeping that lying around the house."

Gautier shook his head. "I doubt he got that in the States. They wouldn't pay him in Canadian dollars and in any event they paid him with a check which he deposited yesterday morning, over fifteen hundred dollars. The deposit slip is in the chest along with all his others. So where did he get this and why didn't he deposit it with the rest?"

"Maybe he withdrew it."

"Not according to his bank book but we can check. Given his life style a thousand dollars would go a very long way."

"Maybe he was planning a change of life style."

"If he was, why would he kill himself?

McNeill nodded agreement adding "And if you were going to use the money around here why would you get it in hundreds? I bet there aren't many places where you could hand them a hundred dollar bill and expect change."

Gautier shrugged. "I haven't checked the rest of the ground floor or the basement. Why don't you do that while I finish going through this chest." For the next few minutes they each rummaged about. The remaining drawers of the chest yielded stacks of old family photographs and a bundle of letters all postmarked several years earlier; the ordinary detritus of an ordinary life.

McNeill did no better. "It doesn't look as if this guy ever used the parlor or dining room. The basement doesn't go under the whole house. There's an ancient oil furnace and a 500 gallon fuel tank that's accessed from an outside pipe on the driveway side of the house. Other than that there are just some old storm windows and a bureau with a cracked mirror. Some shelves near the kitchen stairs are full of empty mason jars. Judging by the amount of dust on them it's been a long time since anyone around here did any canning."

Footsteps sounded on the porch. A moment later the technician came in. Gautier looked up expectantly. "Anything?"

"Yeah, there's a reading on the back of the truck, on the far end on the driver's side—trace amounts of Cesium 137."

"Holy shit." Gautier and McNeill spoke as one voice.

"How much?" Gautier asked.

"Not much, on a scale of one to ten maybe a two or three. And I didn't find it anywhere else. I did a walk-through of the barn and checked some gloves that were up in the loft. Nothing. Couldn't check him, of course, but we could stop at the morgue on the way back and I could take a reading there."

"This Cesium 137," Gautier asked, "where would someone get something like that?

"My guess would be a hospital. It's consistent with medical waste. They incinerate stuff that's gotten contaminated in their radiation lab or the oncology unit; gloves, sponges, tubes ...that sort of thing."

"What do they do with the ash?"

"Usually they store it until there's enough to have it trucked away and buried at a special landfill..."

"Isn't the radiation destroyed when they burn it?" McNeill asked.

"No," the tech explained. "Radiation is an internal process involving the decay of atoms. Burning is an external process changing the form of whatever contains the atoms. Changing the external form doesn't change the internal structure. You can make soup out of radioactive turnips like they did around Chernobyl and you get radioactive soup. Radiation is very persistent stuff. You have to wait for it to decay naturally."

"How long does that take?"

"Anywhere from a few minutes to a few thousand years depending on what kind you're dealing with. Cesium 137 takes about 30 years."

"How would anyone get hold of radioactive ash? Surely the hospitals don't just leave it sitting around?" Gautier asked.

"Not quite that bad but close," the tech replied. "There was a study a few years ago that said a third of the radioactive waste sent to disposal sites in Québec couldn't be traced."

"You say this Cesium 137 is mostly used for medical work," McNeill asked. "Would that include veterinarians? Could St. Germaine have been hauling some medicine or something and maybe spilled a little?"

"I don't know whether vets use it. Maybe they do but I doubt they'd be hauling it around the countryside in the back of a hay truck. That's stuff you use under very carefully controlled circumstances, probably in a lab of some sort."

"How big a bomb can you make out of it?" Gautier asked.

"You can't. It's not explosive. You could use it to dirty up a conventional bomb so that when it goes off the radiation would contaminate the blast area and maybe a mile or two downwind depending on how much there was of it, what the weather was like…a bunch of things…" His voice trailed off but not his interest. Where was the inspector going with this?

Gautier said nothing but pursed his lips, asking himself much the same question.

"Anything else?" the tech asked. "If not, I'll give this place a sweep."

"Yeah," Gautier agreed, "go ahead and see if anything turns up. Be sure to check St. Germaine's bedroom closet. Pay special attention to his work clothes." Once the technician left the kitchen, Gautier turned back to McNeill. "Charbonneau should be back in a few minutes. He'll probably want to know if we found anything."

"What are you going to tell him?" McNeill asked.

"I'll tell him about the money. In fact, he'd be the proper one to go to the bank in the morning to find out if St. Germaine made a withdrawal. "

"And the radiation?"

"No, I don't think so. That's a decision that needs to be made above our pay grade. People get nervous when you mention radiation. We don't want to start a panic."

"What are you going to do with the truck?" McNeill asked.

"We'll impound it. Tell Charbonneau it's part of the border crossing investigation. Put a note on it and park it in the barn. He says he's going to secure everything when he comes back. It should be okay there."

"What do you make of all this?" McNeill asked.

"I don't know," Gautier replied shaking his head. "Maybe if we knew how his truck got contaminated..." His voice trailed off in thought before he continued, "It just doesn't seem to add up. I've got a feeling I'm missing something."

McNeill hesitated before replying. "Are we sure it was suicide?"

"What else? No sign of a struggle and he was a big boy. Strong."

"Maybe it wasn't one-on-one. Maybe there were two or three of them."

"Yeah, but if you see someone making a noose to put around your neck you're not going to just sit there are you?" Gautier asked.

"What if he didn't see it?"

"What do you mean?"

"What if he was already dead? What if they had already broken his neck?"

"And then they hung him to make it look like suicide?" Gautier considered the idea.

McNeill continued. "There's no way the medical examiner would know. The neck was broken. There was a rope around it. What's to question?"

Gautier stood up and started to pace as he thought aloud. "It doesn't look like he was worried about money. His brother says he doesn't know of any girlfriend. Along with poor health those are the most common reasons people kill themselves. But he looked strong as an ox. Hell, he was tossing 80 pound bales of hay around when he died."

"He had to piss a lot."

"Probably nerves. But an autopsy could tell whether there was anything wrong."

"How do we go about asking for an autopsy for an illegal border crossing?"

"We don't," Gautier answered. "We leave that up to Charbonneau. When we show him the money and the bank account and the paid bills he'll do it on his own. He won't want to go to the coroner's inquest without it...sort of an insurance policy in the absence of a suicide note or a motive." They could hear the technician coming down the stairs.

"Will Charbonneau share?"

"I dunno. I'll ask him to keep me informed of anything he learns."

"And if he doesn't?"

"Then I'll send you to the inquest," Gautier said. "It's public." The technician came back into the kitchen.

"Nothing," he told them. "Not a whisper."

"You better get that thing back in the van before our friend returns," Gautier said. Even as he spoke they could hear a car on the driveway. "That'll be Charbonneau now. *Vite! Vite!*" The technician was already halfway across the porch moving quickly toward the SUV.

"Speaking of motive," McNeill picked up the conversation where they'd left off. "What could it be? Apart from his mortgage he apparently didn't owe anything. It doesn't look like there's a jealous husband. The house wasn't messed up and his wallet was sitting in plain sight which seems to rule out robbery. What's left? Road rage?"

"I dunno. Small town people sometimes have grudges that go back generations. Maybe something to do with fence lines or water rights...stuff like that." Gautier didn't sound convinced by his own explanation.

"Or the hot spot on the truck."

Gautier nodded in agreement. "That's what I'm wondering. He sets off the radiation detector at the border. We come to see him the next day. The day after that he's dead." A car door slammed. "We need to get Charbonneau to work with us. Rule out some of these possibilities."

Lunch must have agreed with Charbonneau. He was in an expansive mood. "Have the Mounties got their man?" he asked on entering the kitchen.

"I'm hoping that's what you can tell me," Gautier replied. He sat down at the kitchen table and indicated Charbonneau should join him. McNeill leaned against the sink, present but not participating. This was Gautier's show. He opened it by sliding the envelope across the table. Charbonneau picked it up with a quizzical expression that quickly changed to open surprise.

"I sincerely hope you're trying to bribe me," he said. "Otherwise I think I'm in for quite a story." He was. Over the next few minutes Gautier showed him the accounts ledger and the check book. When he was done, Charbonneau had the same question: "So where did he get a thousand dollars in big bills?"

"I was hoping you could help us determine that," Gautier said. "Maybe he withdrew it from his account yesterday when he deposited the hay money although there's no record of it." Charbonneau nodded his head.

"The bank's closed now but I can check in the morning. And if he did?"

"I don't know," Gautier replied. "Maybe he was going to pay somebody for something. Blackmail? Protection? Drugs?"

"Why do you say that? Couldn't it be for some legitimate purchase?"

"It could be," Gautier conceded, "but, if so, why cash? Why not just write a check as he did with all his other expenditures? What was so unique about this purchase that it required cash?"

Charbonneau had no answer. Gautier didn't expect one. They sat quietly for a long moment.

"And if he didn't withdraw the money from the bank?" the detective asked.

"Then that will leave us wondering where he did get it and why. Presumably it was from someone on this side of the border since it's in Canadian currency. It wasn't for hay because there are no recent Canadian sales in his book. He was doing all his business in the States. So what other service might he be able to perform for that kind of money?"

Charbonneau had a one word answer: "Trafficking."

"I was wondering about that," Gautier replied without saying he agreed. "Since he was going south anyway, was he carrying a little extra cargo?"

"That could account for why he crossed the border illegally. He might not have wanted to take the chance of being searched." Charbonneau paused as the idea grew on him. "But why would he commit suicide if he had money in the bank and two ways to earn more?"

"That," Gautier agreed, "is the question."

"I wonder," Charbonneau replied, picking up the idea Gautier had planted and running with it, "was he skimming some for himself? Was he using? Maybe I ought to request an autopsy."

Gautier nodded his agreement. "I hope you'll keep me informed."

Charbonneau said he would, thinking as he said it that the RCMP was really pretty sharp. "If this guy was a drug courier do you think there's any chance he didn't jump; that he was pushed?"

"We mustn't get ahead of ourselves," Gautier cautioned him. "We don't yet know the source of the money."

Autoroute des Cantons de L'est
Wednesday, September 30th
4:00pm EDT

Apart from a call to the superintendant, the trip back to Montréal was conducted mostly in silence, each man lost in thought, Gautier especially so. He still felt there was something out of place. Something he'd seen that didn't fit. It was the technician who ultimately stumbled on it. "I didn't know the guy but, you know, I feel kind of sorry for him. It must have been a pretty lonely way to live… almost like he was tending the family museum. The place was old but in pretty good shape, neat, tidy, everything in its place. I almost wish I'd taken in his laundry for him."

It took a moment for the reaction but suddenly Gautier sat bolt upright. "My God, that's it!" he exclaimed. "The laundry!" He whirled around in the passenger's seat to confront the technician. "What did you say about St. Germaine's bedroom?"

"I…I dunno. I said it was neat and clean. Nothing unusual."

"No…about his bed." Gautier was suddenly animated.

"I said he had clean sheets on it."

The technician looked perplexed but McNeill, who had seen Gautier in action before, let out an admiring sentence-long profanity.

"The clothes line. There were *five* sheets on the clothesline. There had been six but the Sûreté or the medical examiner yanked one to cover the body."

"So?" the tech asked.

"So St. Germaine lived alone and he had fresh sheets on his bed. Two of those on the line presumably were his but whose were the others? If he's making $1500 a trip selling hay and who knows what else he probably isn't taking in laundry." McNeill was excited. Gautier had done it again. He had seen what was staring everyone in the face. "So he had company after all." Looking at Gautier he added, "You said he looked like he'd been shot when you asked him yesterday if he'd had anyone with him on the trip south. Maybe the thousand dollars was cab fare."

"If it was," Gautier replied, "that raises the question of who would want to get into the States badly enough to pay that kind of money for a ride and what might they have been taking with them?" He paused for a long moment before adding, "And how worried was somebody that their driver could identify them?"

OCTOBER/
OCTOBRE

Chapter Seventeen

The superintendant's first question was brief and to the point. "Was it suicide?"

Gautier looked at McNeill indicating he should take the question. He did, outlining his doubts it was suicide. When he was finished, the superintendent returned to Gautier for comment.

"He may be right. Perhaps the autopsy will tell us for sure. But whatever Mr. St. Germaine's problem was, it wasn't money. He wasn't rich but he had ample income and sufficient savings for the life style he led plus a thousand dollars tucked away from whatever source. And, as Sgt. McNeill points out, he had a fairly prosperous brother living nearby."

"That brother, how did he strike you?" the superintendent asked.

"Nothing out of the ordinary, genuinely distraught—he found the body, had to cut his brother down from the beam. Relations between them apparently were good. He was there because he was bringing a birthday cake and a gift. He said they sometimes went hunting together…" Gautier stopped in mid-sentence and, pulling a pen from his pocket, jotted something in his notebook. "Excuse me but I just thought of something we need to ask the brother." Picking up his narrative he added, "I didn't find anything odd in his story."

Turning to the technician the superintendent said "tell me about the truck."

"It showed low grade radioactivity on the last foot or so of the bed, principally on the driver's side. The reading was consistent with Cesium 137."

"You say 'low grade'. Do you mean it wasn't strong to begin with or that there wasn't much of it?"

"Both. It had the strength you'd associate with a secondary source, possibly incinerated medical or commercial waste. As to the amount, I can't say how much may have been present originally. Some of the contaminant probably was blown away during the truck's travels, perhaps there was a rain shower somewhere enroute which would have further dispersed it or, perhaps, the original amount was minimal, maybe the result of an accidental spill."

"Is there something farmers might carry that could legitimately account for low degree radiation?" the superintendent asked, "Some kind of fertilizer perhaps?"

"I don't know. I doubt it," the tech replied.

The superintendant returned to Gautier. "What's next inspector?"

Gautier cleared his throat. "As I see it, we need to find out where St. Germaine got that thousand dollars."

"Why?"

" It could be the same place his truck got radioactive."

"Who has the money now?"

"The provincial inspector who was there—a fellow named Charbonneau. He's going to check out the bank, see if St. Germaine made a withdrawal."

"This Charbonneau, is he being cooperative?"

"Yes," Gautier thought for a moment before adding, "actually more than he realizes."

"How so?"

"He suspects the real reason we showed up was drug trafficking which gives us a plausible cover to keep looking. We don't have to confirm or deny it; just let him think what he will. If it turns out St. Germaine was not a suicide that will probably further convince him it's a drug case since drugs and violence go hand-in-hand."

"Please continue."

"I also want to get a record of St. Germaine's phone calls for the last couple of months."

"What do you expect to find?"

"I don't know," Gautier answered, "maybe nothing." He gave a Gallic shrug, "But maybe something." He consulted his notebook. "I'd also like to borrow some local manpower from the Sherbrooke barracks. The note I just wrote myself was a reminder to ask the brother—Raymond—exactly where they went hunting. Charbonneau said there are a lot of old logging roads that cross the border. Some may still be passable. If St. Germaine used one of them we might be able to find out which one, tire tracks or something."

"What would that accomplish?"

"If we can find the crossing point, maybe we can find someone at one end or the other who may have seen something."

"Such as?"

"Such as passengers."

"What makes you think he had passengers?"

Gautier told him about the sheets and added, "I'd like to take a forensics team down there to thoroughly dust the place. See if in fact anyone else had been staying there."

The superintendent nodded his agreement. "Go ahead and when you're done, let's get that truck into a safe place. Have it taken over to the Sherbrooke barracks. Anything else inspector?"

Gautier felt there was; something hovering just below the surface of his memory. He raised his index finger signaling a request for a moment's forbearance as he paged through his notebook. "Ah, yes, Fairhaven."

"What's that?"

"It's the boat club where St. Germaine worked during the summer. There was an old letter on the chest where I found the money addressed to someone at the club named Boyden Mann. It had a return address here in Montréal and a phone number scrawled on the back of it. We need to find out who they belong to and I think we ought to talk to this Boyden Mann; find out how come St. Germaine had his letter. We also ought to talk to some of St. Germaine's co-workers at the club, see what they know about him. And, while we're at it, we probably ought to ask the FBI to have a chat with the feed and grain dealer in New York where he supposedly took the hay Monday—find out if he really did and, if so, when did he get there, which might tell us whether he made any detours enroute, did he have anyone with him, does he have any friends there—a general profile of whatever it was he was doing before he tripped the Stanstead alarm."

"Should we ask them to check the hay he delivered?"

"For radiation?"

"Yes."

"I don't know. If word got out it would probably send any accomplices to ground and possibly trigger the sort of panic we're trying to avoid which would make a thorough investigation near impossible. Maybe just say the Sûreté is wondering if St. Germaine was trafficking and while we don't know we're checking it out."

The superintendant looked back at the technician. "How much of a safety factor is there? Would we be putting anyone at risk if we didn't say anything about the radiation at this juncture?"

"I don't know, sir," the technician replied. "Theoretically if contaminated hay was being fed to dairy cows some trace could show up in their milk but given the strengths we have found so far, I'd doubt it would have any adverse effect on anyone but I don't really know... maybe a baby...I just don't know."

"If I may suggest..." McNeill spoke up. "The report from Stanstead went to the U.S. Border Enforcement Team as well as to our people so the Americans have already been officially notified that there was a radiation incident and a farm truck might be involved. So, as I see it, we've already told them."

The superintendant frowned. "Let me think about that." Then, turning to Gautier he said, "We need to consider what we're going to tell the ICC meeting tomorrow."

Gautier nodded as if in agreement. He didn't mean it. The weekly meetings of the Intergovernmental Coordinating Committee were, as far as he was concerned, a waste of time. The fact that they met late in the day on Fridays—supposedly to review the week's non-existent progress in the June bombings investigation—added nothing to their appeal. The only saving grace was that Mayor Ganeau kept them as brief as possible.

Ferme St. Germaine Freres
Thursday, October 1st
11:00am EDT

"Oh hell, here we go again." McNeill groaned. The road leading to the farm was narrowed to a single lane by a row of cars and pick-up trucks parked along the side. Small knots of people were gathered talking among themselves. A fireman motioned for the SUV to keep going. Instead, McNeill pulled abreast of him, stopped, and flashed his ID. The fireman stepped back and waved them into the driveway. Ahead thin whiffs of smoke were still rising from the charred ruins of the barn and farmhouse. McNeill pulled in behind two fire trucks.

The fire chief, a big, stolid farmer whose bib overalls showed under his long rubberized coat, slowly walked over to see who had gotten past his man. Gautier flashed his ID. The chief wasn't surprised. "Charbonneau said he thought you'd show up."

"Is he here?" Gautier asked.

"Left about a half hour ago." The chief looked around at the tangle of hoses and clutter of equipment. "Like I told him, the barn was already gone by the time we was notified and the house was fully engulfed."

"What time was that?" Gautier asked.

"About 4:30 this morning. One of the hands at the dairy in Coaticook lives down this way. He was going to work when he seen it; called right away. We got here just before five."

"So the barn burned first?"

"Yup. There was hay stored in the loft. The fellow who owned this place—Fernand St. Germaine—died a few days ago. Apparently no one thought to check on his hay. Probably thought his brother would do it. Course no one would have got in anyway 'cause the police had the place all taped off."

"Why should somebody want to check on the hay?" McNeill asked.

The chief looked the officer up and down, assessing him to be the city dweller he in fact was. "You can't just let hay sit," he explained, "Spontaneous combustion. Hay with a decent moisture content can hit 150...200 degrees and it'll burn well before it hits 200. You have to check it regular like." He paused and ran a large, gnarled hand over the stubble on his face. "Of course, usually by now the hay's dried out enough that it should be okay. It's generally only the first month you have to be special careful when the moisture's high. I don't know just when St. Germaine had his last cutting but it was probably late August...no later than the first of September. Usually you get most of your heat in the first few weeks," he repeated, "but I've seen trouble as much as two months after cutting..."

Gautier interrupted the chief's discourse on the flammability of hay with a question. "Was there a truck in the barn?"

The chief looked surprised that Gautier knew. "Yup. That probably made it burn all the hotter depending on how much fuel he had in it." Looking toward the smoldering ruins of the barn he added, "Not much left of it now. Burned the tires right off the wheels...

took the paint off…burnt out the wood bed. Damn near not worth towing for scrap." Gautier and McNeill exchanged glances.

"What happened to the house?" Gautier asked.

"Sparks. When that old barn went up it throwed sparks all over the place. We did what we could when we got here but the whole damn place was burning." The chief motioned to a man in a yellow slicker to join them. "This here's the fire marshal," he told Gautier and McNeill. "These men are from the RCMP," he added by way of introduction.

Gautier took it from there. "I'm Chief Inspector Paul Gautier. This is Detective Sergeant David McNeill. The chief says it looks as though the fire started in the barn and sparks carried it to the house." It was a statement which the fire marshal recognized was intended to be taken as a question.

"Yeah, that seems about right. The earliest damage to the house was on the side facing the barn. The wall facing toward the road was still standing when they got here." Gautier looked in that direction. It no longer was.

"No sign of arson?" Gautier asked.

"No, not that I could see. No obvious accelerants, if that's what you mean. This place was probably a hundred years old, maybe older. Wood gets awful dry in that length of time. It didn't help that there was an oil tank in the basement of the house. Probably pretty near full. Hasn't been cold enough to have used much yet." After a few more minutes listening to their explanations for the thorough destructiveness of the fire and parrying their questions about why the RCMP was interested in an out-of-the-way farm, Gautier thanked the fire marshal and the chief before turning to McNeill and nodding his unspoken assent that there was nothing more to be done here. But, before climbing back into the SUV he stood for a long moment, one foot still resting on the ground and looked around, taking in the scene as if to permanently fix it in his memory. Halfway between the ruins of the barn and the house five soot-smeared sheets hung listlessly on a clothes line.

"So, what now?" McNeill asked as, for the third time that week, they turned out of the driveway, past the curious onlookers, toward home.

"Three things. First, we need to tell the forensics team to turn around. There's nothing they can do here. Second, we should request more manpower for the border search since that's about all we have left. And third, we need to think up a damn fine explanation for why we left the truck in the barn yesterday instead of moving it to the Sherbrooke barracks." He paused and then added in a disgusted tone of voice, "And fourth, remind me to ask Charbonneau why he didn't let us know what happened. Theoretically we're supposed to be on the same side."

McNeill pulled his cell phone from his pocket to call the forensics team. "Damn!"

"What's the matter?"

"Battery's low."

Gautier couldn't suppress a grin. McNeill routinely teased him about forgetting to turn on his cell phone. "Here, use mine. Battery ought to be okay."

McNeill took it in silence and flipped open the case. "Hey, you've got a bunch of calls waiting. Don't you ever check them?"

"You've got the phone. You check them."

"Uh, oh," McNeill deadpanned as he did so. "You may be in trouble. There's one from your wife. Came in at ten o'clock this morning."

"I'll do the personal calls. You see if there's anything from the office."

"Yeah. About ten minutes past nine." McNeill pressed a couple of keys and listened to the recorded message. "They say an inspector Charbonneau of the Sûreté called for you. They gave him your cell phone number."

"Damn it."

"Bingo. There it is 9:14." McNeill listened. "He says to tell you St. Germaine's farm burned down early this morning. The fire marshal's there. He wants to know if you're on your way. He can wait around for an hour but then he has to go. And for what it's worth the bank says St. Germaine didn't make any withdrawals since last spring and then only a couple of hundred dollars." McNeill next rang headquarters and asked them to recall the forensics team before handing the phone back to Gautier. "Don't forget your wife's call. I left the phone on."

Gautier accepted the jab without comment leaving it to McNeill to fill the silence with a question. "When St. Germaine was murdered yesterday, why didn't the murderer torch the place at the same time? Why take the risk of going back?"

Gautier, who had been absently staring out the side window, shifted position with a sigh so he now faced McNeill. "I dunno. I've been wondering the same thing. There are a couple of possibilities: number one, maybe the two events aren't related. Maybe it really was spontaneous combustion like the fire chief said.

"You don't actually believe that, do you?" McNeill asked.

Gautier thought for a long moment. "No, I suppose I don't."

"So what's possibility number two?"

"Maybe they *are* related—through us." Gautier paused; eyes squinted as if trying to see the crime scene. When he spoke the words came slowly, each carefully chosen. "If our bed sheet theory is correct and he ferried a couple of visitors across the border he presumably could identify them. Shut him down and you shut down that danger. Make it look convincingly like suicide and there won't be any investigation. But a fire would cover up the presumed suicide and thus probably assure an investigation. So no fire."

Gautier was warming to his theory. He leaned closer to McNeill, emphasizing each point as he made it with a poke in the shoulder. "But then *we* show up—the RCMP. It was hardly a secret we were there. And they—whoever 'they' are—must know that our jurisdiction in Québec doesn't usually include murder or suicide and certainly not the suicide of a small time farmer in the Townships. So if we're there, there must be some other reason—the border. Crossing it illegally is within our jurisdiction. They belatedly realize they silenced the witness but left the evidence."

"The truck?"

"Right."

"But how would they know it contained radioactivity?"

"Maybe they wouldn't. But they might know that—like the house—it contained fingerprints."

"Not anymore."

"No," Gautier sighed, "not anymore."

Chapter Eighteen

Le Café Caché, Montréal
Friday, October 2nd
5:15pm EDT

The meeting at the mayor's office seemed to have been more for form's sake than for any concrete gain. So far the investigation into the June bombings had revealed what, when and where but still not who or why. As the participants pushed back from the table and started for the door he was repeatedly stopped to be told how glad they were to have him back among them. The RCMP superintendant had gone a step further.

"I was wondering if you could spare me a moment, minister."

"Sure. Here or someplace else?"

"Someplace else."

Ten minutes later, having avoided a gaggle of reporters waiting by the elevators in the lobby, and joined by an inspector Gautier, they were seated in a booth at the back of a hole-in-the-wall coffee shop appropriately named *Le Café Caché*. It was not only hidden but virtually deserted at that hour. Two nuns sat at a small table near the front and a workman from the city hall repair project was chatting with the counterman. Andrew's security team sat on a couple of stools near the front facing the street. The superintendant's team waited at the curb in a black SUV, motor running.

Andrew ordered ginger ale explaining as he did that "the doctors say I should take it easy on the caffeine for a while." Under no such restriction the superintendent and Gautier ordered coffee and the three engaged in small talk until the waitress brought their orders. The superintendent asked how he was feeling. His concern was genuine. The service had taken criticism for not having done more to protect someone whose outspoken campaign against separatism had, in hindsight, made him an obvious target.

"A lot better than I did a couple of weeks ago," Andrew replied. "I still get a little tired and the shoulder hurts if I lift anything or lean on that arm which makes it a little awkward for sleeping since that's the side I favor but considering..." His voice trailed off. "...anyway, thanks for asking. How's the investigation coming?"

The superintendant looked down and gave his coffee a stir before answering. "Actually that's why we wanted to talk with you." Gautier watched Fraser's expression. There was no change, no reaction, totally open.

"Anything I can do to help," Andrew replied, "but from a certain point forward you realize I had no idea what was going on."

"I quite understand," the superintendant said. "But it's not Compton where we need the help. We need your help in trying to fit together some pieces we've come up with in another investigation."

"Another investigation?" Andrew's surprise was obvious.

"Yes sir," the superintendant replied. "There was an incident at the Stanstead border crossing at the beginning of this week involving a truck whose owner was subsequently found dead, a possible suicide but maybe not. Chief Inspector Gautier here visited the farm where the truck and the dead man were found and...inspector, why don't you fill Mr. Fraser in on what you found."

Gautier cleared his throat. "We found a four year old letter you wrote to a Boyden Mann at the Fairhaven Boat Club concerning guest privileges. On the back of the letter we found your home telephone number, possibly put there by the deceased, who had been an employee of the club."

"What's his name?"

"Fernand St. Germaine."

It sounded vaguely familiar...somewhere he'd come across that name before. He scanned his memories of the club but no face emerged to go with the name. "I don't know...I can't place the name...what did he do at the club?"

"He was a handyman...groundskeeper."

He shook his head. He didn't know the names of any of the grounds crew. "How would he have a letter from me and, more to the point, how would he have my home number? It's unlisted."

"We believe he broke into the club and found the letter and your telephone number in the membership files. A side window to the office had been forced and a lock on one of the file cabinets had been broken. The alarm company reported getting a signal from the club a little after seven Wednesday morning."

"That's bizarre." Andrew frowned. "Why would he want my number?"

"There's more." Gautier pulled his notebook from an inside pocket and thumbed through several pages. "A phone call lasting less than a minute was placed from St. Germaine's phone to that number—your number—at 8:19 Wednesday morning. About a half hour later at 8:46 a second call was placed to the same number. That call lasted a little over five minutes." He closed the note book and put it back in his pocket. "Could you tell us who took those calls and what was discussed?"

"I have no idea." Andrew replied. His expression was one of total bewilderment.

"Who resides at your home besides you?"

"Only my wife."

"Do you have any household employees?" Gautier asked.

"Just a twice a week housekeeper."

"Was she there at the time those calls were made?"

"I'm not sure. This was Wednesday morning?"

"Yes, sir."

"She may have been but I'm not sure…"

"What do you know about her?"

"I…" Andrew felt foolish. "I actually don't know much of anything about her. My wife engaged her. I'm usually in Ottawa during the week and if I am at home I'm most often gone before she arrives and she's gone before I get home. I mean, I've seen her, especially these last couple of weeks when I've been home, but apart from a 'Hi, how are you?' she does her work and I'm usually in my study doing mine. If she's running the vacuum cleaner I have the door closed."

"Do you know where she comes from?"

"I think she comes from the Eastern Townships. Somebody recommended her to my wife." By way of explanation he added, "Marie-Paule also comes from the townships."

"By any chance from Ste. Herménégilde?"

With the mention of the oddly named village everything suddenly came into focus including the phone page with the name St. Germaine which he had dismissed as one of Marie-Paule's many relatives. He felt a stab of fear and his stomach tightened. For a moment he couldn't catch his breath. The inspector's voice sounded distance and hollow. He thought he might pass out.

The inspector did, too. "Are you alright, sir?" Andrew had turned pale and there was a sheen of perspiration on his face. He nodded unconvincingly. The superintendent wasn't buying it and wasn't taking any chances. They had nearly lost him once before when he was in their care. He called sharply to one of the guards at the counter. "Give us a hand." The corporal quickly moved to Andrew's side and, slipping his arm under his good shoulder, started to help him toward the door. Andrew weakly protested he was okay even as he tried to gain his feet but stumbled and sagged against the Mountie. The other patrons sat frozen, watching the drama unfolding in front of them but if they recognized Andrew they gave no sign of it. Within a minute of his collapse he was in an SUV and it was on the move, lights and siren clearing a path through the narrow cobbled streets of Old Town.

RCMP Division Headquarters, Montréal
Friday, October 2nd
6:30pm EDT

Gautier slouched deep in his chair behind the government-issue, gray metal desk. McNeill had tilted a wooden office chair at a precarious angle so he could rest his head against the wall. They each had a cup of watery coffee from the squad room vending machine. McNeill had been listening to Gautier's story of his meeting with Andrew Fraser. "That's a hell of a thing. Is he going to be okay?"

"The security detail says he refused to go to the hospital. Insisted they take him home. By the time they got there he was looking a little better but he still stumbled once or twice going into the building."

"He should have let them take him to the hospital for a look. Let's face it, the guy's lucky to be alive. If that thing had gone off thirty seconds earlier before he got behind the lectern..."

Gautier agreed, "...or if that trash barrel had been a few feet to one side or the other..."

"But you say he seemed perfectly cool until you mentioned Ste. H? Why? What's with that place? His wife doesn't come from there. Does the maid?"

"Housekeeper," Gautier corrected him with a shrug. "I don't know."

"Maid, housekeeper, whatever...and what's with the phone calls to Fraser's private number by St. Germaine and the money...where did he get it?"

"You know," Gautier said, "sometimes trying too hard to find a difficult answer makes you miss an easy one. Charbonneau asked the bank if St. Germaine had withdrawn a thousand dollars. They said 'no'. But what if he just tucked it aside a little at a time from the odd jobs he did; a little tax free nest egg for a rainy day? A lot of country folks don't trust banks."

"How do you explain that it was all in hundreds?"

"Maybe he changed it whenever he had enough so he wouldn't spend it; self-imposed discipline."

"Okay, for the sake of argument let's accept that St. Germaine was salting away a little something for a rainy day and let's further accept that he offed himself not for financial reasons but maybe because he had an unrequited love or was depressed over something he didn't tell his brother. That still leaves the enormous question of how did the back of his truck get to be radioactive. And why did he find it necessary to lie about where he crossed the border?"

Gautier looked very uncomfortable. "You know, I can't help but wonder if I didn't have something to do with his death."

"You?"

"Yeah. Did I push him too hard? Scare him so much that he panicked and..."

McNeill cut off that line of thinking. "Not a chance. I'd remind you we didn't even know his truck was hot when you questioned him. He wasn't a suspect; he was only a possible witness. We didn't even have a search warrant. No, if it was our visit that unnerved him it was because he was hiding something."

"Or protecting someone."

"Who?"

Gautier shrugged. "You know what else is strange?" He didn't wait for a reply, "That boat club. St. Germaine worked there. Fraser and his wife belonged there but they apparently didn't know him, at least by name..."

McNeill corrected him: "You said Fraser didn't know him, maybe his wife did."

Gautier looked skeptical. "You've got to be kidding. I've met both guys. St. Germaine was no Fraser...not the looks, not the smarts, not the..."

"I know some women who would say you're talking like a man. There are a lot of not so great looking guys married to knock-out women. Look at that Italian model who married the French president a few years ago. Guys look at a woman and say 'wow, I want one of those!' But women are a lot less emotional, calculating even, in picking a man. I read somewhere that men see a date as a tactical exercise; women see it as a strategic move. Besides, if she was at the club and Fraser was in Ottawa...hell, people get lonely."

Gautier looked doubtful but McNeill might be right. As a bachelor he was a lot closer to the action. "I suppose that could explain the phone call and even the suicide—if it was suicide—which I'm not convinced of—but, as you say, that still doesn't explain the radioactivity on the back of the truck...and only on the back of the truck, not in the barn, not on his clothes, not even in the cab."

McNeill wasn't done playing devil's advocate, something they often did when trying to sort through a difficult case. "We don't know where that truck had been between the last time he crossed the border legally and Monday night. What if in between he loaned it to someone? He might not have known where it had been or what it had been carrying."

Gautier wished he had a cigarette to go with the coffee. "What if St. Germaine was hired to carry something across the border and the thousand dollars was payment for making the delivery?"

"So why call Fraser's house? You don't suppose..."

"That Fraser is involved in something? I seriously doubt it; he's the bloody defense minister. In that job he has to go through all kinds of security clearances. We probably know more about him than he does. I'd sooner believe St. Germaine was making a play for Fraser's wife. The money might have encouraged him to tell her he was coming to town and suggest they get lunch or something more."

McNeill picked up the narrative. "And what if she didn't just say 'no' but 'hell no' and chewed his ass out for calling and said she was going to tell her husband and get him fired from the club...really went on a rant?"

"And so he went out and hung himself—unrequited love?" Gautier looked thoughtful. "It's as good as anything else we've got to go on. I think I need to talk to the lady"

"When?"

"Now." Gautier glanced at the clock, "Although my wife's going to hang me. But," he added as he stood up and stretched, "if I had known then what I know now there's one more question I would have asked St. Germaine."

"What's that?"

"Where were you on Labor Day? Compton is only a half hour from St. Herménégilde."

"I wouldn't beat yourself up over that one, either," McNeill replied. "We can ask his brother but I'd be willing to bet he wasn't political."

"Not necessarily political, but maybe competitive? After all, it was the husband of the lady he apparently called who was speaking there. What if he decided to eliminate the competition?" Gautier sighed, checked the number Fernand had scrawled on the back of Andrew's long ago letter and reached for the telephone. "I need to talk to the lady."

4861 Chemin de la Côte-des-Neiges, Montréal
Friday, October 2nd
6:00pm EDT

A short nap had cleared his head and quieted, if not silenced, his anxieties. Splashing some cold water in his face he toweled off and then stood for a moment staring in the mirror. All those conversations he'd needed to have with Marie-Paule but had put off because one or the other of them was busy or on their way out or because he was afraid of the consequences now had to happen. The RCMP knew of the Wednesday morning phone call and if they showed up with a search warrant they would surely impound his computer and discover he'd entered the dead man's phone number and retrieved his address hours before he died. How in hell would he explain that without throwing everything on Marie-Paule? And what was "everything?" He didn't know. That's why they needed to have this conversation...and hope to hell it didn't turn into a confrontation although, in point of fact, he didn't actually have anything to confront her with except what he'd heard of her side of the phone call. What if she wouldn't tell him the other side? Well, in that case, she'd have to tell the RCMP and he wouldn't be able to protect her from whatever might result. Hell, he wouldn't be able to protect himself. An illegal border crossing, a dead man, the club, the phone call...his career would be over by the time the first headline was printed and by the time defense lawyers were paid he'd be broke and unemployable if not in jail. It took a physical effort to stop the downward spiral of his thoughts. Summoning a deep breath he squared his shoulders and headed for the kitchen and whatever might remain of his marriage, career and life.

"Andrew!" Marie-Paule beamed at seeing him. It had been this way ever since the attack. "Did you have a good nap?" He nodded. She came around the end of the counter; cute as could be in a flowery apron that was more theater than kitchen. Cooking was not Marie-Paule's strong suit. She was much better at carry-out. Tonight was no exception; some pasta and chicken concoction from a little family-run café halfway between the gallery and home. She'd been making a salad to go with it and had dressed for the occasion. Beneath the apron was a tight black sweater and beneath that...he began to feel himself aroused as she nestled against him. Against every instinct in him he gently but firmly put his hands around her waist—his hands could nearly meet—and lifted her up and onto the counter. A stab in his shoulder told him that was not a smart move but there were consolations. Her eyes opened wide over a mischievous grin. "Mmmm, you're strong." She didn't weigh much over a hundred pounds. There had been so many times when she was being difficult and he would willingly have had a showdown—the night of the prime minister's reception being one such occasion—but now, when they seemed to be regaining what they had had in the opening years of their marriage and had been losing of late—now was hideously not the time to have this conversation. His tangle of conflicting thoughts was interrupted by the shrill of the telephone. Marie-Paule laughed that deep, sexy laugh of hers. "Saved by the bell!" She picked up the receiver and held it out to him. "It's probably your prime minister." She pretended to pout. He couldn't help but smile. Damn it she was so cute, so desirable.

"Hello," he answered in the bi-lingual, neutral greeting they had long ago adopted to guard against accidentally giving away their identity to a chance caller.

"Mr. Fraser," the voice on the other end of the line was gravelly and familiar and not the prime minister. "This is Inspector Gautier at the RCMP. I met you this afternoon. How are you doing sir?"

"Ah yes, inspector. Kind of you to ask. I'm doing much better. Indeed, I'm just about to have supper." Perhaps he'd take the hint. Marie-Paule still had her arms around his neck, her head resting ever so gently on his injured shoulder. She had seen him wince when he picked her up. From time to time she lightly brushed his shoulder with her lips as if to kiss away the pain.

"I must apologize for interrupting you sir. I'll keep it brief. I would like to come by and finish up our interview and if Madame Fraser is there perhaps ask her one or two questions as well."

"When?" Andrew asked.

"If it would not be too much of an imposition, sir, now."

Andrew suddenly had a feeling of being trapped in his own apartment with the RCMP stationed in the hallway and down in the driveway, ostensibly to protect him but maybe not; trapped as he sometimes found himself in his dreams since the bombing, unable to break his way free to wakefulness. "As I say, we are just about to sit down to supper. If you could..."

Gautier didn't let him finish the sentence. "I quite understand sir: I haven't eaten yet, either. Why don't I get a bite and then come by in about an hour. I shouldn't need more than a few minutes of your time."

Put that way, Andrew had no alternative. He thought for a moment of pleading a headache but he'd already told him he was doing better. "Yes, of course. You know where we live? Yes. Then I'll see you in about an hour." He returned the phone to its cradle.

Marie-Paule lifted her head from his shoulder on hearing that and looked quizzically at him. The added height the counter gave her made their faces level, just inches apart. He kissed her lightly on the cheek. "Someone is coming here in an hour?" she asked. "Who?"

Andrew took a deep breath and helped her down. "We need to talk."

In an instant her mood changed from coquette to cool. "We might as well talk over supper." She divided the carry-out onto two plates and brought them and the salad bowl to the table where she had already laid their places. She tugged the apron off over her head and laid it on the counter, then sat down opposite him. Her expression was studied neutrality. She may not have any idea what the subject of their talk was going to be but instinctively suspected it wasn't going to be good.

Facing her across three feet of table space he took a breath and plunged in. "An RCMP inspector is coming to ask us some questions."

She looked puzzled. "They're already here."

"Not them. They're a protection detail. An inspector is coming; a detective."

"Why?"

"They want to know about the telephone call you got Wednesday morning from Fernand St. Germaine. They want to know why he called, what was said...and I don't know what else they want to ask."

As he feared, she flared. "What business is that of theirs? And..." she looked accusingly at him, "how did they know I got a telephone call?"

He put his hand on her arm to calm her. She pulled back fiercely and started to rise. Her reaction triggered something inside him. He spoke with an unaccustomed sharpness. "Marie-Paule, sit down and listen. This is serious. St. Germaine was found *dead* a few hours after you talked to him!"

She didn't sit but slumped, eyes wide with astonishment or was it fear? He continued. "I did not tell them about your phone call. They found our number in his house and they traced all his phone calls for the past several months, including that one. They even know how many minutes you talked. They are going to want to know what you talked about and they will be trying to figure out whether it relates to his death."

"His death?" It was as if the first time he'd told her it hadn't registered. She looked horror struck. "Fernand's dead?" Involuntarily she put her hand over her mouth as if to stop the words and so undo their meaning.

"Before they get here I need to have you tell me absolutely everything; no omissions, no fibs, everything, no matter how embarrassing or painful."

Her eyes suddenly blazed as if he had slapped her. "Embarrassing? You think I had an affair with him? Is that what you think?" Her voice had risen to a near shout; her cheeks had colored with emotion. She again started to get up as if to flee.

He didn't know where his new resolve was coming from but he was having none of it. He fairly roared at her, "I don't know what to think because you haven't told me anything. You've kept me out of your life. But if you don't tell me now..."

"I've kept you out of my life?" Her voice matched his in volume with an added steely edge that was reflected in her eyes. "You are in Ottawa all the time playing with your tanks and boats. Maybe you should have brought one of your boats down to the lake so we could go for a ride together. You think I have a lover? I don't have a lover. I don't even have a husband! It's you who has a lover. You love your politics. I hate your politics! Maybe I hate you!" The explosion suddenly ended in a burst of tears. He wanted to reach out and hold her but the damned table was in the way. All he could do was take her hand and hold it tightly in his. To his surprise she didn't pull it away until she had to daub at her tears.

Snuffling but without further prompting she began to talk. "Fernand works at the club. He's very sweet, very shy. You surprised him once on the raft when I was tanning. He nearly died of fright." She started to smile at the memory. "He sometimes did little favors for me and not just for me. Cook really liked him, too. But he didn't talk much, he was very shy, so most members didn't know him."

"But obviously you did."

She looked rather blankly at him. "I just told you I did."

"I mean he called here Wednesday morning."

"Oh, that." Her voice sounded dull, flat.

"Honey, you've got to tell me as much as you can remember about that conversation."

Marie-Paule looked around for a box of tissues, tugged one free and took what seemed an inordinately long time to sniffle into it. Then she got up and walked across the kitchen to the trash can. Andrew glanced at the clock. It was almost 7:00. The inspector would be here in a few minutes. He looked imploringly at Marie-Paule. "Please."

She sat back down and, pushing her plate aside, folded her hands in front of her.

"What do you want to know?" She asked and then added "And by the way, who are you; my husband or my member of parliament?" Her voice was steady and cool.

He ignored the barb. "Why did he call you?"

"To tell me the RCMP had been to see him."

"Why?"

"Why had they been to see him or why did he call to tell me?"

"Both."

"I don't know why he called to tell me. Maybe because he was scared and he knew my husband was a big shot in the government." The way she said it, "big shot" didn't necessarily come off as a pejorative although it probably was. "He said they asked him a lot of questions about going to the States to deliver hay. When the club is closed he sells hay from his farm to make money. He said he was worried because he got confused when they asked him where he crossed the border and he told them where he usually crossed but that day he had used a different crossing and they had caught his mistake. He said they were very stern with him." She looked up at her husband and quietly asked "Are they going to be very stern with me?"

In that moment he knew he would do whatever it took to protect her. "No, I'll be here with you."

She smiled very softly. "What else do you want to know?"

"Did he say why the RCMP came to see him?"

"I told you; because he made a mistake about where he crossed the border."

"But they wouldn't have known that until they talked to him. Why did they go to see him in the first place?"

She shrugged. "I don't know. You'll have to ask them when they come."

Andrew already knew the answer to his next question but he asked it anyway. "Marie-Paule, is there anything more you want to tell me?"

She managed a little smile. "I don't think so."

Friday, October 2nd
9:00pm EDT

He couldn't help but notice Marie-Paule's mood had lightened with the inspector's departure. She chattered about her day as she put the pasta/chicken concoction from the carryout in the microwave, re-fluffed the salad and, retrieving a bottle from the refrigerator, poured a couple of glasses of Chablis. She seemed not to notice his silence. He put an ice cube in his wine and played with it, stirring it about with his finger. At last the microwave beeped and she ladled the reheated supper onto their plates and sat down in what seemed a display of triumph, whether over cuisine, the inspector or what he didn't know. "That detective," she said, "his questions weren't so bad."

His reply was out of his mouth before he could stop it. "No, but your answers were."

She slowly put her fork down and tilting her head to one side asked "What exactly do you mean by that?"

He also disarmed himself of his fork and taking a deep breath decided it was again time for some very straight talk. "I mean you didn't tell him the truth about the phone call. It wasn't as simple as you made it out to be."

Her eyes narrowed—a definite sign of trouble ahead—but he knew he was facing far greater trouble if he backed down. "You were listening on the other phone?" The edge to her voice made it less a question than an accusation.

"No, I was not. But I could overhear your end of the conversation and it didn't fit with what you told the inspector. You implied that the phone call was nothing more than someone needing some quasi legal counseling which, I might note, you are not equipped to give. But in point of fact that wasn't what it was about, was it?"

Marie-Paule said nothing, nor did she need to. The look on her face said it all and none of it was complimentary. She pushed back her chair and began to gather up her plate and utensils. "Marie-Paule, put those things down, sit down and do it now." Andrew's voice was controlled but it hinted at a seething rage moments away from erupting. She hesitated as she started to reach for the unused cutlery. "If you walk away from this table I will not be able to help you. And if you don't tell me the truth about that telephone call and the $50,000 in our bank account you will be walking toward more trouble than you can begin to imagine."

At the mention of the bank account her eyes widened and she stared straight at him; her look a mixture of disbelief and fear. "How did you know?" She blurted out.

He sidestepped the question. "The account is in both our names."

For a moment she appeared undecided whether to run or stay and fight. Ultimately, she did neither. She slumped back into her chair but still held the plate and utensils, ready to evacuate at a moment's notice. The look on her face was not surrender but neither was it confrontation. She said nothing but the sag of her shoulders spoke for her. He wanted to embrace her, tell her everything would be alright but, as he'd told himself earlier, until he knew what "everything" was he couldn't promise that, not for her, not for himself. Nonetheless, when he spoke his voice was gentle, coaxing, as with a child. "You said you knew you could count on him; that you wouldn't forget what he had done for you. What did he do for you?"

Her voice was so soft that he barely could make out the words over the hum of the refrigerator. "He was kind. He ran some errands. Carried stuff for me; sometimes brought little gifts—vegetables, corn, that sort of thing. It wasn't just me; he did it for cook, too."

"And that's all?" She nodded assent. Her explanation seemed to square with what he could remember of her end of the telephone conversation. But some handfuls of vegetables were one thing, $50,000 was quite another. "Where did the money come from that's in our bank account?"

"It belongs to the gallery." Her voice was stronger. She set the plate and utensils back on the table and sat up a bit straighter.

"Where did the gallery get $50,000?"

"From a very nice man who likes our pictures; sometimes he buys one."

"But why is the money in our bank account?"

"Because he said he was afraid if word of his gift got out everyone would start asking him for money. So he said I should keep the money in my own account and use it to pay for things the gallery needs."

"And the gallery agreed to this?"

Her head went down again and her voice dropped accordingly. "They don't know about it. If I told them we had that much money they would spend it. They talk all the time about moving, maybe to Sherbrooke Street, where more rich people would come in and buy their paintings. Do you know how much a place on Sherbrooke Street costs? The money would be gone poof, like that." She acted out the last part of the sentence. It was a very Marie-Paule thing to do. She loved to perform and he loved to watch her perform. "They are not practical. They have no sense about money. Their heads are all full of pictures, not numbers. When we get money they spend it stupidly." She was speaking louder, more confidently. "So I did not put his gift in the gallery account. When there is something the gallery really needs—like paying the rent or the electric bill—then I withdraw what's needed and tell them we got a contribution."

A sudden thought arrived with a shiver of anxiety. "Was this gift in the form of a check?"

She looked surprised at the question. "Yes, of course..."

"Who was the check made out to—you or the gallery?"

"To me, of course; if it had been made out to the gallery it would have to be deposited in their account." Her voice implied a question: why couldn't he understand they would waste the money if they got it all at once?

"May I ask the name of this donor?" Andrew asked.

Marie-Paule perked up, not at the question, but at the way it was phrased; a request, not a command. The balance of power had subtly shifted. "I will tell you if you promise not to tell anyone else." She held up her right hand in seeming imitation of a courtroom witness except that she had curled her thumb and little finger together making it look more like a Girl Scout oath. Damn she was cute. He couldn't help but smile.

"His name is Mr. Khashan." She spelled it for him.

RCMP Division Headquarters, Montréal
Friday, October 2nd
8:30pm

G autier heaved a sigh and squinted at the computer keyboard. There was yet another of the never-ending reports to be written before he could go home and he wasn't sure how to go about it. A simple chronology copied from his ubiquitous notebook would come across as disjointed. As an inspector he was expected to pull threads together into recognizable patterns which required thinking through what he had learned after a day of asking questions.

Fraser by himself had been open and unguarded in the cafe, at least until St. Herménégilde was mentioned. But that may have been a matter of timing and not topic. The man was less than three weeks away from nearly being blown to bits. By the time Gautier caught up with him, he had already had a full day. St. H and exhaustion simply may have arrived at the same time. While he looked a lot better this evening he was also more guarded. Was that because he was a little "gun shy" already having keeled over in their first session or because his wife was present?

Madame Fraser was another matter. Although stunningly beautiful she was also stunningly unforthcoming. Of all the questions Gautier had asked her in the course of almost an hour seated in their kitchen he had less than a page of answers in his notebook. He would have preferred to interview her separately—and might still find reason to do so—or, at the least, have interviewed the two of them in some other setting. They ended up on one side of the table with him on the other. That was a configuration for confrontation not cooperation. Insofar as the separate chairs allowed, she had snuggled close to her husband and they held hands throughout the meeting. Having interviewed countless people—law-abiding and not—Gautier recognized the hand holding as an instinctively protective gesture. It said, in effect, "I won't let this outsider get to you." And, as he read through his notes, he realized he hadn't. But maybe he had misread it. Maybe it wasn't him protecting her but the other way around. Maybe she was being unforthcoming because she was trying to protect her husband. After all, someone had tried to kill him and the RCMP hadn't prevented the attack and now here they were asking questions.

Did she take a call at about quarter to nine on Wednesday morning? She thought she had. She wasn't sure what time it was.

Who was it from? Fernand St. Germaine.

How did you know him? He works...worked...at the club where Andrew and I are members.

What was the purpose of his call? He was upset and asked me what he should do.

What was he upset about? Your men had been to see him and he was afraid he was in trouble because he had gotten confused and told them the wrong name of the border crossing he had used. And they had threatened him. That, of course, was not true but given how nervous St. Germaine had been during Tuesday's interview he might have thought he was being threatened when, in fact, he'd been let off with a warning. He had not told her he was the one who had been to see St. Germaine.

Why would St. Germaine call her about something like that? She had shrugged and said she didn't know but guessed it was because of her husband. Maybe he thought her husband could do something but he hadn't actually asked for any help.

Had he ever called you before with a problem? No. He'd never called before. That was one of the few times she volunteered information without being asked.

All his questions about her relationship with St. Germaine at the boat club were met with statements about how sweet and shy he was, always willing to do any little service for a member or other staff. She repeatedly mentioned the cook for whom he also apparently did favors.

Had Fraser ever met St. Germaine? He said 'no' and she corrected him saying he had once on a raft in the lake but St. Germaine was so shy he immediately hopped in the water and swam back to shore. Fraser had no recollection of the meeting.

Had she ever visited St. Germaine's farm? No.

Had he ever talked about his farm? Yes. He said he grew hay and sold it in the States. That was all she seemed to know about it.

Had he seemed depressed? She couldn't tell. She didn't know him well enough.

He'd asked about St. Germaine's brother Raymond. She didn't know him.

Who else among the club members had spent any time with St. Germaine? She didn't think any of them had, "except the cook but, of course, she isn't a member."

He had already telephoned both the cook and the club manager and had gotten basically the same story; "sweet boy…shy…helpful…honest…what an awful tragedy."

Questions about Madame Fraser's activities during the rest of the year when the club was closed brought mention of her volunteer work at an art gallery. She had been politically active when her husband first ran for parliament but in recent years had not. He sensed a little resentment on her part at having been relegated to the parliamentary wives club. She was an honest-to-goodness beauty…with perhaps a little more emphasis on "beauty" than "honest". And yet, for the second time in a week, he felt he had failed to ask a key question; but he couldn't think what it might be.

Chapter Nineteen

4861 Chemin de la Côte-des-Neiges, Montréal
Friday, October 2nd
9:30pm

Although it was early, Marie-Paule had gone to bed pleading a headache while he had retreated to his study where he poured a finger of single malt over a couple of ice cubes and added a splash of water. He felt a little guilty about treating a good whiskey like that imagining frowns of disapproval from his Scottish ancestors which, of course, was silly because half of them were tee-totaling Presbyterians.

Apart from a small circle of light from the desk lamp the study was in shadow. Below, the city sparkled before the blackness of the river interrupted. When the lights resumed on the south shore there were fewer of them and spaced farther apart. It seemed an apt metaphor…but for what he wasn't sure.

The sympathetic gains that followed the Compton attack had begun to fade in the three weeks he'd been sidelined and thus effectively silenced. Marcel had tried to fill in for him but from a near dead heat the separatists had re-opened a small but statistically significant lead. And, while the doctors had now given him the okay to resume limited campaigning, there wasn't much time left to make up lost ground, maybe not enough to turn things around without some game-changing breakthrough. but he had no idea what that might be. It seemed as though every plausible argument that could be made for continued national unity had been made. With a sigh he decided the only thing he could do was to keep making them. As if to punctuate his decision, the telephone rang. He quickly scooped up the receiver hoping it wouldn't awaken Marie-Paule. She'd had enough for one day and, frankly, so had he.

"Hello." As always, his greeting was neutral, unidentifiable except to a select few.

"Now that's what I call a quick response. Guess you were just sitting there waiting for me to call, huh?" Mark had a knack for picking his moments.

"Actually I was just sitting here sipping a bit of 10 year old Laphroaig and wondering how half my ancestors considered it heaven's nectar and the other half the work of the devil."

"I guess I don't need to ask which side you came down on," Mark laughed. "Would I be right that you must be making a reasonable recovery if the learned medicos are letting you imbibe firewater?"

"Strictly medicinal plus which I'm only having a sip and that diluted with branch water. It just gives me a faint memory of what scotch used to taste like."

"But you *are* feeling better?"

"Yeah, I really am...which is not to say I don't have my moments." His voice took on a more guarded tone. "I find I'm not handling stress very well."

"That's hardly surprising...any particular stress?"

"Oh...there was a bizarre little episode this afternoon. I damn near lost it when the RCMP told me they'd linked Marie-Paule to a guy who ended up dead after a border crossing incident Monday night."

"Ye Gods! I wouldn't call that a 'little episode'. What the hell happened?"

In relating what Gautier had told him he felt the tension return along with an unsettling suspicion there were things he either didn't know or was failing to connect to what he did know.

"The poor kid. What a hell of a thing…have someone call up and cry on your shoulder and then off themselves. She's must be all ripped up wondering if there wasn't something she should have said or done. To have that weighing on you…" Mark's concern was palpable.

To his surprise, he found his own was somewhat less so. *That's true*, he thought, *she probably should be all ripped up but she really doesn't seem to be. Maybe it hasn't sunk in.* But he couldn't help wondering if he had heard both sides of her conversation with St. Germaine would her story stand up? Lost in thought he suddenly realized Mark had asked him something.

"I'm sorry, I got distracted. Say again?"

"How's the referendum going?"

"I'm not really sure but I should know in a few days. I've been cleared to resume campaigning."

"Is that wise considering what happened?"

"Actually it's probably the best move at the moment. The TV and newspapers are bound to give me more coverage; free publicity."

"Hardly free," Mark replied, "you paid one hell of a price for it."

"Yeah…well…some paid more…one of the officers who was keeping an eye on me… some of the people who turned out for the rally…I got off comparatively lightly."

Mark's silence suggested he didn't agree but he changed subject. "I see where your friends in Paris are still at it."

"How so?"

"There was an item in the *Journal* today that a French company named Areva is rumored to be considering a major investment in Hydro-Québec."

"That's odd, Areva's their state-owned nuclear company. Hydro-Québec doesn't do much of anything in nuclear—just one plant. They're into water power…lots of big generating stations up north."

Mark laughed. "I love that 'up north' expression you guys use. I've got news for you my friend: you *are* 'up north'. Any further north and you'd be going south!"

"It's all relative," Andrew grinned. "Did they say how 'major' Areva's investment is going to be?"

"Not in the story I saw. And it didn't actually say they're going to make an investment, just 'rumored to be considering' which in this town usually indicates 'trial balloon' to see if anyone pops a hole in it."

"What great timing. A French state company says it's thinking about investing in a Québec state company two weeks before the referendum. No prize for subtlety there."

"I have to admit André the Grand seems to be doing his best to counter you...you ask how an independent Québec will defend itself and his aircraft carrier pops up on your doorstep. You ask how an independent Québec will finance itself and Areva issues a press release. You ought to ask how Québec will procreate and see what he sends!"

They shared the laughter but Andrew couldn't help wondering what the reaction to a major French investment would be. It might well cut at his economic argument for continued federalism. But to Mark he only said "It seems to be the season for people handing out money. I just discovered $50,000 in an old bank account."

"Nice find," Mark whistled. "Where did that come from?"

"Some art lover named ummm...Kagan or Kashman—something like that." Andrew fished among the papers on his desk before finding the slip where he'd written the name. "Khashan. That's it, k-h-a-s-h-a-n. He made a gift to the gallery where Marie-Paule volunteers. She raises money for them and tries, without much success, to keep them from blowing it."

"Maybe I missed a step somewhere but didn't you say you found the money in *your* account? Are you suggesting the beautiful lady is into misappropriating funds intended for starving artists?"

"I'm not suggesting that nor am I suggesting they don't deserve to starve. I've seen their work. No, it's something she cooked up with this Khashan guy to keep his name out of the papers and his money out of the artists' hands."

"Sounds like she hit the jackpot—where'd she find him?"

"I gather he just walked in off the street. Apparently he does so every now and again and buys the odd picture...and I do mean odd."

Mark was silent for a moment. Then his voice took on a serious tone. "May I make a suggestion?"

"Feel free."

"Get that money away from you. Have Marie-Paule set up a separate account or something. It's probably fine but I've seen too many pols in this town take a tumble because someone bought them lunch or gave them a ride home on the corporate jet. Fifty grand could buy a hell of a lot of headlines, especially since you don't know anything about him or his money."

"Your point is well taken and, believe me, I'd already come to the same conclusion."

"Speaking of knowing things...has there been any progress in finding out who set off your bomb or the ones in June?"

"No. We had another meeting at city hall this afternoon and the local police, who are investigating the Montréal bombings, are basically at a dead end; the same for the investigation in Compton, although that's an RCMP matter."

"Because you were the target?"

"Yeah." He didn't particularly like being identified as the target. Somehow it made him feel culpable in the deaths that had occurred. In fact, for a time he had asked himself what if he hadn't gone to Compton that day.

It was Marcel who had disabused him of the notion that he bore any responsibility for what someone else had done. "You had choices Andy and so did they," he had argued. "They could have chosen to get up on the platform and debate you. They could have heckled you from the audience. They could have held a rally of their own. They could have ignored you. They did none of that. Instead they chose to murder anonymously—their names unknown and the identities of those they would kill and maim also unknown ... until the bomb went off." It had been a strong argument strongly put and had gone a long way to helping him climb out of the depression that followed the bombing. Still, as he confided to Mark, he had continuing concerns.

"You know how they talked so much after 9-11 about connecting the dots? I got the feeling at the meeting today we don't even know where half the dots are let alone how they connect."

As his friend related his frustrations in the search for the bomber or bombers, Mark idly toyed with his computer. It wasn't that he was inattentive to what Andrew was saying but, as he had once explained to a frowning Dewitt Hamilton after a staffer fidgeted with his Blackberry all through a briefing, it's the electronic equivalent of doodling. Hamilton had not bought the theory but the more Mark found himself "doodling" on the Internet, the more he liked his explanation.

He tapped "Montréal City Hall" into his search engine as Andrew talked about the meeting there. A picture of a grand pile of civic stone popped up on the computer screen. It reminded him of the building he was in. The accompanying text told how the original 1870s structure had been destroyed by fire in 1922 and rebuilt with Beaux Arts touches. As his eyes wandered through the article, his attention began to shift from the voice on the phone to the words on the screen. Gradually he moved from a comfortable slouch to sitting upright. "This new building was modeled after the city hall in Tours, France" the text said. Mark felt his breath catch in his throat.

"Andy," He stopped his friend in mid-sentence, his voice bespeaking urgency. "Andy, when did the Montréal bombings occur?"

"June 25th."

"No, I mean, what time of day?"

"They were all about seven thirty in the evening," Andrew replied; his bewilderment at the question evident in his voice."The police found timers—actually cheap alarm clocks—in the..."

Mark interrupted. "Can you narrow it down?"

"Not really…except for the one at city hall; there was a time stamp on the surveillance video there. That one went off at 7:32 so the others…"

Again, Mark interrupted; his voice anxious. "Andy, listen carefully. I think you're under attack and not from the separatists. I think someone is using the referendum to cover the real agenda."

"You do." His tone—a statement rather than a question—indicated he suspected he was being set up for a joke.

"Andy, I'm serious." Despite his growing excitement, Mark spoke slowly, even as he tried to recall names and dates from history books and security briefings. "I'm reading from a web site that says your city hall is a replica of the city hall in Tours, France."

"I didn't know that but what does that…"

"Andy, Tours is where the Muslim drive to conquer the West was stopped. The decisive battle occurred there in October 732."

For a long moment Andrew sat silent, still uncertain whether his friend was serious. "Are you telling me some Muslims are trying to pick up where they left off 1300 years ago? And if so, why Montréal? Why not Tours…or Paris?"

"Read their websites. They live in the past. For some of them re-establishing the 7th century caliphate is their whole reason for being."

"But, even so, like I said, why Montréal and not Paris?"

"Maybe the original objective *was* Paris. But what if…just *what if* Legrande, who has a big Muslim problem, found a way to export it? He's forever spouting that 'third way' horseshit of his which doesn't solve problems but dumps them on someone else. He did that when he was a mayor and as president he's routinely been doing deals with the world's bastards. Look who he's crawled into bed with, all the time protesting that it's a 'third way'…the French have an expression for that kind of third way: *ménage a trois* where everyone gets screwed!"

Mark's hypothesis set Andrew's mind racing back over the course of the last few months. When he spoke it was in a hushed tone full of wonder. "Dear God, you may have just connected the dots...some of them anyway. The night of the Montréal bombings we talked and I told you that the list of targets didn't make any sense. But, if you're right, maybe they do make sense but from a totally different perspective. We've been trying to fit them into a separatist framework but maybe that's not where they belong." There was a tone of awe in his voice as he catalogued the bomb sites: "The stock exchange wasn't a logical target for the separatists because one of the things that defeated them last time and is hurting them now is that they chased business out of Québec taking jobs with it and ruining the economy. Renard may have a socialist streak but he's never given any hint he has a suicidal one. So why bomb a symbol of Québec's economy unless you actually intend to cripple it and why would he want to do that?

"Two, the community center was in a largely immigrant enclave likely to oppose the referendum which everyone took as sufficient reason for it being a separatist target. But it was more than that. It was a *Jewish* community center." The excitement in his voice grew as his thoughts began to tumble over each other in their haste to be recognized after months in the shadows.

"Three: city hall. It seemed to make sense because the mayor is opposed to the separatists plus the bomb was placed at the foot of Nelson's statue which honored an Englishman who fought the French. But Nelson was killed by a French sniper. Planting a bomb there symbolically hits both French and English and..." He didn't finish that thought but paused and took a deep breath before concluding. The lines between the dots were getting clearer, bolder.

"The fourth target was the cross on the mountain. That baffled everyone. It made no sense for the separatists to topple a symbol of French history and culture which, presumably, is what they're fighting for. And, it made no sense for the federalists to court a certain backlash if they did it and were ever found out. But it all makes perfect sense from the standpoint of an Islamic terrorist." He suddenly felt exhausted and slumped back in his chair before concluding. "But, if we're right, how do we prove it?"

Mark echoed Andrew's question. "Who the hell would believe it? How do we tell anyone without them thinking we're nuts?" He paused for a moment. "And are we? Have we just tugged the sides of the box so hard to make the evidence fit that we've warped it all out of shape?"

For a time there was only silence on the line and then Andrew spoke first, "No, it fits too well. It all fits...even Le Grande's involvement in what shouldn't have been more than a sideshow for him... maybe even the short-selling of the stocks."

"How so?" Mark asked.

"To raise money without leaving a trail...conspiracies aren't free. We thought the bombs were to influence the vote in favor of the separatists but what if the purpose of the bombs wasn't political but financial...to advance the clock so short sales could provide funds? That could explain why no one claimed responsibility. And from that standpoint it probably didn't matter *what* was bombed so long as the bombing was big enough to stampede the markets. Therefore the selection of targets could just as well serve some ideological end, even one as bizarre as your 732 theory. Why waste an opportunity for jihad?" His own words sent a sudden chill through him. "Oh my God," he slowly exclaimed as the possible implications of what might be happening began to dawn on him.

"What is it?" Mark demanded; concern evident in his voice.

"The money...the money that guy gave Marie-Paule! Is that where it came from, the short-selling of the markets after the bombs? Quite literally blood money?"

"It's possible," Mark replied, "what do you know about this Khashan guy?"

"Nothing. I never heard his name before tonight."

Mark continued. "More importantly, is there any connection between the money and the phone call to Marie-Paule from the dead guy? Did he know Khashan?"

"I don't know," Andrew replied. "I don't know anything about either one of them." He paused and then in a quiet voice added "But all of a sudden I feel like a mouse eyeing the cheese while somebody else is eying the trap."

"So like you say, what do we do with this?" It was a rhetorical question. As a member of the National Security Council staff Mark knew what he had to do...but without something solid to support his suspicions he was reluctant. "We've got a theory that events *seem* to fit but do we have any evidence they actually *do*?"

Andrew noted the "we". It was nice to know he wasn't in this alone. "Not yet. I...we... need to make that our number one priority." He thought of Marie-Paule sleeping in the next room. *Maybe he ought to go waken her and demand the answers she didn't give the RCMP.* But Mark's next words made him hesitate.

"Andy, a word to the wise: be careful. Be *very* careful who you talk to about this. A word in the wrong ear...you know better than anyone how hard these people play."

"Don't worry. I'll be careful but don't forget I'm not without a few resources of my own."

Mark seemed not to hear him. "Andy, I may be way out of line here but I'm going to say it anyway and please don't take offense. Until we know a lot more I'd be very, very careful what I said to Marie-Paule."

He could hear a sudden chill in his friend's voice. "Meaning what?"

"Meaning somebody may be using her to get at you without her knowing it ... certainly without her knowing it. She could be dangerously naive not only as regards your safety but hers as well."

There was a long silence on the line before Andrew replied. "I take your meaning." After a further pause he audibly cleared his throat. "Let's give this some thought." He was about to hang up but before he did so he quietly added, "I do understand what you're saying. I'm also aware that we're racing the clock. It's already October...battle month if you're right. If they set off bombs to raise money and to try to silence a cabinet minister, I don't think we'd better assume there are any limits to what they might do. I need to get up to Ottawa and sound the alarm. After all, I'm the defense minister and if what we surmise is actually happening, I've got to start playing defense."

"And if Marston doesn't agree?"

"Then, if I have to, I'll go public with what I've got and let the chips fall where they may. I can't just sit here and hope that those bastards run out of bombs."

"I wouldn't do that," Mark replied. "You lift the lid without knowing what's inside the box and there could be an explosion the likes of which even you can't imagine. Whatever you do, I urge you not to do that."

"I can't just sit idly by."

"I'm not suggesting you do that either. Go see Marston by all means. I'm going to go see Hamilton. But work inside the system. It's designed to deal with this sort of thing. That's why you have the Mounties and we have the FBI. Hell, they may already know stuff we haven't even thought of. It's their job is to find the dots. Our job is to connect them, put them into some kind of context. And that's what you and I have just tried to do. But like you said, our problem is neither one of us has enough dots to make a complete picture."

There was a long pause from the Montréal end of the line. When at last Andrew spoke there was an edge to his voice. "Mark, do you know something you aren't telling me?"

"Andy, at this point I honestly don't know whether I do or not. It's that Rumsfeld thing: the stuff we know; the stuff we don't know; and the stuff we don't know that we don't know. I'm thinking we've got the first two covered but the last one could blow up in our faces if we start lifting lids without knowing what's under them."

The conversation ended with a promise to talk again after confronting their leaders with their suspicions. Realizing he couldn't deny sleep any longer, Andrew clicked off his desk lamp and, after double checking the security lock on the hall door, went into the guest room and fell into bed.

The White House
Friday, October 2nd
10:00pm EDT

F ar to the south Mark switched off his computer and prepared to lock up and head home. Part of his mind was relieved that at last there seemed to be an intelligible framework for the questions that had been troubling him yet he was still bothered that there was so little hard information to mount in the frame. *But...perhaps... there was something he could do about that.* Putting his keys back on the desk he pulled the telephone toward him, thought for a moment and then tapped some numbers onto the keypad. The line rang only once before a voice growled "Yup." No "Good evening," no "Hello," not even a name.

"Gordon. Mark."

The growl turned into recognizable speech. "Hey pal, isn't it a little after your bedtime?"

"Nah, I sleep on the job."

"Wish I could. So what crisis keeps you sober and in the office on a Friday night?"

"No crisis. Just need some information...informally. I need anything you have squirreled away on a well-heeled guy by the name of Khashan. Let me spell that for you." He felt vaguely uneasy as he did so. He certainly had the authority to request information from the security agencies but this was not entirely official—"informal" as he had said, but maybe rising to "quasi-official". Canada was part of his brief and for the past few months worrisome things had been happening there. At first he'd written them off as coincidence but after tonight's conversation with Andy he couldn't continue doing so. The latest "coincidence"—the $50,000 found in the bank account of one of the leading opponents of the separatist referendum—gave him a starting point and, as such, provided the official part of his request. The quasi part was that the leading opponent also happened to be a longtime friend.

The voice on the phone reclaimed Mark's attention, "First name?"

"Sorry. I don't have one."

"Address?"

"I don't know but he's recently surfaced in Montréal."

"Nationality?"

"I don't know that either although from the looks of his name he's probably some sort of Arab."

"You're really trying to make this easy for me aren't you?"

"I'm sorry Gordy but that was all I was given except that he apparently has an interest in art and is rich enough to be a patron. But I know if anyone on earth can find him, you're the man." He and a battery of very big, very fast computers; search engines not unlike Google or Yahoo where you typed in key words, names, phrases, phone numbers—whatever you had—and they started looking for links. The big difference was Gordon's computers could look in places Google and Yahoo couldn't go or wouldn't dare to go. "Is there anything you can do with that?"

"Without getting into means and methods—maybe. We'll cross-check his name against all the usual suspects...drug runners, other criminal types—plus a few don't-let-them-in lists—although those names usually begin with el or al. And maybe we'll poke around in a couple of other places you don't want to know about. If I do turn up something how far do you want me to push it—listen to a few phone calls, read some faxes or e-mails, look for fetishes?"

"Not at this point, let's just see if we can put a label on the guy."

"Labels are free but if you do decide you want to get into the other stuff you'll have to shoot over some paperwork with a FISA stamp." There had been all hell to pay when the strict letter of the

Foreign Intelligence Surveillance Act was bypassed in the wake of 9-11. Having been singed, there was an understandable reluctance in the intelligence community against being burned. A piece of paper with the right signature could keep careers from going up in flames.

"I understand. How long do you guess it'll take?"

"What priority? Are we cutting into line or waiting our turn?"

"Waiting our turn…but not waiting too long. Like I said, it's informal…at least at this point…informal but not casual."

"I'll see what I can do. Maybe I can get some search time this weekend." As he thanked him and hung up Mark wondered how long it would have taken to get answers if he'd gone through channels. No political science text he'd ever read had mentioned the salubrious effect on the functioning of government that could come from a couple of extra Capitols tickets.

Chapter Twenty

The Ellipse
Monday, October 5th
7:45am EDT

Science teaches that the special look of autumn is caused by the refraction of sunlight through the atmosphere. Literature offers more poetic explanations. For his part Mark only knew a day like this wasn't meant to be spent indoors but there was a briefing paper that had to be done in preparation for the upcoming Paris summit.

To make the moment last, he slowed as he walked the several blocks from his parking space to the EEOB. But even as he was delaying his arrival at work, his work proved not content to wait. He tugged the insistent cell phone from his pocket. Its window showed no calling number.

"Hello."

"Hey pal, I think we've found the fellow you're looking for."

"That didn't take long."

"Interesting character."

"Do tell."

"Not on an open line. I think you'll find this is eyes-only." His caller laughed before adding, "That's a little term of trade craft I picked up at the movies."

"I'm on my way in now."

"Give me a call when you get there and I'll send it over."

"Thanks Gordy. I owe you one."

"Actually two; if we weren't on an open line I'd remind you of what the other one was."

"Two it is then," he laughed. "I'll talk to you in a bit." With that he picked up his pace, the poetry of another autumn day ended almost before it began.

The White House
Monday, October 5th
8:00am EDT

"Is this all?" Apart from the cover page with "Classified—Eyes Only" printed in large type above the routing information there was only a single sheet of paper.

"That's all they sent, sir". The communications room clerk sounded a little defensive. "The cover sheet says there was only supposed to be one page."

Mark thanked him and headed for the stairs, not pausing to read the document. You don't read classified material in public spaces, no matter how tempting. But with his office door closed behind him he eagerly scanned the single page. It contained perhaps two dozen lines of type laid out like a job application. It began with the basics:

Name—"Khashan, Hakim
Age—64
Place of Birth—Beirut, Lebanon
Occupation—Directeur Général, Banque Levant
Address—12 Avenue Foch, Paris 75116

He knew Avenue Foch. It was in the 16th arrondissement, very upscale. Khashan's home address was the same. Apparently he lived above the store. On Avenue Foch it was not unusual to have a tony business on the ground floor and an elegant owner's flat upstairs. The bank's phone was listed but there was no home number. He was educated at St. Joseph's in Beirut, a French-speaking Catholic college, and had an MBA from Insead. There was scant other personal information, not even whether he was married. Nothing that would suggest he was anything but very rich and very discrete. No mention of being an art collector although with an address in the 16th arrondissement odds were good that he had something more than posters on his walls. It wasn't until he got to the last section marked "Additional Information" that he understood why Gordy didn't want to say anything over the phone. It came in a single sentence: "Khashan is reputed to be an informal advisor to President André Legrande." It didn't say what he advised on or whether his advice was taken.

His job demanded skepticism but as someone once observed: "One is chance. Two is coincidence. Anything more is conspiracy." Khashan's links to both the French president and the wife of the Canadian defense minister could qualify as one and two. But was there more?

He stood thinking for a long moment, then unlocked a desk drawer and pulled out a well-worn Rolodex which he thumbed through until he found a number that came with a procedural code. It rang only once before being answered with a medium-pitched tone. He said nothing but when the tone ended he tapped in the code number from the card, hung up and waited, drumming his fingers on the desktop. Less than a minute passed before his phone rang. He let it ring twice more before picking up and re-entering the code number. If the codes hadn't matched he would only be hearing a dial tone instead of a voice which inquired if she could help him. He didn't ask who was speaking. It didn't matter and she wouldn't have told him anyway.

"I'm looking for incident reports from the Québec border last Monday night, probably somewhere in Vermont, maybe New Hampshire. I'll hold." He began to drum his fingers on the desk top.

Surprisingly, the caller returned almost immediately. For the next minute or so he mostly listened, making a few notes on his yellow pad. Once or twice he asked for a spelling. "The one at Stanstead, who else has been actioned on that?" He made a brief notation. "Uh-huh. Yeah, if you could send over a copy. Right. I'll be watching for it. Many thanks." With that he hung up and resumed drumming for a time before locking away the yellow pad and the Rolodex and heading back downstairs to the communications center. They would have brought the fax to him but during the morning rush it probably would take longer than he wanted to wait.

Five minutes later, back in his office with the IBET incident report in hand, he flopped on his couch to plow through the quasi-bureaucratize in which such things were written, in this case by someone named Alain Proust on September 28th. But the first sentence brought him bolt upright. "A radiation detection monitor reported a low level incident at 9:27 pm this date. The coincidence of the alarm with the movement of vehicles was not observable by the agent on duty. However a vehicle in transit through the facility may have been in position to observe the movement of traffic at the instant of the alarm." The Québec license number of what was described as an empty flatbed farm truck followed. In another section of the report headed "Recommended Action" it noted that a request had been made to have the radiation monitor checked and, if need be, recalibrated. A routing stamp indicated that both the RCMP and FBI had been copied on the IBET report.

The second page contained the RCMP response dated a day later. It was brief and to the point. They had traced the truck and interviewed its owner/driver, a man named Fernand St. Germaine. His description of events was consistent with the border agent's report but he apparently had already moved on when the radiation reading occurred. Interestingly, they said he misreported where he had crossed into the States that morning. The "Recommended Action" box was blank but there was a second report attached dated the following day.

They had gone back to re-interview St. Germaine and found him dead, an apparent suicide. That was what Andy had said. What came next in the RCMP report he had not said: "Low level radioactive contamination consistent with Cesium 137 was detected on the extreme rear of the St. Germaine truck bed."

He began to pace the office. Why hadn't Andy said anything about radiation? Surely he must have known. He picked up the phone again and, with a glance at the clock, dialed. It was early enough that he might still catch him at home. The line clicked a couple of times and then he heard the ring tone...once, twice, three times. The line must have rung a half dozen times in all before a husky female voice said "Hello" and then, first in French, then in English, asked that the caller leave a message. She didn't say why, didn't claim they were not in or otherwise occupied. That was left up to the caller's imagination. Her message delivered, the answering machine beeped that it was the caller's turn. Aware of what he'd cautioned, he purposely kept his message light. "Hey, it's me. Don't be surprised if I call back a few more times just to hear that sexy voice! It's about twenty minutes to nine Monday morning the 5th. If you get a chance, give me a holler. I'm in the office. Talk to you later." He rang off feeling more than a little uncomfortable as he did so. Raising suspicions with your best friend that his wife may be party to a plot to break up the country, establish a terrorist base in North America and, incidentally, get him killed in the process, could poison a friendship. But so could radiation.

Monday, October 5th
5:30pm EDT

What had begun as a beautiful fall day had deteriorated until a soft mist enveloped the city. Not quite enough to qualify as drizzle; it had still been enough to make him hurry as he crossed from the EOB to the West Wing. Beyond the Ellipse a line of headlights signaled workaday Washington was on its way home, near gridlock as always. That was one "benefit" of working here. No one's day was ever done until long past rush hour.

Amid work on the briefing paper, he'd searched without success for anything that might add credence to his theory that a malign third force could be at work under cover of the Québec referendum. There had been nothing further from Andy. His phone call hadn't been returned. He'd been tempted to try again but waited; hoping for a reply that hadn't come until now he'd run out of time and was facing his boss with something well short of proof.

"Good evening Mark." DeWitt Hamilton always managed to give the impression that you were a welcome interruption in his day unlike so many in Washington who only acknowledged that you were an interruption. "How are you keeping?"

"Quite well thank you. And you sir?"

"Considering that I once thought I'd be long retired at this point in my life, not too badly. But other than a gracious concern for my well-being, what brings you to see me?" He waved Mark to one of two chairs that sat in front of his desk while he took the other. "Mrs. Reilly tells me you have something you wish to discuss."

"Yes sir," Mark replied. "You asked me to keep an eye on the situation in Québec. I have been doing so and I believe there is a pattern emerging that—while I cannot yet fit it into a formal threat assessment—I felt it should be brought to your attention."

"Threat? To us?"

"Yes sir."

He had Dewitt Hamilton's full attention. "Do tell."

And he did, beginning with the risk of having a rogue state emerge on America's northern border; one motivated more by emotional impulses than rational economic and political policies thus making its ultimate course uncertain and, perhaps, inadvertently creating a strategic outpost for international troublemakers. In that context, he also reviewed the French interest in the Québec referendum including the voyage of the de Gaulle and the potential investment by the state-owned energy company. "French involvement in Québec separation," he summed up, "would almost certainly produce severe strains within the North Atlantic Alliance with both Canada and France potentially demanding our backing, a difficult if not untenable position."

"But not an entirely unfamiliar one," Hamilton observed.

"True enough, sir, but usually played out farther from home. I'm concerned the domestic tensions that have built up over our southern border could easily be transferred to the northern one given a little prompting from Capitol Hill and the press. The effect might well be to further strain relations with Ottawa which are already under some pressure from even the limited measures we've taken to rein-force the border." A requirement that a passport was required to enter the States from Canada and unmanned predators flying along remote reaches looking for illegal crossings had raised Canadian hackles. But, as there was no further response from Hamilton, Mark continued. "In any event, what has prompted my present and more specific con-cern is information I received Friday night from my friend, Andrew Fraser, who, as you know, is the Canadian defense minister as well as a member of parliament from Montréal. As such he has taken a prominent role in arguing the case against the Québec referendum."

"Yes," Hamilton replied, "isn't he the fellow someone tried to kill a few weeks ago? Did they ever find out who?"

"No sir. But he was to have resumed campaigning this past week-end so apparently they think they've got security under control."

Hamilton grunted, perhaps skeptically. It was hard to tell. "Please continue."

"As I said, I rang him up Friday evening to see how he was doing. In the course of our conversation he told me of a couple of incidents which may suggest an effort could be underway to discredit him and, by extension, the federalist effort. A person who worked at a summer club where he and his wife are members was implicated last week in a border crossing incident. A day or two after that the fellow rang up

Andy's wife asking her advice in dealing with the RCMP who were inquiring into the incident. A few hours later, the fellow was found dead at his farm not far from the border, an apparent suicide. The Mounties obtained his phone records and thus learned of the call to Mrs. Fraser although so far they have not made it public."

Hamilton was listening attentively but a slight frown suggested he was uncertain where this was leading. Mark noted the frown and moved quickly to his next point. "He also told me that he had discovered a $50,000 deposit in an otherwise dormant bank account on which he and his wife are co-signers. She told him it was a gift to an art gallery where she volunteers from a donor who wished to remain anonymous and who had suggested that she, in effect, 'launder' his contribution through her account."

Hamilton's frown deepened. Mark pressed on. "Andy of course recognized the potential for mischief and they presumably have moved the funds to an account in the gallery's name. But I was curious whether someone might be attempting to set him up and thus influence the referendum so I made a few inquiries about the donor, a man named Khashan." Mark handed one of the two intelligence reports he had received Saturday to the National Security Advisor. "I would draw your particular attention to the last entry marked 'additional information.' "

Hamilton's frown was replaced by a look of surprise as he quickly read to the bottom of the page. "I don't know him."

"Nor I sir, but it suggests there could be more than we thought to the French connection." Mark paused to rearrange his papers before continuing. "I also asked Homeland Security for any records they might have of incidents on the Québec border last Monday night, the date in question." He handed over the second report. "This one from the Stanstead border station caught my attention."

Hamilton accepted the second report from Mark, quickly skimming down the page to the section marked Description of Incident.

As he read what Alain Proust had written the frown deepened across his brow.

"This is a Canadian port of entry?"

"Yes sir."

"...meaning that whatever set off the alarm was entering Canada, not the United States?"

"Yes sir."

"And this fellow who called Fraser's wife is believed to have been involved?"

"It would appear so, sir. He passed through there about that time and, as you'll note on the third page, a subsequent investigation by the RCMP found traces of Cesium 137 on the back of his truck." Hamilton turned the page and as he read the frown returned.

"Is there some connection between this St. Germaine and Khashan?"

"Other than their both having been in contact with Andy's wife? I don't know, sir. But if there is, Khashan's apparent ties to Legrande could raise some serious questions."

"Such as?"

Mark felt uncomfortable under Hamilton's probing. It crossed his mind that he was facing a one-time corporate lawyer who was not unfamiliar with taking depositions, "Such as whether a third party is taking advantage of the separatist movement and the referendum."

"The French?"

"Yes, but maybe others who would be of greater concern to us. If you could indulge me a moment longer..." Hamilton didn't say anything but neither did he glance at the clock or otherwise betray any impatience. He simply nodded his head signaling Mark should continue.

"You may recall, sir, that after the June bombings in Montréal I told you that the targets didn't seem to make much sense. I would amend that opinion now to suggest that while they didn't make much sense from the standpoint of a Québec separatist, they may have made a lot of sense from the standpoint of an Islamic terrorist."

Dewitt Hamilton was not a man who was easily surprised. While all about him were losing their composure, he could be counted on to remain calm and analytical, even to the point of seeming to be coldly detached. It was one of the qualities that had recommended him for the job of National Security Advisor. Whatever advice he might tender, it would not be an emotional reaction to events. Even now his outward demeanor did not change, although a sharp eye might note that he had uncrossed his legs and was sitting a bit straighter, his hands no longer folded in his lap but resting on the chair arms. However all he said to Mark was "Do tell." And he did, going through the list of targets, ending with the 732 coincidence.

For a long moment, Hamilton didn't respond but sat staring past Mark toward the windows and the street lights outside which seemed to belong to another, distant place. When at last he did speak, it was not to react to the remarkable hypothesis he had just been given but to return to the border incident. What more can you tell me about the radiation alert? What did your friend say about it?"

"He didn't mention it."

"He didn't? Doesn't that strike you as odd?" In the silence that followed the only sound in the room was the distant traffic on 17th street and the ticking of the Seth Thomas clock that sat on the mantle. At last, when Hamilton again spoke, his voice was barely audible. "Are you familiar with Occam's razor?" he asked.

"Yes, sir. I believe that's the principle that says all things being equal, the answer employing the fewest assumptions is probably the correct one." He suddenly felt as though he was back in Professor Bailey's office reviewing the umpteenth draft of his thesis.

"Indeed," Hamilton agreed, audibly drawing a breath as he spoke. "Indeed...and so if in the spirit of Occam's razor we were to shave your thesis to its essentials what would we have left?" It was a rhetorical question which he proceeded to answer. "I believe we would have several expressions of the government of France looking out for French interests and, in the process, seeking to expand French influence in a French-speaking community abroad. I would submit that is not out of keeping with the norms of any state. We ourselves pursue interests which put us in competition—if not contention—with Canada which, nonetheless, we rightly consider a friend. While we are each other's largest trading partner with half our oil imports coming from Canada and while we have a shared economic and security interest in the St. Lawrence Seaway, it is also true that we are not in agreement regarding mineral rights in the Arctic and we clearly disagree about the Northwest Passage which we regard as an international strait and Canada regards as an internal waterway. So in some of our relations we are very sympathetic to our neighbor and in some we are at cross purposes. To keep so complex a relationship on the friendly terms that have long prevailed we must be very careful to set forth our interests and concerns in a clear, forthright manner and assume the Canadians and the French and other friends will do the same. What we cannot do is to try to see the world from their side of the table. We don't sit there. They do."

Not for the first time Mark wondered whether his reasoning was being skewed by his history. For a time, as a McGill student, he had absorbed Canada's memories and ambitions. Had that experience, coupled with a close friendship on the other side of the border, blurred a line that his job required he not cross? Perhaps Hamilton was wondering the same thing for he continued to deconstruct what until now had seemed a convincing case for concern.

"We also have a series of incidents which we suspect may have some common denominator but at present we cannot say what that might be, in part, because one of the principals is dead and because another did not tell you all of what we presume he knew about the most serious of these incidents. I commend you for not taking his report at face value and for ferreting out additional information. I would suggest you now carry that effort a step further and see what follow-up action Homeland Security has undertaken. Since we know the FBI was alerted, let's find out what, if anything, they've learned and ask them to query the RCMP on the status of their investigation. I must say I am a bit perplexed as to why the alarm was triggered going into Canada and not the other way around. Perhaps they can find out."

Mark nodded as Hamilton continued. "As to the conditions Mr...." he paused and consulted the papers Mark had given him, "... Mr. Khashan attached to his gift to the art gallery, I can assure you that having worked with wealthy individuals much of my life, they not uncommonly attach odd conditions to what otherwise would be straightforward transactions. You wonder if it might have had something to do with his apparent status as an advisor to M. Legrande. In point of fact, it might as easily have had something to do with his status as a bank director. Or it might simply have been an effort, as he said, to protect his privacy and not open himself to importuning from other worthy causes."

There was a discrete tap on the door. "Come," he called without raising his voice. Mrs. Reilly's tap and Hamilton's muted response assured that whatever conversation was in progress would stop before she opened the door.

"Your six o'clock is here," she advised.

"Would you be so kind as to ask him to indulge me for a few minutes? There are a couple of points Mark and I need to clarify." Mrs. Reilly nodded and withdrew as quietly as she had entered, the door clicking closed behind her.

Hamilton continued where he had left off as though there had been no interruption. "And then there is the matter of the symbolisms that might attach to the Montréal bomb sites. I think we would have to agree that most dramatic events lend themselves to interpretation, usually depending on where one stands while observing them. You perhaps correctly surmise how the targets might be viewed from the standpoint of an Islamic militant but you do so, if I may note, from Washington. For good reason we tend to see terrorists in many different places, some, no doubt, where they do exist and some, perhaps, where they do not. That is why we maintain a large and expensive intelligence and investigative capability to sort out which is which. Otherwise we are susceptible to constructions of our own making which could take us in unwarranted directions. A few discrete inquiries as to what extent, if any, terrorists are believed active in Canada would therefore be in order. It might also be worth checking to see how accurate the timing mechanism on the city hall camera is. I think it is fair to suggest that 7:35, though only minutes away, might not bear the same significance as 7:32."

Mark felt distinctly uncomfortable, even foolish, in the face of Hamilton's logic. It must have shown in his face for the National Security Advisor's next words contained a bit of balm. "We have had a hard time 'connecting the dots', as they say, and past failure to do so carried a very high price. That is why I frequently must remind myself of Occam's razor and why I pass it along to you for whatever use you can make of it in obtaining *actionable* intelligence."

Stirring in preparation for ending their meeting, Hamilton added, "Do continue to keep your eye on what's happening north of the border, check out that radiation incident and let me know what you learn and would you please write up what you have told me so that perhaps I can pass it along?" Hamilton did not have to say to whom; that was understood. He also did not have to say "therefore you will be working late tonight". That too was understood.

Tuesday, October 6th
8:30am EDT

So far the only part of breakfast he had touched was the coffee. Maybe he'd get to the rest of it in a little while; maybe not. He'd had to struggle until nearly midnight with the wording of the Québec brief for Hamilton, in part because the National Security Advisor insisted that "brief" meant just that and in part because he needed to build a case without reference to the parts Occam's razor had shaved off. The end result was a tightly-worded two pages that essentially said there might be a problem if a) the radiation alert at the Canadian border crossing turned out to be more than a malfunction in a sensor and b) if the separatists triumphed at the polls and subsequently created the equivalent of a no-man's land on the northern border which more malign forces might seek to occupy as the drug cartels had done along the Mexican border or al Qaida had done along the Pakistani border. But, despite having produced a reasoned, non-alarmist document for Hamilton, his own concerns remained undiminished even after six hours sleep. The feeling persisted that there was more to come and it was unlikely to be good. He would not have long to wait for his premonition to be realized. As he returned to his now cold breakfast the telephone interrupted. "Mark, Steve Hanson." Hanson was an assistant to the White House press secretary. "What do you know about a radiation incident last week on the Vermont border?"

"I know there was one. Why?"

"One of the New York papers has an interview with some truck driver who says he was pulled out of line at the border, frisked and he and his truck swept with a Geiger counter. He says the customs agents told him something had triggered a radiation alarm. But he proved clean. So the paper—the *Daily News*—is asking if not this guy and his truck, then who and where is the hot truck? They quote some unidentified asshole at Homeland Security as saying...just a sec... let me find it ...as saying 'this has long been our number one worry that terrorists might infiltrate a nuclear device into the United States through a port or across a border'. The boss is in there now with the old man trying to figure out what to say without setting off a panic."

"Say the alarm went off at a *Canadian* border post, not an American one. The truck was going the other way."

"Is that true?"

"Absolutely. And you can add that it was so low level a reading that the first reaction of the agent in charge at the border station was to call for technicians to check the alarm."

"Did they?"

"I don't know. Like I said, it's on the Canadian side. You'd have to ask them."

"Is there anything else I should know?"

"Yeah, but that's the fault of the U.S. education system and we can't fix it in time for your briefing." The assistant press secretary took the cue and laughed. Crisis contained; at least for now, at least on this side of the border.

The *Daily News* was not one of the papers on Mark's regular reading list. He could have asked the press office to send over a copy but it was quicker to access it on-line. He found the story under the headline "A Ride to Remember". A picture of a short middle-aged man in a uniform standing beside a big moving van accompanied the article.

"Twice each week Joe D'Annunzio leaves Queens for destinations across the eastern United States and Canada. Riding with him are fifteen to twenty tons of dishes, lamps, furniture and family keepsakes. The object is to get them where they're going without breaking any. That calls for care. As a long-distance driver for Allied Van Lines, Joe logs close to two thousand miles in a typical week and has done so for nearly 30 years. At that rate, he estimates he's driven nearly three million miles in summer heat and winter blizzards. With only two fender-benders and as many tickets in all those miles, Joe is rated one of Allied's top drivers. He's survived breakdowns in remote, snow-clogged mountain passes and more than once dodged disaster on a crowded interstate. He says he's had some strange experiences in his travels but never anything like what happened last Monday on what was supposed to have been a routine run from New York to Montréal.

"'It was about nine o'clock at night and I had just entered the Canadian customs post at Stanstead, Québec when all hell broke loose,' D'Annunzio recalls as he sips a beer at the 'D Street Tavern' in

Bayside where he and his friends—many of them drivers like himself—swap stories when they don't have to be behind the wheel the next day. 'Professional drivers, like airplane pilots,' he explains, 'don't drink for at least twelve hours before they make a run.'

"The 58 year old D'Annunzio says he had just pulled into the customs post when something set off a radiation alarm. 'They blocked off the road ahead of me with a prowl car as though I might try to make a run for it. They took my cell phone so I couldn't call anybody, frisked me like you see the cops do on TV, ran a Geiger counter up one side of me and down the other and asked me a hundred questions.'

"D'Annunzio admits he was scared. 'I mean when someone tells you your truck's set off a radiation alarm and you've been sitting in it for eight hours, you'd be scared, too.' He says a customs agent climbed all over his van checking for the source of the radiation while he was held and questioned in the border post. After more than an hour they told him his truck was clean and that he was free to go. A check with the other drivers found none had experienced a similar problem crossing the Canadian border although all said long lines and lots of questions had become commonplace since 9-11. Canadian authorities won't confirm whether there was a radiation alert at Stanstead last Monday night but a source in the Department of Homeland Security says 'this has long been our number one worry that terrorists might infiltrate a nuclear device into the United States through a port or across a border.' The question is, if Joe D'Annunzio's van didn't set off the radiation alarm last Monday night, what did? Meanwhile Joe says it was a night he won't forget. He calls it 'a moving experience.' "

For a moment Mark considered putting in a call to Andy to alert him to the story but he decided to hold off until he could see whether it "had legs" or, unfed, would fade away on its own.

Tuesday, October 6th
11:00am EDT

The business of the morning behind him and some time to spare
before a luncheon at one of Washington's think tanks, Dewitt
Hamilton put the first of the two reports Mark had given him the
previous evening on his desk and asked Mrs. Reilly to place a call for
him. In due course the intercom clicked and she advised that Paris
was on the line.

The greeting from the other end was warm, expansive and friendly.
Hamilton responded in kind. "Jean-Pierre, how good to hear your
voice. It has indeed been too long. Margaret sends along her greetings
to you and Annette. We look forward to seeing you both at the G-7.
We're hoping to tack on a couple of days after it to enjoy Paris." He
paused before continuing, "Well that would be very kind of you.
We'll tentatively accept right now and will work out the details when
we get there if that's all right with you. Excellent."

The requisite—and in this case sincere—niceties dispensed with,
Hamilton got down to business. "I'll tell you why I called. We have
been remiss in thanking you and André for your stand on the sea bed
situation. As you can appreciate it is a little difficult for us to take too
aggressive a stance given its potential for conflict with a neighbor but
we share your concern about Russia's overreach."

He listened for a bit before replying. "Quite. And, of course,
your reaffirmation of the right-of-passage through an international
waterway was additionally welcome here as the principle is of broad
practical consequence to us." For the next several minutes their conversation touched on a variety of issues from the Middle East to
China. While they generally shared concerns they were not entirely
agreed on how best to address them with the Cardinal emphasizing
the value to the United States of France following André Legrande's
nuanced 'third way' which would give it influence in places where

the United States had little while Hamilton emphasized the need for sending clear signals that a firm, united western stand would provide. For his part the French president's foreign policy advisor professed to be concerned lest firm signals harden into opposing camps as had so often happened in the post war years while the American president's national security advisor expressed concern that opponents would seize on any perceived division in the alliance as an opportunity for procrastination and perhaps mischief. At length they agreed that the subject should be revisited over dinner in Paris.

"It has been good talking with you my friend," Hamilton finally said signaling the conversation was nearing its end, if not quite there yet. "But oh, before I go Jean-Pierre, I wanted to ask you...and I'm not entirely sure how to put it...so please take no offense if I word it inelegantly...but *are you entirely okay?*" He carefully separated the last four words giving the question added dramatic effect and then awaited the inevitable question before continuing. "Well, I had an item cross my desk the other day that described someone named Khashan as a foreign policy advisor to André and that, I must admit, raised my concerns since you and I have known each other for more years than I care to admit to and, if I may say so, have worked rather well together."

Hamilton wore a slight smile as he listened to the protestations from the other end of the line and the anticipated follow-up question which he obliquely answered. "His name came up as a 'person of interest' in connection with some inquiries we were making."

His smile broadened as the telephone call finally came to an end. "Well, that's a great relief Jean-Pierre. You have put my mind at ease. It is not often that one gets to work with someone whom you can both respect and like. I do hope I didn't disturb you by mentioning it but I must admit I was concerned. So, I look forward to seeing you. Keep well my friend." As Hamilton hung up he laughed softly.

Chapter Twenty-One

55 Rue du Faubourg Saint-Honore, Paris
Tuesday, October 6th
5:30pm CEDT

"Ah, Jean-Pierre, perfect timing. How nice to see you, my friend. I was just thinking how pleasant it would be to enjoy a modest aperitif before I must suffer through the British trade show dinner. They always serve Beef Wellington at these affairs no doubt thinking they're being terribly clever. But, in point of fact, it only makes me wonder how a mere fourteen miles of water can so affect one's digestion. We know what the British have against Napoleon but what do they have against cows?"

The Cardinal joined the president in laughter before subtly topping him. "Indeed, they seem to forget that Waterloo is not in France but in Belgium and it was a Prussian army that took the decisive action there, not Wellington. Of course, one must acknowledge that he took the decisive credit!" Their further laughter was punctuated by the tinkle of fine crystal which perfectly complemented the Salon Doré with its gold-draped windows that looked onto the gardens. One of those stuffed shirts on TV had once wondered aloud how much influence this gilded room had on the conduct of government policy and whether a more modest space might encourage more modest thinking. If France had wanted more modest thinking, André observed to the Cardinal, it would have built a Swiss chalet.

Equipped with a well-filled glass and comfortably seated, the president spoke first. "So, my friend, is this a social visit, which I welcome, or perhaps a bit of business to which I must attend?"

"I'm afraid there is a bit of business we should address."

Legrande interrupted to lean forward and touch his glass to the Cardinal's. "Santé!"

"Santé!" The Cardinal took a sip before continuing. "I had a telephone call a few minutes ago from Dewitt Hamilton. He pretended it was just a belated 'thank you' for our support in the seabed mining dispute with the Russians and for reinforcing the status of the Northwest Passage with the Canadians."

"So far so good," the president said, "but I take it there was more?"

"Indeed, there was. Pretending it was just an afterthought, Hamilton brought up the name of our little Lebanese banker friend, Khashan. He said his name had surfaced, as he put it, as 'a person of interest'—a term usually used in connection with a criminal investigation. But more interestingly, he said something had come to his attention which described Khashan as one of your foreign policy advisors."

Legrande leaned back, chin in the air, obviously offended at the idea. "That's preposterous. He is no such thing. I hope you told him so. "

"Not exactly, since, in a manner of speaking, Khashan did tender some advice which we did act on."

André let that pass. "I believe you advised we should be discrete, keep our distance from Khashan and wait to see how matters play out in Québec."

"I did and we are; but that does not mean others are being as discrete. In any event, Hamilton did not actually say Khashan claimed such a role but that an item had crossed his desk that so described him. Without knowing what that item is I did not think it wise to offer a blanket denial which could come back to haunt us."

"So what exactly did you say?" The president's voice had an edge which the Cardinal noted.

"I said that like the American president you have many advisors on many subjects, usually specialists who can address a specific area of expertise and no doubt it was such a person in some minor role that was referenced."

"How did he respond to that?"

"He said I had put his mind at ease."

The president grunted. "How do the Americans know about Khashan?"

"An indiscretion perhaps or perhaps Khashan told them, not directly of course—certainly not directly—but through channels. He no doubt knows where such channels run."

"Why would he do that?"

"It could be a matter of ego or..." the Cardinal paused, carefully considering his next words..."or a magnificently structured, double-barreled blackmail; one pull of the trigger for the Canadians, the second for us. If he is about to blackmail the Canadians—which would not surprise me—he may also be about to blackmail us. And for that he would need standing; hence his claim and its advertisement."

"I do not understand," Legrande protested. "Why should he wish to blackmail us? What about his camels needing shade and all that?"

The Cardinal shrugged. "Perhaps he has other plans that do not require shade. Perhaps he intends to move at night."

Legrande persisted. "To perform blackmail you have to have some hidden deed that the victim doesn't want made public. Anything we have done, we have done openly. What is hidden about an aircraft carrier whose travels are spread across the front pages of the world's newspapers?"

"You are quite right. The travels of the *de Gaulle* are not ripe material for blackmail. But the travels of Monsieur Khashan may be, beginning with his visit to Chateau Cher. We know what he suggested we do and we know what we did. What we do not know is what he may have suggested to others and whether they did it leaving us open to assumed guilt by association. That evening at Cher he said enough groundwork had been laid to assure Québec will vote for separation. I did not seek specifics on the premise that some things are best not known but I must admit I'm now a bit uneasy about what that groundwork might prove to be."

"And the Canadians...what could he use as blackmail against them? Has he met with them, too?"

"I don't know but I somehow doubt it...at least no direct meeting...perhaps something more subtle...I don't know. I just wonder..."

There was a long silence as the president digested what he had been told. At length he seemed to brighten and with something just short of a look of triumph asked the Cardinal, "If what you surmise about his blackmailing intentions is true, would he not have to admit to whatever he or his associates may have done and so implicate himself, perhaps even criminally if Hamilton's choice of term was intentional?"

"Person of interest?" the Cardinal looked thoughtful. "Yes, I suppose that is true. What I am not sure is whether it matters to Khashan. We live in a time of intense passions. Some people are not content just to remove an opponent but strap a bomb around their waist and remove themselves at the same time. Admittedly I do not see him as a martyr but I may be misreading him. In any event I think I should find some way to separate us from Khashan when I see Hamilton at the G-7. Perhaps suggest that his inquiry caused us to review Khashan's status and that we found—in addition to greatly overstating a visit to Cher as one of many guests—he may have other agendas which would not be compatible with our thinking...something along those lines. Not too specific, just enough to bring anything that might subsequently surface into question."

"Where is Khashan now?"

"I don't know but likely in Québec. The referendum is less than two weeks away. If he's got some card he intends to play it would seem likely he will do so soon unless..."

"Unless?"

"Unless we could bring him home and keep him under wraps for a couple of weeks."

"How could you do that?"

"I couldn't," the Cardinal admitted, "but I suspect the bank examiners could."

"And if the Americans ask for his extradition?"

The Cardinal shrugged. "Examinations take time."

Again there was a long silence which the president of the republic eventually broke. "How bad could it be?"

The Cardinal did not answer at once. When he did, it was in a flat, unemotional voice. "It could be worse than anything we imagine. It could be that his object is not the return of Québec to France but the export of jihad from Clichy-sous-Bois to America."

"Bring him home."

Chapter Twenty-Two

80 Wellington Street, Ottawa
Tuesday, October 6th
12:00 noon

The PM's press secretary knew most of the reporters lined up against him. Until a couple of years ago he'd been one of them and he knew that if he screwed up this noon he might be one of them again. Even now the news crawl continued to repeat its alarm: "White House confirms radiation alert at Québec border." The midday anchors were struggling to get on top of the story. Urgent calls had gone out to rosters of "experts" to provide opinions while awaiting facts.

From time to time the anchors interviewed their reporters waiting in the Parliamentary press gallery more to assure viewers they were on the job should anything happen than to add substance to the thin gruel of available information. When finally, a few minutes after twelve, the prime minister's press secretary appeared, it was to read a brief statement largely confirming what had been announced earlier at the White House: a radiation alarm had gone off at the Stanstead, Québec border post as several trucks were lined up awaiting clearance to enter Canada. One of those trucks and its driver had been pulled out of line and swept for radiation as it was in the closest proximity to the sensors when the alarm sounded. However, no radioactivity was found on the truck or its driver and he was allowed to proceed to his destination.

"What was his destination?" the *Toronto Globe & Mail* reporter interrupted.

"A company warehouse in Montréal."

"Has the warehouse been searched?" The press secretary was unsure but would get back to him on that.

A CBC reporter wanted to know whether the Marston government, believing the United States to be the primary, if not sole, terrorist target on the continent, had failed to guard against the possibility of terrorists entering Canada. The press secretary firmly denied the premise of the question. "Obviously not; it was our border security that detected the low-level emission and our border agents who quickly and efficiently investigated the incident."

Undeterred, the reporter had a follow-up: "But they only proved *that* truck and *that* driver were *not* the source of the radiation. So what *was* the source?"

"That's a matter that remains under investigation and, of course, we do not comment on on-going investigations," the press secretary replied, "but I would point out that the following morning the radiation detection device that registered the anomaly was replaced and the original unit is presently undergoing tests to determine whether there was a fault in the electronic circuitry that might have produced what is commonly referred to as a 'false positive.' "

Watching from his ministry office on the banks of the Rideau Canal, Andrew had to admire how smoothly the press secretary then began redirecting the reporters away from Ottawa and toward Washington. Each of the next three questions received some variation of the same answer: "You'd have to ask the U.S. authorities about that." Minutes after the Ottawa news conference ended they began doing so but without significantly advancing the story. Official Washington apparently had said all it was going to say.

Changing channels Andrew joined CNN just as an expert from a Washington think tank was also asked whether he thought the Canadians had stopped the wrong truck and, if so, where did he think the nuclear material was now? A veteran of such TV appearances, the expert didn't try to pretend he had any answers but instead managed to look very grave as he nodded his head and said "those are excellent questions." The anchor looked pleased. From there discussion moved to the generally porous nature of the U.S. borders. In the absence of any pictures of the Vermont border, they ran stock footage of swarthy youths scaling a chain link fence somewhere in Arizona.

Andrew muted the sound. Things appeared to be under control, at least for the moment. In a day or two—absent any new fuel to feed the flames—press attention would likely shift to something else. Still, he couldn't help but wonder why someone hadn't let him know about the radiation alarm. They were aware he had returned to the campaign trail. *What if this story had broken when he was in front of an audience with cameras and microphones trained on him?* It wouldn't look very good for the nation's defense minister to have to admit he didn't know anything about a possible nuclear incident on its border. He could envision the headlines that would take his career and the referendum down together.

With less than two weeks to go, the outcome still remained within the margin of error with the margin continuing to favor Renard. As he cleared his desk and stuffed his briefcase with several reports his aides had pressed on him, he wondered what effect the news would have on the referendum. It could buttress Renard's contention that if the federal government didn't know in advance about the Montréal bombings it should have. But the word "nuclear" had a disorienting effect on people. They might not react as expected. In any event, all that was for later consideration; right now he had to get over to the PM's office. His request Monday morning for a meeting had been answered with an invitation to lunch this noon. It would be their first face-to-face encounter since the Compton bombing although

Marston had telephoned twice and had sent a large bouquet of flowers with a hand-written note of well wishes.

He used to enjoy walking the half dozen blocks to Parliament Hill but his security detail had ruled that out. If they had their way the trip would be made with lights flashing and traffic stopped but at his insistence they'd reached a compromise. The flashers and sirens would only come on if there were a traffic jam or a red light that could leave them immobilized and thus vulnerable. Still, even this much security bothered him. Once leaders began to fear the people they were elected to lead where was the democracy headed? Again, it was Marcel Gigiere who offered the best answer. "It isn't the people that you are guarding against," he had argued when the question came up during one of Marcel's visits during his recuperation, "You are guarding against those who would deny democracy to the people. In protecting yourself you are also protecting the right of the people to choose their own government not subject to the violent veto of an unelected minority." And so he settled into the back seat of the car and self-consciously began the short ride to the Hill.

As always, McKinley Marston was the embodiment of graciousness. On being informed that Andrew Fraser had arrived he came out of his office to meet him rather than have his colleague ushered into his presence. "Andrew, how very pleased I am to see you. How well you look! How extraordinarily kind it is of you to come." It took a certain talent to lubricate simple events with elaborate courtesies, in the process smoothing the path for whatever might lie ahead. Marston possessed the talent in abundance, which was undoubtedly a factor in his political longevity. Those who might pose a challenge to his leadership could never arouse enough personal enmity against the man to carry out a coup. Whether the PM knew it or simply sensed it he disarmed the wrath of his enemies with the proverbial kind word the Bible recommended. "I have taken the liberty of asking a couple of your friends to join us for luncheon. I trust that is agreeable with you?"

Of course it would have to be. How could one reasonably say "no, I don't want to see my designated friends, I want to speak quietly and directly with you without any gallery present?" Since good manners thus dictated that collegiality trump candor, he smiled and murmured "How nice" as he followed the prime minister into his office. There, awaiting them, were David Osgood and Mac James, ambition and authority seated side by side.

"Andrew, how awfully good to see you up and about," Osgood made it sound as though he had just recovered from a bout of the flu, not an assassination attempt.

"Indeed," Mac added with the sincerity Osgood lacked, "you had us worried."

As Osgood continued to profess how much he had been missed the suspicion grew that this wasn't a luncheon but a set-up. Mac James and David Osgood had minimum high regard for each other. To bring them together there must be more on the menu than food. Over the next hour his suspicions only grew as the small talk that filled the meal was cleared away along with the plates. The true purpose of the luncheon arrived with the coffee.

"This very pleasant gathering has not only afforded us the opportunity to welcome you back," the prime minister began, "but to catch up on some of what has occurred in your absence."

Andrew decided to play the game. "And what might that be Prime Minister? Apart from the first few days I have been following the news but perhaps I missed something."

"No," Marston quickly replied, perhaps a trifle too quickly, "I doubt you missed anything that was in the news."

"Then perhaps I missed something that was *not* in the news." Mac James took the moment to wipe his mouth, perhaps to remove any trace of a smile.

"Uh...indeed," the PM replied. "Yes. There were one or two matters that on advice we thought it best not to publicize."

"And what might I inquire were those?" Andrew asked, his voice a honeyed mixture of innocence and insistence.

"Uh, yes…of course. It was for just that purpose that I thought we might have this informal opportunity to share that information and consider your response to it."

"Informal" understated the actual setting. While decidedly less elegant than his ceremonial offices across Wellington Street in the Center Block of Parliament, the PM's workaday suite in the Langevin Block was hardly Spartan. The luncheon had been served in a small dining room adjoining his office, the table draped with white linen and adorned with a small vase of red roses. The windows behind the prime minister's chair framed the gothic spires and turrets of the Parliament buildings. The setting may have been many things but it was not "informal".

"These past few weeks have not been without their challenges," the PM said in a remarkable bit of understatement, "though of course nothing like those you experienced and from which, I must say again, we are most grateful that you have recovered." Osgood, ever the cheerleader, nodded vigorously and added a chorus of "hear, hear". Mac James remained impassive, the former prosecutor and law professor, watching as if attending a moot court. Whatever he had to say would probably come at the end, a summing up for a yet unseen jury.

"One of those challenges," the PM added, "was deciding how wide a disbursement to give certain information that came into our hands, especially certain details of the Stanstead incident. It was our intent to bring you up-to-date once your situation could be better assessed but, unfortunately, events have overtaken those good intentions."

Having long ago developed the ability to do simultaneous translation of McKinley Marston's oblique language from what he said to what he meant Andrew immediately understood the prime minister's message as: *We weren't sure whether the blast had loosened your political sense. We decided to wait to see but the talkative truck driver in New York blew that out of the water.*

Marston continued. "We are most pleased that you and your doctors have seen fit for you to resume your campaign against this unfortunate referendum. I believe I may speak for your cabinet colleagues in saying that whatever the outcome we recognize that you have given it your all and for that we—and I dare say a majority of Canadians—are most grateful." Osgood again provided the obbligato to the PM's motif.

"Of course," Marston continued, "we must bear in mind that should the vote not go as we would wish, it fortunately is not the final word on separation. Indeed, it is but a step and not necessarily a step to any preordained conclusion. I believe the wording of the referendum merely authorizes the Québec government to undertake negotiations with the federal government on terms for a possible separation, not an actual disengagement, which would only follow a second referendum on any agreement that might be reached. As some have suggested, it is not unlike the preliminary stage of a divorce proceeding which still offers the possibility of reconciliation, although I hasten to add I have no personal knowledge of such matters, Mrs. Marston and I so far never having had cause to inquire." He offered a small, self-deprecating laugh at what he apparently regarded as a comic impossibility. Osgood quickly joined in. Mac James attempted a weak smile. Andrew maintained a studied neutrality. It was not a subject he found particularly humorous.

Having warmed to his task, the PM continued. "As such, I would expect that men of good will and reasonable disposition might find some agreement short of separation as has been our good fortune on previous such occasions." Andrew fought the urge to bang the table to awaken this man and explain that he was there to warn him that they were not facing men of good will; that they didn't even know who they were actually facing. But some instinct told him to maintain his silence and keep a non-committal expression on his face.

"Should it come to that," Marston continued, "we shall have to impanel a negotiating team to meet with our confreres from Québec.

Naturally, such negotiations would best be conducted in a cordial atmosphere, a pace or two removed from the necessary vigor of the present referendum campaign. Therefore, after much deliberation, I have asked David to lead our side and I shall make that announcement after the vote is tallied thereby making it clear we intend to vigorously continue prosecuting our case. I trust you will agree that David's distance from the battlefield, if I may use such a term, and his keen appreciation for the economic aspects of any agreement that might be reached—a point you have quite rightly stressed in your campaign—makes him well-positioned to lead our team."

He couldn't believe his ears. Marston was conceding defeat before a single vote was cast. And, worse yet, he was proposing to install as lead government negotiator a man who barely spoke French and was intimately identified with Toronto's Bay Street financial community. If the separatists won—and with the polls still so close he wasn't about to concede that—then naming as your chief negotiator the man most closely identified with all that the separatists found most objectionable virtually guaranteed the outcome. Divorce proceedings? This was tantamount to pawning the ring. Renard could and undoubtedly would take the most extreme positions in the sure knowledge that when it came down to a choice between him and Osgood—which is how the French press would portray it—there could be no doubt where the voters would stand. Still, he held his peace. There had to be more to this luncheon than the PM anointing Osgood. If that were all, some Osgood ally would have been invited to attend, not Mac James. So Andrew took a very deep breath and willed himself to remain silent and await whatever Mac had to say.

With his first words, Mac made clear his role at the table. He was there to outline the alternative to backing the prime minister's choice. "Andrew, as you know the RCMP comes under my purview. As such I see a lot of its internal traffic. Following the June bombings in Montréal I gave instructions that anything related to them or to the Québec situation generally was to be brought to my personal attention. As events warrant, I forward summaries to the prime minister. Yesterday I received a report linking your name and your wife's to last week's border crossing incident, the one that's 'gone nuclear' if I may so put it."

Andrew found he wasn't particularly surprised. Intuitively he had already put together what he had been told by the RCMP in the coffee shop with what he'd heard on the TV this morning. He looked from one face to the other before responding to Mac. "I first learned of a suspected illegal border crossing last Friday afternoon from two RCMP officers, maybe the same ones who wrote the report you read. That was also the first time I learned that the key suspect in the border crossing had telephoned my wife." He thought, as he said it, that it was all true. He knew Marie-Paule had received a call and he knew it had come from a Fernand St. Germaine but until the coffee shop meeting he had not known St. Germaine was involved in an illegal border crossing and, even then, not in any radiation incident. "An inspector named Gautier came by Friday evening and interviewed Marie-Paule. There wasn't much she could tell him. The inspector said the fellow got our phone number through a break-in at a summer club we belong to in the townships. He apparently worked there as a handyman. I didn't know him." He didn't say whether Marie-Paule knew him and moved on quickly hoping no one would notice. "I knew nothing about any radiation until I saw the story on TV this morning. And, until you told me just now, I didn't know the two incidents were connected, much less one and the same. But, in any event, we have fully cooperated with the investigation and will continue to do so if there's any way we can be helpful."

Mac pursed his lips but said nothing. He looked like a man who had done his duty under duress. It was Osgood who replied. "I am quite sure what you say is true Andrew but I suspect you will agree our confidence in you likely would not be shared by the opposition much less the separatists who do not know you as we do. Should any element of your situation find its way into the public arena I think you must agree it undoubtedly would have a devastating effect on the negotiations to say nothing of your well deserved reputation and that of Madame Fraser." He noted Osgood's use of the French honorific for Marie-Paule. *Was it a none-too-subtle suggestion that he had divided loyalties?*

How to reply? Obviously the PM had shared the RCMP report with Osgood, probably on the not unreasonable assumption that he had to be aware of anything that might confront him as projected lead government negotiator. What was unreasonable was assuming defeat in the first round and picking a negotiator who was almost certain to guarantee it in the second round. Osgood's feigned concern lest St. Germaine's phone call to Marie-Paule become public was, of course, a threat, coming as it did from the most practiced leaker in the cabinet so he dealt with that first. "I don't have 'a situation' David." There was ice in his voice. "Neither does my wife." He felt less confident about that than he sounded.

Marston moved quickly to head off trouble. "Of course you don't Andrew and I'm certain Mrs. Fraser doesn't, either. It's most unfortunate a virtual stranger tried to involve you in whatever he was doing. That's just one of the trials we in public life have to bear. I'm sure David was only using a figure of speech. We all know we can count on your full support." So that was it. His campaign against the referendum and the public sympathy that came to him in the wake of the assassination attempt apparently, in their minds, had given him a defacto veto. Therefore Mac James had been brought in to say just enough to make sure he didn't exercise it.

"I have always tried to be supportive of you prime minister and I assure you that in the remaining two weeks before the referendum I shall continue to try to make your contingency plans unnecessary." The look on Marston's face made it clear he didn't have the slightest idea whether Andrew had just said "yes" or "no" which in turn left Osgood adrift. He decided to strike out for shore on his own.

"Of course, Andrew, as I said, I am sure matters are just as you say and therefore I hope I shall be able to draw on your wise counsel as the talks go forward even if that counsel must, of necessity, be given privately."

Having once responded to Osgood, he decided not to make a habit of it. Folding his napkin and rising he inclined his head slightly in the direction of Marston. "I thank you for an excellent luncheon, prime minister, but if you will now excuse me I must head back to Montréal and the campaign." Without waiting for a reply, he curtly acknowledged Osgood and James with a nod to each..."David... Mac"...and turned toward the door.

He was halfway down the stairs when he heard Mac call after him. While he and Mac weren't close friends they had always liked and respected each other and consequently had worked well together. That was enough to make him pause to hear what he had to say. "It was a bloody set-up Andy. I had no idea Marston had shared any of that stuff with Osgood. He got me there a half hour before you and made it as clear as he ever makes anything that I had two choices, confront you with the RCMP report or resign. For two cents I'd have resigned then and there but in the wake of this morning's news it would have been seen as taking responsibility for whatever happened at the border and we don't yet know what that was. We don't even have any evidence that a crime was committed. We just have a pile of loose ends that may or may not fit together. If it turns out I screwed up I'll go but I'm not about to give them a blank check. Anyway, I just wanted you to know I'm terribly embarrassed at having been found seated at a fixed game and that I'm praying you can somehow pull out a win. Putting that ass Osgood at the same table with Renard is as good as conceding the country." Mac was so upset that his face had reddened.

Andrew put his arm around his colleague's shoulders. "Mac, for-get it. I knew it was a set-up the moment I walked into the room. You did the right thing. This is no time to have the Public Safety portfolio empty or, worse yet, given to another Osgood." As they reached the front door he stopped and looked inquiringly at Mac. "Are you going back to your office?"

"Yeah."

"Can you give me a half hour?

"Sure. I'm clear at least to three. I expected this affair to run longer."

"It probably would have if the guest of honor hadn't walked out." They both laughed as they exited the building to where two SUVs sat idling at the curb. "Your caravan or mine?"

"If it's all the same to you Andy, I'd just as soon walk. After that lunch I need some fresh air. It's only a couple of blocks."

"Suits me but I'm not sure the security guys will allow it."

Mac grinned. "Relax. They work for me." He turned to a plain-clothes man who was holding open the rear door of his SUV. "The defense minister and I are going to walk back to the office." The man nodded and appeared to speak into his sleeve. One of the SUVs pulled away from the curb. It only went a few feet to the end of the block before stopping almost astride the crosswalk. The other rounded the corner and drove down Metcalf to the next block where he also stopped, again nearly in the crosswalk. Andrew and Mac set out trailed by two plainclothesmen who usually rode shotgun but were now on foot. As they passed the first cross street the SUV waiting there leapfrogged the next one, taking up guard a block further ahead of the two ministers of the crown.

"Reminds me of my first date," Andrew laughed. "The girl's old man followed us all the way to the high school gym to make sure I wasn't leading her astray!"

"You know," Mac replied, "as the father of two teenage daughters I actual sympathize more with him than with you!" Then, turning serious he said, "Quite apart from the potential disaster of putting Osgood in charge of negotiations with Québec, should it come to that, I can't help wondering if the PM is getting ready to step down and has settled on Osgood to be his successor...keeper of his legacy, such as it is. Beneath all his Victorian manners there is an ego."

"Maybe, but if so, why hand Osgood a hot potato like Québec? That could be a career-ender."

"Or a career builder if it goes better than either of us expect. Besides, I don't think he handed it to Osgood. I think Osgood's been campaigning for the job. He's got to know that he doesn't have much support for a leadership run within the parliamentary party. So he's trying blackmail. If the party were to reject him as leader it would be seen as rejecting his negotiations with Québec. That would be a confidence issue if ever there was one sending us into elections badly crippled. The Québec negotiations are his trump card but you and Marcel are in the way."

"But he'd still need to come away with some kind of a win."

Mac shrugged. "Depends on how you define win."

69 Laurier Avenue West, Ottawa
Tuesday, October 6th
2:30 pm

Settled in Mac's office at the Public Safety Ministry the day's events seemed as distant as the muted sounds of traffic from several stories below. "Mac, you should know that luncheon didn't start out the way it ended. I asked Marston for a meeting. He took it from there. I was going to brief him on some things that have come my way and suggest that you and maybe someone from Ogilvie Road should be brought in. But with Osgood present I thought it best to say nothing I didn't want to read on the front page tomorrow." Andrew's mention of Ogilvie Road—the address of the Canadian Security Intelligence Service—made Mac's eyebrows shoot up.

"CSIS?" Mac pronounced the initials as if they formed a word. He leaned forward, concern etched on his face. "What do you have Andy?"

Over the next ten minutes he worked within the system as Mark had urged, telling what was, in effect, the nation's top cop of the theory that the bombing targets didn't make sense to anyone but a jihadist. He explained the possible significance of 732 but didn't say where he got the theory. He wasn't sure why but, seated in the office of the man who commanded the federal law enforcement services, detailing the candor of his discussions with an assistant to the U.S. president seemed inappropriate, maybe even bordering on disloyal, although it had never seemed that way before. In any event, he offered no attribution nor did he mention Khashan. To do that would be to drag Marie-Paule further into the affair. When he was done, Mac sat quietly, seemingly lost in thought. After a long moment he sighed audibly. "Well, as you say, it's intriguing but I don't know that it's actionable. We only had one lead and we lost him."

"St. Germaine?"

"Yeah." Mac fell silent again, then, eyes squinted, looked hard at his colleague. "Andy is there anything specific you can think of? Anybody who's come to your attention, a name, a place, a phone number—anything that might give us somewhere to start? Because right now we're at an absolute dead end and if your theory is correct we could be in for a world of hurt. I must tell you in the strictest confidence it apparently *was* St. Germaine's truck that set off that radiation alarm at the border."

"Apparently?"

"Yeah. We lost it, too. It went up in a fire along with the barn where it was sitting as well as St. Germaine's house...everything."

"Arson?"

"The fire marshal says 'no'...I have my doubts but no proof. In fact, the only material evidence we've got are some tire tracks on an old logging road we think St. Germaine used to enter the States but we can't match them up with anything...the fire burned the tires off his truck and the fire trucks and all the water they sprayed churned the barnyard to mush so we couldn't even cast any old tracks." Mac thought a long moment before continuing. "Andy, I want you to know that I do take your theory very seriously." Again he paused as if deliberating whether to say more. "There was one other thing the Sherbrooke barracks found on that logging road...or actually in a stream that crosses it...an empty lead foil packet."

"Lead foil?"

"Comes on a roll just like aluminum foil—same sort of box and everything, only a lot thicker and a lot heavier. Ten feet of the stuff would weigh around twenty-five pounds. You can get it in scientific supply stores."

"What's it for?"

"It's usually used for radiation shielding."

"My God! You mean he was smuggling a bomb into the States?"

"Probably not a bomb but at least something to dirty up a bomb which could contaminate a chunk of a major city, cost a fortune to clean up and trigger panic in the process. We've told the Americans. They've got a quiet but intense search underway for what we presume was more of the stuff."

"Why would he have tossed some of it in the stream? Is it a public water supply?

"No. The best guess is that something breached the integrity of that particular packet and they had to discard it."

"They?"

Mac shrugged. "Another guess."

Silence hung in the air, a palpable presence, broken at last by a deep sigh that gave little hint of the fierce debate that Andrew had just resolved within himself.

"Mac, I don't know what to say. I came in here with a theory and I realize there isn't anything there to build a case on but..." With a show of resolve he stood up, signaling an end to their meeting. "If I think of something I'll give you a call. Right now I'm going home and do everything I can to upset everyone's plans...everyone we know and everyone we don't know."

Mac also got to his feet. "I sure as hell hope you can Andy. What you've shared with me may only be theory at this point but it could prove valuable down the road. At least it may get us thinking outside the box. Meanwhile, I hope to hell that referendum fails. It'd solve a lot of problems. But you be careful. If what you suspect is true..." His voice trailed off. The rest of the sentence didn't need to be spoken. "Like I say, anything you hear—a name, a place, anything that might give us a new starting point—pass it on."

"I will," Andrew assured him.

"Thank you and believe me, my friend, I'm not unaware of how much it's cost you and how much more it could have cost. As Marston said, win or lose, we're all in your debt."

As they walked toward the elevators they passed a knot of secretaries gathered around a TV set that showed a reporter standing in front of what looked like a multi-lane drive-through at a bank. A few words were audible as they passed "...which began unfolding earlier today with news from New York of an incident here at the Stanstead border crossing."

The two colleagues shook hands and Andrew stepped into the elevator, his thoughts partly on what he'd just been told, partly on Marie-Paule, but mostly on what he had not told Mac.

Epilogue

The rain had eased allowing the windows to be rolled down an inch or so to prevent the windshield from fogging. The slow rhythmic slap of the wipers and the soft shush of the tires on the wet pavement had a pleasantly soothing sound after a tedious day of conferences where long held positions on opening the Arctic to navigation and resource recovery were stated and restated by both sides at such length that the planned supper with Mark had to be compressed into a quick drink and a ride to the airport. "You know what really bites?" Andrew half laughed as he picked up an earlier thread of their conversation, "We defeated the referendum and so everyone thinks it's over but it isn't. There are a lot of questions that remain unanswered...the bombings...the Stanstead incident...the French meddling." Silently he added some personal items to his list. "The questions are all still there but no answers."

"You're right," Mark agreed. "It's frustrating because I have a hunch that the sum of the parts we individually know is greater than the whole of what we don't know ...if that makes any sense."

The dashboard clock read 6:59. "Can you get some news? I feel as if I'd spent the day on another planet. Maybe there's been a big hockey game or a little war we missed."

"There's a difference?" Mark grinned.

The announcer was just talking the station up to the network news as he turn the radio on. "...occasional showers in the morning; clearing by late afternoon...right now in Washington, 52 rainy degrees at 7 o'clock."

A time tone sounded and then over a news theme the network anchor moved quickly into the lead story. "Paris is burning. On the eve of the G-7 summit, gangs of Muslim youths, reportedly inflamed by radical clerics, are battling police across the city. The trouble began several hours ago in the mostly Muslim suburb of Clichy-sous-Bois and quickly spread. Rioters broke through police lines, shattering store windows and setting cars and shops on fire in central Paris. Tourists fled sidewalk cafes as police lobbed tear gas to disperse the rioters. French president André Legrande has appealed for calm. Correspondent Jack Santerre reports this is not the first time trouble has spilled out of Clichy where unemployment, especially among young people, is said to be..."

Mark switched off the radio. "And we think we've got problems. Those poor bastards, 12% of their country is Muslim and every few months their kids burn down part of Paris."

Andrew sighed in agreement. "Yeah and no one has any idea what to do about it."

"Anyway, that's André the Grand's problem. Let's see what his 'third way' out of this one is."

"Probably export them. Best we keep an eye out for anyone crossing the border in a keffiyeh."

"Speaking of the border, whatever came of the mess that guy tried to drag Marie-Paule into?"

"I don't know. The RCMP came to see us once and didn't come back. I assume that in the time honored tradition they got their man."

"Someone got him."

"For sure."

"May I ask you an impolitic question?"

"That's the only kind I'm handling these days."

Mark grunted his disagreement. "I want to argue that decision with you before you go public with it...you haven't have you?"

"No, other than you the only one who knows is Marie-Paule. I don't intend to make a public announcement until the party picks a successor to Marston. So what's your question?"

"How come when you told me about the border crossing and that guy's call to Marie-Paule you never mentioned the radiation?"

"I didn't know about it."

"How so?"

"I don't know. I've wondered the same thing myself. Maybe they thought I knew."

"Why would they?"

"I was a member of that coordinating committee. Actually I still am. Maybe they thought everybody had been briefed and perhaps they were. After Compton I missed a couple of weeks." Andrew sat silent for a moment before adding, "Or maybe it was just more damn dots that nobody connected."

For a time each was lost in his own thoughts. It was Mark who broke the silence, changing the subject back to his friend's future. "You won the referendum—and I do mean *you*. When Marston steps down, you've got to be the favorite to replace him. Nobody's going to back that ass Osgood."

Mark wasn't alone in that view. Several editorial pages had made the same suggestion when, in the wake of the referendum, the prime minister announced that he would resign the leadership at the January party conference in Toronto. "Going out on top" was the way the *Toronto Star* had described his announcement.

"Without commenting on your characterization of a colleague, I would suggest that Marcel Gigiere would be a better choice. Not only does he look like central casting's idea of a prime minister but, politically, picking a Frenchman will help heal divisions faster. Marcel's a good man and I would remind you, he not only campaigned just as hard as I did but when I was out of action he picked up my load, too. He's earned the job and I intend to do what I can to see that he gets it."

"And remain in his cabinet? He'd keep you on wouldn't he?"

"Probably but I also need to invest some time in my marriage. Marie-Paule has been pretty much alone for the last couple of years and especially the last four months. We need some time for each other."

"Fulltime? You're more romantic than I ever gave you credit for."

Andrew grinned but didn't laugh. "I don't know. Maybe only resign from the cabinet, not from parliament. That would still free up a lot of time."

"To do what?"

"I've made a few inquiries. The university may want me back."

"Well at least you'd bring some real world experience to political science."

"Actually I was thinking of something in art."

"Art?"

"You know...connecting the dots." This time it was Mark's turn to grin, but not laugh. Andrew continued. "Actually, after I've had a chance to sort things out and maybe connect some of those dots, I'd like to write a book. This whole referendum debate touched on some pretty serious themes...what it means to be a Canadian, what we can and should be doing with an awfully big chunk of real estate, how we need to deal with our friends as well as our foes..."

"How to tell them apart," Mark interjected.

"That might require a second book."

"Getting back to the other stuff for a minute...whatever happened to the fifty grand that guy slipped Marie-Paule?"

Andrew frowned. "You were right. It smelled of a set-up. So we did as you recommended and put it in the gallery's account the next morning...opening a new one required too much paperwork and too many signatures to be able to move quickly...and, just as she predicted, they ran out and signed a lease on a place on Sherbrooke Street and hired some chi-chi decorator to fix it up. In short, they pretty much blew the money. And Khashan, the guy who gave her the money, hasn't set foot in the new place. He seems to have disappeared from the face of the earth."

"Not exactly," Mark said. "After we talked I sent the bloodhounds looking for Khashan. They found him in Paris. He turns out to be a Lebanese-born banker—a boutique bank in a high rent district—*and*—get this—he's said to be an advisor to André the Grand!"

"You've got to be kidding!"

"Nope. I mentioned it to Hamilton and he seemed surprised, too. He and the Cardinal—Jean-Pierre Dumont—Legrande's Richelieu—are quite close. I wouldn't be surprised if he doesn't make a few discrete inquiries this weekend while he's in Paris."

Andrew nodded toward the radio. "Nice time for a visit."

Mark shrugged and shifted conversational gears again. "Getting back to the referendum...last time I talked with you, you weren't sounding too confident about winning. What happened? Bad polling?"

"No, the polls were pretty close...remember the referendum only failed by a little over one percent, which probably means they'll try again...but I think that truck driver going public with his story turned things our way at the end. The cultural stuff was the separatists' strong suit. We couldn't touch them there and, frankly, didn't much try beyond pointing out that they would be a little French island in a big English sea. It was a sound argument but it never got much traction. They're used to being a minority. So they shrugged it off, in effect asking 'so what else is new?' The economic argument was pretty much a draw for the same reason: the numbers were on our side, the emotion was on theirs. Ultimately, national security turned out to be the thing that turned that last critical couple of points our way. The Stanstead incident made them think. It quite literally hit them where they live."

"The visit from the French aircraft carrier didn't do it?"

"Quite the contrary... I don't know that anyone would phrase it this way but it drove home the point that they aren't *French* French... they're *Canadian* French which, after two or three hundred years is a whole different thing. You know, I think Renard turned out to be too educated for his own good...not too *smart*... but too *educated*. He got his MBA at Insead. Most Québecers have never been to France much less studied there. He thought having lunch on a French aircraft carrier would show how an independent Québec could team up with the fatherland for its defense. But that question simply hadn't ever come up for most people. They were used to Ottawa doing what was needed for their defense and the States being there just in case something more was needed. By raising the national security issue Renard and the truck driver raised the stakes. This wasn't just about sticking it to English Canada any longer; this was about going it alone with the nearest ambulance brigade 3000 miles away. The Stanstead incident drilled that home in a way I could never have hoped to do."

Across the river the white dome of the capitol glowed in the mist. "You know, no offense, because you did a hell of a job stopping what promised to be a disaster, but the truth be told, all that's really happened is that the can got kicked down the road...and maybe not that far down the road.

"You mean they'll try again?"

"Yes, that too, but don't forget, that farmer was returning *home* with a radioactive truck. We still don't know what he delivered or where...or whether he was alone. And apparently there's no one who can tell us."

Andrew wondered if that was so but said nothing. The departure lane at Reagan National was crowded with cabs elbowing their way to the curb. As he reached into the back seat for his coat and briefcase he said his goodbyes. "Remember...you're to join us for a Montréal-style New Years. Marie-Paule says to tell you the guest room is empty and waiting."

ACKNOWLEDGEMENTS

Writing a book is a very solitary activity. Publishing it is not. To those who helped me get the words off my desk and into your hands, I am most grateful.

Canadian author J. FitzGerald McCurdy whose suggestions much improved this story.

Photographer Cedric von Machui of Ottawa's Black Dog Photo who took the dramatic cover photo of the Houses of Parliament as seen from the Québec side of the Ottawa River.

Shelly Coates, at Shellville Design, who patiently laid out both the print and electronic editions of this book.

Melanie Currie who designed and built our website: www.NeilCurrie.net where you can find pictures of some of the places mentioned and leave comments.

CPSIA information can be obtained
at www.ICGtesting.com
Printed in the USA
LVOW07s1330060617
536990LV00028B/108/P